THE
ADMIRAL'S
STEWARD

HOWARD GEORGE

ISBN: 978-1-957956-45-9 (sc)
ISBN: 978-1-957956-46-6 (e)

Rev. date: 09/20/2022

Dedicated to Val, David, Sarah, and Kitty, my supports in life.

"... for there is nothing covered that shall not be revealed and hid that shall not be known."

The Gospel according to St. Matthew, Chapter 10, Verse 26: King James Version.

ACKNOWLEDGEMENTS

My first acknowledgment must be to my late Aunt Clarice, whose research provided the idea for this story and from whom I inherited my copies of *Life of Nelson* by Robert Southey and *Nelson* by Carola Oman. In addition to these works, I have consulted and found useful *Nelson Love and Fame* by Edgar Vincent, *Emma—The Life of Lady Hamilton* by Colin Simpson, *Nelson's Purse* by Martyn Downer, *Nelson the Immortal Memory* by David and Stephen Howarth, *Memoirs of the Life of Vice-Admiral Lord Viscount Nelson* by ThomasPettigrew, *La Marina Militare Della Due Sicilie* by LambertoRadogna, and various editions of *The Nelson Dispatch* and other publications of The Nelson Society.

I must also acknowledge a considerable amount of anecdotal and other useful information provided by my cousin, Beryl Norman, who encouraged me to keep going when I seemed to have run out of useful avenues of research. Similarly, the Gotham and District Local History Society, especially Society Chairman, the late Barry Dabell M.B.E. and his wife Sybil, who became fellow researchers and firm friends. Also, to the late Gordon Thompson for his advice and support.

Among the places of reference I visited and received kindly assistance from their staffs were the Nelson Museum, Monmouth; Lloyds Register, London; the National Archives, Kew; and the WhitbyMuseum.

Finally, but most importantly, I have to acknowledge the unwavering support of my wife, Val, who insisted that this story be written in its present form and travelled across England and Wales, and also on a winter visit to Sicily, in the course of my researches. Her English and history graduate skills were invaluable in critically reading each chapter that emerged from the computer printer.

Howard George

PROLOGUE

The early morning sunlight of late August filtered past the curtain rings of the small upstairs cottage window and made the old man blink. He lay unmoving on his bed, not wanting to make the great effort of getting to the floor and emptying his bladder into the chamber pot by the bedpost. The thought made his nose wrinkle. When he'd struggled out of bed before dawn and lit his candle, the water he'd passed had stunk badly and still did. He hoped one of his daughters or granddaughters would come soon to help him with his ablutions and empty the pot.

He hoped it would be someone other than his widowed eldest daughter, Ann. She was so glum these days because her favored second youngest daughter, Charlotte, and her husband, that terrier- like little man, Edward, had taken their son off to Aston-on-Trent. Hadn't she been back to Gotham twice since then to show him two more baby sons? She knew how to push herself foward that one. He wasn't sure he remembered the names, except he thought one was named John after his own youngest son, just as William had been named after himself and his own William. Then recollection hit him like a blow. His own William was dead. His dependable, sensible son who had lived so quietly, with his equally reliable, hardworking wife, Mary, had gone more than two years before. He calculated that distance in time in the belief that he was now dying himself and looked to the top of his chest of drawers.

He could just see the outline of his Bible. That was a comfort to him, not only to read the printed word but also the faded letter in spidery hand with its three words of signature that rested inside the solid book cover. There was an example in the face of death!

He often wondered why his Uncle William had kept the letter until he died, over fifty years after it was written. Likewise, why had he never told him the correct year of his birth? But that was also true of his parents, if they really were his parents. What should he read into the letter starting, "My dear son ...," instead of "My dear godson ..."?

Perhaps it signified nothing at all, but his musing was not to continue at that point, because female chattering was to be heard as the stairs creaked, and the voices were too young for either of them to be his youngest daughter, Eliza. *Time for some fun,* he thought. With eyes shut and mouth open, he feigned sleep. The door opened,and he heard one say to the other, "He's promised me the ivory shoehorn he keeps in the top drawer of that chest." It was hard not tosmile as they tiptoed to the chest and one eased the drawer open to caressingly display the shoehorn to her cousin. His timing was just right for opening his eyes and saying sternly,

"Thou shalt not steal!"

His words must have sounded sepulchral because both girls visibly jumped before the one said, "Oh, grandfather, we thought you were asleep, and we were only looking."

"Happen you were," he replied and closed his eyes again after he saw the shoehorn replaced and the drawer slid shut. "Take thechamber pot on your way out."

"Don't you want us to help you wash, grandfather?"

"No, ask your mother to come up with the other chamber pot."

"Yes, grandfather," and they left him alone.

She was a good girl, that Emily, although he didn't tell her so. He fell to musing again about his family and thought he'd not done badly for producing healthy children. Apart from Ann and that Edward Pidcock, who'd gone to America, they had all been educated in the village school provided by his lordship. Of course, he could remember when his lordship was the Honorable Richard Curzon, buthe'd been highly thought of by the king who'd been prince regentand made him Earl Howe. King William had given him an appointment at court.

A real gentleman, his lordship, always treated him fairly and allowed the tenancy of the farm to continue after UncleWilliam died. Not a military man, but his grandfather had been Admiral Lord Howe, and his great uncle a general, and now his lordship was long gone too. Was it his grandson who was now the earl?

Time marches on, he reflected. The queen had celebrated her golden jubilee. How long ago had that been? It couldn't have been very long, because he could remember all the free drinks it had gotten him at the Cuckoo Bush, him being such an old codger withall his tales of the great and good. The queen was still going strong, an example of the best improvements in medicine that money could buy after all the babies she'd had! Not like his poor, lovely Lizzie. Their eight together had worn her out, not because they'd been so much poorer than he was now, but due to the sheer strain of coping with those last two births, the baby girl who died and finally Eliza, when they should have been done with making babies.

His thoughts were interrupted again by the stairs creaking, but this time, it was an energetic, firm tread. *Here she is,* he thought, *Eliza.* Aclever girl she had always been, but she reminded him too much of dear Lizzie. He hoped she would treat him gently today and not expect him to drag himself out of bed. As he lay there, his entirebody feeling weak, Horatio William Spencer felt he would not see hisninetieth birthday in this life.

It was too far ahead, and even thinking what a rousing party he would be given at the Cuckoo Bush brought no sense of anticipation, now he was so weak. He wondered how his family would fare when he was gone, and his eyes rested on his Bible again. What the good book said and what lay inside must be their safeguard. He could do no more.

CONTENTS

CHAPTER 1

ENCOUNTER ON THE BAY OF NAPLES

The admiral's barge rose in the dirty-looking swell of the inshore Bay of Naples under storm clouds that seemed to be moving in noparticular direction. Thomas Spencer leaned forward at the stern, gripping the tiller firmly and unconsciously crinkling his nose at the odors blowing off the Neapolitan shore. In reality, the barge wasmore a small cutter, with the mast entirely removed, tricked out as anadmiral's barge, with neatly uniformed oarsmen to emphasize the status of this small vessel from *Vanguard*. Thomas, as an admiral's steward, should hardly have had command of her, even for a short ship-to-ship pull. But every officer and petty officer, from Captain Hardy down, was so taken up with trying to ensure the comfort of their royal and noble passengers that his lordship had said, "Thomas, look you at that transport next beyond Commodore Caracciolo's *Sannita*. That is *Samuel and Jane*, and all of Sir William's bedding and linen has been stowed there. Lady Hamilton requires forthwith all that can be brought. Here is a note for Captain Hopps. List and receipt for him what you bring, and list for Lady Hamilton what remains there. Above all, keep dry what you bring."

What else had there been to say to these exacting instructions but, "Aye, aye, m'lord," as he knuckled his forehead? He could see the strain etched in Lord Nelson's sick, tired face, and the edges of the scar on his forehead were unnaturally red against his white skin. So, Thomas had scurried off to assemble the boat crew, obtain a supply of stout canvas from the sail maker and writing materials from the cubbyhole he shared with Tom Allen. Thanks to Tom's status as a Nelson family retainer, he would forever be "Thomas" to the admiral. Not that he minded, because his lordship was undoubtedly an instrument of God in England's struggle for survival against thegodless, revolutionary French. He was picked to be admiral's steward by reason of having learned his letters so readily at Sunday school back in Gotham and digesting the teaching of the Church so thoroughly that he was transparently devout. That was why he now anxiously conned the barge around the stern of the *Sannita*, with rolled-up canvas stretching from his feet between the two lines of oarsmen to the prow.

As the wind ruffled the fringes of his brown, curly hair below the straw sailor's hat wedged firmly on his head, he reflected that the ship wasn't built quite like an English seventy-four. She was very broad in the beam, with a pronounced squaring of the stern. He wasn't sure if that would make her ride better or worse in a heavy swell, but he'd noted that her forward part was as low to the water asa heavy frigate, which might make her easier to sail in a blow,shorthanded as she was said to be.

He remembered the two Neapolitan seventy-fours built to the English pattern he had seen moored together, their sails removed and no more than an afterguard still aboard, such was the level of desertion from the Neapolitan navy. He supposed better could not beexpected, after King Ferdinand's army had advanced to Rome, only to turn tail and run at the first sight of a French brigade. It left theking and his general, borrowed from the Austrian army, no choice butto return to Naples. That was why the king and his family had now taken refuge on board *Vanguard* to sail away from their own capital city, and General Mack was full of despair. So was his lordship and with good reason after his great victory at the Nile left GeneralBonaparte and his army marooned in Egypt. The French garrison he left on Malta was now blockaded in Valletta by Captain Ball. The French were surely unable to spare a large army for this far south in Italy, even though the Austrians had not yet declared war on them in the north.

His musing on his lordship's anxieties was then brought to a sudden end. Just as the starboard side of *Sannita* came into view, sodid a large launch being rowed furiously toward the ship's ladder, right across his course. He scarcely had time to register that the launch was packed with passengers before pushing the tiller over and shouting, "Cease rowing larboard side." Then, fearing for the safety of those rowers, because the launch might still hit their oars, he called, "Oars inboard." While they slid across, the launch passed them a little over an oar's length on the larboard bow. Thomas saw a woman with copper-colored hair escaping from under a bright, checkered shawl knotted tightly under her chin, peering at him intently between two Italian oarsmen well forward on the launch. He knew they were Italian from their exclamations at the near collision, having heard a great deal of Italian spoken by Lady Hamilton in the past few days.

But what next surprised him was the woman shouting, "Are you English?" in what sounded like a southern English accent.

"Admiral's barge, *Vanguard*," responded Thomas. "Who are you?" The launch, despite being close enough to *Sannita* to back oars, was nearly past the barge when the woman yelled, "Mary, I serve Lady Acton." Notwithstanding the swell, she incautiously stood and somehow kept her balance.

"Take care on that ladder," yelled Thomas before applying his mind to steering the barge back on course to round *Sannita's* fore anchor cable and onward to the *Samuel and Jane*.

"Larboard oars out, and pick up the stroke," he called, and his grizzled stroke oar quipped loud enough for his fellows to hear, "Ye sound like ye've a mind t' be an orficer, young Thomas, steering close 'nough to a vessel t'exchange banter wi' a young leddy."

The other oarsmen smiled broadly, and Thomas retorted, "I'm quitehappy with the lot God has already given me, Will, so you just put your back into getting us up to *Samuel and Jane*, and that goes forall of you. His lordship expects us back with Sir William and Lady Hamilton's bedding during this watch."

That, coupled with a lessening of the swell, was enough to drive them onward, although two bells of the forenoon watch had still to be rung when they rowed away from *Vanguard*. In fact, *Samuel and Jane's* bell only rang twice when the barge was thirty fathoms shortof her side, so it was mere minutes later that Thomas clambered up the short ladder into the low waist of this vessel, which he guessed was short of four hundred tons. The stern wasn't a lot higher than thedeck he stood on, with its large cargo hatches, but in the center of that short superstructure was a flight of steps just below and forward of the wheel mounting. From those steps, ducking low and holding an old-fashioned, three-cornered hat left-handed to his head, emerged a solid, weathered man in a serviceable frock coat. That - and the way a short, dark-haired, tough-looking seaman, who had been making his way across the cargo deck toward him, swiveled hisgaze from waist to stern - gave Thomas the certainty that the three- cornered hat rested on the head of Captain Hopps.

As he emerged fully and straightened, his linen stock, woolen stockings and stout shoes, that confirmed the certainty. Thomasmade along the deck toward him.

"Sir, my admiral, Lord Nelson, has sent this note regarding my orders to bring off as much of Sir William Hamilton's bedding and linen as his barge will safely carry."

"Thee doesn't need to call me 'sir.' Cap'n will do very well," replied Captain Hopps in an unmistakable Yorkshire accent. He movedbriskly toward the rail Thomas had crossed and glanced down at the open boat and its waiting oarsmen. Without giving Thomas a chanceto reply, he continued, "Thee'll not manage it all in that, and what thee takes will need t'be well triced up in yon sailcloth t'keep it dry." Reaching Thomas, he took the proffered note and unfolded it to glance with a grimace at the hand in which it was written. "Who be thee?"

"I be Thomas Spencer, admiral's steward, sir, I mean cap'n," Thomas responded hesitantly, taken aback by Hopps' forthright manner, which now continued.

"Thee doesn't need to tell me who thy admiral is, seeing he's the only one hereabouts, and I shall not trouble my eyes to read his left-handed scratchings, which I recognize well enough. John Parry,bosun, will direct thee below and provide some hands."

He inclined his head toward the dark-haired seaman, whose sunburned features bore an expression of sardonic amusement.Thus identified, Parry adopted a look of studied attention as his captain addressed him directly.

"Have those hospital boys go with thee and Mr Spencer, seeing they stowed it all neat and dry in that store aft the cable locker. Bring that sailcloth up with thee."

This last remark was addressed over the side to the waiting oarsmen in the barge, who needed no further invitation to bring one of them on deck, another on the ladder, with the rolls of sailcloth coming up hand over fist, while Captain Hopps strode back to the companionway leading to his cabin. He still held Lord Nelson's note unread; he had not needed telling of the urgency.

Thomas stared after him, clutching the small bag containing his writing materials, while Parry walked to a forward hatchway and bellowed down for the hospital boys. It had just occurred to Thomas that Parry was Welsh when the first roll of sailcloth brushed past him and he was asked, "Where away?"

So, he hurried after Parry, who led him down a steep companionway to a door that was so tight it seemed to need his entire body weight to force it open. The store beyond was too dark and only the light material used to bundle the bedding showed the outlines of the nearest bundles. Thomas asked Parry, "How do I see what is being moved out to list the contents of each bundle?"

"Spread your lengths of sailcloth on deck. Ye cannot have lighted candles here," came the reply.

"I see I shall only be able to number bundles left behind," Thomas observed.

In the event, it did not prove difficult to achieve a good balance between the major amount of bedding required and other linen and woolen items. The work on deck also moved at a satisfactory pace because the swell abated to the point at which the triced-up bundles could be lowered comfortably into the bottom of the barge, thankfully taking no water. By the time Thomas had five bundles wedged down the center of the barge between his rowers and had counted only four remaining below, six bells had been rung. The sky remained dark.

Captain Hopps returned on deck for Thomas to hand over his

dashed-off receipt and said, "Get thee back to Vanguard, lad; happen there will be another good blow before this day's out. My duty to Lord Nelson, I shall be ready to set sail on his command."

The pull back to *Vanguard* was steady but sure, and it was only when Thomas had given *Sannita* a wide berth, because she swung to her cable, that he became aware of someone waving over her bulwark below the break of the quarterdeck.

Will, who had a better view from his oar bench, exclaimed, "It be that young leddy waving t'ye agin, Thomas!" The latter half turned, confirmed Will's view, and waved back, but when he looked ahead again to check his course to *Vanguard's* quarter ladder, only a cable away, he saw a quarterdeck glass swing away from the barge to *Sannita's* bulwark and guiltily realized, from the bicorn hat worn athwart, that it was his lordship, his good eye to the glass, who had seen his return wave. When the barge hooked on at the foot of the ladder and a pair of seamen supervised by a senior midshipman lowered a cable from a pulley to start hoisting up the bundles, the admiral himself came to the rail and called down, "Get those bundles aboard forthwith, Thomas Spencer, and then come up to explain what you were doing dawdling and mooning over some lady of Naples on board *Sannita*."

Although his facial expression was ostensibly severe, Will, looking up, had caught the gleam of amusement in Nelson's eye but wasn't about to reveal that to spare Thomas's blushes. "You'm for it now, young Thomas."

Very bright his face was as he climbed the ladder and found the bundles in a heap on the deck. He knuckled his forehead to the quarterdeck, where Captain Hardy stood sternly behind his lordship.

"Two and a half hours extra, Lady Hamilton has been waiting for the contents of those bundles, items she requires most urgently, and I see you exchanging waves with a copper-haired lady of Naples rather than attending to your course and exhorting your oarsmen. I had thought better of you, Thomas!"

He, still bright faced, stammered, "M'lord, we were nearly run down by a longboat when outward to *Samuel and Jane*. The woman was a passenger."

"Was she indeed, and how did you and she understand one another?"

"She is an Englishwoman, m'lord. She serves Lady Acton, and her name is Mary."

"You must have been devilish close to being run down." At this, Nelson leant out over the quarterdeck rail, so he could see a few of his barge crew, and called down, "How nearly run down by a longboat were you?"

"Nip and tuck it was, m'lord," responded Will in a very respectful tone for someone having to shout.

"Very well," called Nelson, "get yourselves and my barge aboard. As for you, Thomas, you will remove these bundles below to Lady Hamilton. Give your regrets to her for your delay, and do her bidding in disposal of their contents."

Nelson turned to Hardy, smiling, and said, "I should be obliged if you could spare one or two hands to assist Spencer and Tom Allen, Captain Hardy. It seems Sir William and Lady Hamilton are possessed of a prodigious quantity of bedding and linen."

"Certainly, my lord," responded Hardy uncertainly, still not quite sure how to react to Nelson's rapid change from a severity thatboded punishment to a mild rebuke and dismissal. As Thomas disappeared into the head of a companionway, dragging the first bundle, Nelson smiled confidentially at Hardy, saying, "Thomas is so devout and straight laced; I never thought him likely to attract the attention of so comely a woman as I saw aboard *Sannita*."

At this, Hardy felt it safe to return his Admiral's smile and murmur, "I take your meaning, my lord."

Vanguard was another bell closer to having all battened down that could be, prior to weighing, when Nelson entered the partitioned-off part of the great cabin where Lady Hamilton was to be found nursing the two youngest offspring of their royal majesties of the Two Sicilies.It was evident that some of her linen was already being put to good use.

"My dear Lady Hamilton, have Thomas Spencer and Tom Allen served you as I directed?"

"Most certainly, my dear Lord," she responded, "but why was

Thomas Spencer giving his regrets in such an abashed manner when he had performed the task set him so valiantly?"

Briefly, Nelson told her the story, and an alluring smile accompanied her response. "*Amore* can strike like a bolt of lightning on a wave-tossed sea. It may have done so."

His answering intense and prolonged smile gave cause to hope it was more than a single bolt.

Chapter 2

A Storm at Sea

It was not until the second bell of the last dogwatch that *Vanguard*, with a full set of sails drawing, surged away from the Neapolitan shore under an ominous sky and a wind coming off the mountains inland. Thomas had slipped on deck a short time before darkness fell and quickly noted that *Sannita* and *Archimedes*, the other Neapolitan liner, were preparing to sail. So were a transport and more than a dozen merchantmen to landward of the two warships. Their seamen were clearly impeded by the fugitive passengers crowded on most decks he could see, and the Neapolitan warships didn't look to have that many hands to send aloft, so it was true a good many had deserted. He worried for the passengers on board them.

He knew, now he'd spent some time serving food and drink to King Ferdinand and Sir John Acton in Captain Hardy's cabin, that Sir John's entire household was aboard *Sannita*. To have entrusted his lady, six children, all his valued servitors, which presumably included Mary, and all the movable property they had carried aboard to the undermanned crew of a battleship struck Thomas as an extreme form of putting all one's eggs in a single basket. Sir John had said quite firmly to Sir William a short time earlier, "Whatever his lordship may think of Caracciolo's command of his majesty's ships, I know him to be a first-rate seaman."

Also seated at Captain Hardy's table, while the latter anxiously paced the quarterdeck above with his lordship, was Count Esterhazy.

Unlike his lordship, Thomas ruefully reflected, none of them appeared to suffer from the seasickness. With the wind behind the ship and the swell coming only from that direction, their ability to consume food and drink seemed unabated. All the wine was coming from his lordship's stores! He had no direct access to these because the great cabin had been given over to Queen Maria Carolina, her ladies, and Lady Hamilton. Tom Allen had been ordered to follow all directions given to him by Lady Hamilton, which had earlier included tacking up sheets to partition off sleeping compartments for the queen and her children. As the sheets came from Lady Hamilton's linen he'd brought aboard, someone entering that seat of command might have thought it had become a laundry, without seeing behind the sheets the cots. Captain Hardy had had the carpenter and his mates assiduously knocking these together for three days past.

Despite the lack of an adequate cabin to which to come below, Thomas fretted for his admiral so long in a stiff breeze in a less-than-adequate coat. He tried to tell himself that now that the ship was into the first watch, ensuring the appropriate distances were kept between the masthead lights of all the ships in the convoy needed him, at least until the ship had weathered the final headland of Capri and the yards could be trimmed to alter course southward.

These thoughts very suddenly gave way to tortured recollections of a night just over seven months previous. On one of his nocturnal forays from a cramped storeroom to see to the wants of the distinguished passengers in the cabin, he had no sooner heard the neighing laugh of King Ferdinand at some remark than the regular forward-to-stern dipping and rising motion of the ship was replaced by a violent corkscrewing. The marine sentry by the door of the greatcabin dropped his musket with a clatter, and there came from above and behind him the high-speed series of slapping sounds that told of sails blowing aback.

Pray God nothing gives way, thought Thomas, as he remembered *Vanguard* dismasted and drifting toward the Corsican lee shore. By the time he recollected himself to knock and open the cabin door, bottles and goblets were rolling off the Captain's table, and King Ferdinand had fallen silent.

"Ah, Spencer, what has happened to the ship's motion?" questioned Sir William.

"Doubtless there has been a sudden shift in the wind, Sir William," he replied.

"But we heard a clatter close by before the banging of the sails," persisted Sir William.

"Your majesty and good sirs, that was only the sentry dropping his musket. Tom Allen will reassure her majesty and the ladies on that account," responded Thomas.

Already, Sir William was translating the conversation into Italian to make sure King Ferdinand had understood, but it was obvious from his queasy-looking nod that he had an excellent appreciation of what had just happened. A dripping wet midshipman scurried through the passageway to the cabin door.

"His lordship's compliments to your majesty and noble sirs, the wind has come round to the west, and the ship must tack. It will be uncomfortable, but there is no danger."

With that, the passengers would have to be satisfied because the midshipman darted away. The sound of many feet running wasswiftly superseded by the squeal of gaskets and groaning of timbers,with sails still flogging until they began to draw. Thomas suspected the heading was a long way north of west. If he was right, *Vanguard* was seeking to lead the convoy well away from Capri. So their offing couldn't quite have been good enough for comfort. He went around the cabin removing broken, rolling, and spilled items. It was no use relying on fiddles to sustain the stability of replacements, now they were in a thoroughgoing storm. None of the cabin's occupants were calling for any.

Once King Ferdinand decided to retire to his cot, his companions went one by one to the tiny sleeping cabins, from which the ship's officers had been displaced to house them. Despite no longer havingto attend the captain's cabin, Thomas could do no more than wedge himself in a corner of the storeroom to rest. The motion of the ship clawing tiny distances out to sea on each tack and the corkscrewing and huge increase in noise each time the ship came about to changetack made real sleep impossible. When Thomas dozed, even the sounding of the half-hour bells was enough to bring him wide awake.He doubted anyone lying on his cot would be doing more thanresting and perhaps holding sickness at bay. Upon lurching to a port wedged fractionally open to urinate, it was still dark despite beingwell into the morning watch.

Once he counted off the final bells of that watch, he went to ascertain whether any of his charges of the previous evening wishedto resume the captain's cabin for a cold breakfast. They did not, and it was just then that his lordship was leaving Tom Allen outside the door of the great cabin. He looked pale and unwell, and the edges ofthe scar on his forehead again looked red, even in the dim, early morning light that filtered into the passage. Thomas's mind briefly flew back to that dreadful night of the first day of August, whenamidst all the explosions and percussions, he had mopped Surgeon Jefferson's brow while he pressed together the edges of that same wound, but his lordship left him no time to dwell on the memory.

"Thomas, how fare his majesty and the gentlemen in this storm?" "All wish to remain in the sleeping cabins and require no sustenance, m'lord."

"As well for them all in this blow! Would you make to the larboard gangway, Thomas? Every fresh pair of seamanlike hands will speed our westing."

Couched as a request though it was, Thomas took it to be an orderhe knew his lordship would not have given without the situationbeing desperate and straightaway replied, "Aye, aye, m'lord."

He made his way between decks to come up onto the gangway abaft the mainmast. Immediately, he stepped out from the companionway's shelter; he felt the tremendous force of the wind, which seemed to swoop down on him from both main and mizzen sails and yet sweep horizontally across the deck from starboard at the same time. The yards were trained round well aft to larboard on this southerly tack, and Thomas handed his way along a rigged lifeline to the group of seamen by the braces, taking what shelterthey could from the portside bulwark and awaiting the next order. Luckily, there was now sufficient daylight to see any sign given from the quarterdeck.

No shouted command would carry over the shrieking wind and the working of the ship's timbers.

While he waited, Thomas ventured a glance over the side. Spray, not rain, obstructed his view on the beam. The way the ship rolled, while rising and falling to the wave crests at an oblique angle, was truly stomach wrenching. Thomas reflected he was lucky the Good Lord had given him the robust constitution to cope with these conditions.

He looked aft to see his lordship's one hand and arm wrapped around a quarterdeck rail, while Captain Hardy watched him anxiously. Thomas knew too well the willpower it cost his admiral to keep the quarterdeck like this. He turned to the beam again, and there, as the ship rose and the spray fell away, was *Sannita* several cable lengths away, apparently keeping station on *Vanguard*. *Atleast, the young woman, Mary, is safe,* he thought. Not that she would be able to do other than lie in whatever bed space she had been given, wondering if the ship was about to founder. He wished he could tell her how well the ship had been sailed thus far.

When the time came for Thomas to haul on a rope in companywith others, he found he had lost none of his facility for the work. Indeed, when it came to securing the main yard, upon the tricky evolution of wearing ship being completed, he found himself becoming again the leading hand he'd once been, mainly because his limbs were not so frozen and awkward as those of his temporary workmates. The last leg tacked had been a long one, so it followed that his lordship and Captain Hardy must have calculated somewesting was being achieved.

When a short time into the new leg seven bells of the forenoon watch sounded, Thomas worked his way aft again to see if King Ferdinand and his party would require any dinner that early afternoon. All remained willingly confined to their cots and Thomas was left in no doubt they would remain there until the storm abated. As a result, his lordship saw him resume his temporary position well before the catastrophe which struck at three bells in the afternoon watch.

The ship was sailing well on the southerly tack and, after another up-roll glance to see *Sannita* still on station, Thomas noticed his lordship confer with Captain Hardy then hand his way to the quarterdeck companionway. He knew this led to a small cabin wherecharts were kept. No sooner had the admiral gone down than Thomas was first aware of a huge increase in pressure on the ropes holding the main yard in position and on the port-side top corner of the mainsail. A fraction of a second later, the the shrieking wind rose to a far higher pitch and volume. Before the senses could quite work out where this mighty gust was coming from, the ship rolled over alarmingly to port, and a series of sharp cracks were audible, even above the wind.

Thomas's first thought was, *The masts have gone and we are all dead.* But while they groaned and worked as much as he had ever seen, they were still there. It was only as something flashed by, high above, that he realized the sails had blown out. He saw Captain Hardy shout something to the two helmsmen, and they started toturn the wheel. Gradually, the ship began to come round to a few points east of south, and slowly rolled back to a more normal angle. Thomas ran forward to a locker, wrenched it open, and grabbed an axe. He ran further forward, looking up. It was obvious all the topsails had blown to pieces, but the mast stays were holding. The fore topmast staysail had blown to rags, and a loose cable was lashing around with lethal force.

That was not the most urgent difficulty because the driver was hanging by a number of ropes, in part over the starboard bow. It would have to be cleared, however close to the deck the loose cable was lashing. Thomas ran to where a corner of the driver already overthe side appeared to be hanging from a single rope and lurched against the bulwark. Remembering the watchword, "one hand for theship and one for yourself," he held on with his left for dear life and swung the axe in his right down onto the rope where it was taut on top of the bulwark. It was sliding toward him, so he backed and swung again. It seemed to take too many blows before the rope severed and the overboard end slid away, while the inboard end flewaway from his sight. He had felt rather than heard the axe blows of others as he had chopped frantically.

The inboard section of the driver began to slide toward the bulwark, and he stumbled back aft, partly to be safe as the canvas and severed rope ends finally slid into the sea, but also reflectingthat the main yard might need trimming again. For him, it was not to be. A seaman grabbed his shoulder and shouted, "Our Nel wants ye aft." He looked up to the quarterdeck to see Captain Hardy beckoning him urgently with his lordship close by. He could but climbthe quarterdeck ladder and knuckle his forehead to both.

It was admiral, not captain, who spoke with some with some anxiety. "Thomas, you must go below and reassure our passengers —all of them. Tom Allen has uttered loose words, making them fear our end is nigh. Say I will be down to tell them more when Captain Hardy and I are satisfied as to our position. And send Tom Allen to me forthwith!" Thomas had just got out a swift, "Aye, aye, m'lord," when Nelson waved his telescope to port and continued, "I see your Mary is still sailing snug in our lee."

Thomas continued toward the companionway to the stern cabins. As he well knew, *Sannita* continued to sail with a full set of sails and all her running rigging intact, but he didn't feel the note of annoyance in His Lordship's voice called for him to comment. He just caught Hardy's words, "Caracciolo was so far to leeward; he only needed to be looking ..." Although Thomas thought Captain Hardy could be an overfierce disciplinarian, he did manage to pour oil on troubled waters sometimes. To Thomas's mind that the ship was now riding rather better on the altered course with just the lower sails to drive her. If the wind howled less, Tom Allen's tongue lashing would be very public indeed!

A strange sight met him in Captain Hardy's cabin. Count Esterhazy stood swaying in front of a partly open light on the ship's quarter, threw out some small object, and lurched forward to try and shut out the ingress of waves sluicing along the ship's side.

Thomas launched himself past the count at the light and jammed ittight shut, watched imperturbably from his seat by the cabin's only other occupant, Sir John Acton. The count looked most unwell and muttered, *"Pour le Dieu de la mer ..."* which prompted Sir John to say, "It was his snuff box to placate the god of the sea. Worth a pretty penny it was too!"

Thomas was no French scholar, but he'd instinctively understood the Count's meaning, and rather pagan he thought it. However, it wasn't his place to take exception to the misplaced faith of a foreign nobleman, and he had a message to deliver.

"His lordship's compliments, m'lord and Sir John. A fierce squall blew out the upper sails, but the damage is now cleared, and the ship has come to ride better on a slightly altered course. His lordship will come down very soon to advise you further."

"Very well, I shall so advise his majesty and Sir William. Both are intheir sleeping cabins. His majesty, like myself, has faith in God and the skill of those who sail this ship, but you will have to look to her majesty and those with her. I fear all is not well in the great cabin." Thomas asked after Sir William, and with the terse answer he didn't quite understand, came a question.

"He has ensured he will not drown. Are any others of our convoy insight?"

"*Sannita* is sailing to leeward, Sir John, with all her sails drawing well."

A stream of Italian directed to the Count then followed Sir John's snort of satisfaction at the news. As this included the name Caracciolo, Thomas assumed Sir John was asserting confirmation ofthe Commodore's quality as a seaman. He then reverted briefly to English, in good military fashion, with, "Carry on, Spencer."

When he reached the door of the great cabin and knocked, the voice within that responded, "Enter," over a female cry of pain, was recognizable as Surgeon Jefferson's. The scene that met Thomas was reminiscent of the surgeon's orlop during action or after a serious accident. Mr Jefferson was kneeling over the head of aplump lady, who had bled profusely over her expensive gown before being laid on her side across two chairs, his needle and gut poised inhis right hand. Beyond the woman was a man dressed like in the livery of Neapolitan royal servants but who was clearly holding her down. Just a few feet away, on a small cot was a young boy, in fine shirt and breeches only, with his limbs shaking and twitching uncontrollably. Kneeling to one side of the cot, trying to hold still this boy in a miniature man's undress, was Lady Hamilton. There was a slight froth at the boy's mouth, and his eyes were staring but unseeing. Despite her height and weight above him, she was having little success in bringing the boy's convulsions under control. She looked up, fatigue filling eyes that more often sparkled, and said, "Ha, Thomas Spencer, come aid me with Prince Alberto."

Chapter 3

Royal Tragedy

Downward pressure from Thomas on the arm and knee of the boy prince, across the cot from Lady Hamilton, had no immediate effect, nor did the damp cloth with which she wiped his face and soothed his forehead. There were more cries and groans from the plump lady, held prone, as Surgeon Jefferson rapidly stitched her head wound. These diminished so much when he reached the point of tearing a piece of linen to provide a bandage that Thomas became aware of someone female moaning and retching behind a blanket. This was stretched across part of the cabin's width and tacked to theunderside of the timbers above. Lady Hamilton grimaced at thesound of the ripping material. Some more of her own linen, Thomas surmised, as he looked down again at the shaking little boy. It was amazing that such a small, fragile form could convulse with such uncontrollable power.

Lady Hamilton whispered over the boy's shaking body, "Is it my imagination, or is the ship moving a little easier through the water?"

"The motion is easier, m'lady, now that we sail under the lower sails only," responded Thomas.

"Is dear Lord Nelson still up there keeping the deck?" she questioned further.

"Aye, m'lady, he will come down to keep you better informed when he and Captain Hardy are sure of our position."

"I doubt I should understand very much about our position on the sea, and I have such trust in Lord Nelson's ability. Surely, my husband would follow it perfectly, being a man of science. Have you seen my husband?"

"No, m'lady, but I have been told by Sir John that he keeps to his sleeping cabin," admitted Thomas.

At this point, Lady Hamilton switched her attention away from Thomas and beckoned to the manservant, who had just helped the plump lady with the bandaged head to sit upright on one of the two chairs. Surgeon Jefferson, wiping his needle to replace in a small oilskin pack, also came to stand over the boy's cot, looking down at him intently for a few moments before speaking.

"You understand, my Lady, there is nothing I can do for the boythat you are not already doing. The cause of his condition is notclear, and I believe even a small dose of tincture of laudanum wouldharm him. I will return to see him again in an hour or so, but in themeantime, I must look to an orlop full of seamen injured in this blow.""I am sure you are more needed in your orlop, Mr Jefferson. Ibelieve I detect a slight lessening in Prince Alberto's spasms." Had that reply been given in other than a sweet, reasonable tone, it could have given offence. The accompanying winning smile as she knelt there, looking up at the Surgeon, sealed his acceptance that he was merely being allowed to go without argument. Then, in another ofLady Hamilton's lightning changes of focus, she spoke rapidly inItalian to the liveried servant. He knelt alongside her and took hold ofthe boy, allowing her to stand and move back before telling Thomas what she was about.

"This is Saverio Rodino, Thomas. He is the best of the queen's stewards, so now you can both faithfully steward Prince Albertowhile I look to her majesty and my husband."

With that, she swayed with the ship's motion in a way that looked graceful for such a tall woman and moved to the junction between two blankets where the separated space in one corner of the stern lights started. This was from where Thomas heard feminine groaningand retching, so he wasn't surprised to hear Lady Hamilton speakingItalian in a tone that oozed reassurance, but she received only a halting reply, punctuated as it was by spasms of seasickness. Itdidn't sound as though the queen had anything left inside her to void.After a few further words from Lady Hamilton, she reappeared and left the cabin.

"You steward also?" Saverio questioned Thomas in halting English, curiosity written in his dark eyes. Although he was a handsome, olive-skinned man of medium build, there was nothing superior in his demeanor, despite the grand livery. That was now rather rumpled and soiled, but it was his obvious sincerity and willingness to please that made Thomas take pains to explain his situation, using his few Italian words.

"Yes, *si,* I am, *sono,* Lord Nelson's steward. He ordered me to aid the passengers, and Sir John Acton said I was most needed in here, *qui.*" After saying all this very slowly, he pointed down to the cabin floor in case he was wrong in the meaning of *qui,* but he needn't have worried because a smile came on Saverio's face as he said, *"Bene."*

It was only a fleeting smile because the boy Prince's spasmsincreased in intensity and Thomas instantly regretted moving one hand away. As he resumed a firm grip, Saverio doing likewise questioned him again, *"Il dottore, no aid principe?"*

Thomas felt this deserved a better answer than he was capable of making Saverio understand. "He is only Surgeon for seamen, not really a Physician ..."

Thomas had only got so far with his explanation when Lady Hamilton returned and completed in Italian what he had been trying to explain. Saverio thanked her graciously, also mentioning Thomas. Her Ladyship looked down at the boy for a few moments, seemed satisfied, and then knelt by the chair of the plump lady. The latter had been slumped, as though unconscious, but responded in a slurred voice when Lady Hamilton spoke to her.

After a brief exchange, Her Ladyship called, "Thomas, you willhave to hold Prince Alberto alone for a short while. The Duchess of Castelcicala is sufficiently recovered from cutting her head on his lordship's sideboard that she believes she could lie down and sleep. Safer by far that Saverio aids me to walk her to her cot."

It was during this explanation that Lord Nelson arrived and immediately took charge.

"Stay as you are, Thomas and Saverio. I will assist our ministering angel."

He wasn't altogether steady on his own feet, but he placed his one hand under the duchess's right elbow, while Lady Hamilton levered her to her feet and effectively bore the weight of all three against the roll of the ship for the mercifully short walk to a blanketed compartment in a corner of the cabin opposite the queen.

"Madam," continued Nelson, "it grieves me that you were injured when the upper sails blew out and that my sideboard was the instrument of your injury."

It was obvious the duchess understood not a word of it, so bemused was her expression, but a few words in Italian from Lady Hamilton resolved that. So, it was that from behind the blanket cameNelson's voice saying, "That was none so ill, madam, now the ship's motion is more regular. I wish you a good night's sleep."

Coming from behind the blanket, with his arm in Lady Hamilton's, he said reassuringly, "I am now satisfied our position is far to thewest of Punta Licosa and have hopes of a more favorable shift in thewind overnight."

"Then, my husband can surely lay down his loaded pistols," responded her ladyship.

"What in the name of heaven would he want with those?" asked his lordship in astonishment, as Thomas also stared, open mouthed, awaiting the answer.

"He said he was resolved not to die with the guggle-guggle-guggle of saltwater in his throat, so was prepared to shoot himself as soon as he felt the ship sinking!"

"I suppose the second pistol was in case the motion spoiled his aim," his lordship added, "but Sir William should not fear drowning while he sails on my ship. I have the firm conviction that, should I die at sea, it will be through enemy action, not foundering. That is why I wish my coffin could always sail with me."

It was obvious to Thomas that his admiral had blithely failed to seethe look of consternation that flashed across the face of the lady on his arm. They crossed to the cabin door before she replied and he turned to face her.

"My dear Lord Nelson, we cannot all contemplate our own deaths with such sangfroid. Are you away to your quarterdeck for the night again and in a fair way to killing yourself with fatigue?"

Thomas saw that his lordship's good eye twinkled with delight at Lady Hamilton's concern for him. Beautiful women always brought a florid turn of phrase from him.

"My dearest angel of mercy, the worries of my office might be my undoing, but not fatigue. There is a chartroom I can repair to as occasion allows. Thomas, bide here the night, and follow my lady's instructions."

With that, Nelson's hand reluctantly fell away from Her Ladyship's arm, and he left the cabin. Thomas wondered where Tom Allen now was but thought that he would be unlikely to be sent to relieve him after earlier events. He would just have to carry on helping with the young prince and the cabin's other passengers.

In the event, a better night was passed than he had dared hope. The queen stopped retching as the ship's motion improved further, the duchess snored behind her blanket, and the spasms of the boy prince declined gradually to the point where only one man needed to hold him. Saverio and Thomas could do this in shifts, leaving one free to doze. Sometime in the first watch, the boy's spasms ceased altogether, giving way to what seemed to be a fitful sleep. Lady Hamilton had not slept, but spent long periods with the queen and her other young children. She regularly reappeared to check on the conditions of Prince Alberto and the duchess. In truth, she needed to divide her time in this way. The queen had given birth to the youngest princess very recently, so suckling was essential, seasickness notwithstanding.

Surgeon Jefferson returned twice in that watch, once early on when he had been quite rueful about the young prince but well satisfied with the duchess. On the second occasion, he seemed a little happier with the boy but still doubtful.

"You or Signor Rodino will have to keep a careful eye on the prince, Thomas Spencer. I cannot be sure there will not be another crisis."

When he had gone again, Thomas asked Saverio, "Is there no royal physician to care for the prince?"

The reply was, "I look, no on ship, on altra ship."

"Another ship," Thomas interpreted for both of them. "It was difficult to embark all the people the royal family had need of." There he had to leave the matter and just say a silent prayer for there to be no further crisis.

The only other visitor was Tom Allen, who had the good fortune to just put his head around the cabin door while Lady Hamilton waswith the queen. He told Thomas he was taking care of the male passengers now and in the morning, ending with, "Worse ways to spend Christmas Day."

He ducked away and shut the door not a moment too soon. Her ladyship almost instantly emerged from behind the blanket abruptly

"Did I hear that miscreant Tom Allen?" When Thomas confirmed the accuracy of her hearing and the content of the message, the response was more measured.

"I had better look to my husband again to be sure he has created no further alarm."

Thomas smiled to himself as she left the cabin for a short time. Saverio, who had woken at the sound of Tom Allen's voice, first looked at Thomas quizzically during the exchange with Lady Hamilton then solemnly tapped the side of his nose in response to the smile. Truly, it was hard to regain the lady's regard once lost!

Right through the middle watch and more than the first two bells thereafter, the only real movement in the great cabin was LadyHamilton padding around all her charges. She seemed to ride the ship's motion with ease and amazingly able to hold fatigue at bay. It was while she was looking down at the boy Prince again that the marine sentry, contrary to his orders for the time being, banged his musket butt on the passage floor. This could portend only one visitor and, slightly abashed though he was by the noise of his entrance, Lord Nelson exuded cheerful, wind-borne vigor.

"My dear lady, my regrets that the sentry forgot his orders, but we are so near a much fairer first light that I felt impelled to be first to wish you joy of the day of Our Savior's birth. The wind is moving round to a much more favorable quarter for our passage to Palermo, and I have hopes of greater comfort for a swifter passage."

"My dear Lord Nelson, after all your endeavors for the safety of their majesties and all of us, it is yourself who most deserves joy of this Christmas Day."

"How does her majesty now fare? I should like to wish her joy of this day."

"Sadly, she and the little princesses remain prostrate with the seasickness. Best that I convey your good wishes to them in a little while."

At this, Lady Hamilton moved impulsively across the cabin floor to take both of Nelson's hands in hers and turned him to face Prince Alberto's cot.

"See how much better our young prince does."

Indeed, the boy was blinking as though in the course of waking, and Saverio began speaking to him softly and reassuringly in Italian. It was only at this point that his Lordship appeared to notice Thomas and Saverio.

"I see you have both had a long night of this duty. No matter, Ihave now put Tom Allen back to caring for his majesty and all of those in the wardroom." Turning again to Lady Hamilton, he continued, "If your ladyship should be able to cope with only Signor Rodino to assist for an hour from five bells, it will help in raising the spare set of upper sails to have Thomas on the larboard gangway again, once we have beat to quarters and there is sufficient light."

As if on cue, the boy prince opened his eyes and piped a couple of words, to which Lady Hamilton responded at greater length, pointing to the blanket behind which his mother and sisters lay. The boy looked reassured; her ladyship turned back to Nelson.

"There is your confirmation, my Lord, that we shall cope in here while Thomas is absent, useful though he has been all night. Pray, send him back at sometime today and not Tom Allen to replace him. *He* can stay under Mrs Cadogan's feet."

"Most assuredly you shall have Thomas back, dear lady."

24

Thus it was that Thomas found himself making his way within the ship again to the gangway close by the quarterdeck ladder and forward to the little knot of seamen above the waist. *What a difference from the last time,* he thought. Will waved to him from the starboard gangway. There were two more seamen than on his side, presumably through injuries in the gale. The scudding clouds wereno longer a single dark mass and the wind no longer looked to have excessive force for both topsails and topgallants. Better still, so far as he could judge where the light was coming from without actually seeing the sun, the direction was southeast.

The result of all this was that well over an hour elapsed withThomas reverted to leading hand on the larboard gangway. The upper sails were raised and all were reset to best effect, so when the last brace was tied off, all was well above deck.

It was a fearful shock to return to the pandemonium in the great cabin. Saverio was on his hands and knees with bucket and cloth, trying to wipe around the cot of Prince Alberto. The boy was screaming in pain, curled into a fetal position from which Lady Hamilton and Mrs Cadogan were trying to straighten him sufficiently for Surgeon Jefferson to examine. The queen had ventured from her own cot but was slumped on a chair close by, tears rolling down her cheeks. The duchess, with her bandaged head, was kneeling the far side of the queen, trying to comfort her but sounding and looking as though she was merely wailing herself.

Thomas could see both blood and bile amongst the lumps of undigested food that Saverio was trying to remove with cloth and seawater, and the smell was even more unhealthily pungent than it had been earlier. He could not help a shudder of foreboding thatsuch a small body should be capable of voiding so much.

His arrival was spotted by the waiting surgeon. "Spencer, come and assist Her Ladyship and Mrs Cadogan, but gently, man."

Hesitantly, Thomas moved forward, not wanting to spoil the progress Saverio was making in his task, at the same time anxiousto avoid showing revulsion or reluctance. "Here man, hold his shoulders, and leave his legs to the ladies. They have gentler hands," said the impatient surgeon. Thomas held onto the soft skinof the boy's delicately small shoulder blades, thinking his hands mustfeel like two especially rough lumps of holystone. Immediately, Surgeon Jefferson's hand touched the boy's lower abdomen, heconvulsed and shrieked, his skinny arms flailing. The realization hit him that the poor boy's pain would be making him insensible to any other feeling. He could tell Surgeon Jefferson was steeling himself against the young prince's reaction to his touch while gently and methodically feeling the flesh all around his groin. Soon done, the surgeon said, "Let go of his legs if you please, ladies. It does nogood now, but you hold on, Spencer, so the boy doesn't fall."

He then whispered urgently, "My lady, I must beg your aid inspeaking with her majesty." Lady Hamilton, looking distraught in a way that Thomas had not seen before, which aged her in his sight, merely nodded her assent, let her hands slip away from the boy's legs, and straightened up with head bowed. Mrs Cadogan held her grip on the boy but moved with his legs as they curled again before she let go. A tear rolled down her cheek, as she faced Thomas and watched her daughter move to the unoccupied side of the queen's chair, while Surgeon Jefferson stood resolutely in front of the queen and bowed before speaking.

"Your Majesty, I believe there is no treatment I can give your son tocure his condition." He halted while Lady Hamilton translated and then continued, "Something has burst inside him to cause him the great pain he suffers." After another break for translation, he added, "I can relieve the pain with tincture of laudanum to an extent, but it may have the effect of so weakening the prince that he expires before we reach land."

As this was translated, the queen threw up her arms, flung them around Lady Hamilton, buried her face in the latter's dress, and gave a series of great, muffled sobs. In order to try to continue speaking with her friend, Lady Hamilton slowly sank to her knees by the chair, caressed the queen's hair, and murmured several words to her. Thomas could see that Saverio, who had now finished with the cloth and bucket, was straining his ears to catch the gist of his queen's reply, but the repeated sobs made that impossible.

Her ladyship then addressed a question to the Surgeon. "Hermajesty asks if a physician and surgeon expert in this kind of ailmentwould be able to save the life of Prince Alberto, should he survive to reach land?"

"It is my opinion that, even if such a physician and surgeon were present now, he would be able to do no more than I suggest. I am very sorry to have to say this."

When Lady Hamilton translated this, another outburst of heaving sobs followed, interspersed with incoherent words. Nonetheless, the translation given was, "Do as you suggest."

Stiffly, Surgeon Jefferson responded, "I will need to ask his majestytoo."

Wearily, Lady Hamilton rose after another brief exchange with the queen, who still sobbed and reluctantly let go of her. "We are surehis majesty's view will be the same, Mr Jefferson. I will take you to him," and with that, Lady Hamilton led the surgeon from the cabin.

Thomas did not know if he should release his grip on the prince to allow him to curl up on his side. He whimpered pathetically in his nakedness, with his legs up, but Surgeon Jefferson would need him face up to administer tincture of laudanum, so it was kinder to hold the boy firmly as he was. Saverio brought a cover and draped it over the boy, up to his chest.

When Lady Hamilton returned, the king and Prince Leopold came with her and Surgeon Jefferson. It was obvious they had come tosay farewell to son and brother. Thomas found it very hard to avoid showing the emotion he felt whilst continuing to be the deferential servant. His lordship joined those gathered to ask if more assistance was needed and to give the estimation that Palermo would be reached in the middle of the night. Although his extreme discomfiturewas obvious, he let it be known quite eloquently, through LadyHamilton, that he would pray for Prince Alberto and his royal parents and that he would send his chaplain, the Reverend Comyn, to pray with them. He had no choice but to offer spiritual comfort in this way, seeing that the Reverend Comyn was a Church of England clergyman, but no offence was taken in this sorry situation. Thomas could see his lordship was struggling to cope with the atmosphere of grief in anticipation amongst those in the cabin and relieved to be able to escape back to the quarterdeck.

The rest of that Christmas Day was too full of sadness for Thomas to remember more of the comings and goings. He did remember the body of the boy prince visibly relaxing when Surgeon Jefferson had poured a small phial of laudanum mixture down his throat. A fresh nightdress they had put on him and brought a chair so that Lady Hamilton could sit with the boy in her arms, reasonably close to his sobbing mother, who was still unable to take food or drink. Once, when her majesty dozed, he managed to persuade her ladyship to take a few mouthfuls of coffee, but out of deference to her friend, shewould not eat as the day wore on and daylight gave way to dusk, then darkness. The breathing of the child against her bosom grew progressively shallower, and Thomas, with nothing now to do, other than go on his knees while the Reverend Comyn prayed for this child and for those to whom he was dear, was not surprised when Surgeon Jefferson held a mirror to the boy's open mouth, saw no moisture form, and whispered, "My lady, the child has gone."

What did prove a surprise and a lasting memory, after the queen had given a great moan of grief and flung herself across her dead child and her friend, was Lady Hamilton, white-faced and whispering,"I could never go through such an ordeal with a child to whom I had given birth."

Thomas did not understand the look Mrs Cadogan gave her daughter, which might have been a warning to speak no more. He reflected that, in the presence of grieving royalty, perhaps it was simply a mother-to-daughter expression that quietly comforting her friend would be best. Her Ladyship began stroking the queen's hair and murmuring to her in Italian, but her expression remained just asit had been when whispering her fervent utterance, until Saverio gently lifted his queen away.

Chapter 4

Strange Introduction to Palermo

The sailmaker was summoned to the great cabin and assessed the quantity of canvas needed to fully wrap the corpse of Prince Alberto but not before Lady Hamilton had led the queen tactfully back intoher sleeping compartment. In voices as low as they could manage, Thomas and Saverio let the sailmaker know that the wrapping was not for a burial at sea, but only so that his laid-out body could be parceled and carried ashore for a funeral mass. A measured piece ofthin board, the recovered end of a blown-out sail, and the small amount of cordage required were rapidly and quietly agreed.

Little time elapsed before he returned with the necessary material. The canvas had been cut to shape and looked suitably clean. Using the small, stripped-down cot, Saverio carefully draped the canvas over it, placed the board on that and then the body wholly on the board in a clean nightgown. With hands together on his chest, eyes closed, face clean, and hair tidy, the frail body would have lookedlike a small boy saying his prayers, had it not been for the unearthly pallor of his skin in the candlelight. It was at this stage that Thomas advised Lady Hamilton, with the sobbing queen on her cot, they might wish to come and see the Prince before he had to be covered for his final bodily journey.

The resulting outburst of grief was especially hard for the two men to bear. The great wrenching cry as the bereaved mother threw herself to her knees by the makeshift bier and pressed her lips to those of the dead child had tears coursing down their unshaven cheeks as they stood silently with heads bowed. It was only when Lady Hamilton took advantage of a brief steadying in the rolling ofthe ship to lift the queen bodily to her feet that she noticed the two men, seemed briefly to recognize they shared her grief, but allowed herself to be turned away wordlessly.

Lady Hamilton briefly returned from behind the blanket to tell them softly to do what was necessary, and the canvas was duly folded over the small body. Thomas fed the cordage beneath, three times across and once end to end, all lines neatly joined, as befitted his calling. When he had tied off the ends, he stuck his arms beneath and lifted.

"No great weight," he whispered to Saverio, who took in the lack ofstrain in his shoulders and responded, *"Si,"* his eyes expressing the understanding that pained them.

Much later, when the first watch was virtually over, his lordship returned. Tired though he obviously was, he had to temper his exhilaration at the progress of the voyage upon entering the great cabin and paused by the makeshift bier.

"Is that the body of the prince you have parceled, Thomas?""Yes, m'lord," he replied, likewise in a low voice.

"The queen and Lady Hamilton?" Lord Nelson next asked, pointing to the hanging blankets. He scarcely waited for Thomas's answer before pacing briskly to the point where they joined.

His entrance and low-voiced words to the queen prompted another outbreak of sobbing, but another intervention from Lady Hamilton helped bring it to an end, and there ensued a three-way conversation in both English and Italian before he emerged and, on this occasion, addressed both Saverio and Thomas.

"The queen has asked that you go ahead together, carrying the body of Prince Alberto to the palace when we land. I intend to follow with her majesty and the princesses before his majesty is greeted byhis leading subjects in Palermo. All being well, this can be done before dawn, but your appearance must be suitable to impress thoseyou will need to deal with. Freshwater rather than seawater, methinks. I will see you are free to draw some off. You have about three hours to ready yourselves. Galley fires will be lit sooner."

Once these orders were imparted, His Lordship quit the greatcabin, leaving Thomas to try and explain to Saverio the parts he had not understood. Fortunately, miming the cleaning of clothing, shaving, and drawing water from a barrel got Thomas through the preparation needed. Saverio had understood the order to carry the prince's body to the palace, but not the time available to prepare. "Quando?" he asked, and Thomas, guessing what that meant held up three fingers. "*Tre ore,*" said Saverio, answering his own questionjust before Lady Hamilton reappeared to repeat it all in Italian.

They were then free to depart so Thomas could first help Saverio smarten his livery, seeing that he lacked any alternative clothing. When they reached the nearest water butt, the marine guard alreadt had his instructions, so Thomas drew off a canvas bucket full. They had watered only five days before in the Bay of Naples, so it was clean enough to do most of what was needed to Saverio's livery. By the time that was done, the motion of the ship had become so much more regular that Thomas thought they might safely shave. He mimed this to Saverio, left him in the storeroom he was currently sharing with Tom Allen, and went off with his bucket to the galley, returning with a copper bowl of reasonably hot water. With that and alittle soap, each in turn gingerly applied Thomas's cutthroat razor to the other's bristles. By the time Thomas had changed into his best uniform and the odd spot of soap and hot water had been applied to the more obdurate blotches on Saverio's livery, they were able to return to the great cabin looking fit for duty, if still exhausted. The change was promptly observed by Lady Hamilton.

"Now that you are both prepared for the next duty, I must look to her majesty and myself."

She then continued in Italian, which had Saverio headed for the Queen's sleeping compartment. Just as he did so, there came a slight lurch of the ship and a scraping noise from forward, which progressively moved aft. Thomas recognized this as rope fenders rubbing on a durable surface. There were a number of shoutedorders above, and he then heard the sound of feet on a stonesurface as well as those on deck.

"I believe we are in harbor m'lady." "Heaven be praised," she responded.

Saverio had obviously gone to one of the stern lights and peered out into the darkness because he called out, *"Molo di Palermo,"* but the queen still sobbed intermittently. Thereafter, activity in the great cabin dramatically increased. Lady Hamilton had them rushing around bringing more water for the queen to wash and dress for outdoor travel. Then she woke and similarly prepared the two princesses who were old enough to have outdoor clothes. For the baby, cleaning and a handy carrying blanket were readied. Only thenwas word of their availability sent out.

His lordship was the first visitor, just to check that there were no last orders to give. Tom Allen had already put him in his boat cloak and given him his hat, a sure sign he was all of a fever to beonshore. With even the duchess now in her outdoor clothing, he saw there was nothing further to be done and withdrew so that the King, Prince Leopold, Sir John, and Sir William could enter. His majesty cast one look at the parceled body of his dead son and went to embrace his wife, which brought on a brief renewal of the sobbing, until Sir John and Sir William in turn addressed her majesty withwhat Thomas assumed to be condolences. It was when Sir William had finished speaking that the queen, broken voiced, launched into aspeech about Lady Hamilton, which would no doubt have been a paean had the circumstances not been so tragic. The old man looked slightly embarrassed by the praise of his wife, although he was doing his best to conceal his feelings. King Ferdinand joined in with the effect of bringing the praise to an end. Thomas thought Sir William had aged during the voyage, while his wife seemed to have reinvigorated herself with all her exertions. He noticed that His Lordship had been staring at her with a rapturous expression during the expressions of praise and gratitude.

The King gave instructions to Saverio, which repeatedly used the word *prete.,*

Lady Hamilton, seeing the look of mystification on Thomas's face, whispered, "You have to find a priest who serves as a royal chaplain and do as he directs."

He, Sir John, and Sir William then left, and it was time for Saverio to take up his burden. He did this reverently, and Thomas led him out of the cabin and through the ship to the larboard waist. A reasonably level gangway had been laid from a sally port to the quayside.

Despite the swell within the harbor being muted, it was still a shock to their legs and balance to feel the stone of the quayside underfoot. Thomas motioned to Saverio to stop a moment. Better to allow a chance to regain balance than risk a fall that would look very poor, given his burden. The ship was moored short of the point where the mole curved to the landward. Glancing back to the seaward end, Thomas could see that *Sannita* had also moored and other ships of their previously scattered convoy were nosing past into the inner harbor. Unlike *Vanguard*, they probably wouldn't need to be warped out again in a hurry.

Now they had regained their land legs, there was nothing for it but to make carefully in the darkness over the worn stone surface, ships'lights behind them. A few lights showed from the inhabited city somedistance ahead with, fortunately, a clearing sky. A wall to the seaward side of the mole did not quite cut off the view of inky water that lay to both sides and around the curve. The walkway narrowed before it came alongside some low buildings that cut off their view of the inner harbor for upward of a hundred paces, although the sea was still visible to larboard. Saverio had clearly been there before because he was stepping out with a confidence Thomas would not have felt if alone. The walkway opened out into an extended wharf, before which there stood two massive ornate stone structures. Hugely solid timber gates lay open between them. In the gloom, Thomas could just make out a wall running away from the tremendous gatehouse on the left, which was less than half the height of the gatehouse. To the right, a similar wall seemed to bend away in front of another taller building behind it, but he could see thatwas dictated by the way in which the inner harbor ran inland to that side.

"*Porta Felice*," said Saverio, pointing a finger from below his burden into the gap between the two gatehouses.

"A city gate," responded Thomas, which had Saverio mouthing the words to try and remember the expression, by which time they could look directly through the open gates. Thomas saw that a pavedroadway, lit by oil lamps at regular intervals, ran arrow straight, gently ascending into the far distance. The paving was smooth and shone nearly white below the nearest of the oil lamps.

"*Via del Cassaro*," informed Saverio, pointing with his finger along the roadway.

They continued through the gateway, and Thomas just had time to see a broad stairway some yards to his left before Saverio's steady pacing took them alongside the tall stone building on their right. The rising wall to the left and the steps at it's beginning suggested some kind of walkway on top of it.

This would have been claustrophobic had they not rapidly come to a point where steps up to a church entrance on the right werematched by the opening of a large, paved area to their left. Briefly, Saverio halted, first inclining his head to the right.

"*Santa Maria della Catena*," said Saverio, as if reading Thomas's thoughts, adding, "fishermen's church." Then, looking left, he said, "*Piazza Marina*," before continuing on up the straight roadway. Thomas tried hard to memorize these names, fearing he wouldstruggle to find his way back to the ship with no Italian vocabulary to seek directions. He would just have to mime what he meant and tryto remember more Italian words to include in what he said, if he was left alone at some point.

He walked more quickly, so he could be fully within Saverio's sight once past the large, open *Piazza Marina* and into a section of the straight road flanked by tall, unlit houses.

He held out both arms, pointed to himself, and asked, "I carry?" Saverio thought about it for a moment then responded, "A little."

He stopped, faced Thomas, and allowed him to carefully slide his arms under the wrapped corpse before withdrawing his own. Although the weight was slight, carrying in that arms-outstretched manner over hard stone paving with shadows between the lights must have soon tired Saverio. As Thomas followed him along the road, with the occasional darker alleyway leading off into a jumble of unlit buildings, his shoulders began to ache with carrying in this manner. However, the sky visible above was beginning to lighten, and he was encouraged by the lack of deviation since entering the *Porta Felice*.

He hoped he'd got that name right! It seemed like several minutes' walk to reach one substantial crossroads that Saverio didn't name and quite a few more to reach a crossroads where the high buildings on all four corners were fronted by columns, carvings, and statueson several levels.

Saverio turned and said, "*Quattro Canti* is name," then carried on walking while Thomas, trying to keep up, pointed his finger up to the armored statue of a man bearing a sword and asked, "Who is he?"

"Spagnolo King, all Spagnoli Kings," responded Saverio. Thomas thought he meant Spanish Kings of bygone centuries and nodded sagely. Beyond this grand crossroads, they passed two narrower crossroads and were just coming to an opening on the right when Saverio turned and held out his arms to receive Thomas's burden.

"*Prete* no see you *portare*." Thomas had no difficulty working this out and in no way felt offended, seeing that he was not of the Roman persuasion.

He stood still while Saverio retook the burden from him and responded, "*Portare* in English is carry."

With a grin, Saverio added, "You learn *Italiano*. I carry is *porto*." They reached the opening, a street that looked to lead to a square,

but the view that really caught Thomas's attention, over the tops of the buildings the far side of this street, was a circular stone structure surrounded by a latticework of timbers. There were ladders leading up the timbers, so Thomas assumed a roof was still to be provided. "*Duomo,*" explained Saverio, and when Thomas looked mystified, added, "*Cattedrale.*"

But when Thomas exclaimed, "Ah, you mean the dome of the cathedral that isn't yet finished," it was Saverio's turn to look puzzled. Thomas pointed to the ongoing construction and circled his hands to show what he meant. Saverio merely nodded his understanding and continued walking past another short street on the right. This gave a view of a high and apparently crenellated wall to one end of a building.

"Cathedral also," grunted Saverio and walked on some distance to the next opening on the right. The huge building stretching from the corner up the side street had two high stone arches linking it to the building further up the near side. With his head, Saverio indicated the building opposite.

"*Palazzo Arcivescovile,* we go."

He led Thomas along the side street and across to double doors set in well-maintained stonework with a metal bellpull set high up thedoor frame. With a forefinger poking out from under his burden, Saverio pointed up to the bell pull, so Thomas duly reached up to it and pulled. There was the muted sound of a bell jangling within the building, but for nearly a minute, no sound from within.

Then came the unmistakable sounds of top and bottom bolts beingdrawn. One door was opened by a man with a brown, well-lined faceand silver hair below his priest's hat. No taller than Thomas, his cassock showed him to be spare of build, and his reaction to Saverio's answer to his first question was an expression of great sadness. He then made the sign of the cross over the bundledcorpse of the boy prince and said a prayer in a language that didn't sound quite like Italian, so Thomas assumed it was Latin. At its end, Thomas said, "Amen." The priest looked at him curiously and addressed another question to Saverio.

With its answer, he turned to Thomas, saying, "Bless you, my son, for your reverent aid to our king's servant," in heavily accented but fluent English. He continued, "I am Father Francisco and will do whatI can to aid the two of you in your sad task."

There then followed a voluble Italian conversation, at theconclusion of which Father Francisco added, "Wait while I leaveword for the Archbishop of our sad errand."

Saverio's face bore a look of relief, despite still having to hold his burden in the street. Father Francisco had closed behind him the door, which looked to lead into an internal courtyard. However, he was gone no longer than a minute and returned holding a small book in one hand. When he closed the door, someone else bolted it from inside. He stepped in front of Saverio, motioned Thomas to Saverio's side, and led them back to their original route. As he looked back toward the harbor, there was a group on foot in the distance but too far to make out anyone, although it was now virtually full daylight. Father Francisco was murmuring a prayer as they went past a seriesof low-walled rectangular enclosures on the left.

Beyond them was an open space, onto which they turned, to head for a short flight of stone steps upward. This gave access to a space so broad, left to right, and so deep before it fronted what seemed to be a massive fortress, that Thomas assumed it was a military parade ground. Father Francisco led them forward then veered left almost along the face of the building. Thomas noticed what he thought was the strangest thing about the building. There was an abrupt change from a crenellated fortress to a rather old-fashioned looking mansion that rose in successive storeys, judging by the windows, which were very narrow on the ground floor.

They halted by a pillared doorway with a strange birds and animals sculpture above. This door also had a bell pull, but the response to Father Francisco's pull was tardy.

The door was eventually opened by a shuffling, white-haired servant wearing the same livery hose as Saverio; he had obviously just pulled his shirt over his tousled hair and luxuriant moustache. Helooked baffled by the three in front of him, while Father Francisco spoke crisply. When the nature of Saverio's burden was explained, his face crumpled. His voice cracked as he responded to the sad tidings, and it seemed his expression of grief for his royal employers was only brought to a sudden end by both priest and fellow servitor successively telling him their requirements.

He then bowed them into an anteroom while he shuffled off for his keys. It was on his return to unlock a door on the far wall thatThomas realized an inner courtyard lay beyond. The winter daylight had scarcely penetrated this space between the conjoined buildings that made up the palace. As the old servitor led them through the door into the courtyard, Father Francisco turned again and said, "Now you will see the wonder of this *Palazzo dei Normanni,* the *Cappella Palatina,* which is the chapel royal."

The shuffling servitor led them slantwise across the tiles to a broad and grand stairway, which they ascended. Even in the still poor light, Thomas could see that the stairs were made of polished red marble and that the staircases wound around the courtyard to at least two levels above the ground floor. All around the courtyard were graceful stone arches supported by columns. Between each substantial plinth was a balustrade, also delicately carved in stone.

After the stairway had reached a broad, covered passageway, a view between the columns to his right and those at the far end of the courtyard on this level showed some kind of painting high on the wall. It was only when they had rounded the passage corner and come up to a point virtually below the start of this artwork that Thomas realized it was divided into more than one picture by columns on that wall, running up to brick arches. Below the first picture, whose significance he didn't understand, was a border with a series of circular head-and-shoulders portraits with names around them. The old servitor selected a key on the ring he was holding and fumbled inserting it in the door's keyhole. Thomas thought the portraits could well be of the Apostles, with their names in Latin, because the word to the left of each one was *Sanctus,* and he could certainly pick out *Thomas!*

A clink as the lock mechanism worked echoed around the courtyard. Initially, all Thomas saw as the door swung inward was a candle resting in a sconce. The servitor returned his ring of keys to aresting place in the top of his hose and took up the flint resting on thesconce. He struck it repeatedly on the metalwork near the tip of the candle's wick before he achieved a spark adequate to light thatcandle. This he then removed and carried to the next wall-mounted sconce, lit another candle, and moved on.

As he followed the others through the doorway, Thomas was totally unprepared for the transformation from the subdued decoration of the stonework around the courtyard to the array of interior colors that seemed to grow and grow with the lighting of successive candles. The pillar-mounted arches seemed to rise up and up to where the daylight had begun to percolate into the chapel from high above. While his eyes slowly swiveled round, he realized the decorations of frescoes, angels, and saints covered one arch and one recessed wall after another. Not just the outer sides of the arches, but their undersides and high, high above them. There was so much gold, both in the images that contained so many other vivid colors and in elaborate designs between the images, that his senses were virtually overwhelmed.

While he stood rooted and staring, the servitor dragged a trestle from somewhere to erect before a rail and steps leading to the altar, high above which was a seated the Virgin Mary, flanked by other figures, with a domed Christ in blue and gold glory above all.

"It is a depiction of Christ Pantocrator, reigning in Heaven," said Father Francisco, interrupting his prayers. "The whole chapel was decorated by the best artists from Constantinople, this island, and beyond that the Norman kings could persuade to come and work for them."

Thomas was staring around still when a purple cloth was draped to cover the trestle, and Saverio carefully and reverently laid his burden on it. Father Francisco's prayer then just about registered in his brain, which was fuddled even more by the smell of incense from the burner in the priest's hand. Where that had come from or how it had been lit he had no idea, but when he saw where Saverio was kneeling before the draped trestle, he automatically went to join him in prayer. Father Francisco moved around the makeshift bier, incanting from his little book and gently swinging the incense burner until he seemed satisfied that his ritual had been completed. At that point, he made the sign of the cross over the two kneeling men and had just got out, "Rise, my sons," when Lord Nelson entered the chapel, bicorn hat in the crook of his left arm, looked briefly around him, and spoke rather too loudly.

"There you both are; mission faithfully accomplished, I see."

His words echoed in the vaulted space above them as Thomas

regained his feet. Father Francisco, who had put down the incense burner while the two had knelt, turned to face his lordship.

"Have I the honor of addressing Milord Nelson?" he asked.

"Indeed you have," replied his lordship, taken aback and reducing his volume.

"I am Father Francisco from the palace of our archbishop," said the priest in a gentle tone. He then continued, "Now that I have completed the postmortem last rites for our dear little prince, I can commend our king's servant and yours for the faithful and decorous completion of this, their duty."

This was said with such humble sincerity that Nelson's response sounded defensive.

"His majesty's confessor had broken his arm in the storm. I did have my chaplain, Reverend Comyn, pray for Prince Alberto's soul while he still breathed, father, but of course, he is a priest of our English Church, not your Roman Church."

"Just so, milord, as I understand are also your own father and brother," the priest responded smoothly, "so I am sure Our Lord will have heard your devout prayers."

That this pleased Nelson was evident in his smile as he reached the reason for his visit to the chapel.

"I have brought her majesty and the princesses to habitable rooms here before his majesty is received by his subjects at the quayside. Her majesty's distress is such that time must be allowed for her to bemore composed before any public duty. I have left her in the care of those servants who attended on our arrival."

"Your kindness does you great honor, milord. I shall go with Saverio to assure her majesty that all needing to be done here has been reverently concluded and that she may come here to pray in due course."

The good father and Nelson bowed to each other, and the former then departed, leading Saverio, who smiled gratefully at Thomas as he moved away. Once they had gone, his lordship gazed around the chapel for long moments before reflecting,

"Well, Thomas, I do not suppose any royal palace or great church in England had quite such a chapel as this, even before the time of

Cromwell's despoilers. St. Paul's in London has noble proportions but is bare compared with this. How do you find it?"

"I don't know, m'lord. I've never been in a cathedral."

His lordship looked surprised. "Not even that of your own diocese?"

"No, m'lord, it's not in Nottingham."

Realization then dawned on Nelson's face. "Of course, your cathedral is York and even your Minster in Southwell. Is it not near Newark, easier by boat from Nottingham than road?"

"Yes, m'lord, but a long, hard pull back upstream."

This made his lordship smile again. "Well, Thomas, I only needyou to make the long walk back to the ship before I return for his majesty. See if you can find some kind of cart to carry Sir Williamand Lady Hamilton's bedding, linen, and other possessions here, including that which you had to leave in *Samuel and Jane*. She has moored."

Hopefully not too far out, thought Thomas, as he saluted and said, "Aye, aye, m'lord."

The knowledge that he had to be back on board before his lordship left Thomas no time for sightseeing. He had no difficulty finding the long, straight road back to the *Porta Felice*. Once he went through the gate, the inner harbor looked crammed with vessels, yet sail- bearing masts still coasted in to find a mooring. Hurriedly, he walked round to the mole and along its top.

A few local inhabitants were now gathering close to the open sally port and gangway, which boasted two marine sentries. Judging by the richness of the clothing of those who had so far arrived, *they were local dignitaries,* he thought, but his attention was instantly drawn away from them by the sight of a stationary horse and cart alongside the mooring of *Sannita*. Seated on the driver's bench, alongside him, was Mary. Without meaning to, his feet took him past *Vanguard's* stern just as the final items were thrown on the back of the cart and it started to move toward him. As they converged, he waved, and she recognized him and waved back.

"You sailed well through the storm," he called. "And you too, admiral's barge," she called back.

The realization she didn't yet know his name made him gabble, "I be Thomas Spencer, admiral's steward."

She looked at him and laughed, head thrown back and copper curls escaping from under her headscarf, gaily asking, "What are you doing off your ship, Thomas?"

"Sad duty to the *Palazzo dei Normanni* and back," he responded.

Her face and voice now sobered, and she asked, "Was that to do with the young prince we heard had died? That is why Lady Acton and her children have already gone ahead. I am sorry I did not connect you with that."

She then spoke a word of Italian to the driver, and the cart stopped again. She reached her hand down to him.

"You remember I am Mary? Mary Hever is my full name, and I am seamstress to Lady Acton." He took her hand in both of his and got out, "I remember," but only that. All he could think of was her soft hand and concerned, blue-green eyes.

"Well, Thomas Spencer, I am glad to make your acquaintance properly but must also be away to the Palazzo with Lady Acton's belongings."

He held onto her hand and rushed his words, "I am glad to properly make your acquaintance, Mistress. I am also in need of a cart for Sir William and Lady Hamilton's belongings but do not speak the Italian to find one."

"I knew it was too good to be true that you were glad to know me for my own sake!"

However, she followed her response with a few more words with the driver, and when he seemed to respond affirmatively, she turned to Thomas.

"He will return to pick up Sir William and Lady Hamilton's property after his majesty has left the ship. I will ask to be allowed to return with him, so long as you address me as Mary."

The cart moved off slowly, and Thomas walked alongside still holding Mary's hand.

"I will surely do that," he blurted, "and I am glad to be acquainted for your own self."

He reluctantly let go of her hand as the cart moved a little faster, and she called back.

"Your hands feel like I expect a proper sailor's to feel."

"But, I am a proper sailor," he responded, following on. Then he realized his feet had carried him back to *Vanguard's* gangplank.

Chapter 5

Private Conversation After
a Royal Progress

The door of the great cabin was wedged open, and the specially made cots were being removed by the carpenter's mates. Inside, Lady Hamilton's bedding was being rolled up by a party of seamen under her supervision. All the tacking along beams had gone, so the carpenter's mates must have been busy very soon after the passengers left.

"Ah, Thomas Spencer," exclaimed her ladyship as soon as she spied him, "is there a wagon for my bedding and linen?"

"There will be after his majesty has left the ship, m'lady. Mary Hever off *Sannita* has arranged with Lady Acton's carter to come back and hopes to herself."

"And here was I thinking you were only wasting time in idle chatter with her on the quayside! She sounds a useful woman, your Mary Hever."

Thomas felt a flush creeping up his neck and into his face. He had no idea they had been watched from the cabin stern lights. *How many other pairs of eyes from other parts of the ship had done the same,* he briefly wondered, but her ladyship was surely a sharper observer than most. To cover his embarrassment as best he could, he added,

"She has some of the Italian but nothing like as much as your ladyship."

Flattered though Her Ladyship obviously was by the comparison, her face bore a look of calculation. "Enough to be of help, clearly. I will trust you, Thomas, to bring after me to the palace what I have here and also that from *Samuel and Jane*. Captain Hardy has promised me a boat and crew with a senior midshipman, so you need only take delivery on the cart. Where is your list?"

"I will fetch it directly, m'Lady."

In the admiral's storeroom, Tom Allen was grumbling about the hurry everyone was in, as though it would not have the effect of restoring their own working space to them. Thomas recovered the list from where he had secreted it, told Tom he was under Lady Hamilton's orders, and rushed out again, missing Tom's knowing smile.

Back in the great cabin, the working party were lashing their bundles in sailcloth.

"Leave them in front of Lord Nelson's sideboard," ordered Lady Hamilton and dismissed them as soon as the bundles were stacked. There was also a stack that resulted from the bedding having been brought in from the cabins which had been used by the male passengers.

"Thank you, Thomas," said her ladyship graciously as she received his list. "If you could remain here with my property, I shall have Captain Hardy send away his boat."

Thomas was not left alone for long. The King, young Prince Leopold, Sir John, Sir William, and Count Esterhazy all entered to wait for the admiral's return. Even Prince Belmonte, the Royal Chamberlain, put in a belated appearance. Although all were restored in sartorial terms, they made a somber group, seated on chairs in a semicircle by the stern lights.

Thomas came to Sir William's side. "Should I offer any refreshment, Sir William?"

"No, young man. We have all breakfasted and are ready to depart."

The elderly knight did not look well, he thought, *no wonder, with the rigors of these past days.*

There was now a hubbub from the quayside, as well as on board while the ship was frantically put back to rights. The noise ashore reached a brief crescendo and was followed in less than a minute by the arrival of Lord Nelson and Captain Hardy.

"Your majesty's leading subjects in this city have noted your royal standard flying from our main and wish to pay their respects. I have returned with both closed and open carriages from the palace stables," announced his lordship.

"The people do not know of the loss of his majesty's son, nor is it fitting it should mar their wish to receive his majesty joyously. Quitting the ship should be done with due ceremony, as should be the greeting of the leading subjects. Thereafter, his majesty and Prince Leopold will proceed by open carriage to *Palazzo Colli*," responded Sir John.

Thomas noticed that Lady Hamilton had entered the great cabin quietly behind Captain Hardy and stood close to the door, unwilling to draw attention to her presence at this otherwise male gathering.

"I cannot have salutes fired while the ship is moored to the mole, but the marines will form a guard of honor from the ship's side to the point where his majesty receives his subjects. From quarterdeck to bowsprit and along the yards, officers and men, indeed the entire crew, will line the ship to cheer his majesty ashore," his lordship detailed.

Sir John looked at Prince Belmonte, who looked at his royal master, and it was evident from their expressions they had understood with satisfaction how the royal dignity was to be respected. His lordship looked around the faces intently and continued.

"Very well, Captain Hardy, set it all in motion. Sir William, will you and Lady Hamilton remain aboard while his majesty greets his subjects? There is a closed carriage available for you to follow his majesty's party to the palace."

"By all means," responded Sir William promptly. For a man who went to pains always to sound equable, his relief at being spared the standing around in the breeze on the quayside, whilst King Ferdinand and his heir received the felicitations of his subjects, was obvious.

Captain Hardy having already departed, further conversation now became impossible. The beating of a drum, the blowing of fifes and whistles, shouts of command, and above all, the pounding of a few hundred pairs of feet on decks combined to create a din. To those who knew, the measured tramp of the marines had a completely different cadence to the sound of watches of seamen running to theirstations. Thomas barely had time to reflect on this before his lordship, moving briskly to the door, only smiling at Lady Hamilton in passing, said, "Come, Thomas."

He and Tom Allen were detailed off to the port gangway, and boatswain's mates passed rapidly along the ship's sides, ensuring the lines of seamen were continuous with no bunching. For those aloft on the yards, whistles, shouts, and arm motions had to suffice. In just a few minutes, the orderliness of their display was surprisingly good, enhanced as it was by the twin lines of the red-coated, musket-bearing marines forming an avenue away from the side of the ship.

On the quarterdeck, Captain Hardy had his officers lined in seniority, with Lord Nelson by his side. Beyond the civic dignitaries waiting the far side of the lines of marines, Thomas could see the few Sicilian troops who had been turned out. They vainly tried to keep the populace clear of the line of carriages and coaches waiting some distance away toward the fishermen's church. It was obvious that people were still arriving, and the drivers of some waiting conveyances were having to keep their horses under tight control.

At the first sign of King Ferdinand reaching the gangplank down from the ship, the marine captain barked orders to present arms. As the marines smartly presented their muskets, the order, "Hats off," rippled along the side of the ship, and hearty cheering immediately accompanied the hat waving.

It would not have been such a brave and noisy spectacle if his lordship were not such a popular commander, reflected Thomas.

As it was, officers and men alike were giving their arms and lungs good exercise. The cheering and hat waving went on as the Mayor of Palermo and other dignitaries one by one bent over the hand of their gracious monarch. The marines sloped arms and reformed in line alongside the ship.

The acclaim was infectious and taken up by the crowd looking on from the quay. Only when the king and his young heir mounted the step of their open carriage did Lord Nelson give a final left-handed wave of his hat and replace it on his head, closely followed by Captain Hardy and Lieutenants Vassall, Compton, and Parkinson. They set about clearing the quarterdeck as a preliminary to getting

47

working parties of seamen back to their tasks. A great deal remained to be done to put *Vanguard* back into fighting condition, and no more time could be lost.

As Thomas saw his lordship begin descending to the great cabin, he also began to make his way there to stand guard over Lady Hamilton's property until the rest arrived and the cart returned. Onhis arrival, Tom Allen was trying to make himself invisible by the doorwhilst his lordship was deep in conversation with Sir William and Lady Hamilton.

For a few moments, Sir William was far more animated than earlier.

"I beseech you, my lord, to accompany my lady and meyself to remove the Queen and her daughters from *Palazzo dei Normanni* to *Palazzo Colli* where the king has gone," the knight pleaded as Thomas reached the door, but then he seemed to lose his energy.

However, Lady Hamilton had lost none of hers and took up the persuasion.

"The *Colli* is as far again beyond *Normanni* on the edge of countryside. It is a hunting palace and unfit for ladies. It needssomeone to drive the cleaning out and furnishing of the most suitablerooms."

"I am not sure what I can bring to that work. There is still much to do here to make the ship battle ready," responded His Lordship.

"The king is only going there because he wants to hunt oncePrince Alberto's funeral is over. He will listen to you, my dear lord, onwhat needs to be done rather better than he will to myself. Thequeen is quite unable make her needs plain at this time of sorrow. Between us, we must do it for her."

"You are sure she is not better where she is, with the priests," his lordship tried.

"Assuredly I am not," began her ladyship firmly. "Maria Carolina willrecover the quicker with all of her family around her and by seeing that her husband must be dragged back to his royal duties."

"That is indeed the nub of it and sound in logic," added Sir William.

"The king will certainly have to take action in the defense of his realm. We cannot just leave him in the hands of Acton and Belmonte," reflected his lordship, finally warming to the idea of maintaining a grip on royal decision making. "But I cannot be so far separated from *Vanguard* and my other ships for more than a day or two."

"That is all my husband and I beg of your lordship. I am sure the king will have accommodation near the shoreline found for us when he sees he has too much of a crowd at *Palazzo Colli*," added her ladyship with a winning smile.

The decision now made, his lordship turned toward the door and rapped out an order to Tom Allen to put up a bag for a few nights andbe ready to accompany him. In so doing, he noticed the return of Thomas and promptly issued his orders too

"As for you, Thomas, you will first see all Sir William's property assembled, loaded, and transported as her ladyship informs me you have arranged. Then make haste here to ensure I can return aboard and find all in proper order."

Minutes later, when Tom Allen returned, suitably laden, the party offour swept out, and the last Thomas saw or heard of his lordship for the next two and a half days was his advice to Sir William to be careful with his footing until used to being on land. This in no way lefthim at a loose end. There was waste to clear and a start to be made on repositioning his lordship's furnishings as he liked them. He seemed to have achieved very little when a young midshipman put his head around the door.

"Officer of the watch says the boat sent away at Lady Hamilton's request is returning. You must go to the quayside astern to take delivery of the cargo."

"Thank you, young sir. I will need hands to reload on a cart, when itarrives, and to remove and load this," responded Thomas, pointing to the pile by the sideboard.

"Don't know about that. You'll have to speak to Lieutenant Parkinson," added the youth, not very helpfully.

Up on the quarterdeck, Thomas explained his predicament over the two separate quantities of property to the extremely busy officer, who listened patiently.

"Very well, Spencer. I suppose we must be thankful to have got them off the ship and now their property too." He then bawled, "Mr

Austin," and the one-armed boatswain came running up the ladder. An unknowing observer would have been amazed to learn that he had only lost the missing limb at Aboukir Bay, so speedy was his response. Very effective it was too in providing Thomas with the muscle power to haul up the bundles the boat had brought from *Samuel and Jane*, and it was just as the last of these was on the wayup to the quay that Lieutenant Parkinson hailed.

"Ahoy there, Thomas Spencer, I believe your cart approaches with a woman aboard."

"Thankee, sir," replied Thomas, saluting, and screwed up his eyes to peer past the people between him and the cart. Once he picked out Mary's distinctive hair, he asked the seamen to start bringing ashore the pile of bundles in the great cabin. Fortunately, they were able to do this without disrupting other work aboard. When he scrambled up to the driver's bench of the fully laden cart, he pressedclose to Mary. She was squeezed between the driver and himself, soit was to envious glances from those working on the yards and in therigging and an ironic wave of the hand from Lieutenant Parkinsonthat the cart pulled slowly past Vanguard's stern.

"We are for *Palazzo Colli* this time," he said to Mary as though confiding in her.

"I know," she replied dryly, "Lady Acton is already there and not a room clean!"

"How did she know to go there and not *Palazzo dei Normanni?*" asked Thomas.

"Word came to us from Sir John just as Lord Nelson was leaving your ship with the queen and princesses, so she went direct toPalazzo Colli, which you said very well."

"I have heard the name many times now," said Thomas, rather brushing aside the compliment. "Why did the king allow the queen to be taken to the wrong place?"

Mary turned her face to look at him very directly and quizzically.

"I imagine that he did not want the body of his dead son in *Palazzo Colli*. The queen is rather more fervent at prayer than is the king.

Likely he knew she would insist on being close to the chapel where the boy lies."

Thomas drank in what he felt was the beauty and truth in her eyes, still oblivious to their surroundings, although they had now left *Vanguard's* bowsprit far behind and were now approaching the *Porta Felice*. Up the first part of *Via del Cassaro* they went.

"Here is Santa *Maria della Catena*," Mary observed. "What is the chapel called, where the body of the boy prince lies?"

"*Cappella Palatina* and I have never seen so much gold and decoration!"

"You do speak the Italian names very well for someone who has been here for such a short time," Mary insisted.

"I had good teachers when I was there, Saverio Rodino and Father Francisco," responded Thomas modestly. "But I do not take the meaning of their words like you."

"Well, I have been here a year or two now, so I pick up more and more of their speech and a lot of the ways of this royal court, thanks to Sir John's position," mused Mary.

"Did you say Saverio Rodino? He is someone I know to be loyal to the queen."

"Yes, that struck me during the storm when he served so well," replied Thomas. "How did you come to be employed by Lady Acton?"

"She was in Dover, waiting for a fair wind for a passage to Hamburg when I was also staying there, and a friend of my aunt's recommended me," said Mary.

"So, she then saw your needlework and was impressed by it?" Thomas questioned.

"Not exactly," responded Mary carefully, "but she did come to be so, and who would not be, with six children to keep from looking like ragamuffins. They do so love to chase around getting into trouble."

Her tone had now become so bantering that Thomas wondered if she had deliberately steered their conversation away from her being taken into service in Dover, and he didn't wish to press the subject on so short an acquaintance, especially now having the desire to extend his time with Mary.

"My parents and brother live in Gotham, near Nottingham. Do you still have family in Kent?" he asked in a hesitant way.

"Oh, my parents still live in Ryarsh. I am, after all, only twenty-seven years, and they were young when they had me," she replied without noticeable reluctance.

"I have twenty-eight years, and my parents were both more than twenty when I was born. Perhaps it is living in a small place in the country that keeps them hearty."

Mary's response to this was immediate. "Ryarsh is small too. The air smells good, not a stinking town like this."

She gestured around her, while the carthorses plodded up the slow incline of the long, straight road, where the narrower roads off were flanked by huddled dwellings. Many looked as though they could be stinking hovels.

Fortunately for them, the winter breeze off the sea was not allowing the city odors to be oppressive, thought Thomas, *although it was possible that in warmer weather, with a breeze off the land, the smells could be nearly as bad as those of Naples.*

"Surely it will not be truly as bad as Naples," he said, putting thoughts into words.

"Well, it does not seem as huge a place," she observed, shuddering, "Now there was a stinking city where the poor died like flies. No wonder, with filth everywhere!"

The cart reached the place Saverio had called *Quattro Canti,* but here, the carter turned his horses to the right and flicked his whip. The crowds who had turned out to greet their king would just have to part to allow him passage. The cart was too heavily laden to really accelerate and moved slowly forward as the people seemed to part in a good-natured way.

Thomas thought the road was trending northwest but wasn't given chance to reflect on that or the miserable appearance of some of the narrower streets and alleys. Mary now questioned him. "Have you left a wife or sweetheart in this Gotham of yours?"

"I have never been married, and there is no woman awaiting my return," he replied. As a hurried afterthought, he added, "other than my mother."

"Were you thwarted in love and ran away to sea to forget?" she probed, laughing.

"I enlisted in his majesty's navy in the hope I could help save our country from the godless French, who seek to destroy one country after another," he replied stiffly.

"And what progress do you believe you are making in that aim?"

Thomas realized her tone was still bantering, so he looked her in the eye as he replied.

"While I serve his lordship, the progress is clear to see. He will save this kingdom, whatever happens in Naples, now we have left."

"Precious little help he will have from anyone not in King George's navy," she responded in lowered voice, suddenly serious. "The ships can do much to keep us safe on this island, but what is to stop the French in Italy?"

Thomas thought about it. "Surely the Emperor in Austria will not letthis kingdom fall? Is not the queen his sister? The Russian Emperor is our ally too."

"Well, Thomas, from what I hear Sir John say to Lady Acton, you are a deal too trusting of foreign allies. They will blame Lord Nelson for having General Mack lead the King's army to Rome before they were ready for war," said Mary.

Thomas was so depressed by this that he looked away from Mary and took in the gate through the city walls they were now approaching. It wasn't as high or ornate as *Porta Felice,* but nonetheless composed of sturdy stonework. With the gates shut andbarricaded, the wall looked as though it could withstand cannon fire for some time. A distance ahead was a small fortress from whose ramparts cannon poked.

"That is *Castel Nuovo,*" said Mary. "I don't know why it stands where it does."

"With an alert garrison, well supplied with powder and shot, it could raise the alarm for this *Palazzo Colli* we are going to. So make this city gate impossible to attack, while its garrison holds," Thomasaverred.

"So, now you are soldier as well as sailor, rather like his lordship," teased Mary.

Thomas saw the joke and just added, "I know a little about cannon fire."

The deterioration in the road the cart was taking now became marked, and there were small, stony fields between the buildings they were passing. No longer were there crowds of people but just a few passing along the road or talking outside houses. No one was working in the bare, winter fields. This would have made him feel worse, had he not remembered it was the day after Christmas Day. He had no idea how it would be celebrated in the Roman Church on this island.

"This being St. Stephen's Day, how will the people here celebrate it?" he asked.

"Like any other saint's day, they'll go to mass. Do no work they can avoid and eat and drink to their hearts' content whatever they have," came Mary's dry response. "Look ahead, Thomas. You can see *Palazzo Colli* with woodland behind it."

This did little to raise Thomas's spirits. Beyond the next small farmstead rose a gaunt and rather mean-looking palace with windows no wider than those he had seen in *Palazzo dei Normanni*. However, it lacked the interesting external detail he'd seen there. His impression was not improved upon the final approach by a drive bordered by poorly maintained gardens. The carter steered his horses around the front of the building to a mean-looking doorway, where a male servant was brushing out rubbish and large quantities of dust and soot. Two elderly and currently dirty women were using carpet beaters on rugs that were pocked by burn marks.

"This is where Sir John and his family, Sir William and Lady Hamilton and Lord Nelson and his servant, all have rooms," said Mary and called in Italian to the man.

He brushed the mound he had accumulated to one side of the door, dropped the brush across the doorway, and hurried to the cart. Mary spoke at greater length and with emphasis, at which the man said, *"Si, signorina,"* and hurried into the building.

"You have a way with your fellow servants, Mary," observed Thomas.

"They respect my skills and know I stand no nonsense," she declared.

The same man emerged with three others, and they began unloading the cart, two to each bundle, at which Mary turned to Thomas.

"You have done all you need to. I will pay the carter, and he will take you back to *Quattro Canti*."

"When shall I see you again?" he blurted."All in good time, Thomas," she replied.

Chapter 6

Cares of Command in New Quarters

Two afternoons later he had the great cabin tidy and organized exactly as his lordship liked it. He had even tidied the hutch - cabin would have been too grand a description - he shared with Tom Allen. Out of the blue, he was summoned by Captain Hardy.

The summons was to the quarterdeck, where the Captain was standing with Lieutenant Westcott. He had previously been Master at Arms and still carried himself in the disciplined manner one expected. He stood ramrod straight in his naval lieutenant's blue, listening intently to his captain's instructions. Thomas approached and stopped a few paces away, so did not give the impression of deliberately earwigging these instructions.

Captain Hardy had noted his arrival and deliberately raised his voice so that Thomas could hear him speak in his firm Dorset accent.

"You must see that no man gives offence to the local population." He then shifted his eyes to Thomas and continued, "Here is Thomas Spencer, who will be one of your working party and has conducted himself satisfactorily on shore already."

That this was as near to praise as Captain Hardy ever came made Thomas feel slightly uncomfortable as he knuckled his forehead. The captain continued expansively.

"You are to make up a bag of his lordship's writing materials andgo with Lieutenant Westcott to Villa Bastioni. His lordship requiresthe villa be made fit for habitation. He will arrive there this afternoon and must write to Lord St. Vincent before nightfall."

"Aye, aye, sir," responded Thomas, thinking Captain Hardy was being rather kind in alerting him to the need to take his lordship's best-quality paper.

"Be down at the gangway forthwith. The men required are being assembled."

When Thomas arrived a bare minute or two later at the open sally port, a significant portion of the crew, seamen with brooms andbuckets and carpenter's mates with bags of tools, were already making their way down the gangplanks. He joined the tail end of this procession, his drawstring bag over his shoulder. Once lined up by a boatswain's mate on the quay, for Mr Westcott to walk from the rear, Thomas reckoned there were about fifty men in the column. Down to where the top of the mole broadened out Mr Westcott led them, but then bore south, past *Porta Felice,* along a way that was separated from the seashore by a grassed area that had parched in summer and had too much rain in recent days. To their right, several paces away over bare, compacted earth stood the city wall, constructed of huge blocks of dressed stone. The solid masonry, which seemed to be a good twenty feet high, had a concave curve to it. The projectingmassive coping was surmounted by a short, thinner-looking parapet. It seemed strange the windows of a terrace of grand mansionsshould tower above a wall built for defense, but the mansions stood back from the top of the wall.

Also, there were one or two intervals in the parapet, through which cannon muzzles poked, so there had to be an elevated walkway to serve them. Loopholes clustered at intervals in the lower wall suggested passages to these for musketeers to shoot down any attackers who survived the cannon fire. Thomas reflected that the stonework was well weathered. He remembered what Saverio had said about the statues of the Spanish kings just as the column of sailors drew level with a narrow stonework arch, into which was set asolid timber door. This broke up the continuity of the wall, emphasized by the door standing open to reveal a narrow street leading away. It wasn't full of people, but those who were there seemed very interested in where the sailors were going.

The fitful winter sun slanted over their shoulders as they walked. Seamen never quite managed to march, even when armed. Equipped as they were, there was no possibility of the column behind Mr Westcott looking orderly. He marched on ahead, affecting not to notice, until he had passed a bastion that marked a corner where the wall swung inland. It was possible to see another bastion set into the wall, not far away. This had to be part of a gateway, judging by the streams of people headed in and out of the city just beyond it.

At this corner, set many paces apart from the city wall, was the strange sight of a building constructed of shiny stone. So near white that one's eyes were dazzled when the sun shone on a portion of it! On the far side of this building was some kind of garden set behind railings jointed at regular intervals into columns of the same near-white stone. Surmounted by urns in the same material, there was no adequate respite for any eyes looking in that direction.

Mr Westcott then bore right, making directly for the portico to the front of the building, where the two recessed doors stood open. He turned and faced his large party of seamen and shouted. "Gather in front of me for your orders."

Upon this men crowded forward, spilling out to the sides in order toplace themselves within earshot.

"Those of you with buckets will have to go through the villa to the kitchen, where I have been told there is water. Those with brooms should go straight to the highest rooms, bucket holders and those with cloths and leathers to follow. The whole villa must be cleaned out; top to bottom, windows and such furnishings as there are."

At this, he stood aside to allow the boatswain's mate to lead the bucket holders in search of the kitchen. The men with brooms also filed past to the first flight of stairs, and the remaining seamen went to crowd the villa's hallway. This left only the carpenter's mates and Thomas with Mr Westcott for separate instruction.

"We must now see whether the furnishings include usable beds. If not, you must return to the ship to bring back the cots made for Sir William and Lady Hamilton. Likewise, his lordship's second cot must be found and brought. Do not say a bed is capable of use if it has woodworm or is flea ridden. Thomas Spencer, you must see if there is a writing table that can be placed suitably in a downstairs room. If so, equip the table for his lordship."

A quick sortie through the ground floor rooms revealed nothing other than a good view of the sea from a window. The room could be easily shut off from the noisy work getting under way in the rest of the villa. It had a door so solid that Thomas concluded it must have served as the study for the gentleman of the house. Making a mental note there was a good position for a desk facing seaward, set back from the window, Thomas headed for the flight of stairs to the first floor.

Like the door and window surrounds, lower walls, and floors, these were constructed of highly polished marble. There was stylized plaster above and up to moldings at ceiling level. Boots rang on the stairs, and there was a chill in the musty air of the building that had not been noticeable outside. When he was going from one large chamber to another, it struck Thomas that he had not seen a single fireplace.

There was likewise no furniture on the first floor. A narrower staircase, constructed of dark timber that creaked only slightly, led up to a number of rooms of varying size with low, sloping ceilings. In the largest of these, directly off the head of the staircase, was amass of furniture all piled together and covered in dust. The seamen who had reached this floor before Thomas were busy making the dust worse by sweeping the floors to the top of the staircase. A couple of them were busy moving the items of furniture piecemeal to enable the entire floor to be swept. Thomas caught a glimpse of slender table legs, surmounted by a top that looked to contain drawers. He launched himself forward and wiped a sleeve across a corner of the tabletop to reveal a beautifully smooth, mottled brown finish.

"This one for His Lordship," he sang out as a seaman was about toplace a leather upholstered chair upright on the tabletop.

Fortunately, this had the effect of the man freezing in mid-action, and Thomas took in that the chair had legs that looked the same shape as those of the table. He ran his hand down one of them and, sure enough, it had the same finish.

"That also," he said, removing the chair from the seaman's grip, and taking it to a vacant corner already swept. He darted back forthe table.

It was only a few seconds' work to drag that to the same corner, borrow a clean dusting cloth, and wipe the whole tabletop. The backrest of the chair, its verticals, and leather seat cleaned up equally well. Thomas concluded he had seized a lady's writing table and matching chair. Downward pressure on the chair seat showed it was firm in build, well padded, and of ample size and height for His Lordship, notwithstanding it's delicate appearance. He was on his knees, cleaning the table legs, when Lieutenant Westcott marched straight in from the top of the staircase. He took in all that was happening in the attic room with a single sweeping glance, andapparently without drawing breath, started giving his instructions.

"Elegant enough for his lordship, Spencer. Two of you carry the table down to the room where Spencer takes the chair. Carefully, mind, I should not wish to see so fine a piece damaged. The rest of you clean up all that other furniture and carry it down to the bedchambers. All of it will be needed and more besides."

Thomas needed no more prompting to pick up the chair and make toward the head of the staircase. After a moment's hesitation, the seaman from whom he'd taken the chair and one other came over tothe table. Each took hold of an end. Thomas took his time over starting down the stairs to give the other two sufficient to follow him. He knew Mr Westcott would follow down, and heaven help the other two if they damaged the writing table!In the event, they did very well and on the lower staircase kept to the center.

Once in the chosen room, Thomas placed the chair facing the window that looked out over the bay. The writing table was being set down with its drawer fronts facing the chair, Lieutenant Westcott looking on from the doorway, when the sound of hooves was to be heard from the front of the villa.

The lieutenant disappeared in the direction of the entrance. The hoof beats merged into the unmistakable sound of a carriage halting and then ceased. Mr Westcott's voice boomed through the vestibule.

"Spencer, here at the double," and Thomas ran.

The sight that greeted him was Sir William, looking ghastly pale and ill, being virtually carried between her ladyship on his left and his lordship on his right. His good left arm propped Sir William under his armpit. Thomas hurried forward to his lordship's side of the trio.

"Relieve her ladyship of the weight first, Thomas," barked His Lordship in obvious distress for the condition of his friend and hisown inability.

Thomas ran behind them to prop Sir William's shoulder with his lefthand and put his arm around Sir William's waist, saying, "I have Sir William's weight, m'Lord."

In truth, the Knight was so frail and light that Thomas was able to take virtually all his weight. Lady Hamilton released her husband andmoved a few paces forward so she could turn and see her husband being carried closer to the villa. Lieutenant Westcott came forward and saluted his admiral.

"The villa is near ready for occupation, my lord. There are chairs brought down from the attic. I will have one brought directly for Sir William."

"I trust there is also a bed that can be made up for Sir William so soon as the carter and Tom Allen arrive with the bedding," responded his lordship briskly.

Mr Westcott saluted, said, "Yes, my lord," and turned smartly to march up the doorstep.

He called for an armchair and footstool to be brought, then directed a boatswain's mate to take half a dozen men outside to await the arrival of the bedding. Thomas had to take firmer hold ofSir William. Between His Lordship and himself, the shivering knight was safely guided over the doorstep and into the vestibule. Here, there was space for the seamen ordered outside to file past, trying not to gawp. The frail, ill old man was lowered gently into the high- backed armchair some quick-witted member of the company had identified as suitable for the distressed gentleman. Lady Hamilton stood to one side, worry etched on her large features, which seemedless rounded in her tense state but obviously more beautiful to at least one of those observing her distress.

"My dear lady, please go around this accommodation and select a bedchamber for Sir William," his lordship gently advised.

"Only if you have Thomas Spencer in constant attendance on my husband while I do so," she responded and, leaning over, asked, "Is there aught you want now, dear William?"

"A blanket over my legs; it is so cold," quavered the old man.

"You shall have one immediately Tom Allen arrives, my sweet," and with that, she turned to Westcott, saying, "Now, lieutenant, show me the rooms and furnishings."

While she swept from one ground floor room to another, Mr Westcott virtually running behind her, his lordship turned to Thomas above Sir William's head.

"Have you set up a position for me to write, Thomas?"

"A good table and chair, m'lord, in a quiet room facing the bay. I was called away before I could set out your paper, quills and ink."

"See to that when good Sir William is settled," ordered his lordship. And then, bending to the armchair, said, "When her ladyship returns, I must take me to the writing table to write to Lord St. Vincent and Lord Spencer on the subject of the Swedish knight, Sir William. Ah, here comes Tom Allen with your blanket."

"Of course you must, my dear Nelson. It grieves me to be sounwell as to be unable to assist you," Sir William shakily replied, withTom tucking the blanket about his legs.

Her ladyship arrived back at the foot of the staircase and started ascending, the dutiful Mr Westcott just behind. his lordship bentsolicitously to Sir William again.

"We shall soon have a bedchamber organized for you, Sir William." Straightening again, he murmured, "Now would be a good time,Thomas."

So it proved to be, thanks to Tom Allen hovering to one side of the shivering knight. He had made him as snug as could be in that draughty vestibule. Thomas set out inkwell, quills, best paper, sealing wax, and the sand container before he heard through the open door her ladyship and the Lieutenant returning down the stairs. WWith the noise of seamen carrying in bedding and linen, it was onlyher ladyship giving orders that alerted him to dart back beside Sir William. On arriving by her husband's chair, she straightaway made her requirements known.

"I believe it best, my dear, that your bed should be on this floor in the south-facing room across from the kitchen. There is not a single fireplace in this villa, only a cooking range in the kitchen with some charcoal and firewood his majesty has sent down. We must have our warming pans out of the ship's hold."

In prompt execution of her orders to Mr Westcott, two seamenwere already carrying a heavy timber bed frame down the staircase, sweating not just from the weight, but in case they missed their footing. Others followed, more comfortably, carrying separate pieces to make up the whole. She also directed suitable bedding in thesame direction before speaking to His Lordship.

"My dear Lord Nelson, I have taken the liberty of assuming a bedchamber overlooking the sea, also on the warmer side of the villa, would meet your satisfaction. I shall take the chamber above my husband's, the better to hear should he need me during the night."

"Dear Lady, I am sure your dispositions are as perfect as may bein this place. Although it lies further from the mole than I would have wished. Allow me to send for the additional galley stove that I knowis stored in *Vanguard's* hold. While we have the carter here to carry, sacks of coals can also be brought."

This reply from his lordship brought a relieved expression to Lady Hamilton's face before she smiled very tenderly at him and announced her temporary departure.

"I fear I must be away again to the palace in the coach to weepwith Her Majesty."

Thomas wondered if anyone else caught the flicker of annoyance that crossed her husband's face at that point.

"Allen and Spencer can make up the bed, while we await the means of warming. Handle the bed linen carefully. It has been well repaired, due to Lady Acton loaning Spencer's Mary to me for the work."

She was making to leave, under Nelson's admiring gaze, before she recollected what else needed to be brought from the ship.

"Our court dress will have to be recovered from the ship's hold and brought here for cleaning and hanging. His majesty's reception is in two nights' time."

"I shall not be well enough to go. I do not know why his majestyhas to hold the reception so soon, when his own family have to recover their dress likewise."

In response to her husband's tremulous complaint, Lady Hamilton assumed a patient and tender expression.

"My dear husband, I shall be sure to give their majesties your regrets. I know they have to show their subjects here that theirgovernance is still firm, despite mourning the loss of poor little Alberto. King George will still be well represented by Lord Nelson and a good number of his officers. I shall also be there, poor substitute as I am for yourself."

With that, she swept out of the front portico, followed by more than the gaze of the admiring Nelson. His order to Mr Westcott to dispatch a party to *Vanguard* to bring all that was required seemed to be a little delayed in coming. Thomas and Tom Allen slipped away without bidding to make up Sir William's bed. Once in the designated chamber, where a couple of carpenter's mates had completed the bed assembly and moved away to the next job, he questioned Tom.

"Who is this Swedish night his lordship mentioned?"

"That will be Captain Sir Sidney Smith, as flash a cove as was ever made post," came the swift reply.

"So, what has this Sir Sidney Smith done to anger his lordship?" pressed Thomas.

"Claimed his orders put him in charge of throwin' Bonaparte out of Egypt an' he c'n call on as many o' his lordship's vessels as he wants."

"Who is supposed to have given him such powers?" asked Thomas incredulously.

"Their lordships in Lunnon," responded Tom in his broad Norfolk. "Lord Spencer be the boss of 'em. Yo bain't be related, be ye?" he added, laughing at his own joke.

Thomas smiled to show the thought he might be related to

aristocracy was indeed funny and then commented, "No wonder his lordship is angered."

"That be why he has the courier brig on standby for his letters," added Tom with sangfroid, "an' I reckon Lord St. Vincent won't stand for it either."

Their bed making done, he walked to the door and sniffed toward the kitchen. "Reckon it'll be warmer if'n we bring Sir William through. Some'uns lit the range."

Back to the vestibule they went, and Tom made the suggestion. Because it included carrying the armchair with Sir William riding in it, the idea was well received. As they carried, one each side, hislordship called after them.

"Thomas, bring candles and a lighted taper. Daylight is fading too fast."

With his hands well and truly occupied, Thomas could only nod hisassent. So soon as the old gentleman was positioned comfortably bythe bed, Thomas left him in the care of Tom and strolled into the kitchen. A pair of plump Sicilian women were chopping root vegetables very small to throw into a large, black pot - some kind of broth that already stood on a grid above the range fire. On a trestle table in the far corner stood a few candelabra and several sconces, already loaded with candles. Thomas just called *"Buonasera"* to the women, walked over to the table, selected a candelabra and a singlesconce. He picked up a taper he saw lying there and walked over to the range.

"Per ammiraglio," he said, now that he was close to the two women. Their smiles showed his small number of Italian words was improving. He walked off to what had now become his lordship's study. He found him already seated at the writing table, staring out atthe darkening waters of the bay. With daylight faded, he was alreadycomposing his thoughts for the laborious writing to come. Thomas lit the candelabra candles from that in the sconce, placing the candelabra to his lordship's left.

"Is that sufficient light, m'lord? I can bring more."

"That is enough, Thomas. Leave me to write, and aid Tom with poor Sir William, but stay within call. I shall need you to carry letters to Captain Hardy."

Remembering what Tom had told him about the courier brig, Thomas drew the natural conclusion that the commander of the brig would receive his orders on board *Vanguard*. He merely responded, "Aye, m'Lord," withdrew, and closed the door.

Fortunately, the warming pans and a sack of small coals arrived soon. Tom, who had some expertise with loading them at a suitable heat, bustled off to the kitchen. There wasn't much Thomas needed to do for Sir William. He assisted him to the chamber pot, albeit rather frequently, and did the emptying. Tom came back from histask with a single warming pan, which he spat on to make sure it wasn't too hot.

"Ther'll be devil to pay, if'n I burns Her ledyship's linen."

"Aye," said Thomas nervously, but Tom judged it well, and ten minutes later they were tucking the shivering, old gentleman into a warm bed. His lordship was writing when Tom left again to warm the other two beds on the floor above, and he was writing still when Tom returned. Thomas, now in a chair close by the sleeping Sir William, thought he must have dozed off when the sound of horses brought him alert again. Within a few seconds, her ladyship was coming into the room. Immediately, she saw her husband was asleep. She put her finger to her lips and walked as quietly as her shoes on the marble tiled floor would allow. Coming right up to Thomas's ear, she whispered only, "Lord Nelson?"

To which he whispered in reply, "Still writing," at which she left again, visibly on tiptoe.

Later, she reappeared and beckoned Thomas. He also left the sleeping knight quietly and followed to his lordship. He was still atthe writing table, sealing a second letter. He looked tired and strained when speaking to her ladyship.

"It is done. I have only sought clarification of the Swedish knight's orders from Lord Spencer in neutral terms, but I have been very forthright in my private letter to Lord St. Vincent."

"What a deal of trouble SSS causes," responded Her Ladyship. Ina deeper and mock-manly voice, she added, *"pour un homme qui parle le francais si bon que les gens croyent qu'il est une personne de langue maternelle francaise."*

It was just as well she had shut the door behind Thomas and herself when they entered, because His Lordship threw back his head and laughed out loud, then got up, placed his hand on Lady Hamilton's forearm, and raised her hand to his lips.

"My dearest Emma, if your talent for mimicry could only make the Swedish knight's claims as ridiculous as he is wont to sound."

"Well, my dearest lord, simply believe his claims will prove to be soridiculous."

This was said so lightly and smilingly that Nelson continued to smile broadly himself, quite revived by Her Ladyship's capacity to make light of cares and fatigue. "You do so much to lighten my tired mind that I can almost concentrate my thoughts on the defense of this island."

It was as though his final instructions had been forgotten, thought Thomas. Her ladyship's reply helped restore his memory.

"Best only after a night's sleep, my dearest lord."

At this, Nelson turned to him and said, "I had best send you offwith the letters, Thomas."

"Take the coach, Thomas," added her ladyship. "The driver still waits, and you are needed back in this villa tonight. If Tom Allen and yourself will take turn and turn about to sit with my husband, I may even rest for an hour or so before he wakes. I have endured more than a week of sleepless nights and must weep with the queen againin the morning."

"Do as her ladyship says, Thomas," confirmed his lordship, admiration and concern for her chasing across his face at the same time.

In no time at all, he was in the coach, with her ladyship calling out instructions to the Italian driver. Before long, he was looking out of the coach window down the mole to where the lantern-hung side of *Vanguard* rose above it. There seemed to be some activity on the gunwale. Before he could make out exactly what, the coach stopped short by the forecastle, leaving him no choice but to open the door and jump down. Once able to look past the horses, he saw that horses pulling a cart faced those of the coach.

His heart jumped because he realized it was the same carter, again accompanied by Mary. They had not seen him for the simple reason they were gazing up to where a large timber case was being swayed out above the gunwale. Seamen on the back of the cart waited to receive it. The brow seemed to be more permanentlyrigged than hitherto but so steeply, that swaying out the case direct from hatch to cart was safer. He didn't expect Mary to know this, but the urgency of his own mission precluded explanation, so he stepped smartly up to the driving bench.

"Mary, I have letters for Captain Hardy. I'll be back directly."

He stopped only long enough to register her astonished face dropping to him. He strode quickly on below the lowering case to thefoot of the brow and up the footholds to the marine sentry at the top.

"Thomas Spencer with his lordship's letters for the courier brig," hecalled. Word was passed to the officer of the watch and duly came back down the chain of command.

"Come aboard and proceed directly to the captain's cabin."

On arrival, he found Captain Hardy seated with a young manwhose uniform coat bore a commander's single epaulette. Knuckling his forehead, he awaited attention.

"Ah, Spencer, I understand you have arrived in some style," said the captain dryly.

"Lady Hamilton loaned the coach for speed, sir. I have the letters. His lordship says they can go in one bag for Lord St. Vincent."

The Captain looked at how they were addressed and then looked up again at Thomas.

"Very well, Spencer, do not become accustomed to riding in comfort. You will have to aid the coachman and get around our otherevening visitors. Just as well you are already acquainted," said Captain Hardy with the ghost of a smile on his normally stern face.

"Aye, aye, sir," said Thomas, knuckling his forehead again and departing, hearing only as he left and before the marine sentryclosed the door, "Well, commander ..."

Back at the brow, he found the cart was fully loaded with the large case on top of smaller ones that must have already been there. It had moved forward right to the edge of the mole, below the forecastle. He ran down the gangway and walked over to the coach horse nearest the far side of the mole. The coachman saw what he was about, so when he took hold of the halter, a click of the tongue set the horses ambling, allowing Thomas to circle them round. Coming back toward the side of *Vanguard*, but still circling, he managed to come up alongside the cart, and Mary leant down.

"You gave me a fright, Thomas, walking under our cargo."

"No danger," he responded cheerfully. "Now, had it been a thirty-two pounder cannon, I might have been hesitant."

"Now that we have court dress loaded for the king and queen and Sir John and Lady Acton, we must away to the *Colli* again. Where are you bound for, Thomas?"

"Only *Villa Bastioni,* close to the shore. Sir William is sorely ill," he replied.

"So, he will miss the king's reception and the annoyance of seeing the queen fall weeping on his lady's bosom, like she did when poor little Prince Alberto's coffin was carried into the royal vault," she commented, but not in a condemning tone.

"Were you there at the funeral?" he asked without reflection on herwords.

"No, but Her Ladyship and Sir John were talking about it afterward."

"I did think Sir William looked annoyed about his lady going to weep with the queen," Thomas ventured, trying to work out what he thought about the words Lady Acton had used.

He took Mary's hand in both of his, thinking what further he could say, other than that they both had to go their separate ways, butMary spoke first.

"You begin to see what it is like at this court your admiral has vowed to defend."

"Take good care of yourself, Mary, until we meet again," was all hefelt able to say.

CHAPTER 7

RELATIONSHIPS AND INTRIGUES

The third day after King Ferdinand's Sunday evening reception, Sir William's condition had improved. He was sitting up in bed when his lady returned from her morning visit to *Palazzo Colli*. Thomas had just been reading to him from a scene in *Two Gentlemen of Verona,* despite his obvious lack of experience in how to read drama. Tom Allen was idling in the kitchen, trying to romance one of the plump Sicilian women. Thomas had pointed out they had husbands who were likely to turn nasty if they heard about his attentions. As a result of the lure of "a woman wi' a noice bit o' fleesh aboaut 'er," Thomas would have to cover for him.

Lady Hamilton swept into the room, untying the ribbon of her black bonnet to throw that headgear on to a chair. She ran a hand over her bouncing, brown curls. "How many times have I been to the *Colli* to weep with her majesty? I have entirely lost count after twelve nights without sleep."

At this, Sir William looked irritated but said only, "It is natural to weep over all we have lost, but if you did not weep so readily, sleep would come more easily."

At that, his lady bridled a little and responded in a surprisingly dogged tone.

"After all we have lost, that beautiful boy in especial, there is nothing two women of sensibility can do other than weep together."

The look on her face was so stubborn that Sir William's facial muscles visibly tightened. His yellowed skin stretched like parchment over his cheekbones.

"Well, you are most certainly not yet a philosopher," he ground out."The stoics would not countenance such behavior."

This and the outburst in response came just as his lordship entered the room to request loan of the coach to take him to *Vanguard* for conference with Hardy.

"I am sorry I came to you with so little education," she raged, "but my mother and grandmother had to pay for my schooling, poor though they were. I did not have the privilege of being tutored at Windsor with his majesty King George."

Even his lordship paled at the fury of this outburst, although he hadthe presence of mind to intervene with his request for the coach, to which the lady's response was still wounded.

"Do as you need, dear Lord Nelson, for it appears my use of their majesties' coach is less than appropriate."

She stormed out and up the staircase.

"Good Sir William, I very much regret I must away to the ship, leaving things here as they are," said Nelson in an effort to break the sudden silence tactfully.

There was no doubt he had found the confrontation between his two friends as painful as could be and really did wish he was somewhere else. Sir William looked like a man who knew a situation had got out of hand but didn't know how to undo what had been done. Thomas just wished the floor would open up and swallow him and the book he was holding so tightly.

Tom Allen, who had heard the raised voice of her ladyship and her departure, chose that moment to sidle into the doorway. He had been careful to avoid her catching sight of him, knowing full well he would have been an alternative target. His lordship looked wordlessly and appealingly from Thomas to Tom and back again, butit was Sir William who first recovered something approaching equanimity.

"Of course you must be away, dear Nelson. You have our defenses to look to, so do not trouble yourself about this difference of opinion. It will blow over presently."

So, Nelson left, but the consequences of the difference of opinion were far from over.

Her ladyship sharply reduced her visits to *Palazzo Colli,* but her bad humor with her steadily recovering husband continued, perhaps slowing that recovery.

But with a gentleman so elderly and downcast by recent events, who could say, thought Thomas. What was noticeable, when his lordship was in his study in the villa, was the time the two of them spent there alone. Only the snippets of conversation he heard, when she walked in unannounced, gave him some idea whether their talkstogether were important for people around them. Did they bear on matters of state or, alternatively, were they little more than gossip? Sometimes, it was hard to tell, as on the day in early January when she rushed in.

"Dear Lord Nelson, our cooks have given me distressing news of Lady Knight and her daughter, who are now lodged not far away in rather a mean hotel."

"My dear, dear lady, I am so sorry to see you distressed. Shall I send Thomas out while you tell me the entire story?" he asked.

"No, no, I believe you will need to send him there with a message that we shall call."

Then she related the story of how in the flight from Naples, the filling up of *Vanguard* and other ships properly prepared for passengers had left the two ladies all night in an open boat. Only thenext day had they been taken on board the flagship of the Portuguese squadron, where passengers were left on deck. Thefollowing day was Christmas Day, and *Alliance* had arrived, so they were able to transfer ship a day later and, by courtesy of Captain Bowden, be allocated decent accommodation for the voyage. However, the damage was done to the health of Lady Knight, the widow of Rear Admiral Sir Joseph Knight, long deceased, who was too elderly to shrug off cold nights in an open boat and on a ship's deck.

When his lordship had heard the sorry story, he was agitated and upset, so this was not merely gossip, regardless of its source.

"What a shameful piece of mismanagement, that the widow of a fellow rear admiral should be subjected to such privation. It will have been hard on her daughter too. We must visit as soon as they can receive us and ensure Lady Knight has a competent physician and ample medicines. I will give you a note to take, Thomas."

"My dear Lord Nelson, allow me to pen the note for both of us. Iam sure Lady and Miss Knight will not take offence when we areboth to visit," added Her Ladyship.

Promptly agreeing, His Lordship paced the floor while she sat at the desk and wrote.

"Niza and his squadron are no more use in an evacuation thanthey would be in a fight," he fulminated, "to leave gently born passengers on deck all night!"

"My very dear lord, do not give yourself further anguish over poor conduct you were not there to see and correct," counseled herladyship, signing the note.

When she had sealed and addressed it, she looked up at Thomas. "Here it is. The hotel is one road in from the city walls and best reached by that doorway through the wall halfway to *Porta Felice.* There, you can turn right, and it has a small sign saying *Albergo* when you reach it. If you have to speak there to someone with no English, say, *'Una lettera per La Baronessa Knight.'* Can you
remember that, Thomas?"

He repeated the required expression accurately, and they sent him on his way. He entered the tall, narrow building when he'd found it and put the expression to the sallow-faced, little man behind a table to the left of the entrance.

He pointed upward and said, *"La Scala seconda, numero due."*

Up two narrow and steep staircases he went, then turned onto a cramped landing where just three doors led off. He knocked on that with a painted number two and waited the few moments it took for a slim woman to open the door. She was his own height, but about his lordship's age. As she looked him coolly up and down, he took inthat her dress looked expensive, although the colors were somber.

"Do I have the honor of addressing Miss Knight?" he asked politely.

"First tell me who is doing the asking," she responded in a refined accent.

"I am Lord Nelson's steward with a note for Lady Knight," said Thomas, holding out the note, thinking that dealing with this woman was less than easy. She reached out and took the note as though it had been carried in a diseased hand.

"My mother is indisposed, but I will carry it to her. Wait here for the reply."

She closed the door, leaving him staring at the number. While he contemplated how badly painted it was, Miss Knight opened the door again.

"You did not tell me your own name," was her opening foray. "Thomas Spencer, ma'am. Is there a reply?" he then promptly asked.

"If Lord Nelson and Lady Hamilton could allow an hour, Lady Knight and I will be ready to receive them. Please convey that message to his lordship and her ladyship."

Following that response, he was thankful to take his leave and hurry back to the villa.

It was a few days after the successive visits to the hotel that her ladyship swept into her husband's bedchamber. Tom and Thomas were clearing away after Sir William had enjoyed a light lunch sat up in bed, during which he and his lordship kept each other company. Sir William's stomach and bowels had thankfully been restored to regularity, although he was still weak.

"Well, the queen is in a rare taking. She surrounds herself with guards because she believes the French have sent agents to murder her. It is all made worse by the king surrounding himself with hunting companions and shutting her out of matters of state entirely," her ladyship announced to all in the chamber, removing her hat.

"Surely there is no risk of either French agents or even local malcontents managing to evade the royal guards?" his lordship queried.

"I believe it is the morbid fear of the same fate catching up with her as overtook her sister, the queen of France," responded her ladyship, now addressing her answer to Nelson alone.

While he pondered this, Sir William gently interposed a view. "Iwould call it paranoia, after the Greek, *paranoos*. It is an irrational fear, no doubt brought on by her extreme grief at the loss of her son." His lady appeared to ignore his opinion, although Thomas, whonow had a high regard for the old gentleman, thought it must be sound thinking. It was evident his lordship thought so too. Feeling such embarrassment at this continued evidence of her ladyship's long maintained sulk, he felt obliged to acknowledge the value of Sir William's contribution.

"I am sure your learned analysis is correct, Sir William. This news gives me concern for her majesty's health, but it also concerns me that we are now deprived of reliable information on the conduct of affairs of state by his majesty and Sir John. We must give some thought to how we might overcome that problem."

"My dearest Emma, perhaps your next visit to her majesty should not be long delayed, just to be sure the situation has not changed," conceded Sir William quietly.

For just a moment, there was a look of satisfaction on her face before a bland reply.

"I shall of course do as you say, dear husband. I may yet aid her majesty in overcoming her groundless fears, although that could take some considerable time."

"That matters not, if the outcome is the restoration of her majesty's health, but do keep a careful eye on the situation between king and queen. My dear Nelson, I believe I would better reflect on what else we might do after a period of rest."

In truth, the old gentleman did look fatigued by the conversation but a shade happier. His Lordship likewise seemed to feel the sulk was lessening and took the hint to go.

"Then I shall leave you to rest in the tender care of your lady, good Sir William."

However, no sooner had his lordship started to move towards the door than her ladyship retrieved her hat.

"Tom and Thomas will settle you down, my dear."

She made to follow Nelson. Clearly, the route to marital peace in

Villa Bastioni would not be straightforward.

Nonetheless, aided by the warmth from *Vanguard's* reserve galley stove, the elderly knight made good progress in his recovery. One day, when he had resumed dressing for the day and ambling around the villa, he saw Thomas coming out of his lordship's study late in the afternoon with a note he had to deliver to Captain Hardy. He signaled to Thomas not to close the door but to announce him and walked in.

"Still toiling, my dear Nelson. Even were I in a condition to assist you, the ministry would still blame me for the loss of Naples. As well we sent my treasures home in Colossus, for we shall soon be following."

"Surely not, Sir William ..." was all Thomas heard his lordship say, while he crossed the vestibule before leaving the villa.

The atmosphere continued to be depressed as January advanced. Mrs Cadogan had moved in a few days after the others but kept very much to herself. She sensed that the strained relations between her daughter and son-in-law were not conducive to any intervention by herself. There was no news from Naples, other than that the French army of General Championnet was advancing on the city. Seeing that all the news from the mainland was bad, there was no improvement in the queen's condition. His lordship worried about the defense of the Straits of Messina and had written to Minorca for troops. In the meantime, he could only rely on the thousand Russians left behind in Messina by Admiral Ouschakoff. Those troops had not been left behind for the defense of the Straits when Ouschakoff's squadron sailed on with the object of capturing Corfu from the French, but only because the Czar Paul also had designs on Malta. The French in Valletta were under siege by Captain Ball without the benefit of any British army troops.

This exemplified His Lordship's dilemma. He had sixteen ships of the line and as many lesser vessels as he could manage to keep within the Mediterranean, but they were scattered in small numbers from the Levant and Egypt to Malta and Minorca. Apart from allies such as the Turks, seeking to force Bonaparte's French army out of Egypt, land operations depended on taking sailors out of ships.

So, when his lordship decided to send Thomas back to *Vanguard*, essentially to run messages between himself, Captain Hardy, and Sir John Acton, it was with a sense of release that he trudged back to the ship. Sir William was sufficiently recovered for Tom to see to both male residents of *Villa Bastioni*. A room was allocated in the villa to Mr Tyson, the admiral's secretary, so there would undoubtedly be more letters for Thomas to carry around Palermo.

After his first night back on board, it was a surprise to be summoned to the great cabin in the forenoon watch and find his lordship seated behind his desk with Captain Hardy seated to one side. Had they not looked so relaxed and welcoming, Thomas might have thought himself in trouble. After his salute, his lordship spoke affably.

"Thomas, Captain Hardy and I believe you could be of assistance in obtaining accurate intelligence. You have heard her ladyship say that the queen is now kept away from the king's deliberations with his ministers, so it would assist me to have a better knowledge of matters to which few other than the king and Sir John Acton are privy. Ah, I see you are looking mystified. Let me begin to tell you how you might help by saying that her ladyship has arranged with Lady Acton for some work to be done on her wardrobe by Mary Hever."

Thomas swallowed hard, seeing that this was leading to someone asking Mary to spy on her employer. He cleared his throat rather noisily.

"Did you have something to contribute to our consideration?" asked his lordship.

"I doubt Sir John will be telling Mary what is decided," he replied diffidently.

"No, that is true," responded his lordship, crisply, "but Sir John will sometimes talk to Lady Acton while Mary is in the room. It is what may be revealed of matters of state in that way that is of interest."

"That is why you will be sent to *Villa Bastioni* with some message or other each time Mary Hever is there," added Captain Hardy.

"I am sure you understand that her ladyship cannot question Mary about what has been said in her presence in case Lady Acton shouldask her about her conversation at *Villa Bastioni*. She will need to be able to answer truthfully that Lady Hamilton spoke to her only of dresses and hats and fripperies," elaborated his lordship.

Thomas, of course, could now see whose thinking was behind the instructions he was being given, but that wasn't the aspect of this plan that troubled him.

"Is there any risk to Mary in this, m'lord?" he asked.

"Why, of course not, Thomas. It does you credit to be concerned for the young woman," answered His Lordship with a smile. "There is no need to tell her what you are about and so no reason to make her feel she has some kind of secret."

"Mary has no good opinion of the court, m'lord. I believe she wouldfreely tell me things if she knew who would hear them," stated Thomas nervously.

His Lordship and Captain Hardy looked at each other before his lordship replied.

"I am sure Mary is as loyal to King George as we are ourselves, but perhaps it is best not to burden her now with knowing who else will hear her confidences. Do not think that you are deceiving her in behaving so, only seeing how it goes at the start."

With that, Thomas had to be satisfied. A couple of days later, whenhe was called to *Villa Bastioni* to receive a note for Captain Hardy regarding the actions taken by Commodore Mitchell of the Portuguese squadron, Mary saw to it that temporizing had to be cast to the wind.

She was in a small, rear, ground-floor room, sewing the hem ofone of her ladyship's dresses, when Thomas knocked and put his head around the door. She smiled at his bashful expression, butgave him no chance to speak first.

"Where did you spring from, Thomas?"

"From the ship," he replied, "I have to pick up a note from His Lordship to Captain Hardy about ships burnt off Naples, but it's not finished yet."

"Who told you where to find me?" she asked.

"Well, her ladyship, who passed me between here and the kitchen," he admitted.

Truthful though this was, taken by itself, Mary's response was cool. "Now, why would her ladyship be encouraging you to interrupt my work?"

"Perhaps she thought you could sew and talk to me at the same time," Thomas started hopefully, seeing a smile in her eyes, "and I'm out of the way to kick my heels here."

"And perhaps she thought you would pick up gossip from the king's council, now that the queen is shut out and can no longer tell her," retorted Mary tartly.

The smile still played around her eyes and mouth, which made Thomas want to rush across the room and kiss her on that very pretty mouth. However, he realized he was quite incapable of turning Mary from her present train of thought.

"His lordship knows only what he is told when he is called to the King's Council to say what measures he is taking for the defense of this island," he justified.

"Ah, so it is his lordship our conversation will serve. No doubt, that puts a better face on it, but why should I tell you what I hear?" mused Mary.

"Well, his lordship is fighting King George's war against the French and is our best hope of victory," he started, then in a rush, "and I can see you the more often."

Mary stopped sewing, threw back her head, and laughed, but not derisively.

"Oh, Thomas, you would never make a courtier because you have no idea how to deceive," she got out, with tears running down her cheeks, once her laughter had subsided. "That you appeal to my loyalty to our country, which I left when I was friendless, shows touching faith in the justness of our cause. The notion that I should pass on gossip for the great pleasure of us being together more often ..."

Thomas gently took hold of the hand holding the needle and thread aloft.

"But, you do enjoy being with me. I will never put you in danger,

Mary, or fail you," he insisted, gently lowering and caressing herhand in both of his.

"Have a care where you take my hand. The needle is long and sharp," she warned in a soft voice carrying no threat. "I know you sailors; here today, sailed the morrow!"

"I will never leave you for longer than duty requires," he soothed, still caressing her hand.

He lent forward to kiss her. A fleeting kiss was all she allowed before pulling back to speak with a look of appeal in her eyes.

"Is there not something wrong here in myself having to make thepayment to give pleasure to you, my fine, true Thomas?"

"I cannot deny it, but I have this feeling we are caught up insomething."

"That we surely are, Thomas. What do you wish to know while Ifinish sewing this hem? How many councils a day the king holds?"

"Surely one would be sufficient," he responded weakly.

"Not a bit of it," Mary continued briskly, "some days it can be as many as three."

"And, do they decide aught, apart from begging his lordship tosave this island?"

"Well, the other day, the king allowed Cardinal Ruffo and eight companions to have themselves landed on the coast of Calabria to raise an army and drive out the French."

"What, a priest?" he asked incredulously.

"He is no priest. He was Treasurer to the Pope in Rome and made Cardinal when he retired from the position."

"Departing with some of the Pope's treasure would have beenmore to be expected," commented Thomas.

"Never mind dreaming of treasure, I have this hem to finish. Here, hold a length of it instead of my hand, and I shall be quicker," Mary mockingly scolded.

"Commodore Caracciolo is also going back to his estate outside Naples to protect his tenants. It is said that, when the king consented to his going, he warned the commodore he must not aid rebels or the French."

"It seems strange a naval commander of the king would want torisk himself there now that a French army is in the offing," reflected Thomas, moving the dress material through his hands as Mary furiously stitched to make up for lost time.

"There are those who wonder if he has not simply thought the king's cause is lost," Mary added dryly, reaching for her scissors to cut her thread, "but that is all I can tell you for today, so we must part until my next summons also brings you rushing here."

She didn't sound exactly wistful, but her smile did show that she quite looked forward to that next occasion, so Thomas felt his hopes for their relationship rising.

A call to Sir William's chamber swiftly followed Mary's departure. There, his lordship was seated close to the knight, while his lady was ostentatiously at the far side of the room. Not withstanding the cool atmosphere between man and wife, Thomas's interrogation wasswift and effective. There was no consternation that Mary had so quickly tumbled to what was happening, merely satisfaction that she would do as they wished. The news about Cardinal Ruffo had his lordship's full attention.

"He spoke earnestly when I met him at the *Colli*, but I do not know what a swelled-up priest with so few companions can do to raise an army."

"Perhaps more than you imagine, my dear Nelson," put in SirWilliam, saving Thomas the need to correct his lordship as to the priesthood.

"Fabrizio Ruffo is a younger son of an impoverished noble family, but he was both Treasurer and Minister of War to His Holiness, so was given his red hat on relinquishing those offices without being required to take holy orders."

"But, what kind of army will he be able to raise in Calabria?" His Lordship probed.

"Oh, it will be a peasant army, but do not forget the influence of the Church and that Ruffo is a Calabrian. The King's army was lamentable; Ruffo could do no worse."

"Well, I bow to your knowledge of Calabria, Sir William. At the very least, Ruffo will tie down numbers of French troops, so long as he evades capture."

"Thomas mentioned there was a second piece of information from Mary," interposed her ladyship, who had been uncharacteristically silent up to this point.

"What was that about, Thomas?" asked His Lordship, turning back to him.

"Commodore Caracciolo going back to the mainland, m'lord," Thomas answered.

"Yes, I knew the king had consented to him going. Was there something particular about it?"

"Only that when he asked the king to allow him to go to look after his tenants, the king warned him on giving consent not to consortwith rebels or the French."

"Foolish decision to let him go, wise warning," snorted Sir William. "I fear we have not heard the last of Caracciolo by a long chalk!"

"I fear events will prove you correct, my dear, wise friend. Was there any view given by others at Court as to Caracciolo's reason for going back?" queried His Lordship.

"Only the feeling it was merely an excuse, m'Lord," answeredThomas.

"Ha, so they liken him to the proverbial rat," mused His Lordship, smiling, "but if he is one, I believe he is abandoning ship as prematurely, as Commodore Mitchell burnt the two Neapolitan seventy-fours abandoned by their crews. Not that *he* should sufferfor being overzealous! Here is the note for Captain Hardy, Thomas."

"Before you send Thomas on his way, my dear Lord Nelson, I believe we should advise him how soon he will be having another conversation with Mary."

"Not *too* soon I hope. We should not make Sir John suspicious," broke in Sir William, sounding a shade nettled at his wife's further intervention.

"Not until Monday afternoon of next week," responded her ladyship in a very level tone.

His lordship looked ruefully from one to the other.

In this vein, matters continued for the remainder of January andthe early part of February, not withstanding the arrival of *Bellerophon* with a convoy and the flag shift into that ship, so his lordship could send *Vanguard* and *Minerve* away to aid Captain Ball on Malta. Mary would allow Thomas no more than the occasional kiss. Each time, Thomas was questioned after their conversations, the distance between Sir William and his wife continued to be evident, until the thirteenth.

It was as Thomas walked into the kitchen that Wednesday afternoon, to find Tom Allen with an arm around the darkly handsome, plump Sicilian cook and she with a ladle laughingly raised towards his head, that Tom called out.

"A word wi' ye, Thomas, afore ye gows threw."

He halted by the door to the passage that led past the room where Mary worked. Tom let go of the Sicilian woman, gave her a swift, playful slap on the bottom, and equally swiftly moved out of range of the ladle. Coming up to Thomas, he was bubbling with suppressed excitement he could no longer contain.

"She aas finally snared irs lordship. No more virsits to Leggorn, a' reckerns."

Struggling to take in what Tom was saying, he just asked, "Who has snared him?"

"Why, err laidyship o'course. Come out irs chamber irn err nightgaown wi' a smoil orn err faice," answered Tom, the excitement broadening his accent.

"What d'ye mean about no more visits to Leghorn, Tom?"

"Well, irs lordship wont be a goin' terr see irs opery singin' laidy, Adlaida Corellyah, no more. Err laidyship irs steerin't course naow."

That was something he hadn't known about, thought Thomas,keeping the smile off his face at Tom's rendition of "opera," but he reflected her ladyship had a good singing voice too. He decided his best reaction was to be noncommittal.

"You saw that this morning, did you, Tom? How did you find his lordship?"

"Tyerd, but very aappy an' needin' a good swill doawn, aforedressin'."

It sounded consistent with what Tom had seen, as Thomas now acknowledged.

"Thank you for telling me, Tom. I will be careful what I say later, butfor now, I must go in to see Mary."

"Naow don't ye get all fired up an' imtatin' irs lordship, Thomas."

Little chance of that, reflected Thomas ruefully as he walked into the passage, but he was nonetheless eager to tell Mary what he'd just heard.

CHAPTER 8

INTRIGUES CONTINUE AND SIR WILLIAM TAKES A LEASE

Thomas must have burst in on Mary too precipitately because there was initially a look of irritation in her eyes at the interruption of the intricate needlework she was engaged in, renewing embroidery on a bodice. Once she had registered who was rushing into the room, a look of sardonic, but welcoming, amusement took over.

"You must be burning to tell me something for a change, Thomas. Iam agog to hear it, whatever it is, after her ladyship looking like the cat that got the cream."

"Tom Allen tells me that she shared His Lordship's bed last night, beyond doubt."

Mary looked at him with an expression that managed to be both sad and tender.

"Oh Thomas, you are such an innocent if you have not seen this coming. I do not know what his relationship with his wife is like, and Isuppose you don't either.

Truly, his memory of Lady Nelson had faded, he realized with a feeling of guilt, but said nothing.

"I've heard Sir John talking to Lady Acton about Lord Nelson's longassociation with the opera singer, Adelaide Correglia, in Leghorn. That Lady Nelson is not here, and he makes no move to bring her here, meant that he would resort to one or the other."

"Tom told me about her too," he confessed, "I now see that Her

Ladyship was determined it was going to be her. I feel we are caught up in her web."

"You are not alone in that feeling," she said archly, resuming her needlework, "but there is nothing we can do to alter things. From what you have told me of the old gentleman, nothing he can do either, even should he want to bring it to an end."

"All he wants is for his wife to be kind to him," Thomas statedfirmly.

"Well, she was certainly being that when I arrived. Fussing over him she was, and he looked so pleased, even if the rest of us do see him wearing a pair of horns!"

"Was his lordship there?" Thomas asked her, moving over to hold her free hand.

"Not that I saw, and don't think you'll be imitating him soon. It will be a long while before I trust another man and certainly not out of wedlock," she retorted.

"Have you been let down by a man in the past?" he asked tentatively.

"You might say that." She laughed harshly, drew in a deep breath, and continued.

"You may as well know the whole story before you decide if you want to bind yourself to me. A man in Ryarsh, some years older than me, who had a sickly wife, paid court to me secretly. He was a well set-up man and handsome. He made a good living from buying produce and manufactures and selling them at a profit. I do not knowwhat you call that sort of trade, but smooth tongued he certainlywas."

"A higgler is what we would call him where I hale from," prompted Thomas, still holding onto her hand and stroking the back of it,realizing this was taking courage.

"Higgler doesn't sound at all kindly and rightly so in his case."She again paused and laughed bitterly.

"He told me his wife was dying and so he would soon be free to marry me, but he lied. Fool that I was, I lay with him in a glade where we met during the warm summer weather. When I told him I was with child, he said he would have to deny our coupling to avoid theshame putting his wife in her grave. It then became clear to me why he had been so careful not to be seen with me."

Thomas looked at her sadly but didn't release her hand. "What became of you then?"

"My parents also wanted no shame, once I brought myself to tell them. That was before my body started to show thickening. So they packed me off to an aunt in Dover who was a childless widow and still lived frugally in her late husband's house. I would take in needlework until the birthing to earn my keep. Then we would decidewhat was to be done with the child. My mother had taught me well,so my aunt soon found me plenty of work from the well-to-do ladiesof Dover."

Thomas looked mystified at that point but said nothing, so she continued.

"When the birthing came, it was so painful. My aunt did not know what to do, and the midwife she paid for from the money I earned was drunk. The baby was a boy, but breathed poorly from the moment he came out of me. She cut the cord badly, and he bledfrom the navel until he expired in less than two days. It was a miracleI did not follow the babe with childbed fever, the way she handledme. But I thrived and took it as a judgment on the higgler that his sonhad died. I was alive, with my breasts full of milk, the very night that Lady Acton was awaiting a ship for Italy – with her baby son and in sore need of a wet nurse. Very sore indeed, as I found out."

"What happened to the corpse of your own baby?" asked Thomas, gripping her hand.

"He had not been baptized so could not be buried in consecrated ground. A field edge outside the church burial ground was found. At my aunt's request, the rector of the parish did send his curate to say a prayer as we laid him in that unmarked grave. It was well enough done. I would have loved him had he been a lusty babe, but I fearthe way he was conceived doomed him not to be. Of course, Lady Acton knew I had given birth to a bastard who died the day before she saw me. I came well recommended for my work by the lady with whom she stayed. She could see my aunt was respectable and Iwas clean and tidy, so she offered me employment and passage. I accepted as a way of avoiding return to Ryarsh or staying in Dover."

"Did it not make you miss your own babe the more, suckling another woman's child?"

Thomas had tears in his eyes, almost overcome with the tragedy of it all.

"No, it was strangely comforting to take the youngest of LadyActon's sons to my breast, greedy little squaller though he was. It seemed I was doing penance for my sins with the higgler, at least until the babe was weaned. I had not realized how much I would continue doing penance with my needle until we were on passage. The contents of Lady Acton's travelling chest led me to believe that Sir John could not be a rich man," she replied, speaking these last words in a strongly ironic tone.

"Well," said Thomas reflectively, "I can recall one saying of theLord from the Good Book that applies to you and one to your dead babe. I recall he said, 'Let him that is without sin cast the first stone,' and–"

He got no further because Mary squeezed his hand tightly, her eyes shining in response to his sad, intense stare.

"I know what you were going to say for my babe. It is, 'Suffer the little children to come unto me,' and I love you for both of these thoughts, Thomas Spencer."

"And I love you enough, Mary Hever, to ask you to marry me. I have a few pound put by, but I shall have to seek permission from his lordship and the captain."

Mary suddenly looked thoughtful.

"I will gladly marry you, but better not to say ought at present, whileour meetings are to serve his lordship's needs."

Thomas would have felt foolish for not having contemplated that obvious problem, had not Mary then flung bodice and needle to an adjacent table. She pulled his arms around her waist, and moved her lips up to his.

"You have not yet asked me what I have heard," she pointed out.

Her breath warmed his face and she kissed him lingeringly, her tongue running across his lips. His own tongue touched hers, and a shock ran through his body, compelling him to press his tongue into her mouth and start running one hand up the front of her dress, at which she pulled her head back and put a finger to her wet lips.

"Thomas, you had better listen, rather than just one bit of you standing to attention while the rest of you is all over me. I must have the wedding ring first, however long it takes. All I can tell you today isthat Cardinal Ruffo has been given a good welcome in Calabria. The formation of *The Christian Army of the Holy Faith* has been announced. He has reported thousands flocking to the royal banner."

Thomas looked at her sheepishly, his erection diminishing as he took in her words, but he still held onto her waist wordlessly, while she continued in her usual practical way.

"There will be times when no one interrupts us, and I can give you a little more pleasure to be going along with. Today, you havealready been with me too long for so little that is new."

Thomas realized the truth of this with a start, disengaged himself, and stood up. He bent again only to give Mary a swift kiss on the lips before he spoke.

"Now that Sir William has introduced me to dramas by William Shakespeare, I know to say, 'Farewell, parting is such sweet sorrow,' and bow my way out."

"Desist from bowing; you could injure yourself," said Mary, picking up her work.

When he went out and walked to the vestibule, it was from his lordship's study that three well-recognized voices were heard. He knocked, and her ladyship let him in.

"Here is Thomas, come to pass on a few more secrets to us," she breathed, ushering him to the center of the floor.

She went to the corner of the desk, where a coffee pot stood on a tray. She bent to pour another small cupful for her husband. She waswearing a dress with a loose, low-cut bodice that left little to the imagination as she bent over her husband. and Thomas could see his lordship's eyes on the opposite side of the desk were riveted on her breasts. He shuffled and cleared his throat.

"Well, let us hear what you have from the *Colli,* Thomas," his lordship said quite gently, reluctantly lifting his eyes.

"M'lord, it is very little. Cardinal Ruffo has raised the royal bannerof *The Christian Army of the Holy Faith*, and thousands have gone tojoin him," Thomas managed.

He need not have worried about it being so little. his lordship now looked toward Sir William with an admiration that Thomas could see was really to disguise the fact that he was shamefaced. He focussedhis eye away from a now upright Lady Hamilton.

"My dear Sir William, your judgment of what Ruffo might achieve inthe Calabrian situation is proved perfect. I do believe it would be worthwhile to send one of my captains with a small squadron to monitor events on land from the Calabrian coast and render any assistance he can. It may reduce the threat to Messina."

The elderly knight, now basking in the close attention of his wife, was modest.

"Ruffo is making a good start, and the sight of a King's ship or two should encourage his recruiting, but time enough to add more ships when the French retreat before him."

"Good and wise Sir William, you are right; we should be cautious for now. I have more calls on my sixteen of the line than can be managed," his lordship praised.

Her ladyship placed her hand on her husband's shoulder andspoke gently.

"You see the benefit to naval and political strategy of my dear husband being restored to health, your lordship."

Sir William lifted his head and looked up tenderly into his wife's eyes and in His Lordship's one good eye. Looking across the desk atboth of them, Thomas discerned a change from that slightly shamefaced look to one of pure relief. With a flash of perception, he realized that the tired, old knight didn't really care whether his young,ennobled friend was bedding his lady, so long as she continued to bekind to himself in his old age. Her ladyship picked her moment to confirm her control.

"I am sure our difficulties will recede, given time. So long as we three remain *Tria Juncta in Uno,* we shall yet save this kingdom and defeat the French. Now, shall we set a day for another of Mary's conversations with Thomas?"

Nelson smiled at the reference to the knights of the bath emblem and gave his view.

"Let us leave it a few days in case I am asked to provide support to Ruffo. I am afraid it is back to *Bellerophon* for you, Thomas, whatever the noise of her repairs."

"Aye, aye, m'lord," he said, saluting and trying to avoid showing his disappointment at the lack of an early assignation with Mary.

His Lordship looked at him quizzically as he left, and from the vestibule, he could hear muted laughter. Surprisingly, he was back less than two days later, asked to accompany Sir William in the coach to make a visit to a nobleman who was willing to lease his mansion. When he walked into the vestibule of *Villa Bastioni,* Lady Hamilton was also there to see them away. The coachman was standing by, with his horses finishing their feed buckets in harness. The old gentleman was wearing a heavy frock coat and muffler over his elegant household wear. His lady was holding his three-cornered hat in readiness. He looked pleased that Thomas had arrived promptly that morning.

"I am glad you are here, Thomas. I have the prospect of leasing a fine mansion with proper fireplaces, although I fear it will be very expensive."

"Do not fret over the money, my love. Dear Lord Nelson has promised he will share the cost with us, needing a shore base as he does," soothed her ladyship.

"Well, I trust that need will last for the term of months to which I have to commit."

"Do not fear, my love. He has far too much still to achieve here to take himself home this spring," her ladyship confidently asserted. "It will be so much better if we can entertain again in the style expected of his majesty's minister."

The old gentleman looked pleased at that prospect and yet still fearful of the expense. Thomas helped him up the coach step and her ladyship spoke to the coachman.

"Palazzo Palagonia, Via del Quattro Aprile, per favore."

"Do you know what *Via del Quattro Aprile* means, Thomas?" asked Sir William, settling back on the seat cushions.

"It sounds like way of the fourth of April, Sir William, but surely not?" said Thomas.

"Well done, my boy, you have it exactly right," said Sir William as the coach set off along the foreshore track toward *Porta Felice.*

"It refers to an event in Sicilian history, known as the SicilianVespers. An uprising against the Angevin King took place on Easter Monday in the year 1282."

"Was it a successful uprising, Sir William, to have a way named forit?"

"All too bloodily successful," sighed Sir William, "not that it freedthe Sicilians from foreign rule for very long."

"I do not understand how Spanish kings came to rule here," queried Thomas.

"Ah, that is simple, my boy. After the Angevins had all been killed or evicted, the Sicilians realized they needed a foreign protector against both Barbary pirates and Princes on the mainland of Italy. Sothey asked the King of Aragon to be their overlord and he accepted. You perhaps know the last King of Aragon, Ferdinand, was the one who married Isabel la Catolica, Queen of Castile, and so became a joint monarch of Spain. After they had conquered the Moors inGranada, the Sicilians still needed their protection. The Barbarypirates had been given new heart by the rise of their fellow mohammedans, the Ottoman Turks."

The coach had now rumbled through the *Porta Felice* and along the first section of *Via del Cassaro,* but on reaching the corner of the stone wall to the left, followed it round to hold to that rising side of *Piazza Marina.* Sir William pointed out a building ahead.

"You see that large, old building up on the left; that is *Palazzo Chiaramonte.* The Spanish Inquisition housed their prisoners inside, so their rule had its dark times."

It looked forbidding as they passed, but Thomas had no time to respond because the coach rattled on forward over the paving into a narrow street, still rising. The coach had not gone far along thisstreet before the coachman pulled the horses almost to a stop sothat he could slowly pull the horses round to the right. As the coach itself came round, its windows started to pass under an arch and into shadow before emerging into a lighter, open courtyard, which the direct sunlight had not reached.

Once stopped, with the horses a little way short of an arch, the far side of the building, a little, elderly man in a black frock coat, with a black, three-cornered hat jammed on his white wig, opened Sir William's coach door, bowing.

"Benvenuto in Palazzo Palagonia, Barone 'Amilton."

Sir William responded in equable-sounding Italian, then turned quickly to Thomas.

"This is the nobleman's agent."

He stepped down. Thomas opened the other door and got down his side of the coach, where there was a door into some kind of gatekeeper's lodge. He walked round the back to join Sir William and the agent, who was pointing up a stone stairway virtually opposite the lodge and speaking volubly. With his silver-handled walking stick on one side and Thomas the other, the old knight followed the agent up the stairway quite nimbly. The stairway had a landing where it turned back on itself to run up to the door of a reasonably well- plastered and decorated receiving room. Once inside, other doors led off to further rooms each side along the front of the *Palazz,* All three were of reasonable size and decoration for entertaining, but badly in need of a thorough cleaning. Spiderwebs before the dirty windows meant to overlook *Via del Quattro Aprile* and in ceiling corners attested to the lack of recent occupation. Sir William let the agent show them first the room on the *Piazza Marina* side of that by which they had entered. Then the room to the far side, where the street was running uphill. At its end was a short flight of steps leading up to a smaller front room with another access from an internal passage. Thomas made a mental reservation of this to be his lordship's study.

The agent led them through the rooms and passages of this slightly higher section of the first floor, which ran round the corner to the upper side of the sloping courtyard. The coachman was leading the horses round in a tight curve to edge the coach around to face the way they had come in. An internal staircase led to a higher floor with quite pleasant sleeping chambers, *garde* robes, and dressing rooms. The bedchambers, like the receiving rooms, had fireplaces, which Sir William noted with approval. They worked their way back from the rear of the building on this floor, which seemed to overlook some kind of garden on the uphill side.

Thomas wondered where the servants' quarters were to be found. On resuming the first floor, an internal, narrow, stone staircase to the ground floor soon revealed a kitchen of decent size with a pump over a wellhead. There was a large fireplace with roasting spit, cooking ranges and stone sinks. Empty shelving ran up the walls and overhead racks were held in place by cords and pulleys. It was off a passage leading from the kitchen that a series of small, dark rooms were to be found. Clearly, these were the servants' quarters, Thomas realized. With their whitewashed stone walls, they madehim think they must be like prison cells. Not that anyone would want to spend more than nighttime sleeping hours under a blanket in one of them on a winter's night! All waking hours, working or not, would be best spent in a nice, warm kitchen, once the mansion was occupied.

From this part of the ground floor, they went to the other side of theentrance arch and started again. Sir William was counting under his breath, occasionally forgetting not to say the numbers out loud as they went from room to room. Upstairs they went again on thisdownhill side of the *Palazzo,* finally coming back to the first roomthey had entered. They walked toward the door leading out to the staircase.

"Thomas," said Sir William, taking his arm, "pray walk over to that window, open both sides, and step into the mock balcony, then look down to *Piazza Marina,* while I discuss matters with the agent. Afterward, you can tell me what you see."

When he had done as bidden, Thomas realized why he had been required to do this. He could see right into the paved area below the steps of the fishermen's church, with the city wall behind. The forest of bare masts beyond told him that the inner harbor was directly in the line of sight from this window. Across the room, a low-voiced Italian conversation was ongoing. Thomas concentrated his gaze on the masts and saw two more float in front of the moored vessels and stop. He considered how signals could be passed to this mansion from bunting raised up a mast on a signal halyard. Attention could beattracted by shining a mirror from a crosstrees. This wouldn't have tobe very high up a mast, given his current height above the city wall. Better than keeping a man on the parapet, unless they were under attack.

Behind him, the conversation stopped, and he turned to find the agent bowing to Sir William and heading out of the room for thestone staircase.

"Well, Thomas, what did you see out there that held your attention so long?"

"I looked right over the city wall to the masts of ships moored in theinner harbor, Sir William, and I was considering means of signaling."

"Excellent! My estimation that this would be virtually unrivalled as ashore base for Lord Nelson is vindicated, albeit at a high price. Still, the agent has confirmed his principal, Ferdinando Gravina Alliata, will consent to subletting in addition to use by Lord Nelson, and the building is a sound, fifty-roomed mansion, so I have said that, subject to consultation with his lordship, we will take it."

"I believe his lordship will only have to see the *Palazzo*, Sir William. Do we need to take a look at the rear of the building fromthe alleyway behind?"

"Yes, that is a good suggestion, Thomas. *Vicolo Palagonia*, I believe it is called, also named after the owner's Gravina grandfather, who was Prince of Palagonia."

"Has he fallen on hard times, to be willing to let this mansion, Sir William?"

With a wry smile, the elderly Knight leaned on his stick.

"Would that were so, young man, but it is more a case of his making every asset work for him to sustain the grand style in which he lives at Bagheria, along the coast."

He waved his free hand vaguely eastward then continued.

"He lives in a mansion far more ornate than this, called *Villa Palagonia*, with fantastical statues of his own design in the garden, I am told. Some young traveler from the Court of Saxony viewed the statues in their setting many years back and wrote a critique. He is supposed to be a great poet and writer in the German language, by name of Goethe. He also stayed in Naples on his progress south, rather a pretty boy. I fear I digress. Lend me your arm to take the stairs, Thomas, and we will ensure there is no disrepair to the rear walls."

There wasn't, and the coach was soon rolling back along the track below the walls to *Villa Bastioni*. They arrived just as a naval officer with a single epaulette to his uniform coat entered the vestibule. In the minute or two it took Thomas to assist Sir William down from the coach, someone had alerted her ladyship to their return. She stood just inside the door, smiling and solicitous.

"I can see the *palazzo* proved suitable, my dear husband, I have not seen you so invigorated since we arrived on this island."

"At a high price, my love, on which we shall have to speak with ourdear Lord Nelson ..."

At that moment, a sudden shout of triumph was emitted in his lordship's study. The door was flung open and his lordship emerged clutching an opened letter. The young officer who had brought it stood rooted before his admiral's desk, a look of slight bemusement on his face.

"Wonderful tidings, my dear, dear friends, Lord St. Vincent has given me carte blanche to deal with the Swedish knight. Thomas, have Mr Tyson come down—there is work to be done—and remain on standby for carrying to the harbor."

His lordship then swung back to the young naval officer and spoke in a more measured tone. "Well, commander, not only have you brought the best of orders from Lord St. Vincent, but you have also guaranteed your urgent passage to the Levant. Please make allhaste to take on such stores and water as you need. I will give you a brief note to *Bellerophon* to replenish you. Your written orders and dispatches will follow as soon as they can be written."

That was all Thomas heard as he ascended the stairs to call Mr Tyson. He would be busy with his quill and ink on His Lordship's best paper all the sunny hours of that afternoon. When he came back down behind Mr Tyson, the young commander had gone. Sir Williamand his lady were closeted in the study with his lordship, and an enthused discussion was audible when Mr Tyson opened the door toenter.

Whether this concerned the enterprise on which he had assisted Sir William, or one or more of the numerous opened letters that had come with the all-important dispatch from the Commander-in-Chief, Mediterranean, Thomas did not know. For him, at this point, it was enough to know that His Lordship was cheerfully embarked on energetic action with the support of his dear friends. Surely events would now take a decisive turn for the better?

CHAPTER 9

THE INTRIGUES FOSTER A RELATIONSHIP

Surprisingly, the firm action taken to bring Sir Sydney Smith under his lordship's control did not initially bring about the decisive shift in fortunes Thomas had anticipated. The fast courier brig carried eastward his orders to simply assist the forces of the Sublime Porte against the stranded French army of General Bonaparte. However, itwas a case of everything seeming to go slowly. News of Ruffo's advance northward in Calabria seemed only to trickle in. The *Bellerophon* repairs went slowly because timbers and spars had tobe shaped. News from Naples was intermittent, although it was clearthat the rulers of *Republica Napoletana* were not having an easy time, even with the iron fist of General Championnet to support them.In one local respect, matters seemed to be made worse by information that emerged from the next conversation between Thomas and Mary, a week after the day of optimism.

Mary was still readying herself to start work in the small room, examining one of Her Ladyship's dresses to see where the hem needed restitching. Thomas quietly opened the door and walked in.

"My, we are in a hurry today," she said, laughing and carefully laying the dress over an adjacent chair.

Thomas needed no further invitation to move right up to her and put his arms around her waist. He pulled her tight to him, feeling the shape of her breasts against his chest as he planted his lips on hers.He strove to move his legs closer, but voluminous skirts and petticoats defeated him. Gently, she disengaged her lips.

"I am still dressed for a winter's morning, Thomas, like the Sicilian women."

"It doesn't feel cold to me," he said glumly, almost as if it were just to hold him off.

"Now don't go into a sulk with me. I've plenty to tell you today."

He brightened a little at the thought of prolonging his stay that morning.

"Perhaps I should first tell you, my dearest, that we shall soon be meeting elsewhere than this villa. Arrangements for a move are well in hand."

"Oh, you mean to *Palazzo Palagonia;* better for dark corners, I hear," rejoined Mary.

"I thought Sir William's arrangements were meant to be private," said Thomas incredulously, still trying to pull her closer.

"I told you nothing is ever secret for long around this Court," she said, laughing again and lifting a hand to his chest to hold him back. "Why haven't they moved already?"

"Well, some redecoration is needed to receiving rooms and main bedchambers even after cleaning. her ladyship wanted to do more, but Sir William said we would be merely increasing the Palazzo's value to the owner. His lordship agreed, then, there was a delay for the tradesmen to become available," he informed.

"You can't be surprised about that delay, with all the houses let to families escaping from Naples. The king and queen are adding to the problem," Mary responded.

"How is it they are adding to the problem?" asked Thomas, letting go of Mary's waist with one hand and trying to lower the other around her bottom.

"Why, they are having another *palazzo* built, far out of the city to make the Queen feel safer. They are calling it a *palazzina* to show it is smaller than you expect a *palazzo* to be," Mary intoned mockingly, swinging away from his groping hand.

"Just where is it and how grand?" questioned Thomas, although the disappointment in his voice had nothing to do with the question.

"Just landward of *Monte Pellegrino,* and it has been designed in the Chinese style, so you may expect the decoration to be very costly. *Palazzina Cinese* it is to be called. Then there will have to be separate accommodation for royal guards, gardens, roads, and walls, so it will all be costly," Mary reported in a cynical tone.

"I doubt his lordship will consider it money well spent," Thomas despaired. "Have you nothing better to tell me?"

"Fabrizio Ruffo is about to advance into Northern Calabria unopposed. A bandit called Michele Pezza has joined him. He has a fearsome name for ambushes in the mountains. People call him *Fra Diavolo,* which means brother devil or in the devil, so the French prefer to sit in fortified towns. Also, Cardinal Ruffo is in touch with loyalists in the Papal States. They are about to rise against the French, and General Championnet does not have enough troops for everywhere."

"That does sound better," admitted Thomas. "Give me another kissbefore I go."

"Now you sound like every other sailor," mocked Mary, "and seeing that her ladyship still looks like the cat that got the cream, I dare say his lordship will still be enjoying his oats right up to the moment he sails away and takes you with him."

"I don't think that will be for a while yet," Thomas said cautiously, putting an arm around her waist again.

Mary didn't resist the embrace or kiss.

His lordship was alone in his study, still laboriously working his waythrough the remainder of the large numbers of personal letters of congratulation on his victory at the Nile. Most had arrived at the end of January, although a few only the previous week. Tom Allen was quickly sent for to invite Sir William and her ladyship to join him. He was then instructed to go and check that dinner could be served at one. Tom was away at his most agile with those instructions, seeing they contained an excuse to visit the Sicilian women in the kitchen. Thomas wondered what they made of lunch being called dinner according to Royal Navy custom. They understood a bare handful of English words.

It took only seconds for her ladyship's voice to become audible from the door of Sir William's ground-floor bedchamber. His lordship had Thomas sand and fold his latest letter until they came in and sat down side by side. Thomas then straightened up for the usual interrogation, having already decided to repeat first what Mary had told him about the Calabria situation.

"Well, Thomas, tell us What Mary has heard this week," orderedhis lordship.

"M'lord, the French are not daring to confront Cardinal Ruffo's*Christian Army of the Holy Faith*. It appears he has been joined by Michele Pezza, a bandit some call *Fra Diavolo,* who is feared for mounting ambushes in the Calabrian Mountains."

His lordship leaned back and laughed before turning to Sir William. "Is this not a contradiction in terms that the devil should join the *Christian Army of the Holy Faith*, Sir William? Have you heard of this bandit before?"

"I have heard of him many times, my dear Nelson. Usually when King Ferdinand's troops have been trying ineffectually to capture him after some outrage or other against merchants or tax gatherersfailing to travel in armed convoy."

"He begins to sound like the great devil," rejoined His Lordship,"but do you have any knowledge of why he has been able to evade capture?"

"Oh, he has his supporters among the Calabrians, because it is said that, when he relieves tax gatherers of the king's taxes, agoodly proportion is returned to the payers," replied Sir William witha hint of amusement.

"By the saints, Thomas, he sounds like a Calabrian version of your Robin Hood," his lordship exclaimed, "clearly a man to be watched very closely, especially by Ruffo!"

"Calabria, being in Italy, someone is more likely to write an opera about him than a saga," chimed her ladyship, also laughing.

"There is more from Calabria, m'lord. Cardinal Ruffo is in

101

touchwith loyalists in the Papal States, who are about to rise against the French, so General Championnet cannot commit more troops to the south," added Thomas, capitalizing on the humor.

"Am I correct in believing this should give us grounds for some optimism, my dear Sir William? If I but had English troops for Messina, the Russians could go to Ruffo."

"Assuredly, if loyalists rise anywhere south of Rome, even should they stay in the mountains for their own safety, Championnet will be forced to concentrate his troops to hold the cities. It occurs to me, mydear Nelson, that he will retain his garrison at Salerno in an endeavor to deter Ruffo from a direct assault on Naples along the coast," Sir William reponded.

"I believe the time has come for Captain Hardy to send an officer to Ruffo, with a corvette inshore to relay that officer's reports. I shall have to make sure the officer reaches Ruffo himself, rather than falling in with the great devil," said His Lordship with an air of decision. "Now that I have the benefit of your counsel, Sir William, onthe return of *Vanguard* and *Minerve*, we shall have a look intoSalerno and assess its seaward defenses."

"Is there anything else for Thomas to report?" asked her ladyship, who had been keenly following every word of her husband's advice and her lover's decisions.

Swallowing hard, when two pairs of eyes and a single penetrating one swiveled back to him, Thomas said, "The king and queen have had building start on a small palace to be called *Palazzina Cinese* to the landward of *Monte Pellegrino*."

"Has the queen not told you of this, my dear Lady Hamilton?" asked his lordship.

"She has repeatedly told me that her entreaties to her husband to live safely outside the city were being listened to and that he was formulating plans. This of building another small palace she had not told me," replied her ladyship bitterly.

"It will cost a fortune to build even a *palazzina* in the Chinesestyle," added Sir William morosely.

"Small wonder we had to accept a delay in tradesmen starting work on Palagonia. They are too busy lining their pockets from the king's treasury."

"From which money would be far better spent recovering the Italian mainland as part of his kingdom. He would even do better giving the money to the Great Devil himself to have him launch his bandithorde on the French," railed his lordship.

"Perhaps they will fight better if they have to capture French army pay chests and supplies to pay themselves," reflected Sir William. "The king seems determined not to part with his gold in the direction of the mainland. That would run the risk of a goodly proportionsticking to the fingers of those through whose hands it passes."

"I think you will find my dear husband is very perceptive on such matters. In any event, the money is as good as spent on the *palazzina*," added Her Ladyship.

"I am sure both of you have the right of it," responded his lordship ruefully. "Those of us assisting his majesty to recover the greater part of his kingdom must rely on our own resources and any we can capture."

So saying, he pushed a clean piece of paper in front of himself then picked up his quill.

"A brief note for Captain Hardy, Thomas. I am sure he will be well pleased to be quit of *Bellerophon* once Captain Darby brings back *Vanguard*."

That, thought Thomas, meant Captain Hardy would have to detach a swift vessel for the look into Salerno and ensure the orders were drawn up. It was all part of being the flag captain. It left his lordship free to think about how to carry the fight to the enemy, knowing the preparation he'd ordered had all been carried out. He did hope that the commander of the swift vessel detailed to look into Salerno and would be equally competent in his steering and sail handling. Standing in close enough to assess the quality of the fortifications and count the muzzle flashes when the garrison opened fire was a risky business for the crew of a small vessel. He was just at the pointof reflecting these were nearly the worst of times, because the French artillerymen would be exceptionally nervy, when His lordship's quill stopped scratching. His one good eye looked up.

"There, it is done, Thomas. You are right to think it will be hot workfor someone."

"Aye, m'lord," he replied, waiting while the ink dried and Her Ladyship went to fold the paper carefully. It was sometimes uncomfortable how his lordship read his thoughts, but he now stood expressionless until the note was handed to him.

"Back to the ship with you, Thomas."

He responded as usual with his salute and departed. He didn't think going to Calabria was a safe mission either!

The turn of the month passed without apparent progress otherthan the days growing longer. The weather became sunnier and *Bellerophon's* repairs came to a conclusion.

There was no doubt that it was now as warm as Nottingham in a good April, thought Thomas. Two large working parties were formed,one to clean out *Palazzo Palagonia* and the other to remove all the property at *Villa Bastioni* that would accompany its occupants. Royal permission allowed removal of all the furniture brought into usethere, so it was to the *Villa Bastioni* party Thomas managed to have himself attached. He could not allow the furniture in His Lordship's study to come to any harm. He would have to see it installed in the selected first floor room on the front of the *palazzo*.

Not that he or either of the other two principal residents were present on their villa to *palazzo* removal. The coach had taken them off on another visit to Lady and Miss Knight, to be followed by a visit to some *palazzo* on *La Nova* for a reception and musicalentertainment. According to Tom Allen, despite now being better housed than in the miserable hotel, Lady Knight was ailing andunlikely to be well enough for the visit to La Nova. Indeed, he gave the gloomy opinion she was not long for this world.

"And then whur will Mirs Knight be? Moved wi' urs into thirs pal- latso wirse steerin' fur," he added with a regretful shake of the head

He was doubtless influenced by the thought that Miss Knight,being prudish, could make romancing kitchen women rather more difficult.

It was late afternoon, the daylight fading, when Thomas had his lordship's study arranged satisfactorily. The coach rumbled over the uneven paving of the courtyard. Sir William must have been shown his bedchamber and stayed to rest there for a while. Lady Hamilton entered the study first by the door off the corridor, his lordship's left arm falling away from her waist as he followed behind.

"You see, my dear Horatio, that Thomas Spencer has protected your furnishings and set up your writing desk very satisfactorily," said her ladyship silkily.

His lordship tore his good eye from the contemplation of her luscious body and marched the few steps to the window. He opened one side and stuck his head out.

"That is exactly the view I need to be at the heart of things," he enthused.

As his paramour joined him and bent to follow his gaze, his eye must have dropped to her breasts because dismissal followed.

"Thank you, Thomas. You may go and find your quarters with TomAllen.

As Thomas was closing the door behind him, his lordship's lips were virtually on one of the breasts, prominent as they were in a low-cut gown.

Sadly, this was the way of things for over a week ahead. Now that the old gentleman had a room with a fireplace, he was having the firelit in the late afternoon when the temperature fell. It was then kept alight into the night, so he did not wake up cold in the morning. Only when they were out at entertainments or soirees did the pattern vary.One evening at the end of the first week there, they also hosted a musical entertainment. The more the elderly Knight kept warm, the more he enjoyed periods of rest and so the more time his lordship was closeted alone with Lady Hamilton.

He did, however, spend an entire day on his correspondence when Mary arrived early in the morning for her ladyship's planned review of her entire wardrobe of gowns. This to ensure each one was fit to wear in company, now that they were going to entertain regularly in a way that befitted a minister. Thomas showed her in but was then told to wait on his lordship's requirements until four in the afternoon, or however many bells in the afternoon watch he called it. He was to ensure food and drink was sent in just after midday.

Therefore, his impatience mounted when he returned from the ship with messages responding to his lordship's earlier queries. There were still over two hours to go. In the *palazzo*, being so large forcurrently so few occupants, the room he shared with Tom was reasonably large. Also, not quite so dark as it had been before a good coat of whitewash. They each had a chair as well as a timber bed, and Tom was seated on his, cleaning his belt and shoe buckles. "Well, I don't knaow 'ow theay arr cowpin nart seein eech orther terday," he chortled.

"Both keeping too busy to be worried about it," Thomas responded, forcing a smile.

"And err ledyship hargin your Mary's toime. It'll get wers when shay's lertin out."

Thomas looked mystified at Tom's last laughing comment.

"Wan o' therm kirchen wimmen reckerns err ledyship irs werth child, burt errly."

Thomas's eyes narrowed at this piece of gossip, and he decided to test it.

"How does the woman claim to know this?"

"Err ledyship ars aankerrins for particerlar kindser food," Tom now responded.

"We will have to wait and see," reflected Thomas. "How would it change things?"

"Well, irt baint th'old gernulman's. Therd bey ern owseful o'erm otherwise an' whart will err ledyship back irn old England 'av tersay?" said Tom with glee.

"I don't know," confessed Thomas. "I never really got to know LadyNelson."

Tom then volunteered his not very flattering opinion, based on his long experience during the "on the beach" years. His lordship had not coped well with being shackled and had taken himself off more than a few times. In truth, the start of the present war and the relationship he had formed with Adelaide Correglia had livened him. Then he was Captain Nelson of the *Agamemnon* with the breath of freedom, although he would never admit to it. Thomas listened intently to all of this, suppressing his smile at the continued mispronunciation of the opera singer's name. Tom continued that he wasn't too sure what the effect of the relationship with the lady now in his lordship's life would be. Seeing she and Mary had drunk wine with their dinner, Thomas might be in luck.

At this, his patience was nearly snapping, and he had to take himself off to see if the old gentleman was awake and had any requirements. As it happened, he was seated comfortably in a chair, reading and quick to discern Thomas's impatience.

"I am afraid ladies are wont to spend long hours over their gowns, Thomas. It is fast approaching the hour, so you could put your head around the door and say Sir William is concerned that his lady may be overtiring herself."

With fervent thanks, Thomas bowed himself out and worked his way around the *palazzo* corridors to Lady Hamilton's dressing room, where a small, low table was positioned before the chairs Mary and she were using. When Thomas had given the excuse provided by the old gentleman, his wife smiled and got up.

"I shall go for a conversation with him. I believe I am seriously in need of having Mary join this household as dressmaker. I have seen the lack in my wardrobe and the yards of silks I shall need."

So saying, her ladyship smiled at them both in turn and left. No sooner had Thomas closed the door behind her and turned back to Mary that she spoke sharply.

"Do not come rushing to me and trampling on this gown. It has been the devil's job to repair neatly."

Fortunately, her eyes didn't look cross, so Thomas replied insouciantly "I believe you drank wine with your dinner."

The "yes" in response would have come out with a flounce had Mary not been sitting and unwilling to add that the effect of the wine on her eyesight made her cross. She put the gown aside and leaned back, not yet catching Thomas's implication.

"The daylight in here is not so good either.... . Oh, you think I am ripe for taking after a glass of wine, do you, Thomas Spencer. No doubt that naughty man Tom Allen has been talking and puttingideas into that woolly head of yours."

"He's not been naughty where you are concerned, has he, Mary, my love?"

"Oh no, he's very respectful to me because he knows I am yours."

By now, he was leaning across her chair, one hand gently on her cheek, and she leaned forward to lightly kiss his lips, but then looked him seriously in the eyes.

"Do not imagine I am lifting my skirts to you this afternoon. It has been a hard day, and we have to talk before I can leave. The queen has been opening her heart to Lady Acton only yesterday, and she has received word from Vienna."

"Without Lady Hamilton having been told?" asked Thomas.

"No time, and I believe the queen is much abused for the influence Lady Hamilton is said to hold over her. Her husband will no longer listen to her thoughts on anything. You saw her grief on board*Vanguard*. Surely, you feel sorrow for how she is treated?"

Thomas thought back to how the large, expressive eyes of this woman had welled with grief at the loss of her son. All those babies she had borne and knowing the French revolutionaries hadmurdered her sister in public by chopping off her head with one of their infernal guillotines. She had to be a woman of character to keepgoing. True, her large jaw diminished her fading attractiveness, but itdidn't make her any less a woman of great presence.

"Yes, I did at the time and still do, even though his lordship says this *Palazzina Cinese* is a waste of money that could be better spent," Thomas replied quietly.

"Perhaps there is now no need to worry," Mary commented, "because the word from Vienna was that, by the time the letterreached her majesty, the emperor would have declared war on France."

"That was long overdue. Three months ago would have beenbetter," said Thomas.

"I know you are only giving the commonly held view here, but there is more. The army that attacks the French in the north will be a joint Austrian and Russian army, and it will be commanded by the great General Suvorov, who has been made Field Marshal of the Austrian army," Mary added, sounding pleased with herself.

When Thomas left her after a few more tender kisses, Mary sounding pleased with herself was quickly justified in his lordship's study. Tom Allen had carried the message for Sir William and hislady to come and hear this latest information. Thomas told all of it at once to the three of them, and His Lordship was optimistic.

"Well, I believe Suvorov personifies the Russian bear at his most savage when I think back to the way he extinguished Polish independence for the late Czarina Catherine, aye, and beat the Turks back to the Caucasus before that! I can think of no better fate for these French revolutionaries than to be slaughtered by his troops."

"We must hope his army treats civilians well," Sir William commented, "so that we do not see loyal subjects of the Emperor being made turncoats."

"I am sure you are right on that score, Sir William, but if he moves quickly, he will less antagonize the people of Lombardy than the emperor's own generals did. You will recall some had little success against Moreau in the southern German lands. Now that General Buonaparte is locked up in Egypt, we have those new young generals, MacDonald and Joubert to face."

His lordship still persisted in pronouncing Bonaparte as "Buonaparte," despite the General's change in the spelling of his name.

"Do not forget Bonaparte may attempt escape overland," Sir William cautioned. "I am not sure the Turks can stop him short ofAsia Minor."

"Surely, it cannot happen at speed with such a distance for his army to cover?" suggested her ladyship, anxious to keep her menfolk in agreement.

"No, he need not worry Suvorov in the short term," conceded her husband.

That was as far as the discussion went because a mirror flash caught the window pane.

His lordship jumped up and pulled open one-half of the window to look out.

"The flag of the brig come in from Messina is showing. If I am not mistaken, here comes our news at the run. He looks happy, but he may just be enjoying himself."

However, when the young commander came breathlessly into the room and panted that General Stuart had arrived at Messina withone thousand two hundred English soldiers from Minorca, his lordship's ebullience scarcely knew any bounds.

"Now, my dear friends, we are free to start the recovery of Naples. We can be sure this island is safe, even should his majesty do nothing. Now, we can support Ruffo wholeheartedly and see what comes of his venture. I shall plan a squadron."

Sir William, on this occasion, saw no need to urge caution and *TriaJuncta in Uno* proceeded with the commander to a receiving room. Refreshment for all four was well justified!

Chapter 10

Naval Support for the Calabrian Fight Back

According to Tom Allen, the nocturnal toings and froings between his lordship's bedchamber and that of Lady Hamilton continued unabated. This was aided by the way in which the corridors of *Palazzo Palagonia* baffled sound. That depended on soft footwear for the stone surfaces, but there was a clear desire by both parties not to cause upset. It struck Thomas that Sir William had been the instrument of making life easier for his faithless wife and friend by his very decision to rent the *palazzo*. Yet the improvement in his own comfort and happiness were so evident that it was easy not to think he was only occupying a fool's paradise.

Moreover, the pace of life in this shore-based command post had increased hugely. First, there was the need to keep King Ferdinand and Sir John Acton informed of preparations to go over to the offensive. Although that did not mean they would agree to His Lordship putting to sea to lead his squadron. The solution to that problem presented itself with the arrival of a dispatch from Lord St. Vincent. He had relieved Thomas Troubridge of the task of blockading General Bonaparte's army in Egypt and ordered Sir Sydney Smith to replace him. Thomas had arrived to collect another note for Captain Hardy to find the usual trio closeted in his lordship's study. The admiral was holding forth on the King's views.

"King Ferdinand thoroughly approves of all my dispositions but will not hear of my leading any one of our attacks until success in retaking Naples is assured."

"And her majesty says she would likely swoon and die if dear Lord Nelson, her noble protector, were to leave this island," added her ladyship.

A look of exasperation passed between Sir William and his lordship at the mere prospect of once again seeing her majesty swoon, but equanimity soon returned.

"Well, it matters not they are agreed on this, now that I know Thomas Troubridge and *Culloden* are returning to me from the blockade of Egypt. I shall make him commodore of the squadron for the bay and request my Lord St. Vincent to confirm him, so he is not outranked by any Russian or Turk and can deal with Ruffo."

"I applaud your reasoning, my dear Nelson," Sir William contributed. "Have you yet resolved how to deal with this of the Bashaw of Tripoli?"

"My note to Captain Hardy, which Thomas will take, advises *Vanguard* must be ready to put to sea immediately after *Culloden* has arrived. I will transfer my flag into her. We shall then have a show of force at Tunis. I pray it will be adequate to end his communication with Bonaparte but fear it will not. No matter, we shall give him the benefit of the doubt for now and bombard only if he fails us."

"An excellent ploy," enthused Sir William, "we give him a chance to show the loyalty to the *Sublime Porte* he pretends and keep retribution for later proof of disloyalty."

"I shall rely on prompt word from your informants along the African coast, Sir William, to avoid keeping *Vanguard* idle on her return. I have also not forgotten the need to take Salerno. Sam Hood and *Zealous* will suffice, I believe."

The elderly knight looked pleased and added only, "They will not fail."

So, it was back to the ship for Thomas again but very quickly now La Cala was so close. The one drawback of all this positive activity, he thought, was that there was no mention of when he would be ordered to meet with Mary again. Relations with the *Colli* were now so close and cordial again!, He wasn't even needed to ply between ship and *palazzo* for the two days it took *Culloden* to appear from the direction of Messina. He spent the time packing the furnishings and stores his lordship would need for the temporary stay in the ship. Notthat the flying of his flag meant he would be on board regularly, whilethe delights of the *palazzo* were available. It seemed he was destined ever to be packing and unpacking, from permanent to temporary flagship and back again.

Vanguard was moored near the seaward end of the mole, prow facing the open sea. Thomas came up onto the larboard gangway to watch as *Culloden* tacked northwest under all plain sail. She came round due south, taking advantage of the offshore breeze to glide into the harbor, reducing sail as she came. She bore no resemblanceto the forlorn ship that had sat aground at the entrance to Aboukir Bay. That afternoon at the beginning of last August, she acted as a marker for the rest of the fleet to avoid the shoals while they boreinto the bay. One after another, driven by fighting topsails only, they came both sides of the leading moored ships of the French line.

Thomas momentarily shivered at the recollection of the opening crash of gunfire. It had seemed to go on endlessly into the night, even after his lordship's wound had taken him and others below.

An effort of will brought him back to the present, and his seaman's eye took in the superb condition of *Culloden's* upper works and sails.He compared her with the knocked about, but still workmanlike,condition of *Vanguard*. Movement on the quarterdeck to his leftcaught the corner of his eye. A glance round told him that his lordship had hurried down from the *palazzo* in response to the usual signal for the sighting of a sail. Captain Hardy had lined up his officers for the ceremony that would attend the shift of flag. It acted as a sign to Thomas that he must get below again. His lordship was in an obvious hurry, so there could be no delay in shifting his dunnage.

At the head of the companionway, he caught a glimpse of the upper works of an open conveyance with two female passengers, one of whom had the so familiar red hair. He squinted to lookthrough the rigging and verify that it was actually Mary in a carriage with a lady. He had to continue down the steps before his delay in doing so drew attention. When he accompanied helpers bringing his lordship's property into the waist, they were directed into a boat below the larboard beam. *Culloden* was dropping a stern anchor before entering La Cala, to bring her head parallel with the end of themole. The admiral's barge was already being rowed across theintervening, ruffled water. Before the boat bearing Thomas and the dunnage had cast off, he was being piped aboard *Culloden* to be greeted by Captain Troubridge.

By the time the second boat had been rowed across, his lordship's flag had been raised. He had done with the assembled officers and was still conferring with Captain Troubridge. Thomas was admitted tothe great cabin to have the boxes deposited in a cleared space.

"You stay, Thomas. I shall have a note for Sir William. The boatcan stay too and carry him to *Porta Felice*," his lordship called after the departing helpers.

When the door was closed, he turned back to Thomas. He had meanwhile briefly and happily noticed that Captain Troubridge still had that eager, open look on his large face. He and his lordship wereseated by the stern lights, which much reduced the Captain's excessof height.

"You must not approach the carriage in which your Mary is apassenger, Thomas. She is accompanying Lady Acton, who has been poorly and needed some air. What better tonic than the sight of this fine ship!"

Captain Troubridge smile at His Lordship's compliment had a boyish look, for all he was a big and mature man. Nelson turned back to him.

"So, the Swedish Knight really believes the Turks can hold General Bonaparte, with his assistance at Acre of the Crusaders?"

"I believe he does so with some justification, my lord," responded Troubridge. "He was landing guns and having them restoreemplacements before I left. Bonaparte has difficulty bringing up his artillery train outside the walls. The terrain of the Holy Land is rocky and unforgiving."

"Just so," his lordship murmured, as though he were recollecting all the Bible stories from his youth that gave him a mind's eye view of that land. "I must write."

Thomas hurriedly set out writing materials on the table that belonged to Captain Troubridge. The note was very short, and the accompanying instruction a little less terse.

"Say to Sir William and her ladyship that I shall return this evening. We shall arrange another meeting with your Mary, never fear."

Thomas could see Captain Troubridge looking mystified, but aquick look in his direction from his lordship seemed to communicate that he would be enlightened soon. Thomas just saluted and left, the note in his hand.

Back at the *palazzo*, Sir William was vitally interested to hear what Captain Troubridge had said about the prospect of halting Bonaparte at Acre. He had only commented when Thomas had recounted all.

"I do hope Sir Sydney can supply his gunners adequately from the sea. If Bonaparte can be held there and falls back, the Turks may be persuaded to attack."

However, her ladyship seemed rather anxious this should not delay attacking Naples.

"It has come to a sorry pass that the safety of the *Sublime Porte* should depend on SSS. We must hope dear Lord Nelson does not feel impelled to reinforce him. It is bad enough he must send Captain Hardy to Tunis!"

"I doubt Captain Hardy will be gone for more than a week or two, my dear. Tunis lies not so far away," Sir William placated.

"Well, I hope so. We must not go back on the promises we have made to their majesties when all is in our favor," his lady indicated firmly before changing tack.

"Who else have you seen in the port today, Thomas?"

"Only Lady Acton in a carriage with Mary to care for her, m'lady," he replied.

"Yes, I heard Lady Acton had been unwell," mused her ladyship, "even in this mild spring weather. Well, she is not the only one. I despair of poor Lady Knight making any recovery. Perhaps Mary has some knowledge of Lady Acton's malady."

The obvious implication was that Mary would be quizzed about the nature of the illness on her next visit. Thomas was so eager for that to be very soon that he completely neglected to ask himself how indelicate such a line of questioning would be until Sir William intervened, looking and sounding careworn.

"I must caution against any offer to nurse Lady Acton, my dear. Generous nature though you have. We must remember the commitment we have given to Lady Knight, for Miss Knight. I have today promised rooms here to a second English family."

"Are you ordered back to your ship, young man?" Sir William asked Thomas, looking easier now that he had averted the arrival of any further nonpaying guests.

"There is no need for Thomas to return to the ship before dearLord Nelson arrives, my love," her ladyship quickly averred. "It may be Thomas is needed here."

That latter view was the one to prevail, upon his lordship conferring with the tenant of the *palazzo* and his lady. By then, Thomas had already heard from Tom Allen about the recruitment of the Gibbs and Noble families as paying guests. Tom's opinion was that Sir William was strapped for cash and dubious he would obtain adequate recompense from London. Before the evening entertainment HerLadyship had organized for invited guests, they were both summoned to the study for orders.

"I see no reason for you to return to the ship, Thomas, either tonight or for a week hence. I intend to allow Captain, nay Commodore, Troubridge full use of *Culloden's* great cabin while he orders his squadron. You shall serve the wine with Tom tonight. As for the days ahead, we have many tasks for you here."

He dared not look sideways at Tom's face as they saluted and left. The use of the royal "we" showed all too clearly her ladyship'sinfluence over the decision. No doubt it made good sense not to place the lowly representative of an invisible admiral under a commodore's feet. Tom soon voiced his other thought.

"Oi feelrs a virsit frawm yore Mary cermin' awn," he muttered when they were safely round the corner of the corridor from the study door, and Thomas grinned in reply.

It was not a struggle, living in *Palazzo Palagonia* with her ladyship in charge. She had no difficulty finding fine musicians, suppliers of fresh produce for her skilled cooks to fill a buffet table to overflowing with tasty dishes, and an excellent wine merchant. Her reputation for recognizing quality and being prepared to pay for it had spread throughout Palermo and beyond. Agents and tradesmen saw her taste was backed by the combined purses of her husband and Lord Nelson.

The beauty of their location was that any delicacy produced in another part of Sicily could be sailed around the coast, if it had to come too far for the mountainous and poor roads to bring the item fresh into Palermo. All Tom and Thomas had to do was move around the evening's gathering with quiet, respectful demeanors, filling and replenishing glasses of guests with wine. They knew the choice of leftover food and drink would be theirs, when the guests departed.

The small number of Italian words Thomas had mastered were more than enough to serve the guests who weren't English. Her ladyship's eye, roving around the gathering would find no fault in the competence of his service. He noticed that she held her wine well, her observation unimpaired, while his lordship was very rapidly affected by a glass or two. This had the effect of making him talk loudly and nearly endlessly. The guests mostly didn't seem to mindor become bored. Sir William's good manners and learning were unfailing in conversation, but Thomas knew that he would be fretting over the expense.

Only two mornings after that first evening of being a wine waiter, Mary came again, ostensibly to do work for her ladyship. Alerted to her presence alone in a workroom, Thomas rushed along the corridor and through the door. The noise of his approach had alertedMary to swing around upright to face him. Breathlessly, he charged into her with arms outstretched to encircle her upper body, only to find her arms braced to prevent their bodies colliding.

"You are like a tempest, Thomas, but better that than creeping up on me."

At that moment, he was not so sure. He pushed his head forward to kiss her. She didn't resist the kiss but broke the contact of their lips after only a few moments.

"You are forceful this morning, Thomas. What has got into you?"

"I saw you two days ago in the carriage with Lady Acton,"

heraged, "but I was forbidden from coming onto the mole to speak with you."

At this, Mary looked him seriously in the eyes, but a smile played on her lips.

"It is just as well you were forbidden, if you were in a fever tospeak to me. If it was Lord Nelson did the forbidding, he was right. Lady Acton would have been upset if we had been accosted. I had enough difficulty persuading her that sea air and the fine sight of one ship coming in and another leaving would aid her recovery."

"Is she better now?" Thomas enquired, the tone of his voice betraying humiliation.

"I do not believe she will ever be truly better. Her condition is one brought on by too many babies. Not just those living, but those that didn't too," Mary replied sadly.

"Have the Court Physicians no treatment for this?" asked Thomas, without thinking for the moment that they would already have been consulted.

"They say only sleeping draughts to give her pain-free rest. As much rest as she can be allowed and only the freshest foods that can be provided. That has to be all soft stuff because her teeth have rotted, and most have already been pulled out. I do the best I can to help her rest. She devotes what energy she has to her children," Mary recounted with a glum and despairing air.

"It must be dispiriting for you to cope with, my love," Thomaswhispered, lifting her fingers to his lips and thinking.

How easy his own life had become in comparison.

Mary treated him to a wan smile and made a visible effort to straighten her back.

"Well, I am not the one who is ill, so we can both thank the Lord forthat. I can give you what else I've heard. The first is that work on *Palazzina Cinese* is going on apace. The second that, when capture of Naples is assured and the Bashaw of Tripoli has been dealt with, the king and queen will consent to Lord Nelson going to Naples."

"But I would have expected the king to want to take the surrender!" he expostulated.

"Sir John's opinion is that the king will take a great deal of persuading to go back to Naples, that is, if he will go at all," Mary responded with a knowing smile.

"Surely, he will have to see his government set in place?" Thomas probed.

"Perhaps he will leave it to others, like Cardinal Ruffo and Lord Nelson. Ruffo's army is in the mountains near to Vesuvius, Sir John says," Mary replied sweetly, "and now that I have told you all I've heard, you had better leave me to my work."

"I don't seem to have been in here very long," Thomas observed. "It's no use looking like the child who's had a sweetmeat snatched from his hand," Mary teased. "Questions will be asked if you stay toolong for too little."

As Sir William would perhaps have put it, the logic was inescapable. Thomas had to go, so his reporting session in HisLordship's study involved no questions as to his personal conduct. Admission to a mere parting kiss with Mary would have done nomore than make his audience smile. Important decisions needed to be made.

"The people in the mountain villages all around Vesuvius will not hold any truck with radicals and revolutionaries. I have visited enough of them in my ascents to know that. It seems that the timefor decisive support to Ruffo has come," asserted Sir William.

"My own sentiment, dear Sir William. I shall send Thomas with a note calling Commodore Troubridge and his captains to a shortcouncil of war. We must work day and night to see his squadron Naples bound this month," his lordship added.

"Will Captain Hardy have brought *Vanguard* back in time?" asked Sir William.

"It matters not, so long as I have the intelligence he is returning," replied his lordship.

"Do you not need to have a ship from which to fly your flag?" probed Sir William.

"I have a plan for that contingency," murmured his lordship, quill to inkpot, before he started to scratch his note left-handed.

"You will not take umbrage with their majesties over their refusal tolet you sail, even now?" her ladyship asked.

She did not disclose the cause of her anxiety.

"There is no point before we have control of the Bay of Naples," breezed His Lordship, quill poised over his note, "but I believe I shall ask their majesties to join my party on the mole to wish the squadron Godspeed and good fortune."

"I must applaud that sentiment, my dear Nelson. It is the piece of diplomacy most likely to win us free of this Court in a month or two," Sir William enthused.

"The day for that cannot come too soon," His Lordship grated, scratching away with the quill. He did not see her ladyship's tight-lipped, anguished expression.

Thus it was that Thomas carried messages between *palazzo* and ships by day, while Tom Allen attended to the messages arising from the social calendar of the *palazzo's* occupants. At least four nights a week, they were both pouring wine into the glasses of guests. Thomas frequently found himself considering the ruinous cost of itall.

Sir William and he were not the only ones to see it that way. Commodore Troubridge, despite the immense amount of paperwork he had undertaken to have his squadron ready for sea that month. He was a *Palazzo Palagonia* guest a few times before he pleaded pressure of work to justify declining subsequent invitations. His glances around at the other guests showed his distaste for some were, just as his expression in watching her ladyship hold court as though she were both minister and admiral, was troubled. Thomas suspected his lordship would soon know what troubled Commodore Troubridge. His reputation was for being forthright and honest, however respectfully he put his views.

It wasn't until the day *Culloden* and her consorts sailed that Thomas was close enough to hear another of their conversations. This was the occasion of the unorthodox flag shift into a transport *Vanguard* had not actually returned from Tunis but was known to be only a couple of days sail from Palermo. What made it unusual was his lordship's selection of *Samuel and Jane*. This was not a regularlyhired transport and was not subject either to naval discipline orbookkeeping.

"Captain Hopps will make suitable space for us," his lordship had airily prophesied the previous day. He ordered Thomas to pack up his property again for transfer out of *Culloden* at first light.

With such an early start required, it was just as well that the weather was springlike, with a mild breeze out of the southeast. Thomas was just seeing the last of the boxes lowered to *Samuel and Jane's* boat when his lordship and the commodore came to the quarterdeck's edge to witness the lowering of the rear admiral's flag and bending on the commodore's broad pennant.

"Well, Commodore Troubridge, I give you joy of a full day's sailing with a following breeze. I shall expect to hear great things, with such an auspicious start,"

His lordship spoke in a very good-humored way for someone who had been roused in the dark, shaved and dressed by Tom Allen in candlelight, fortunately without mishap.

"I only wish you were coming to see great things for yourself, my lord, rather than being kept here at the whim of the court and mired in entertainments."

"It will not be for overlong, Troubridge, so long as you make good progress clearing the revolutionaries out of the islands and bay," his lordship promised. "Remember to have all ships ignore Salerno. Sam Hood will be only a few days behind you."

There was no mistaking the look of eager anticipation on the Commodore's large face. His mop of unruly hair was ruffled by the breeze, hat held in his left hand. The sense of cheerful anticipation carried right through his lined-up officers.

"I look forward to the day I can attend you on your flagship in the bay, my lord, free of shore-bound ties," responded the commodore, saluting.

His Lordship made to the head of the ladder that ran over the side. Thomas had already gone but was still listening intently as he shinned down the ladder to take his place near the boat's prow. There was a clean and vacant space in the stern sheets for his lordship.

Even as oarsmen propelled the boat toward *Samuel and Jane's* mooring, *Culloden's* anchor was up and down, and the sheets were allowed to fall and catch the wind. Once aboard the small merchantman, with her handful of four-pounder popguns, the admiral seemed uninterested in the arrangements Captain Hopps had made for his accommodation. After his flag had been raised at the ship's mizzen and saluted, he simply walked to the side to watch thesquadron make sail to the north. This left Thomas to set out the contents of his boxes in what was normally Captain Hopps' cabin. That bluff Yorkshireman had already indicated the use of sometemporary partitions in the upper tier of cargo space. These hadmore than doubled the sleeping spaces aboard, although head roomwas minimal.

When Thomas had finished, to what he believed would be his lordship's satisfaction, he came back on deck. His lordship was still watching the fine sight of the five ships of the line and their smaller consorts under full sail, bearing a few points west of due north. Only the slight working of the stump of the Admiral's right arm told Thomas the emotion that was stirred by sending off this squadron.

"The cabin is laid out ready for your inspection, m'lord," he deferentially reported.

"Not now, Thomas. I must take the boat to confer with Captain Hood," he responded.

He half turned and waved his left hand across the deck in the direction of the solitary ship of the line lying at anchor with sails furled. Just to seaward of her lay an anchored sloop. his lordship turned back to look wistfully at the departing squadron.

"Did you ever see such a fine sight, Thomas?"

"Not with such a true following breeze, m'lord," replied Thomas truthfully.

His lordship turned to him, smiling, but spoke with a rueful expression in his voice.

"No doubt you are right to qualify it so. Nothing so fine as a blue water sailing you hoped to have made yourself. I will send the boat back for you, Thomas. *Zealous's* boat will bring me back to shore. Her ladyship will have need of you at the *palazzo*."

"Aye, m'lord," was his stolid reply.

There was to be another entertainment!

CHAPTER 11

AN UNWANTED PREGNANCY AS THE FIGHT BACK GOES ON

That night's entertainment went on into the early hours. the bleary-eyed clearing up of the following morning made April fools of those who had to rouse themselves to do the work. No tricks were played by those who were English and understood the tradition. Her ladyship seemed to have slept badly and was prowling around issuing orders. Within minutes, the noisy activities of the kitchen women forced Tom and Thomas to stir themselves and bring down all the empty wine bottles. At their first glimpse of her ladyship,coming along the corridor toward them, the lead, Thomas thoughther face and neck seemed to glow with health and vigor, yet hereyes looked tired.

She stood aside to let them pass before speaking.

"Be quiet in clearing away. Sir William and His Lordship are still sleeping. Do not go in and rouse his lordship for another hour, Tom Allen."

"No, m'leddy," he responded humbly, inclining his head in passing. Thomas did likewise, after the split second in which he saw the look in her tired eyes was more indulgent than her tone. They moved smartly ahead. It would not do for her ladyship to think he wasstaring at her. The question whether there was truth in the Sicilian women's claim to Tom Allen did cross his mind, as did the reflectionit was obvious how she knew both husband and lover were still asleep.

Her body looked no fuller, although she was such a tall woman that she carried her weight well. Her bosom was always prominent, even in loose-fitting clothing like her current night attire and dressing gown.

He would have to put it from his mind. Otherwise, he would befound staring at her and he had no intention of being accused of insolence. This was only the first of a number of such mornings because the entertainments seemed to go on night after night, broken only by *Vanguard's* arrival back from Tunis.

Her sails were seen, far out beyond *Monte Pellegrino,* in the clear visibility of a bright morning. Thomas was sent off to call in *Samuel and Jane's* boat. His lordship, accompanied by Sir William and her ladyship would greet her arrival and make the flag shift back to her. The weather was fine, so there was no swell within the shelterprovided by the mole. The sea was little more than ruffled by the breeze when the boat passed its outer end, yet her ladyship still managed to look queasy until the boat drew alongside *Samuel and Jane.* Thomas was able to hook onto her chains so his lordshipcould considerately hand her first onto the ship's ladder, then Sir William, before going aboard himself. Captain Hopps received them, hat in his hand. He was questioned by her ladyship so soon as she was aboard.

"You must show me the accommodation made available to His Lordship, Captain."

"Time enough for that when we have seen *Vanguard* anchored, dear lady," called Nelson as he followed Sir William aboard.

By the time Tom and Thomas brought up the rear, *Vanguard* was making her final tack to come about no more than a cable's length *from Samuel and Jane.* Her own anchor splashed down and flapping sails were rapidly clewed up.

"Can we now see the accommodation Captain Hopps has provided you, my dear Lord Nelson? We are both of us avid to see what a small ship can provide."

"Could you lead the way, Captain Hopps?" prompted his lordship. "Bring up the rear, and provide assistance on the ladder, Thomas."

Snug it was, with six of them standing in the space before thedesk, its chair next to the stern lights. A cot occupied the space to port, while a sea chest stood to larboard. Only a set of his lordship's writing materials occupied the desktop.

"As you see, Sir William and dear lady, it was adequate for my temporary needs."

No reply was needed to this assertion, but her ladyship had not quite finished.

"What have you done for your own accommodation, Captain Hopps?"

Clutching his hat and mildly embarrassed to be directly questioned by this tall, fine-looking lady in the presence of her husband and his lordship, he gabbled

"We have put in a 'tween deck above the hold, now the cargo's gone."

"Would you be so very kind as to show all of us?" asked Her Ladyship, smiling.

"Gladly, milady," he responded, more at ease, but adding hurriedly, "with your permission, milord."

His lordship smiled too and gestured with his one hand for the captain to proceed.

Back on deck, there was an uncovered hatch abaft the mainmast. Upon approaching this, a companionway of freshly worked timber came into view. Captain Hopps walked to the hatch frame, turned his back on the opening, and stepped over the frame to descend. Thinking this would be a tricky piece of balancing, Thomas instinctively moved to the far side. His lordship held out his hand to her ladyship, who only took it after turning her back on the hatch as the Captain had done. She held on only for the first couple of steps before descending steadily unaided. His lordship followed.

"Assist Sir William, Thomas, and follow down." He was then gone into the gloom.

Sir William balanced himself with his walking stick left-handed on the deck by the hatch's edge. He held out his right hand for Thomas to take and managed the first three steps very well. He took some time to bring his walking stick behind him, while his eyes adjusted to the lack of light below. Thomas knelt and handed the elderly knight down a few more steps. The dim glow of a lantern further into this 'tween decks structure enabled Sir William to see the bottom few treads. He let go of Thomas, who made haste to follow the party. Tom Allen brought up the rear this time. To starboard at the foot of the companionway was a partition with a doorway.

"This will be my cabin, Milady. As you can see, there's plenty more deck forward."

Her ladyship was having to bend slightly, owing to the limitedheadroom. She looked forward to where the ship's carpenter and mate were working by the light of their nearby lantern. The posts of another partition were being fixed under the deck beams.

"It is a far larger space than I imagined, captain, if rather low for a tall man."

"It is high enough for all of us used to minding our heads, dearlady, and most competently done, Captain Hopps. There will beaccommodation for my little crew should I need to bring them aboardon another occasion," his lordship averred.

"Perhaps we should now go above and leave Captain Hopps and his men to complete their work," added Sir William, his walking stick planted on the decking so he could sway easily to the ship's motion.

"An excellent suggestion, my love," her ladyship replied, as she still looked appraisingly around. "We have tomorrow's entertainment to plan, so must move on to *Vanguard* and be away again within the hour."

Thomas thought only he saw Sir William's grimace at the prospect of more expense. Her ladyship had already swept back to the foot of the companionway and needed no steadying hand on the steps. Everyone's eyes other than his followed her. His concern was to see Sir William safely on the open deck and over the side into the waitingboat. He was last on deck and first over the side to assist the knight down the ladder. His lordship's flag was lowered with due ceremony and placed in the care of Tom Allen. This accomplished, the row across to *Vanguard* was short.

Captain Hardy greeted his lordship and guests with due formality. Following the re-raising of the rear admiral's flag, the party was for a considerable time in the great cabin. Finally, Tom was ordered that he and Thomas should call the admiral's barge aft. His lordship was in good spirits as he led his guests and the captain out from under the break of the quarterdeck.

"So, the word along the African shore is that Buonaparte hasadvanced far into the Holy Land and is now besieging Acre, where the Swedish Knight has galvanized the Turks into firm resistance?"

"Aye, my lord, but it sounded from the word in Tunis that his army lacked siege artillery, while Sir Sydney and the Turks were being resupplied by sea."

"Well, it would be helpful if the Swedish Knight could spare one of his smaller vessels to send me word of how the siege progresses. I do not doubt from what you tell me that, should Buonaparte break off the siege and return to Egypt, the Bashaw will resume his conspiring. We shall then have to deal with him severely."

At the tumblehome, where his two servants stood ready to assist his guests down the ladder, his lordship moved forward to take her ladyship's right hand as she turned her back to the sea, in order to descend. Thomas stood ready to take her left hand if need be.

"Well, another shift of flag accomplished. We have it off to a fine artnow!"

"Aye, m'lord," they chorused, while Captain Hardy looked on impassively.

Thomas reflected he was merely accepting the loss of his great cabin with equanimity. They certainly did have flag shifts off to a fine art.

It was not naval activity that most required adjustment on Thomas's part as April progressed but domestic changes in the*palazzo.* despite the rapid flow of naval and military tidings. The first of these changes, not truly welcome to Thomas, was the arrival of Miss Cornelia Knight as a resident. Lady Knight, who had been ailingever since her ordeal during the flight from Naples, had died even asthe spring weather became beautifully warm. Despite her offhand way with servants, the promise his lordship, Sir William, and her ladyship had jointly made to Lady Knight to take her daughter into their household did have benefits to *Tria Juncta in Uno*. Miss Knight's flawless mastery of Italian, with grammar reliable in correspondence, her ladyship could not match. Her knowledge of French was to the same standard, so her usefulness to his lordship and Sir William was immediately apparent.

The flow of dispatches from and to the mainland, which included captured documents, had vastly increased.

One of the earliest pieces of intelligence via Messina was confirmation that the joint Turkish and Russian assault on Corfu had captured that island. Thomas was with his lordship, receiving messages to be taken out to *Vanguard*, when Miss Knight brought inthe translation of the message that had arrived from Cardinal Ruffo'sCalabrian headquarters. He leaned back after reading it through.

"This is excellent news. The Russians and Turks now established on Corfu intend to move forces across the Adriatic to assist us in recovering the eastern coast of His Majesty's kingdom. I begin to hope I shall soon be able to put to sea for Naples."

Miss Knight looked pleased to be taken into his lordship's confidence.

"Will you need me to translate a reply, my lord?"

"Most certainly," he replied, "I shall suggest which ports they should take, to hasten the French out of the kingdom."

His lordship has the bit between his teeth, thought Thomas.

His mind strayed back a few days to the occasion on *Vanguard's* quarterdeck when he had been seeing Captain Hood on his way in *Zealous* to capture Salerno. A signal gun had banged out from the ship and the sloop to accompany her was heeling over to the wind with her huge triangular foresail billowing high above her hull. She took the lead northward in response to the line of signal flags that accompanied the gun. The signals had come down as the liner's sheets were let fall by the watch aloft out on the yards. With her anchor up and down, *Zealous* had also begun to surge ahead andhis lordship raised his bicorn hat to. The solitary officer on the weather side of the liner's quarterdeck then returned the salute.

"See how well Sam Hood handles his ship. Both he and Thomas Troubridge will achieve great success," his lordship had exclaimed to Sir William.

"My dear Nelson, they cannot fail with you as their example. Your plan to allow the Salerno garrison to see the commodore sail bydays ago, as though they are ignored, is truly masterly," the elderly knight had responded.

"They shall not see *Zealous* until she follows her boats out of the dark. By that time, the outlying batteries will already have been seized, and the weight of shot will be in our favor. It only wants the sloop to look in and see no guns have been moved since she was last there," his lordship had explained wistfully.

He left none of the party in any doubt he wished he was there for the capture.

Her ladyship had been unwilling to allow him to dwell on the prospect.

"I must take a boat to shore and coach to the *Colli* to assure her majesty that you, her protector, are still here, my dear lord, rather than away to risk shot and shell."

For the few moments Thomas was remembering this, his lordship again had that far-away wistful look in his eye and visibly struggled to dismiss his thoughts and Thomas.

"Here are the messages, Thomas, both addressed as you may see."

"Aye, aye, m'lord," he responded, taking the sealed letters, saluting, and turning.

"My Lord, should I stay and take down your reply? It seems unnecessary to call Mr Tyson when I am already here ..." he heard Miss Knight say as he left.

The next harbinger of domestic change was more pleasurable for Thomas, being a visit from Mary. Chance had it that he saw her turn a corridor corner just short of the room she used for sewing. He dashed behind her through the door and pinned her to the wall with his embrace, his mouth on hers in an instant. Gently, her lips pushed his head back until she could disengage to speak.

"Thomas, my love, glad I am to see you and find you so needy, but the door is open."

He couldn't close the door without removing a hand, so she came off the wall, twisting away from him with more reproving words.

"What if her ladyship had been here when you burst in? What would you have done then?"

"Given my regrets and left as quickly as I could," he mumbled, lurching forward again.

"Not before she'd have seen which bit of you was standing to attention!"

He stopped and held out his hand to her, now visibly wilting, but unrepentant.

"You said yourself you were glad to find me so needy. It gets harder to bear."

"I know, my lover, I find it hard to bear too, but we have to be strict with ourselves."

She twined her fingers in his, but held her body away, and continued.

"Let us sit and talk. Tell me, who were the children I saw playing inthe courtyard?"

"Oh, they are the Gibbs and Noble children. Both families are now lodging here to Sir William's pleasure in helping meet the cost of this mansion. He finds her ladyship's entertaining ruinous."

"She has been much with the Queen these past few days. Sir John says she has asked her majesty to obtain a potion for her, to make sure she miscarries."

Mary's eyes had narrowed thoughtfully while passing on this piece of gossip.

"No doubt he has someone listening behind the Queen's door!" Thomas grated with indignation, adding, "are our kitchen women in his pay?"

"I doubt that, but it may be he has heard from another what they are saying."

Mary's tone was so measured and serious that he felt impelled to continue listening.

"He says she will be ruined in society if she is seen to be withchild. Sir William will have to divorce her unless he says the child is his. Then he will be a figure of ridicule because no one will believehe is the father."

"It will scarcely be good for his lordship, if that is how it is," Thomas dryly observed.

"Believe me, it is never a serious matter for the man. He merely pays for the upkeep of the bastard, should it live," Mary spat out but then controlled herself to add, "I had better give you other news, so you have something you dare tell his lordship."

"It would be better. He already knows Sir John is no friend of her ladyship because of her influence over the queen," he conceded.

"Sir John's spies in Naples tell him that General MacDonald has advised the Directory he should withdraw all of the French armynorth of the Arno, to counter the threat by the Russians and Austrians in Lombardy," Mary recounted.

"Soon enough, he will be threatened by Russians and Turks from the east, now they have captured Corfu," Thomas added, "but who is this General MacDonald?"

"Oh, just another young French general, says Sir John. Obviously of Scotch descent, perhaps in France for generations, because they were of the Roman Church."

"So, has he mentioned any more young French generals, other than Buonaparte of course?"

"Well, he has heard that Joubert threatens to be better than Bonaparte. Why do you insist on calling him Buonaparte? Then,there is Massena who defeated the Swiss last year, but it is said heis a Jew."

"King David in the Books of Samuel was a Jew, and he never lost a battle," Thomas commented gently.

"I forgot how well you know the Scriptures, but being generals is not what you hear of Jews doing now. You still haven't told me why you call the one in Egypt Buonaparte."

Thomas smiled at Mary's riposte and explained.

"His lordship insists on calling him Buonaparte because that is his original family name from Corsica. He has only changed it to Bonaparte to make it sound more French. His lordship says weshould insist on still making him sound Corsican."

"But, why should we see any gain in doing that?" protested Mary. "Because Corsica is an island full of murderous bandits, and

Buonaparte is just one of them. His lordship knows the island well. It was at the siege of Calvi he lost the sight in his right eye, but he still went on to capture the fortress," Thomas explained.

"I see why he has your devotion. He really is a lord of battles with the wounds to show for it," said Mary quietly, "but this with herladyship will bring only grief."

"Perhaps we shouldn't think about that," Thomas doubted.

"Is there anything else Sir John has said that I can tell his lordship?"

"Only that he doesn't believe he can control Ruffo treating with therepublican rebels."

"Why on earth would Ruffo do that?"Mary smiled sadly.

"He doesn't believe the Lazzaroni should merely be left to taketheir revenge for their suffering in January. He wants to recover the King's lands with the least loss of life he can manage."

"Truly Christian of him, but I'm not sure how his lordship will view that," Thomas exclaimed. "What does Sir John want to do?"

"Set up courts to try and condemn captured rebels, I believe," Mary said hesitantly.

"There can be no harm in telling his lordship so," asserted Thomas.

"And there I believe we had best leave things for today," Mary concluded, treating him to a lingering kiss before she reached for needle and cotton.

The reporting to his lordship was unusual in it being just the two of them. Somehow, he seemed too distracted to send for Sir William and her ladyship. Although he professed interest in General Buonaparte's potential young rivals, there seemed to be something troubling him. He heard Thomas out with only the occasional question or prompt before commenting.

"Young General MacDonald may be, but he realizes he will behard pressed between ourselves and the savage old Russian bear in the north. Thank your Mary for me when next you see her, Thomas. Now enquire whether her ladyship is back from the *Colli*."

That curious dismissal had Thomas wondering exactly what was happening. Her ladyship wasn't back. Sir William was resting during the warm afternoon and Tom had been sent out with invitations to yet another entertainment. In the event, there was no time for pondering because a signal from La Cala drew attention to the arrival in the bay of a sloop. Nothing would do but summoning the admiral's barge so that he could be rowed out to *Vanguard* to take the commander's report.

Fortunately, Tom sauntered back and took over the job of ensuring his lordship was shipshape. He had his decorations pinned on and bicorn hat aloft, distinctively athwart, for the walk to the water's edge. As usual, Tom and Thomas fell in behind his lordship. Captain Hardy had sent off a senior midshipman, a gangling twenty-one-year-old hoping to pass for lieutenant. He had the prow of the barge drawn up on the shingle, where the shore sloped down to the water's edge. Now, he stood forward of the barge saluting.

"Very well, Mr Woodin, let us proceed forthwith," ordered his lordship lightly.

Flattered his name had been remembered, but nearly tripping overhis own feet as he turned, Mr Woodin hurried aboard and back to hisposition on the tiller. Tom, as his lordship's body servant, followedthe length of the barge to settle himself in a corner at the stern. Although a little plump, he made sure there was a good space for hislordship. His unruly, curly, dark-brown hair settled around his tanned face when he stopped moving. Thomas should have been next, buta look at the prow showed it would need more than the two most forward oarsmen to heave the barge fully afloat.

His lordship followed Thomas's eyes, took the hint, and embarked. A couple of good heaves later, at the expense of one wet foot, Thomas was aboard. He kept clear of his fellow heavers, who needed to regain their places at the foremost oars. No wonder Mr Woodin was known by the crew as Wooden. Perhaps he'd had a difficult time before coming to *Vanguard* out of the brig *Mutine*.Captain Hardy had been Captain of that vessel at the time. At the ship, Thomas hooked on the barge's prow a little past the ladder to give his lordship a good, solid platform. He could see the signal flagsout for the commander of the sloop. Captain Hardy looked about to have his admiral piped aboard. His slightly protuberant eyes took in all that was happening in the barge and on deck. Tom Allen went up after his lordship, but the rest of them were ordered to stay where they were. The sound of the sloop's boat hooking on the far side came soon after.

It was always amazing how quickly scuttlebutt spread from under the break of the quarterdeck on such occasions. The word was that Salerno had been easily and cheaply taken. Cheering broke out all around the ship, which wasn't unwelcome to his lordship when he emerged. The commander was wished Godspeed north again. Indeed, with the commander going over the side, he brought the cheering to a crescendo by raising his hat to all of them. Captain Hardy wore a bland smile at the theatricality of it all.

When Tom descended to the barge before his lordship, he was clutching a package of correspondence. On arrival at the *palazzo,* the coach was in the courtyard. Thomas was sent to invite Sir William and his lady to the study, while Tom carried the package up to that room. Sir William was his usual self, refreshed by his afternoon rest, but her ladyship looked tired and strained. His lordship had all the letters from the package spread across hiswriting table and the tension between her ladyship and himself was palpable. He handed her a couple of letters in Italian. Thomas backed to the door but was stopped.

"Stay Thomas, and repeat for Sir William and my lady what Mary heard Sir John say," ordered the admiral, looking as though hehoped it would reduce the tension.

Thomas had to go through all the items Mary and he had agreed could be repeated. Those about the young French generals were of little interest to Sir William and her ladyship. When it came to Ruffo's attitude toward the Neapolitan republicans, her ladyship's face became anguished as she blared out her feelings.

"What will we be able to tell her majesty if Ruffo pardons thousands of republicans in his majesty's name? She believes she isin mortal danger from them, even here. We cannot countenance this when she has been our friend for so long."

Her bosom heaved, and her face was red with anger. His lordship seemed anxious she should say no more and moved swiftly to cut off her flow.

"Was there more, Thomas?"

"Only that Sir John wants to set up courts to try and condemn rebels," he stammered, without realizing he had given Sir William exactly the right means to douse the fire.

"There, my love, you see that Sir John has the perfect solution to the problem and a solution that the outside world will see as fair *and* reassuring for her majesty."

"And, there can be courts-martial for any who have deserted his majesty's armed forces for the rebels, for which purpose we shall be there to make sure it happens," his lordship added grimly. It seemed to Thomas he was desperate to turn the subject away from her ladyship's relationship with the queen.

That he had succeeded in this was borne out by the question she then put to him.

"You are suggesting that we might sail for Naples, my dear Lord Nelson? But when?"

"Quite soon. Sam Hood's dispatch says that Ruffo's army already dominates in the mountains north of Salerno. You have in your hand, my dear lady, his first letter to Sam Hood and another addressed direct to myself. There are letters from Ouschakoff and Kadir Bey, both in French. I can just about make out that they are promising support on the Adriatic coast. Also, Kadir Bey believes that the army of the Sublime Porte, with the help of the Swedish Knight, will halt Buonaparte at Acre. So he should, with three of the line I can ill afford, but we will have Miss Knight translate fully to confirm I have it right."

"We cannot undertake a sea voyage just yet," responded her ladyship with an expression that was suddenly calculating, hastily adding, "as there is an entertainment for which invitations have already gone."

"Oh, it will not be too hastily planned. Sam Hood says the rumor amongst fishermen is that Commodore Troubridge is going well. I need his own confirmation to put the suggestion to his majesty and Sir John. You may leave us now, Thomas."

None too soon, the latter thought after knuckling his forehead and sliding out of the door. What a hothouse of intrigue the study had justbecome! That feeling had still not left him the following morning. Tom's return from his early morning foray into the kitchen was with eyes twinkling and brimming over with excitement.

"Err leddyship took a poshun laast night. Shay wars given un by ther queen, but it 'as only given err dyer-rear."

"What malady would this potion be for?" Thomas asked carefully. "Why, getting rid of er baby," answered Tom scornfully.

He returned the look in Tom's laughing eyes levelly. He wondered quite how he had managed to glean quite so much from the plump, brown-skinned woman to whom he'd taken such a fancy, when she could only converse in her Sicilian dialect. The sign language must have been truly arousing, but he reflected at the same time that it all rang true. He grinned and contented himself with commenting knowingly.

"I thought something was afoot when they were in his lordship's study last night."

"Well, oi never. Waat 'appens naow?"

"We just watch and wait and see," Thomas replied, lifting his hands in helplessness.

In the few days that took, a sloop had beaten back in contrary winds from the commodore's squadron to report all the islands near to Naples had rehoisted the Royal standard and that the loyal islanders had delivered up traitors to the commodore with their own recommendations which of them deserved death. By reason of that, he was in sore need of a Royal judge and troops. It was not only her ladyship who next travelled in the coach to the *Colli,* but his lordship as well. Her majesty was able to confirm that she and her husband were in agreement on sending a judge and troops. His majesty,whilst unwilling to allow considerations of justice in his recovered realm to interfere with hunting, was not convinced by Ruffo's appeasing policy. His lordship then naturally saw Sir John to arrangethe detail of sending a judge and troops in a Neapolitan warship. Thecurious thing Thomas then found out from his usual highly reliable source, was that her ladyship had spent some time with Lady Acton.

The coach returned with an extra passenger. Mary had to do a littleextra work for her ladyship. There was only time for a whispered conversation in the courtyard before the coach returned her westward. The two ladies had met alone, so Mary had no idea of the purpose. The next day, for Thomas, was taken up by the visit on board *Vanguard* that sent the commodore's sloop bowling northward with the reply he desired. Another entertainment was to be held that night, so suspicion was suspended until fairly early the following morning, when her ladyship unexpectedly ordered the coach to visit her majesty. Her return in the afternoon produced an order to the Sicilian servants to prepare an upstairs bedchamber. Although she smiled at Thomas when he poured her wine that evening, there was no hint of what could be going on.

Two days later, the coach was called out again, this time for her ladyship to visit Lady Acton again. No sooner had it rattled over the cobbles than his lordship sent for Thomas. He looked up from the letter he was writing, and Thomas could see anxiety etched in his brow.

"I believe you should be the first of my little crew to know that your Mary is joining my Lady Hamilton's household. She will be returning with her ladyship."

Thomas could not keep the happy grin off his face, whatever lay behind this news.

"Yes, I thought that would please you, Thomas," His Lordship added, also breaking into a smile, "but she will have to live upstairs and suffer no unwelcome visits."

"M'lord, Mary and myself are promised to each other in marriage when it becomes possible," Thomas replied with some trepidation.

At this, His Lordship's smile broadened into the one of great charm that he exerted when leading men into terrible danger. Had Thomas looked closely, he would have seen it was initially tinged with relief. However, he missed the moment, and his lordship responded.

"Then, I shall put your joint wish to her ladyship, but mark you thatwe may have to leave Mary here for a time when we sail for Naples.""It would be safer for her, m'lord, and she knows I have to do my duty."

"Very well, I shall suggest to her ladyship that you should marrybefore we sail, and given her agreement, I shall speak to Reverend Comyn. You should, after all, be married according to the laws of England."

"I am much in your debt, m'lord. Is Lady Acton fully recovered that she is willing to release Mary from her service?"

His lordship shifted in his chair and said, "Not exactly, but Sir John has sent for a young niece, who he believes will be a fitting companion for his lady, with no duties other than to cherish and lift her out of despondency."

With that, Thomas had to be satisfied, for it was said sincerely enough. It was only later, when the coach returned and Thomas finally had a moment with Mary in the room prepared for her, thatshe gave her reaction.

"I do not know what I have been brought into here, but I do know that Lady Acton, poor soul, is most unhappy at my departure. Sir John has only sent for this young niece because her majesty insistedhe release me to this household."

"Mary, my love, it is our one sure chance to be married. Even if I have to sail with His Lordship, it will not be for long."

"Do not doubt, Thomas Spencer, that I intend to become your wife,however soon after you put a ring on my finger you have to sail awayin that great ship."

"We must get to a goldsmith," he responded. "I have a few pound put by."

"Then you are fortunate, but it will soon go," she ribbed him. "There is still prize money for the Nile to come," he protested. "Then my cup runs over; both our cups run over! So, why do I feel there is something more to this than we can see and that it is herladyship's doing?" Mary worried.

It was then that Thomas told her of Tom's latest information from the Sicilian kitchen woman. Her eyes widened, the implications sinking into her woman's mind.

"As well that I love you dearly, Thomas Spencer, and care less about what allows us to be together than the actual coming together.Now, be off for the night before more than your cup runs over."

A lingering kiss was all he had as parting gift, but he still rancheerfully down the stone stairway.

CHAPTER 12

A RELATIONSHIP ENCOURAGED AMID CAMPAIGN MOMENTUM

It took only a couple of days for Mary to gain the confidence of the plump Sicilian woman who worked in the kitchen and was Tom's current romantic interest. Her name was Letizia, and she had ahusband with a fishing boat. There were times when some of his catch found its way onto the *palazzo's* table at a very fair price. That was as far as humoring Tom went. That Mary could converse in Italian and was a working woman like herself, was sufficient to endear her to Letizia. From the first full day, her ladyship made it plain she intended to take full advantage of Mary's command of colloquial Italian in a general housekeeping sense. She was anassistant relaying orders to the various parts of the *palazzo*. How busy she was kept was evident from the fact that half a week had passed before she whispered an instruction to Thomas,.

"Sewing room tomorrow morning."

Fortunately, it was a day of his lordship writing replies to letters already received and digested. Once Thomas had placed all the necessary materials to hand, he was not required for nearly an hour. The sealing and packaging for different destinations would be when he was next needed.

He eased into the sewing room, with the door as little ajar as he could manage. Mary had one of her ladyship's gowns spread wide across the floor for rehemming. Closing the door and stepping very carefully around the wall to where Mary had stood up to receive him, he took hold of her around the waist. She gave him only a perfunctory kiss and held her back very stiffly.

"This is a serious mare's nest we have been pulled into," she shot at him.

"What do you mean by that, my love?" Thomas asked cautiously. "My talks with Letizia have made me sure she is telling truth that Her Ladyship is still with child. For one thing, she is still having morning sickness. For another, she has already said to me that his lordship will soon speak to you about the arrangements for ourmarriage."

"I do believe that is welcome, whatever else may happen," mused Thomas.

"I do not doubt how welcome you will find it to be in my bed and more besides! Now, that is another thing to make me uneasy. I arrived to a chamber and a bed plenty big enough for two," Mary reflected. "What did His Lordship say?"

"Only that I couldn't visit you there, until I said we wanted to be wed. Then he was very keen for us to get on with it, so long as her ladyship agreed," Thomas replied.

"I've had no doubt of that since I arrived," Mary commented dryly, "so much so I asked if her ladyship would help me provide a wedding breakfast. I found her quite eager to oblige."

"That was bold of you, my love, but clearly well judged," Thomas responded carefully.

"I doubt His Lordship would welcome common seamen in this

palazzo."

"Such were not in my thoughts," Mary advised firmly.

"You can splice the main brace or whatever you call it in some shoreside tavern with any number of your common seamen the night before we are wed. Settle for Tom Allen alone on the day."

"Then, who were you thinking of, my love?" asked Thomas, caressing her hand.

"Why, Lady Acton would appreciate being asked, but where will webe wed?"

"His lordship and Reverend Comyn will have to advise me on that," he reflected.

However, a little later, on returning to assist his lordship, he found itwas all decided on the advice of Sir William, although he was not present when Thomas was told.

When he knocked and walked into the study, his lordship stood before his writing table with Lady Hamilton holding his one hand in both of hers, close to her breast.

".......and I fear it has not worked on me."

Thomas could see his lordship's face was ashen and shocked, while her ladyship's bosom heaved with emotion. With delayed reaction to his entrance, they awkwardly turned to face Thomas. Shefirst let one hand fall to her side then gently removed the other.

"Ah, here is Thomas Spencer to be informed of his marriage arrangements."

His Lordship forced a smile onto his face before he was able to speak to Thomas.

"Well, Thomas, her ladyship and I have had a learned discussion with Reverend Comyn and Sir William. As you know, all the churches here are of the Popish persuasion, so none of their priests willconduct a marriage according to the rites of the Church of England. Nor would one of them consent to Reverend Comyn using his churchto sanctify your marriage."

From a hesitant start, he was now in full flow.

"We considered a shipboard marriage but thought Mary would find it disconcerting with an entire crew looking on. Then Sir William reminded us that this *palazzo* is an embassy, while he, His Britannic Majesty's Minister, is in residence. Reverend Comyn can marry the two of you here after reading your banns for three Sundays' church on *Vanguard*. What do you say to that?"

"Thank you for your kindness, m'lord," Thomas replied, adding hurriedly, "and m'lady, for your kindness to Mary and me."

Now that she had mostly quelled her emotion, her ladyship was able to respond.

"Reverend Comyn is still with my husband. If you could but bring them here and Mary too, we could carry our plans forward."

His lordship nodded assent, and Thomas bowed his way out, not fooled for a moment that it was to give them a minute or two longer together. However, exultation at the progress toward his marriage to Mary prevailed. Given his respect both for the old gentleman and his lordship's chaplain, it was with a light heart that he strolled around the corridor corners to Sir William's chamber to find the knight andhis guest seated in conversation that Sir William interrupted once Thomas arrived.

"We have lately been discussing how best to arrange your marriage to Mary Hever, young Thomas."

"I thank you for your kind consideration, Sir William and reverend sir," replied Thomas very respectfully. "Your presence in his lordship's study is requested."

"It seems his lordship is in a hurry to press arrangements along, Sir William," the bluff-featured cleric commented.

Thomas smiled. He liked and respected Mr Comyn as much as the old gentleman. He was not the kind of parson who gave himself airs and graces but demonstrated his faith in a direct way. He just got on with what he believed needed to be done. It brought back the memory of that hot night when the sounds of battle still raged above them. With his lordship's wounded head newly bandaged, Mr Comynhad calmly sat on a small bench writing orders at his lordship's dictation, for these to be carried off around the victorious fleet. Only his untidy hair and sprouting bristle had shown the emergency with which he was coping on that occasion. Now, his chin was clean shaven and his hair swept back in a neat, gingerish quiff on the topof his head. His side whiskers, nearly down to his starched white stock, were of a browner hue. He grasped an arm of the settee prior to standing.

"It is as well I know you to be a good Christian man of mature years, Thomas Spencer. Otherwise, I would have to give you my homily about marrying in haste. But I have seen your intended wife about this mansion. I know her to be also someone of mature years and seemly behavior. Rest assured, however, that I shall have to speak to the two of you together."

"I am asked to bring Mary to the study also," Thomas humbly revealed.

"Very well, I shall take the pair of you away afterward. There is no time to be lost in providing you with instruction for the married state. A little time spent in prayer for your marriage would be no bad thing,"asserted the earnest cleric.

"Allow them some scope for enjoyment and happiness, my dear Comyn. The smooth running of this household depends on their endeavors," chuckled the old knight.

Thomas would not have enjoyed the banter half so much had he heard the continuation of the conversation in the room he had just left.

"Much depends upon the loyalty and silence of Thomas Spencer," said Her Ladyship, focusing her gaze upon her lover's one good eye. "Do not worry about Thomas. He is completely loyal and knows how to keep his mouth shut. But, what if his Mary should herself get with child?"

"There is no danger of that. There is a reason she is no longer capable of conceiving."

There was a sly look in her eye as she made this point in support of her plan. She had spent over an hour convincing her lover it was now the best hope of saving them from losing everything they had each worked for. She also wished to avoid a millstone hangingaround their necks for the rest of their lives.

"I shall not want to be here when the time comes. There are too many prying eyes and wagging tongues," she continued, the look in her eyes now imploring.

"We have *Samuel and Jane* out in the bay, my love, with her'tween decks accommodation. When the time comes, Mary and yourself can be rowed out there."

"But, that is months away! You mean to keep her lying idle and earning nothing for her owner all that time," she expostulated.

"Not entirely. Where we go, she goes. When we sail to recover Naples, as we undoubtedly will, she will carry extra troops 'tween decks. Captain Hopps will do as I require at every stage. Those are the instructions of his owner in Whitby, arranged by a good friend in the service who is connected to him."

As the little admiral spoke, he saw the light of reassurance returnto the eyes of his lover. Her arms reached out to clasp him to her before she spoke again.

"I fear you will have to be very patient with me, my dear, dear lord.I am so fearful of complications if we continue as we have these last two months and more."

Notwithstanding her words, her fingers moved below the waistband of his breeches to feel him harden, but his devil-may-care smile showed the fortitude he proclaimed.

"Your health in this is my only concern, my dearest love. If abstinence gives you the confidence to live through this, then somust it be. We must carry out our plan to cause the least harm to anyone, or our nation in a time of trial."

"And, how will you feel six months from now, if I should provide youwith a son?"

His brow furrowed while he thought.

"You know my experience of being a parent to Josiah has been less than a happy one. In the event of having a son society will not allow me to acknowledge, I do believe I would need to see how well he does. Then, I may take a hand in making a man of him."

"So, in the meantime, you would trust his upbringing to Thomas and Mary?" she asked.

"Entirely," he confirmed with an instant smile, "they are a good andreliable couple."

With that, she twirled away from him with a look of reluctance inher eyes.

"Those we have summoned will be here instantly. We must be composed to show that all our concern is for the happiness of the couple to be married."

"Assuredly, my dear lady," he replied, his good eye twinkling as he got into the act.

Just seconds later, the study was crowded with four more occupants.

His lordship was now primly seated behind his desk and her ladyship the other side on one of the audience chairs. Seeingthat there were only two more of these chairs, Thomas held back, with Mary just behind him. Sir William took one of the chairs, but Reverend Comyn hovered, unwilling to take the final chair and leave Mary standing.

"Please do come in and sit down, Mary. Then, Thomas can shut the door, as is his duty when we need to speak privately," hislordship commenced in a kindly way.

"Your help to Sir William and Lady Hamilton and myself, has given us a good opinion of your moral character. Your desire to make an honest man of Thomas Spencer even more so. Therefore, we are going to suggest how best to arrange your marriage. Let me allow Reverend Comyn to explain how it should be done."

"Thank you for your consideration, my lord," Mary replied primly. "Now, we will have to read banns, and 'church' on *Vanguard* is the

place to do that. With two Sundays left in April and the fifth of May to follow, that means you could be married the following week. I believeit would be more comfortable for the ceremony to be here rather thanon board ship. That is entirely proper because this is the ministerial residence of Sir William. However, it is customary for the bride and bridegroom to be present for the calling of banns on at least the first occasion."

"Then we shall all attend church on board this next Sunday," Her Ladyship chimed in.

She looked from her husband to the admiral for confirmation. Thomas had sidled round the wall to a point where he could catch

Mary's eye. Although she looked very wary as these plans and suggestions were put to her, she had the wit to catch the pleading expression in Thomas's eyes and look pleased.

"It is very kind of you to put so much thought into how Thomas andI might be wed with no undue delay, my lord and reverend sir. I shall not feel uncomfortable at Church on board, but your support for the banns is truly welcome."

"You have presence of mind to add to your other virtues, my dear young woman," said Sir William with sincerity.

Thomas felt a pride in her welling up to the point that he could hardly contain his feelings. Mary blushed in a very becoming way and produced another intervention from Her Ladyship.

"You must not embarrass Mary, my dear husband. Can we mention the wedding breakfast we shall also provide here for a small gathering?"

"We have not mentioned the date yet," put in his lordship.

"We are thinking of Tuesday, the seventh of May. Owing to the demands of the service, a wedding breakfast may well be all we have time for. The signs are that May will not be far advanced beforeI have to order Mr Comyn, Thomas, and Tom to accompany me on board and sail. You will recall, Thomas, that something similar interrupted Sir Ed'ard Berry's happy occasion before we sailed ayear ago."

This brought Thomas back to earth with a jolt. He remembered all too well the young Captain having to tear himself away from hisbride. This may have explained why his lordship replaced him with Captain Hardy, so he could carry the news of their victory at the Nile back to England. Then, he had been wounded and captured in an action at sea and had to be exchanged before reaching home.

He just responded, "Aye, m'Lord," trying to seem imperturbable where duty was concerned.

"Before we reach the point of causing consternation to Mary and Thomas, perhaps we should decide on witnesses to the marriage and who shall be invited to the wedding breakfast, my dear Lord Nelson," her ladyship intervened again.

"Just so, and I have it in mind that the fourth witness, after ourselves, should be Mr Charles Lock, the Consul," added Sir William.

"And that means we shall have to include his gossiping wife in the wedding breakfast party."

Thomas, who was trying to keep one eye on Mary throughout this, saw her eyes narrow at this interchange between husband and wife. He realized Mary thought this was a ploy by Her Ladyship to ensure that Mrs Charles Lock would have to attend the wedding breakfast. He spoke hurriedly before Mary's expression could be noticed.

"We are very happy with all the arrangements, m'lord, Sir William, m'lady."

He bowed to each of them in turn as he spoke, not daring to lookat Mary again.

"Well, that is settled then, for I see that Mary also agrees," His lordship said crisply.

"I believe we should allow Thomas and Mary their private homily from Mr Comyn."

Now, Thomas looked at Mary and saw she was as glad of their dismissal as he was.

Neither that interview nor the banns that followed on Sunday were painful. In fact, members of the crew cheered after Reverend Comyn had finished reading them. Captain Hardy looked skyward with atight smile, as if to say the Lord alone knew what indiscipline was being encouraged. His lordship smiled beatifically all around, reciprocated by Sir William and her ladyship. Thomas saw Mary was too nervous to smile, so he gave half a smile in order not to appear miserable. It wasn't forced, thanks to his dearest wish being to marryMary. What else was going on around them was of no account.

The following fortnight passed very quickly, thanks to all the comings and goings. Thomas seemed to be almost continually crossing *Piazza Marina* and exiting or entering *Porta Felice*. The small vessels available to Commodore Troubridge were constantly plying between his squadron and Palermo. Other small vessels from home also came in with something like regularity. The problems the commodore was having all stemmed from the disunity of the Neapolitan allies he was fighting to restore to their capital city. King Ferdinand had sent him a judge and troops, as requested, but hewas being frustrated by the timidity of the judge, Vincente Speciale. Hence the laudable effort to apply judicial process to those accused of rebellion, so they did not merely become the victims of old scores being settled by opportunistic accusers, was failing. Perhaps thiswas explicable on account of the extreme reluctance of the troops to be landed anywhere, although the French garrison of Naples had withdrawn into Fort St. Elmo.

His lordship gave frequent, angry voice on reading dispatchesThomas carried to him. This never included the conduct of his commodore. He would have been compelled to deal with the situation in the same way himself had he been occupying *Culloden's* great cabin. He could only express his frustration and appeal to King Ferdinand to send explicit orders to the commander of his troops. Heassured Commodore Troubridge of his support in whatever action hetook to break the deadlock, consistent with the King's policy. However, that policy was not consistent with the approach of Cardinal Ruffo. He more than ever wanted to grant amnesty to the rebels and agree to generous march-out terms for the French garrison of Fort St. Elmo. The problem was the king's only force on the mainland consisted of Ruffo's army.

Only a day or two after Thomas had attended Church for thesecond reading of the banns, a courier brig arrived from home. This vessel deposited letters with *Vanguard* and sailed forthwith to the northwest for Minorca. The salute to his lordship's flag was the only sign her master and commander recognized there was someone senior to Captain Hardy. The scuttlebutt was that Army dispatches toMinorca were urgent. There was only a private letter for his lordship, although with an Admiralty seal. When Thomas took this into the study, Nelson followed his usual practice of scanning the contents before dismissing him. He often commented, and this was no exception.

"Their Lordships are sending me *Foudroyant*, with Sir Ed'ard to captain her, now that he is recovered. Well, that is truly welcome now that poor *Vanguard* is nearly worn out."

He read on, and his expression suddenly became grave before he looked up.

"Bring Sir William and her ladyship quickly, Thomas, and staywhen you come."

He had no clue what the bad news could be, but it was obviously of importance. From initially dashing around the corridors, he slowed himself to make the adoption of a neutral demeanor credible. He must have passed it off well because Sir William and her ladyship were surprised to see such a grave expression on Nelson's face.

"My dear, dear friends, a private letter has come from Lord Spencer, and I fear it contains grave tidings for you. Colossus went down with all hands off the Scillies," his lordship began. Instantly, herladyship sat down, but Sir William was that much slower and started to sway.

"My treasures!"

"Assist Sir William," his lordship rapped at Thomas.

He quickly moved to take hold of the elderly knight's shoulders andlowered him into his chair.

"Does the ship lie in water shallow enough to recover anything?" he quavered.

"From the description of her position, I regret not," his lordshipconfirmed gently.

"Thomas, a glass of brandy from my cabinet for Sir William, and one for her ladyship too."

When he served these, Thomas saw her ladyship's eyes were blinking back tears and she was trembling as much as her husband.

"I shall not by any means be destitute when we return home," Sir William reflected philosophically between sips of brandy, "but it is grievous that most of the collection I wished to leave to posterity should lie on the seabed. There were also some other items that would have brought a fair price."

Her ladyship's lip quivered at the voicing of this last thought, but Thomas did not think through the significance of that until a later discussion with Mary.

"No doubt Sir William would have allowed her to receive a good amount of the money raised," she speculated.

"Well, we had better not expect too much of a wedding breakfast."

"Surely, she will never be poor, even as a widow!" Thomas protested.

"Lady Acton said she lives extravagantly, and I can see she was right. She also said Sir William's lands have to pass to a male heir of his family."

"Wasn't she saying that to put you off joining her ladyship's service?" he probed.

"No, she said the heir was someone called Greville, and she's not a spiteful Lady, nor yet a schemer, so she just accepted I was coming here," Mary responded calmly.

There, Thomas had to leave the subject.

CHAPTER 13

THOMAS AND MARY MARRY

The remaining days to their wedding sped by in a great flurry of message carrying for him and frantic preparation for Mary. She put Thomas's best rig into perfect order and worked behind a closed door, altering a gown her ladyship had provided. Accurate cutting down and restitching were needed.

The day after the final banns reading was the day before theceremony. Mary's attention had shifted to the kitchen with the menu her ladyship had provided to instruct Letizia and her assistants. The only invitations outside the *palazzo* household, to Lady Acton and Mr and Mrs Charles Lock, had gone out with Tom Allen days previously,so there was nothing to impede Thomas being sent down to *Vanguard* late in the morning. A schooner under full sail had been spied many miles eastward, coming in from the Messina direction. The ensign and press of sail indicated urgent tidings. Thomas rushed down as the schooner came round to spill the wind and drop anchor just beyond the ship. He had no sooner arrived and seen the schooner's boat already hooked on than there was an outbreak of cheering from his fellow members of the crew. Clambering up the rope ladder to the main deck, he was met by James Quick, a coxswain.

"What are the lads cheering?" asked Thomas.

"Serm Roosiern viecterrie arn land. Cap'n's expectin' yousel take word to our Nel."

Giving his hurried thanks to James, Thomas rushed to announce himself to the first marine sentry. He summoned the captain's clerk. The second marine sentry stood on duty outside the captain's door. The clerk leaned toward him and whispered confidentially.

"The captain is still questioning the commander of the schooner."

Thomas could hear that for himself without hearing the actual words. Captain Hardy's measured tone was followed by a jerky, nervous-sounding voice and a pause before the Captain resumed speaking. Upon this ending, a skinny, sweating officer with a lieutenant's single epaulette on his ill-cut uniform coat came through the door. Captain Hardy was seated at his desk and still writing. The marine sentry smartly shut it again.

Poor fellow, thought Thomas of the schooner's commander. He would have been terrified Captain Hardy would find fault with his conduct and report his failings to his lordship.

"The Captain likes to finish what he's writing before calling us in," whispered the clerk unnecessarily.

"Come," was called from within.

The marine sentry smartly threw open the door. The clerk preceded Thomas, who came side by side with him before the desk and knuckled his forehead.

"Ah, Spencer, here is a sealed letter for his lordship from Admiral Ouschakoff, which I am assured contains both French and English versions. Here is also a note from my word with the commander who has just left."

He folded and sealed this last. Thomas stepped forward to receive both packages as the captain briefly instructed the clerk.

"No copy needed."

Receiving the packet and folded sheet from Captain Hardy's hand, Thomas stepped back and knuckled his forehead again.

"So, it is marriage for you tomorrow, Spencer. Not an institution to be entered into lightly," said Captain Hardy with a wintry smile.

Thomas was so surprised to hear a personal remark from the captain not in the line of duty that he almost forgot to stammer, "Aye, Sir."

"Be sure to have a sober, clear head for the occasion. That is the surest way for all to go well for you and your bride from the start."

"Aye, aye, captain, and thank you," Thomas got out.

The Captain, with a wave of his hand, indicated the interview was over.

In the boat across La Cala, Thomas reflected that the Captain's advice was well meant and sound. That night, Tom and he were meeting a few of their fellows, including James Quick, in a tavern. The hard drinkers amongst them, and that included Tom and James,would drink the rough Sicilian red wine as though it were beer. That he would have to be careful was his last thought before he stepped out of the boat, clutching the missives. He worked his way to the *palazzo*. There was plenty of noise from the kitchen, but the corridor outside his lordship's study was still. He knocked and entered to find his admiral studying a chart of the Bay of Naples.

"A note from Captain Hardy, I see, Thomas, but from whom is the packet?"

"Admiral Ouschakoff, so Captain Hardy said, m'lord," he replied. "Let me read Captain Hardy's note first. Open the seal for me."

Thomas did so and opened it out to pass across. His ordship scanned it speedily.

"Ask Sir William and her ladyship to be so good as to join me. Also ask Sir William if he has a passable map of Northern Italy to bring here."

"Yes, m'lord," Thomas responded, moving swiftly.

On reaching Sir William's chamber, where the old gentleman was reading, Thomas related his lordship's request for the map, which produced a question he briefly answered.

"The scuttlebutt says a Russian land victory, Sir William." "Does it indeed, young man," exclaimed the old gentleman.

He went to a chest and rummaged until he brought out a tight rollof parchment.

"Here I have it, but it may be a poor map by his lordship's standards. Her ladyship is with your Mary, so come with me to collecther."

Back in the study, after Thomas had been told to keep out of Mary's sewing room, the package from Admiral Ouschakoff hadbeen opened.

"It is good of you to come so promptly, Sir William and my lady.

This letter in English is written in a manner so peculiar that I can barely understand it. Would you see if the French version is any better?"

Sir William picked up the indicated French version, seated himself, and started to read.

A minute or two passed in silence before he handed the rolled map to Thomas.

"May we have the map unrolled on your desk, my dear LordNelson? The French speaker available to Admiral Ouschakoff iscompetent and precise."

The desk was promptly cleared of the other papers so Thomas could unroll the map and weight down its corners. Sir William studiedit then put his finger on a blue line.

"Here is the River Adda. Field Marshal Suvorov has defeated the army of General Moreau so severely twelve days ago at a place called Cassano d'Adda, that the French are abandoning Verona and falling back on Milan. The letter says Field Marshal Suvorov will give pursuit forthwith. He believes he now enjoys superiority in all arms over the French in Lombardy."

"Savage old Russian bear he may be, but he is a man after my own heart when it comes to pursuing the French," cried His Lordship, "and we must support him."

"How may we do that, hundreds of miles to the south?" interposed her ladyship.

Thomas thought he caught a note of anxiety in her voice and he reasoned she would not be happy if his lordship sailed far to the north.

"Why, my dear lady, by driving the French entirely from their majesties' kingdom and capturing any fortresses south of Rome in which General MacDonald has seen fit to leave garrisons."

"If Suvorov could lead this combined Imperial and Russian army to victory over an experienced and successful general like Moreau, then I give MacDonald little chance against him. Our support need be no greater than you suggest, my dear Nelson," added Sir William thoughtfully. At this point, Thomas could see that Her Ladyship was looking positively reassured, but his lordship left him no chance to observe further.

"Thomas, would you find Mr Tyson and send him to us. Sir William and I will need to send letters of congratulation and say what weshall be doing to help drive out the French. Ah, ask Miss Knight to attend also for the translating."

After this excitement, Thomas's tavern evening was not quite an anticlimax, but he was being careful. After the numerous toasts to himself and his bride, he took only sips of wine. He proposed counter toasts to their allies, his shipmates, his lordship and Field Marshal Suvorov. So, it was he who led Tom home through the warm, stinking alleyways to the *palazzo*. The result was that he awoke to the cooler air of morning with only a slight headache. This cleared after he ate bread and dripping, washed down with bitter coffee. The letters had all gone to Vanguard the previous afternoon so as not to hold up the schooner's return journey, so he needed only to rig himself out in his best, ready for the forenoon hour appointed. Tom needed some help to do likewise, thanks to imbibing with the best of them the previous night, which caused Thomas to spare a thoughtfor his shipmates and pray they had returned to the ship sufficiently orderly to avoid any trouble with the watch on duty.

They went to the large reception room a little early, Thomas in possession of the thin gold ring he would give to Mary, to find the Reverend Comyn already there, rehearsing the ceremony from his prayer book. The ring was entrusted to him and he said a prayer fora fruitful and happy marriage. Knowing what he had been told by Mary, he felt a little guilty about the fruitful part of the prayer, but he had to respect Mary's confidence. In came Sir William and his lady, followed by his lordship, talking to a youngish-looking couple. Thomas recognized the man as Mr Charles Lock. All of them sat ona row of chairs facing the Reverend Comyn, who then drew out his pocket watch. He looked at the time and asked whether the bridewas ready. Sir William got up, left the room, and reentered a minute or two later with Mary on his arm.

Her auburn hair was coiled high on her head and she wore a gown in a delicate shade of ivory. The edging around her neck was of a near transparent, lighter material that plunged to a central point just above her breasts. The sleeves were of the same material. What she was wearing on her feet, Thomas could not tell, but she looked taller than usual. Her face didn't look pinched today, but rather flushed with happiness in a very pleasing way. Thomas found her more lovely than on the first day he had set eyes on her.

The consequence of this vision was that he went through the entire ceremony as if in a dream, until Reverend Comyn concluded.

"I now pronounce you man and wife. You may kiss the bride."

He took Mary in his arms and knew it was real. Tom also gave Mary a good kiss, but then he'd told Thomas he would! So did Sir William, her ladyship and his lordship. Her ladyship said what a pity it was that Lady Acton had felt too poorly to attend. Only Mr and Mrs Lock held back and offered stilted congratulations.

Glasses of wine were poured for all, and the bride and groom toasted before moving to a smaller room with places laid at a single table. Letizia waited with the other woman who normally worked in the kitchen. Mary went ahead with Sir William and his lordship to find Mrs Cadogan and Miss Knight also waiting to offer their congratulations. Thomas heard her ladyship speak French to Mrs Lock. He didn't understand the words, but recognized the tongue. He could see from behind Tom that her ladyship was looking at Mary. Although he didn't know it, the words he actually heard were, *"Je croix qu'elle est enceinte."*

He knew *ey* in Italian meant *is,* so he guessed it was the same in French and concluded he would just have to remember *ansant,* as he heard it, to see if Mary knew what it meant.

Naturally, the food they were served consisted of Sicilian dishes, although eaten at the time of dinner in a king's ship. Mr Tyson joined them as well as Reverend Comyn. Thomas found it extremely strange that Mary, Tom, and himself should be sitting to eat with those they would normally serve. His lordship, the two senior members of his "little crew," and Sir William were the ones who behaved as though this was quite natural. Her ladyship and her enemy, Mrs Lock, were too busy eyeing each other across the table to act truly naturally. Mr Lock was too jumpy to handle the situation well.

Eventually, a delicious creamy and alcoholic dessert was served.

His lordship had consumed two large glasses of wine, which always made him particularly garrulous. He stood to propose a further toast to bride and groom.

"I ask you all to charge your glasses and drink with me to a long and happy marriage for Thomas and Mary. They are trusted and valuable members of this household. We can at least join with them in this one day of celebration. Then we must all become slaves to duty and much of this household be removed to *Vanguard*."

At this point, his lordship swayed as though anticipating the ship's motion. Tom forgot his status as a guest and took up his usual position behind his master. However, no physical assistance was needed, and his lordship continued speaking.

"Sadly, that cannot include Mary, who must remain to help keep this, the land base of our operations, in fair condition for our return. Such is the lot of a sailor's wife, who must always loyally accept absence in the cause of duty for king and country. We know she will do this as a stouthearted Englishwoman, so we wish Thomas and Mary the joy of their time together before a temporary parting."

He drank deeply, and others stood and drank with him before he slumped down in his chair to Tom's obvious relief. Thomas looked across at him and stood up.

"M'ord, Sir William, m'lady, and honored guests, Mary and myself thank you for your wishes and for this generous repast. If you would be so kind as to allow us to withdraw, we could enjoy a walk along the foreshore."

"Well, that is a novel activity for a newly married couple to aspire to," brayed his lordship, now slurring his words a little.

"A little gentle exercise before something more strenuous may be good for the constitution. Do allow them to go," declaimed Her Ladyship, laughing.

"It is a worthy sentiment to commune with nature," added Sir William.

"Very well, you are excused until tomorrow, Thomas," his lordship conceded.

Later, backs to *Monte Pellegrino,* their heads were shielded from the sinking sun by broad-brimmed hats. Mary looked into Thomas's eyes, his arm around her waist as they strolled.

"That was clever to ask to be excused this early. We can take ourselves to bed with no one around."

"Not really. I just wanted you to myself alone, without being a laughing stock going to our chamber in daylight," he responded.

"I wanted to ask you what something I heard her ladyship sayabout you in French to Mrs Lock means."

"But, I only speak some Italian. Tell me what you heard."

"It sounded like 'shu crewwa kell ey ansant,' but I find it hard to say," he confided.

Mary stopped suddenly and faced him, eyes blazing. "I know what *enceinte* means. I have heard it said by ladies in Dover. It means 'with child.' She who is really with child claims I, who cannot be, am the one with child. Now I know fully what is to be. Well, you and I had better enjoy our repute while we can."

She turned him forcibly toward the seaward-facing city wall and seized his arm, dragging him toward the nearest gate. Only when they neared the *palazzo* at its upper end did she slow her pace to enter quietly. She led him by the hand up the steps and round totheir chamber. Closing the door, she seized his breeches front and deftly unbuttoned them before unhooking her gown at the back. The top fell for her breasts to swing free, then she took his rapidly rising penis in her equally hot hand.

"Fancy me being fool enough to do without this until now," she breathed.

She wriggling the rest of the way out of the gown and pulled him down onto the bed. His lips around one of her hardened nipples, she guided him into her, legs gripping his back.

Chapter 14

An Interrupted Honeymoon

Daylight streamed through the single, high, uncurtained window.It hitthe wall facing the foot of the bed on Thomas's side. It was this that woke him from too brief a sleep. Mary slept on, her face against his chest. Her hair was all around her head and shoulders. her breath onhis body would have aroused him, but for the pressing feeling that heneeded the chamber pot again. Small wonder it had been so well used in the night and that he had awoke exhausted. and without an erection! He had never expected that Mary would wake and want him so many times in the night! Nor that she would cry out in ecstasy while wildly working her body on his weakening prick, after he was spent inside her.

He gently disentangled himself and eased off the bed to stand groggily. He walked unsteadily to the corner and pulled the board off the chamber pot. His wrinkling nose told him that it had been one of Mary's wise and practical arrangements. He knelt to make sure his aim was true. His reflection how the love of a good woman could drive her to take the lead in their lovemaking came to a sudden end. The sound of his urine flowing into the capacious pot was enough to wake Mary. Her head lifted as he shook off the last drops and turned towards her, naked.

"Come back here, and I will stop him looking so tired," she murmured throatily.

"Look at the daylight, my love. His lordship will be got up by Tom before long. I shall be expected to be ready for work," he protested, making for his heap of clothing.

"*She* will not be out of her bed until near noon," Mary wheedled, rising on her knees to show her delights, but his body was sadly slow to respond.

"Now I need the pot too," she shrilled crossly, "so you had better get dressed and carry it down to the drain."

Thomas turned away to pull his shirt over his head. He did not mention that his prick was sore. He doubted that would be regarded as any excuse. When he had also pulled on his breeches and heard her urinating cease, he turned back to watch her stretch and pull on her shift.

"Yes, my love, of course."

He felt a first stirring in viewing the perfection of her charms, whichthe shift did little to conceal. Sadly, the moment had passed for her, and she quickly moved to her gown.

"Well, what are you waiting for? We shall never break our fast before his lordship calls you if you do not get down there and swill under the pump," she chivvied.

He did as he was told and went down to find that the kitchen was bustling. The drain and pump, fortunately, were not in use by anyone else. He would have to organize a bowl of water for Mary andhimself to be kept in their chamber. Frequent replacement would ensure they always had clean water to wash in private. Wedded blissin an upstairs chamber in the *palazzo* had practical consequenceshe needed to sort out quickly. Back he hurried with the washed-out pot and his suggestion.

"You will have to buy a large jug and bowl from the pot stall on *Piazza Marina*. It will not be costly if they are plain," Mary advised, fully dressed and pinning her hair.

"I have a small bowl her ladyship gave me, but it doesn't hold enough for two."

"I'm not sure I would know which bowl and jug are best," confessed Thomas.

"You bring your coins, but only silver, not gold, then leave the buying to me. All you have to do is the carrying back here," Mary stated, putting in the final pin.

"Now, let me get down to Letizia in the kitchen before we both faintfrom hunger and thirst."

Her smile was loving, so his hand went straight to the purse hisbelt looped through. No thought he was trusting her to spend his money frugally entered his head.

"We really should have done this long ago," she laughed, taking his hand and leading him through the door.

Down in the kitchen, Tom was not in fine fettle. He received scant sympathy from Letizia, so it was with relief he greeted the arrival of the newlyweds. He rightly deduced that the friendship between the two women would work to his advantage in securing a share of the freshly baked bread she would produce for the couple. The jugLetizia placed on the table for them had a strong smell of lemons. The drink it contained was soothing for Tom, but refreshing for the newlyweds, as they chewed the bread with gusto. Tom chewedcautiously and slowly. Eventually, he was done.

"Errs lordship will be frettin' if'n I doerrs not get erm dressed. Ye can take yoor ease a while longerr, Thomas. Err laydysherp errs prowlin, Mary."

He rose from his stool and ambled away. Mary's eyes followed him to the door.

"Tom was being really helpful there without knowing. If we hurry, we can buy jug and bowl before we're wanted."

With that, she jumped up, and Thomas rose rather more slowly, taking a final swig of his drink. He brought with him a bite-sized remnant of bread.

Their purchases were made in good time. The half hour it took for Mary to strike a good bargain and carry the their weighty purchases back to their chamber was the last free daytime for many days. His lordship was driven by the need to prepare for sea and her ladyship by a frenzy of entertainment organizing. It was as though therewould be no time left to her in Palermo within days. Sir William just went along with both of them, helping with advice and soothingfrayed tempers. However, there was little he could do about Consul and Mrs Lock. The wife's family connections made it impossible to persuade Queen Maria Carolina that the couple weren't Jacobins. Mrs Lock was convinced it was the influence of her ladyship over thequeen that resulted in the suspicion with which they were treated at court. This misapprehension was not helped by his lordship demonstrating no desire for the assistance of Consul Lock in victualing *Vanguard*. The gathering of other vessels to sail northwardwith the flagship represented substantial demand. This was exactly the type of role a consul in a foreign port frequented by British shipping was supposed to fulfill, but his lordship would not have it.He took a close, personal interest in ensuring his ships were supplied with food and drink that would keep their crews healthy. Histime at *Villa Bastioni* had convinced him that the trade in lemons just outside the city wall gave him the means to cheaply keep scurvy at bay. An officer from *Vanguard* made regular purchases. Now, thanksto her ability to converse in colloquial Italian, he enlisted Mary as a kind of value adviser and interpreter in the task. Thomas was also sent with the party, not just to keep Mary safe but also to make abrief second record of the quantities and prices paid. The walk to thegate close by the *de Vega Bastion* didn't feel too long in the early morning. Returning to the *palazzo* in the hot sun, to then face household chores for Mary and more message carrying for Thomas, was enervating.

That the nights were their own was no great help. Their highly physical enjoyment of each other the rest of that week took stamina. Thomas could scarcely believe how energetic Mary could still be during the working day, when he was struggling to hide his exhaustion. The time passed so quickly to the following Sunday's Church on board that his response to Mary's frantic lovemaking had no chance to falter. Now came the event that gave lovemakingadded urgency in the days before they were parted.

His lordship led his little crew down to the ship, discussing with Reverend Comyn the issue of sobriety. With the entire crew packed into the waist by divisions, Reverend Comyn, on the quarterdeck, had just started when the officer of the watch swung his telescope toward the base of *Monte Pellegrino*. From that point on, attention to the homily on sobriety was sadly lacking. Any man positioned to see what the telescope was trained on darted glances through gun ports or over bulwarks.

Within a minute or two, his lordship had edged to the clergyman's side and whispered in his ear. Following this the sermon concluded in stentorian tone.

"So, you should remember the guidance of the Scriptures for moderation in all things. It will assist you in maintaining that level of sobriety essential to capable and prompt performance of your duties. Particularly now you are about to return to battle his majesty's foes."

A fervent "Amen" from the entire assembly followed. Whispered word had spread like wildfire and the service was brought to an end as swiftly as was decently possible.

Tom and Thomas had been on the seaward gangway for theservice. They had an excellent view, once they could properly turn away from the quarterdeck. The incoming vessel was a large, well- armed brig. Really not much smaller than a small frigate. She carrieda full and billowing set of sails until very close to harbor. Close in, a signal could be seen flying. Captain Hardy, with no less than four lieutenants, now had telescopes trained. They read the flags to one another with the signal book. Soon, one called out the entire signal.

"She is Espoir with an urgent dispatch for His Lordship."

Captain Hardy barely had time to turn and repeat this before his lordship's order.

"Signal master and commander to repair on board with the dispatch."

Even as the brig swung away from the wind and sails began to be clewed up, her anchor hit the water. and she swung broadside to *Vanguard* a couple of cables distant. A boat was swung out in great haste, and Thomas turned to Tom.

"Do you not have the feeling that trouble has arrived?"

"Yerrs I do. We murst get aaft and be ready fer errs lordship's orders."

Outside the great cabin they waited while the large and experienced-looking officer entered and made his report. He was in there with his lordship and Captain Hardy for quite some time and emerged with a rather smaller package than the one he had taken in.He looked eminently at ease, so the onlookers of the little crew concluded his lordship must have viewed this officer's conduct with some favor. They were not long in finding out. Tom and Thomaswere soon called on to carry orders to small vessels in harbor. Mr Tyson was also in the great cabin, although seated separately at a small desk, writing out fair copies of his lordship's orders. Thesewere not just to Espoir's commander but for Commodores Duckworth and Troubridge and Captain Ball on Malta. Likewise,orders to the other commanders who would do the carrying.

That afternoon, when Thomas reported back to the *palazzo* with signed receipts, Sir William and her ladyship were closeted in the study with his lordship. He gestured for Thomas to place the receiptson the desk and carried on speaking.

"Just to send Commodore Duckworth two of the line, I am obliged to recall Troubridge and all his liners. I must leave a small flotilla in the bay, but to have it commanded by a post captain, I must leave Foote in Seahorse, which deprives me of a frigate. It is now thatthree of the line with the Swedish Knight is a grievous deficiency. Well, Thomas, what is the scuttlebutt as to my direction of sail?"

"Why, west m'lord," he responded cautiously.

"There you have it, Sir William. All of my sailors know I must put to sea in support of Lord St. Vincent. How to be an adequate support isthe question."

"I am sure you will find a way, my dear Nelson, however difficult you find it, to put a squadron together. Shall you take the Portuguese?" Sir William enquired gently.

"For all the use they are, which is none at all!" his lordship responded grimly.

"I must also take Ball away from the blockade of Valletta."

"Surely, the more ships you have together, the less likely theenemy will be willing to risk joining battle with the great Nelson," added her ladyship.

To Thomas, this had all the appearance of someone wishing to convince herself.

"Would it were so, dear lady, but I shall make haste nonetheless. Thomas's Mary will soon be deprived of his presence in her bed,."

This last notion not only caused the lovemaking in that bed to take on a truly desperate quality. It also became a household joke as the days and nights stretched out to a week, before a halfway adequate force was assembled.

Accordingly, the next Sunday leading-out of the little crew was to the sight of Sir William, her ladyship, Mrs Cadogan, and Mary gathered at the *palazzo's* entrance arch to watch them away. Mary was blinking back the tears, with her ladyship's arm around her in ostensible comforting to cover her own distress.

Then followed a day of easy westward tacking. The arrival from that direction of a fast sloop bearing another Lord St. Vincent message was alerming. He had seen the French fleet and five Spanish liners slip through the straits whilst he was ashore.

It was as well there were small vessels to carry messages. His lordship reacted with his renowned speed of decision. Lord St. Vincent had to be advised of a concentration point for the squadron. Those still to rendezvous had to be chivvied, and the ships to Minorca were recalled. Thus it was a fleet of thirteen liners and numerous small craft that brought up the sight of the island of Marettimo. The early evening sun played on rocky headlands that plunged down to the nearing shoreline.

Tom and Thomas had both gone below, once they had seen that the sea north, west, and south of the fleet was clear. Tom knew his lordship would need a snack and glass of wine before taking to his cot. Thomas had the rather different consideration that the admiral usually wanted to continue his correspondence by candlelight when the sea was calm. It was now, and clear of sails even toward the distant Barbary Coast. There would be no desire to antagonize such a major force. Now, they stood just outside the great cabin, preparations completed. His lordship's conversation with CaptainHardy was clearly audible, but apparently not being attended to by the marine sentry, who stood easily with musket grounded. He took no notice of the two of them listening.

"Send off the small craft that have my written orders, Hardy. The sooner we have a line of eyes and ears both northward and southward, the better."

"Aye, my lord. I shall follow with a 'heave to, well spaced, lights showing' signal for all other ships. There is no good holding ground off this island's western shore."

"Make it so, Hardy, make it so. This is a tolerable swell on which torock the night."

"Errs lordship will be daown directly," Tom muttered.

The prediction proved correct. Only notes for Sir William and her ladyship were penned and sealed after supper. Thomas was dismissed and Tom saw His Lordship to his cot.

Next morning, not long after first light, a boat from *Swiftsure* hooked on. It bore Captain Hallowell and a large timber item that looked all the world like a coffin. When hoisted aboard and carried to the break of the quarterdeck, it was indeed a coffin. Captain Hardy, upon greeting his fellow captain, lost no time in ordering Tom todress his lordship to receive Captain Hallowell. Thomas he ordered to stand by the coffin with *Vanguard's* carpenter, pending his lordship's arrival. Thomas watched as Mr John Cooper ran his professional eye over the coffin. He walked around it to inspect the workmanship from every angle. Then he stood back to check if the line was true, at which point his face registered that he'd found no fault. His lordship arrived, talking with animation.

"You say it has been made from a single piece of *L' Orient's* mainmast, thrown clear when she blew up, Hallowell?"

"That is so, my lord. It was a good length that hit the waters of the bay very conveniently. I knew instantly from the size of the splash what had come down close enough to be brought under Swiftsure's side. The lashing on and hoisting aboard took rather longer, my lord," responded the lean and energetic Captain.

"Well, it is a fine piece of work, and I am honored to accept the gift. It will be a continual reminder that no one can count himself immune from shot and shell when battle is joined."

His Lordship still ran his hand over the smooth, polished grain of the well-fitting lid. He caught John Cooper's eye, then added other commendations.

"My compliments to your carpenter and my thanks to all who assisted in the recovery and working of *L'Orient's* severed mainmast. This timely gift, knowing the likely odds we shall be facing very soon, can sit behind my chair."

The officers and men who had gathered cheered his lordship's words. John Cooper supervised the carrying of the coffin to the greatcabin with care to ensure that the willing hands doing the carrying kept it damage free as if it had been his own work. Tom and Thomas heaved sighs of relief when they and others were able to lay the coffin flat, a comfortable space behind the admiral's chair. JohnCooper and his mates would fit wedges to hold the coffin fast during the day's cruise.

A good many days cruising it turned out to be. The late spring heatwas made bearable by the breeze as the liners beat north then came about to tack southward again. They repeated the same track many times and after a time, it became boring. Only the day another fast sloop from the west hurtled across the noonday swell into the midst of the small fleet, with word that Lord St. Vincent was now in the Mediterranean with twenty of the line, did excitement mount. The lieutenant commanding the sloop had gone again and Nelson had resumed the quarterdeck when Tom and Thomas were listening after preparing the Admiral's dinner table.

"Now that his lordship has ordered Lord Keith to break off the blockade at Cadiz, I believe the Dons will follow him through the straits. We shall be faced with forty or more French and Spanish."

"That seems more than likely, my lord," Captain Hardy agreed flatly.

"Why did not Lord Keith sail out and attack the Brest fleet when he saw them sailing past him in line ahead?" his lordship asked rhetorically and incredulously.

"Could there have been a likelihood the Dons would rapidly get to sea behind him?" wondered Captain Hardy.

"Not the Dons whose expedition and sailing skills I know!" exclaimed his lordship.

"Could be a good fight then," whispered Tom to Thomas.

It was not to be. A good many days cruising, with his smaller vessels spread out north to south to cover the likely tracks, convinced his lordship the French and Spanish were not comingeast. There were far too many other priorities needing his attention, so the small vessels were called in. Signals were relayed over long sea miles in sparkling late spring weather and the ships allowed the wind to fill their sails eastward in company. This was only to the pointwhere Captain Ball's ships bound for Malta had to part from the remainder.

Although the liners were now reduced to ten, even counting the Portuguese, they must have made a brave sight rounding *Monte Pellegrino* with their consorts. A good many of the local populace gathered along the shore around La Cala to wave and cheer them in when June was not three days old. Some only looked forward to relieving the sailors of their pay. Wiser heads must surely haverealized that the return of undamaged ships meant no battle had been fought. His lordship was eager to moor and be carried to*Palazzo Palagonia,* for the coach stood prominently waiting. While *Vanguard* warped in, Sir William got out to show he was waiting.

"I must be on my way, Hardy. His majesty will expect reassurance that we shall resume removal of the French from Naples."

"Just so, my lord. There are too many of us to be moored here for long," the captain replied.

He looked around at the ships of the fleet dropping anchors in the bay.

"My little crew can follow. Thomas will return with any messages and, I dare say, an invitation to celebrate the king's birthday tomorrow," his lordship ordered.

With that, he was gone, leaving Reverend Comyn and Mr Tyson tolead off on foot towards the *palazzo*.

"Did you see her ladyship was also in the coach?" Mr Tyson asked the reverend.

"I was unable to see," replied Mr Comyn.Tom slyly winked at Thomas.

They were approaching the downhill end of the *palazzo* and Thomas could already see Mary standing at the near edge of the entrance arch.

"Your dutiful wife awaits you, Thomas Spencer," Mr Comyn said with a smile.

Thomas's heart was too busy skipping a beat at the sight of her to reply.

"Ah, 'tis lurve," murmured Tom.

"Then, he had better go in front of us," laughed the reverend.

Off Thomas went to embrace Mary and lead her up the stone flight of steps. Around the corner toward their room, he stopped to kiss her properly. The heat of their bodies coming together was overpowering in its intensity.

"I'm sure I should be reporting," he murmured, after disengaging tongue and mouth.

"Never you worry, lover, the coach stopped only moments, and then they were off to the *Colli*." she flung herself along the corridor toward the door of their room, holding his hand tightly so his feet were obliged to follow. Slow he might have been to start with, but unwilling he was not. He speeded up when she threw the door open. He just had time to slam it shut before her urgent hands were under his sailor's smock. He wasn't too slow with the buttons at the back of her dress. It seemed to take no time before they were virtually naked on the bed. while his shoes had gone, he still had his stockings on. He gazed rapturously down from her jutting breasts and past her gently rounded belly to the triangle of dark hair and groaned with ecstasy as her hand went round his erection.

"Do you think it is sinful to take so much pleasure in our bodies," she teased.

"Careful with your hand. I have missed you too much not to come quick," he groaned.

"Then, we had better not waste it, even if we know we won't be procreating."

She giggled and rolled onto her back, pulling his arm above the elbow so that his shoulder was above her. Then, in a trice, all of him was above her, her legs were wide, and he was deep inside her. Later, when he was spent but still in that position, her hand came round his back to tease at a point just behind his testicles and she spoke softly.

"Her high and mighty ladyship has been in a stew while you've been away."

"For missing his lordship you mean?" he asked ingenuously.

"Not missing him like this, while she has still been so sick," she breathed, "but being fearful what might happen to him in a battle.She has worked me nearly to death, letting out waistlines just enough for comfort now."

"Will it not show when she walks about?" he questioned, enjoying her tickling.

"Not for a while yet, but I will tell you what I noticed the one timeher belly was bare. She has the marks I have each side, which is a sure sign she has given birth before."

"I wonder how long ago?" he pondered.

"Probably years ago, before her belly got more rounded, because they were harder to see than mine. I had to stop looking when she snapped at me not to stare. Oh ... oh, that is better."

She groaned as he hardened again and her fingers ceased to do their work. His body began to move on hers and he found her lips with his to enjoy her tongue teasing his. They made less sound that way.

Later, sleepily, with a humor that produced a surprised look on her face, he said, "I believe I should now look at the marks each side of your belly while there is yet light."

CHAPTER 15

HONEYMOON DISRUPTED TWICE MORE

The inspection of Mary's stretch marks was sadly interrupted by the sound of hooves and carriage wheels on cobbles, nearly belowthem.

"His lordship is back," Thomas gasped.

He collected up his clothes and hopped from one foot to the other to pull on his breeches. Mary lay back and laughed. When he was hunting for his left shoe, she pulled on a shift, kicked the shoe from under the bed, straightened his collar, and smoothed his hair.

"Hmm, you no longer look like a man come straight from a woman's bed.

"She dabbed a small cloth in their water bowl and wiped his face, while he secured the second shoe buckle.

"I shall be sewing if her ladyship wants me."

She pushed him through the door and closed it again quietly. He could stroll around the corridor, presentable once again. He reached the door of the large reception room in time for the coach passengers arriving at the top of the stone staircase.

"Ha, Thomas, bring some wine to the study. We have a party to plan."

"Aye, m'lord. Is there aught else?"

"Find Mary after you bring the wine. We must get in supplies," added her ladyship.

Thomas went down to the wine store, uncorked a bottle, and put it with three glasses on a tray. w Back up the steps he carried and into the study.

"Sir Ed'ard Berry should be here in *Foudroyant* within a few days," his lordship was saying to Sir William.

"I shall send poor *Vanguard* home when I transfer my flag. She is terribly knocked about, but I shall keep Captain Hardy for another ship."

"Do I recollect you saying *Foudroyant* is a larger ship, my dear Nelson?" Sir William asked. Thomas poured three glasses of wine and handed one to her ladyship. He placed the tray to hand for Sir William and His Lordship and bowed his way out as this answer was begun. Mary would have had good time by now.

"We shall be spaciously housed when we sail for Naples ..."

Round the corridor in their room, he found Mary fully dressed. Her hair neatly braided, she looked for all the world like a young, competent housekeeper.

"They are calling for you to help with what they're doing to celebrate King George's birthday." he spoke with as much enthusiasm as he could manage, knowing all the work it wouldinvolve.

"Ah Thomas," she responded, stroking his rather bristly cheek and smiling sweetly.

"What a marvel you were gaining me so much time. I doubt we willhave to work desperately hard to keep them happy. Tom will do his share and so will Letizia. I can always ask for her to be allowed to bring in others if it's a throng that comes."

With that, she was through the door. Thomas followed in her wake,stopping short of the study door when she knocked and entered.

In the event, it was a throng that assembled the following day just after noon. Mainly an English throng, seeing the occasion demanded invitations go out to Commodore Troubridge and all the ships' captains. A good proportion of lieutenants and marine officers were also invited. Although the timing was for what the service called dinner, it was to be served buffet style. Tables were laid out and atop table for the three hosts, the Commodore, and those courtiers who had accepted their invitations. As Tom and he circulated to pourwine for toasts to the king's health, Thomas found himself wonderingwhat the foreign guests would make of it all.

That would depend on how much they could remember when they were as drunk as everyone else, he reflected.

Her ladyship was seated between his lordship and Sir William, with Commodore Troubridge to his lordship's right. It was noticeable that the commodore was very lively in conversation with his male hosts, but restrained and anxious when responding to her ladyship. Miss Knight was on hand to interpret for the princely guests who had too little English to follow the speeches proposing toasts. Tom winked at Thomas over the heads of those seated as he poured for her the requested small glass of white wine. Mary was at the far end of the large reception room by the groaning buffet tables, ensuring that hosts and principal guests were served.

While captains and others below top table were being serveddrinks by a handful of reliable wardroom stewards, her ladyship was watchful that the top table food serving was being done properly. Hermother, Mrs Cadogan, was controlling the access of the throng of marine and naval officers to the buffet tables. She hardly touched theglass of wine that stood before her. His lordship, however, was both drinking quickly and talking volubly, mostly how he would restore King Ferdinand's kingdom in Naples. Once *Foudroyant* arrived, he would sail in company with the entire squadron.

"We shall each take on board contingents of His Majesty's troops, Troubridge. We can have done with Ruffo's temporizing when we land them and put the remaining forts in French and rebel hands under siege. Do not think I am relieving you of command of the squadron. Once we have the seaward forts, I shall send you awayup the coast to harry the French. We must aid our allies to drivethem out of Italy. Suvorov and his Russians present us with a goldenopportunity."

A smile broke out on the commodore's earnest, large face at this reassurance.

"My lord, it gladdens my heart that we wait only for the newest andmost powerful ship we shall have on this station. Who will control theking's troops?"

"I shall have plenary powers from his majesty to control all landand sea forces in his absence, but I intend to bring Sir William and her ladyship with us."

Thomas caught the expression of dismay that briefly flitted across the Commodore's open face. It was instantly replaced by a look of concern.

"Surely your lordship will not risk carrying Sir William and his lady into danger?"

"Have no fear on that score, Troubridge. If there is any risk of *Foudroyant* having to join battle, I shall transfer Sir William and her ladyship to *Samuel and Jane*. She has ample accommodation now and will sail with us."

"My lord, I thought she was merely your temporary store ship. Thatyou had no control other than the contract to carry your stores," the commodore prevaricated.

"She has been refitted with a 'tween deck forward of the break at my request. The master has instructions from the owner to meet my requests, seeing that he has some kind of family connection with my friend, Moorsom," confided his lordship.

A knowing look crossed the Commodore's face at this mention of aname he knew.

"I believe he has lately returned to active service, my lord."

"Yes, I doubt he will have much time to continue growing his family, as he seems to have been doing since the American war ended. I am sure their temporary loss is our gain and he will do very well for us," his lordship reflected with a smile.

There, Commodore Troubridge left the subject. The expression of admiration that had overtaken disquiet showed he well understood why others in the service and in commerce had such confidence in Nelson to do all manner of things for him.

Thomas moved on to replenish Sir William's wine glass, noting that the elderly knight had been drinking intermittently whilst listening to his lordship holding forth.

He murmured his thanks to Thomas before leaning forward to speak around his wife.

"I fear this occasion will cost us a pretty penny, my dear Nelson."

"It has to be borne, good Sir William. Think of the benefit to the morale of our officers, now that we are so near to sailing," his lordship responded ruefully.

Her adyship wore an expression of annoyance during this exchange. Either she felt there was an implicit accusation of extravagance in her catering or simple chagrin that discourse was going past her. She was not slow in putting a stop to that.

"We shall soon enough be depending on the protection of these officers, my dear husband, so we cannot begrudge them food and wine bought cheaply enough."

His lordship caught her expression with his good eye, clearly having recognized the nettled tone in her voice. He drew her into the conversation in a placatory manner.

"My dear lady, I have the utmost confidence that you manage our household expenses with great prudence. Just seeing the manner in which Mrs Cadogan so nobly assists you, for no benefit to herself, could not lead a sane man to think otherwise."

It was laying it on a bit thick, thought Thomas, but Sir William felt similarly obliged.

"You must forgive me for seeing all expenditure in a negative light after hearing of the loss of my treasures, my dear love. It is just the unreasonable fear of an old man. After all, I still have my lands to provide income when we go home."

"And, some of those are along Milford Haven, the finest deepwater anchorage in Europe. We shall have to set about securing mercantile developments to increase the return on your lands," His lordship, looked closely for her ladyship to thaw.

"It is not just my mother, but Mary too, who help me ensure there isno waste," her ladyship finally responded.

Thomas quickly moved along to Count Esterhazy and a noble Italian couple. He did not want any more attention drawn to either Mary or himself.In one sense, the rest of the grand party was just work for those serving. It was also a goodwill-building occasionamongst the captains, lieutenants, and marine officers, which might well affect their future service for good or ill. Toward the end, after numerous toasts, Tom was resorting to subterfuge. He moved glasses around on the top table to ensure his lordship drank as little as possible before the party broke up. He averred to Thomas thatthe peer would be ill enough in the morning without drinking any more. He made sure Thomas was elsewhere, serving a small group of Captains, so he alone was left to serve wine on the top table.

Only her ladyship, who drank sparingly throughout, appeared to note with sardonic amusement what Tom was doing. By this time, Miss Knight had withdrawn to her room, the expression on her face demonstrating that she found naval officers in drink too uncouth. She was not present to see Tom assist His Lordship to rise and besteered toward his chamber. Thomas likewise assisted Sir William, while her ladyship swept away imperiously to bid farewell to thenoble guests. Commodore Troubridge gathered his little coterie of captains and led them to the anteroom. In this manner, a general dispersal began.

Tom had the rights of it. His lordship was ill the following day. As a result, Thomas and Mary were required by her ladyship to spend most of that day clearing away and cleaning up after the party. Meals were restricted to party leftovers, as if to demonstrate how frugally she could manage. However, the hard work of two days and stale food fried in oil did nothing to diminish the desperate lovemaking of the recently married couple. They believed they had only a fewnights left before prolonged separation for a second time.

In the event, plans proceeded a little slower than anticipated. The following morning, the grandest-looking two decker Thomas hadever seen rounded *Monte Pellegrino* under full sail and drove intothe bay. Thanks to watching that fine ship being well brought aboutto a mooring off La Cala, hardly anyone noticed a sloop far out, coming from the direction of Messina. His lordship received Sir Edward Berry aboard *Vanguard* and acquainted him with the arrangements he required to be made for the transfer of his flag to *Foudroyant*. Despite his wounds in *Leander's* fight with *Le Genereux*, Captain Berry was still the slim, young-looking gentlemanThomas remembered. He took with good grace the news that Captain Hardy would be joining *Foudroyant*, to retain his services on the Mediterranean. Also that Sir William and Lady Hamilton would besailing with them, in addition to a contingent of Neapolitan troops. Somany more to accommodate other than the "little crew" was undoubtedly going to tax his ingenuity. He had sailed from England sufficiently shorthanded to be pleased by the addition of officers from*Vanguard*, which his lordship was ordering. He was straightaway at pains to put in hand the organization needed. He acknowledged Reverend Comyn, Mr Tyson, Tom, and Thomas most graciously when they were taken aboard Foudroyant to assist. Thomas thought him a welcome change from Captain Hardy, although he had toadmit one knew where one stood with the latter. Clearly, the band ofbrothers spirit of the Nile lived on in different ways with each captain. What made a great impression was not just the newness and solidity of this ship but its roominess in every part. The increase inheadroom might not matter greatly to his lordship, but a good manyofficers and men would benefit greatly. This was immediatelyobvious from Captain Berry not having to duck below beams the wayhe had needed to do when flag captain on *Vanguard*. That he hadconsiderable feeling for that time was borne out when he gazed outof the great cabin's stern window across the anchorage to his former command.

"Poor Vanguard is sadly worn by overuse."

He turned back with pursed lips and a furrowed brow and got on with allocations. Even Tom and Thomas found they were better accommodated on this ship, thanks to some separation from his lordship's stores.

Only when the little crew returned to *Palazzo Palagonia* that early evening did they become aware of the importance of the sloopclosing the port from the east. The written record of Captain Berry's dispositions had found his lordship jubilant for an entirely different reason, revealed as he laid aside their papers.

"Sir Ed'ard has assured me he will come here in the morning to receive my decision on these. We shall transfer flag the day after, following which loading shall begin forthwith. There is splendid news from the east. Buonaparte was compelled to lift the siege of Acre. His army departed the Holy Land across Sinai, back to Egypt."

"May all the saints be praised," Reverend Comyn responded on behalf of them all.

"Wait, there is more," his lordship continued, warming to the task. "The Sultan in Constantinople is encouraged by the success of his garrison in the siege. He will assemble an army to descend on Egypt by sea. He hopes the French will be crushed between that force and the remaining Mamelukes."

"A fitting fate for the heathen French to be crushed so," added Mr Comyn.

"Let us not count that blessing prematurely. However well supported by our ships and their guns, the troops of the *Sublime Porte* will be up against a European army, no doubt refreshed by regaining Egypt. However, we can say that General Buonaparte will be too busy to make mischief elsewhere. We can safely sail for Naples without the slightest worry," his lordship concluded.

When Sir Edward visited the *palazzo,* a significant party gathered in the large reception room after business. It was clear that this earnest and well-spoken gentleman had made a great impression onMiss Knight. She made a point of monopolizing his time while tea was taken. She asked about his wounds on *Leander,* treatment by the French, convalescence on exchange, and attendance at Court tobe knighted. Thomas wasn't at all sure they hadn't met before, so easily had they fallen into conversation. He had to grin when Tom looked over their heads at him and winked. Being a gentleman couldbe a mixed blessing!

The transfer of flag went well, but the loading started that day took an interminable six days. No surprise when 1,700 troops, their equipment, and supplies had to be spread around the entire squadron and the few other vessels. At last, with the Hamiltons and Prince Leopold also embarked, the little armada sailed on 15 June. *Monte Pellegrino* had not dropped below the southern horizon when an eastward sailing brig intercepted *Foudroyant,* hove to, and dropped a boat. The same experienced-looking commander whohad come previously from Lord St. Vincent clambered between his oarsmen to the stern sheets. The boat skimmed across the swell to the flagship's side, while all the ships of the squadron backed wind. When the commander had been received and departed again, Thomas had never seen his lordship emerge from a great cabin so glum looking. Both captains also looked very serious.

"We must turn around and disembark most of the troops. Certainly, all that are incapable of serving as extra marines. Also, Sir William and her ladyship, then put to sea again to face whatever the French and Spanish throw at us, with Lord Keith's niggardly reinforcement. Thomas, I shall need you to accompany Sir William and her ladyship back to the *palazzo*. No lingering with your wife when there is workto be done!"

Captain Hardy smiled grimly at the last sentence. He had looked extremely worried at his lordship's outburst openly criticizing Lord Keith. The expression on Thomas's face became as serious looking as Captain Berry's, but for an entirely different reason. Mary had been complaining how snappish her ladyship had become in recent days, so although he had been sailing away himself, there was at least the satisfaction that only Mrs Cadogan and Miss Knight were being left behind. The one was a hardworking old lady, always in hermob cap. Her double chins wobbling above her blouse as she applied herself to any task. She would chat away to Mary in her Cheshire accent, while they both sewed, during her daughter's was absence. The other needed Mary's skills for her own wardrobe too much to treat her with anything but studied courtesy. However, he now had to accompany ashore the person who would get under Mary's skin. The Lord knew how long it would take to see off the French and Spanish!

"Aye, aye m'lord," he replied mechanically.

"Do not look so glum. You at least will *see* your wife. Come,gentlemen, we will acquaint Sir William and his lady with what must be."

Sir William looked bemused and her ladyship anxious when Thomas led them across the upper end of *Piazza Marina* and into *Via Quattro Aprile*. Mrs Cadogan and Mary were waiting under the entrance arch. That part of the city was buzzing with curiosity as to why the squadron had so suddenly returned.

"Have the coachman make ready, mother," her ladyship called, taking charge. "We must collect Prince Leopold and his lordship from the ship and take them to the *Colli*. The soldiers are being taken off."

As they rushed away, Mary squeezed Thomas's hand. "What is happening?"

"The French and Spanish fleet is likely to attack our squadron, so his lordship is dispensing with passengers and soldiers so we can sail ready for them."

On hearing this, Mary flung her arms around him and fiercely held him to her, with tears in her eyes. Thomas realized how terrified she was and tried to allay her fear.

"It will probably be a false alarm like last time. They have little stomach for joining battle with his lordship."

"Even when there are so many more of them?" she asked anxiously.

He could hear the two horses being led over the cobbles from the stable to where the coach stood in the courtyard and gently pried her away to hold at arm's length.

"his lordship is not given to leading us into death traps. I must go, so as to be back at the ship before the coach. I have strict orders, my love," he replied and kissed her.

"Men are killed even in running sea fights. Let you not be one such," she entreated.

"I will not put myself in harm's way without need," he promised, detaching himself.

Mary just stood and bit her lip as he walked down the slopingstreet again, watching until he was out of sight. She barely noticing the coach rumble past.

Thomas hardly needed to have worried he would not regain the ship before the coach. Crowds of soldiers blocked the mole the whole way to where it joined the foreshore. Quite apart from theships alongside the mole, others which had only heaved to in the anchorage were sending in boatloads more. Those were now coming to the end of La Cala, where it shelved, for want of other space. There was nothing for it but to weave his way around one group of apparently leaderless men after another. They had brought off only their muskets and marching packs. There were loud arguments going on at gangways between their officers and naval lieutenants. On reaching *Foudroyant* at the seaward end of the mole,the marines had disembarked. Their captain was assisting a senior officer of the royal guard to explain to others that the men needed to be formed up and marched off the mole. The assistance was more physical than verbal, thanks to the solid line of armed marines slowlymoving landward across the whole width of flagstones. His lordship and the two captains were impatiently pacing the quarterdeck, but there was now no obstacle to ascending the flagship's gangway.

At the top, Thomas found himself being beckoned by Sir Edward, so he knuckled his forehead. a "Coach on its way, Sir."

His ordship turned on hearing this and lifted a small telescope toward *Porta Felice* but only murmured, "I have it," before he rapped out an order.

"Have the marine officer still on board go to his captain and say I need a route cleared through that disorderly rabble."

He was clearly furious with the delay, but Captain Hardy dryly took the sting out of it.

"We have disembarked them without most of their equipment and all of their provisions, my Lord. it is difficult for their officers to explaintheir return to barracks is only temporary."

"Well, the sooner the coach can reach me to take Prince Leopold back to his royal father, the sooner his majesty can arrange to feed them while we are gone. I wonder whether such an undisciplined rabble are worth feeding. Ha, look, Culloden's marines are joiningour own. At least they make a fair showing."

"Indeed they do, my lord. There goes our marine lieutenant. Let ushope they clear a path for the coach as quickly as Spencer slipped past all of them."

His anger defused by Captain Hardy's interventions, his lordship faced Thomas.

"You made good time, Thomas. Go down and see Tom has Prince Leopold ready."

Tom had the nine-year-old dressed in his miniature uniform and near the gangway. The boy was volubly stating in broken English his unwillingness to be disembarked.

"I want sail with great Lord Nelson to battle."

"An' very brave of you it ers, y're 'ighners, but y're father will not allow," said Tom.

"Padre, il Re' non e permesso," tried Thomas.

That only produced a stubborn look on the boy's face, a stamped foot, and a shrill, "I sail!"

At that point, her ladyship's head appeared as she ascended to the deck speaking a stream of Italian to the boy. Tears rolled down his cheeks, but Her Ladyship wiped them away. Then his lordship was with them both, allowing Tom to heave a sigh of relief. The boy was led down to where Sir William waited in the coach.

It must have been one of his lordship's speediest visits to the *Colli.* Nonetheless, the ship was ready to be warped away from the mole. She was pulled round by a line from a ship merely heaved to and ready to sail. With surprisingly little confusion, the squadron formed up in the bay and sailed westward.

If any had anticipated either the appearance of the French and Spanish fleets, or that his lordship would beat up and down off Marettimo again, they were mistaken. He had called Captain Ball with his two ships off the blockade of Valletta. Lord Keith's two ships by way of reinforcement had joined them off the western tip of Sicily. The squadron was now a small fleet! On only the fifth day out from Palermo, a sloop arrived from Minorca with news that Rear Admiral Cotton had arrived with twelve ships to reinforce Lord Keith. The "heave to, captains repair on flag" signal was flown. Tom and Thomas were directed to ready wine for serving.

From the pantry, they could not help but overhear his lordship with Sir Edward and Captain Hardy while they waited for the other Captains' boats to arrive.

"After all the letters I wrote entreating, begging him to retain his command, whether or not he needed to stay ashore to recuperate, Lord St. Vincent has resigned and gone home three days since. LordKeith is Commander-in-Chief in his place,"

His lordship's high-pitched voice contained a venom in this final piece that Thomas had never heard from him before, except inrespect of General Buonaparte.

"That ee haas written many letterrs," whispered Tom.

"Is that so bad, if Lord St. Vincent was so sick?" they heardCaptain Hardy say.

"I have no confidence after he failed to break off at Cadiz and attack Bruix's ships. Then there is the matter that we have been sent here on faulty intelligence. If the French and Spanish were coming, we would have had word of them by now. Well, I tell you, gentlemen, we shall not remain a moment longer but return to the task we were ordered to perform: Restore his majesty to Naples."

"Will your Lordship return Bellerophon and Powerful to Lord Keith?" asked Sir Edward in a worried-sounding voice.

"Oh, I think not. With Rear Admiral Cotton's twelve, Lord Keith has thirty-one. I may return Commodore Duckworth, who knows the Balearics and the Catalan coast better than any other. We also have the blockade of Valletta to resume, thanks to no glimmer of understanding at Horseguards that troops are required to reduce the fortress,"

Minutes later, there was no dissent. Commodore Troubridge spoke strongly in favor of bringing the entire Italian mainland under allied control. Captain Ball stressed the urgency of having ships of force back in position at Malta. Hence, it was back to Palermo. The messenger sloop returned to Lord Keith with details of his lordship's plans. The fastest ship forged ahead to have the troops ready for embarkation.

What a different and orderly scene met their eyes on the mole. Narrow columns of troops were ready to move forward. Thomas with his lordship's small escort picked their way to *Porta Felice,* where the coach waited. Thomas detached to the *palazzo* to ensure Sir William and her ladyship would be ready for the coach returning from the *Colli.* Precious little time they would have to pack for the Lord knew how long! Mary clung to Thomas with no fear and perhaps a little relief. Her ladyship, dressed ready for the coach to return, was now all sweetness and light.

Chapter 16

Vengeful Return to Naples

The afternoon of Monday, 24 June, was very warm, even in the breeze that drove *Foudroyant* into the Bay of Naples. The remainder of the impressive fleet sailed spread out behind her. Of course,transports like *Samuel and Jane*, which were not really armed at all, made it look more impressive than it really was. The fact remained that it was the most powerful armed force anywhere on the Tyrrhenian Sea. Thomas had briefly come on deck to judge speed and distance. Tom or he could make sure his lordship came on deck soon enough to miss nothing of significance. He stood in the shade just below the break of the quarterdeck. A bulky shadow cast from above, which he recognized Captain Hardy, suddenly gave voice.

"Those flags mean trouble."

He looked over the quarterdeck rail and called. "You had better advise his lordship now, Spencer."

Thomas reacted like a scalded cat, having believed he was invisible to the quarterdeck. He should have realised that two captains aboard meant one had freedom to rove around. His lordshipwas galvanized into action when Thomas repeated Captain Hardy's words.

"Find the signal lieutenant."

Tom provided his hat and Thomas departed quickly for the lieutenants' cabins. On the heels of that startled officer, he heard Captain Berry speak "Captain Foote must be in a lather to tell you something, my lord.

He is already in his boat and casting off before being summoned."

"So, he should be with flags of truce flying from Fort St. Elmo, the sea forts, and his own masthead. He has some explaining to do," hislordship responded tightly.

All on the quarterdeck watched with everyone else as Captain Foote's boat crew made the long pull to reach *Foudroyant's* side. Although a lean-looking man, Captain Foote's face was flushed as her came over the side. He saluted the quarterdeck, and was ushered to the great cabin. His lordship, Sir William, and Captain Hardy awaited and Sir Edward joined them. Tom and Thomas were in the pantry, able to hear most of it. Captain Foote was not invited tosit, only to explain how he came to be party to a truce. It had not been authorized by King Ferdinand, or Commodore Troubridge before he departed. Captain Foote sounded like a man under pressure.

"My Lord, my orders were to cooperate with Cardinal Ruffo and theCommanders of the Russian and *Sublime Porte* detachments in the blockade of the forts. I had supposed that, in his command of the royalist army that entered Naples, Cardinal Ruffo was the confidential agent of his Sicilian majesty. He had already signed the document on the twenty-first, as had the commander of the Russian detachment. Although I was concerned that the terms of capitulation of the sea forts were very favorable to the republicans, I felt obliged to sign the document yesterday. It had been ratified by GeneralMejean in Fort St. Elmo, as to the three weeks armistice with his force."

"Well, Captain Foote, I fear you have allowed yourself to be humbugged. You have allowed yourself to be imposed upon by that worthless fellow, Cardinal Ruffo. He is endeavoring to form a party hostile to the interests of his sovereign,"

His Lordship's tone was even.

"My lord, I had no idea that such was his intention. I lacked instructions or any document to assist or guide me in my dealings with the Cardinal," added the Captain.

"Well, you have at least brought the Nuovo and Uovo Forts to the point of surrender. I give you credit for dealing with attacks by Republican ships with all possible zeal, but I must now ask you to withdraw. Compile for me a detailed narrative of your dealings with Ruffo to better inform my future action toward him. Rest assured thatI exercise the powers given to me by King Ferdinand to repudiate thefavorable terms for capitulation of the sea forts and the three-week truce given to Mejean."

"I shall prepare the narrative forthwith, my lord," said Captain Foote and withdrew.

"Ers Lordship ders 'ave a way wi' simple-minded officerss," Tom whispered.

Thomas grinned and whispered back.

"I feel a Captains' conference comin' on."

Seeing they were in agreement about this, there was nothing for it but to ready the wine. Signal flags flew to annul the armistice and summon captains. They were not the only ones requiring wine. When dusk fell, there came on board a darkly mustachioed fellow who announced himself as Egidio Pallio, leader of the Lazzaroni. He sought audience with Sir William and her ladyship. This fellow, who looked like a brigand, was allowed into their cabin. Her ladyship called for Thomas to bring wine. It was tricky by candlelight to distinguish between Sir William's bottles and his lordship's. He consoled himself with the thought that, if he made a mistake, it wouldbe easily corrected next time around.

He could not follow the voluble Italian that poured out of this excitable man. Only demeanor told him some of it was a protestation of loyalty. Nor could he follow the questions put by Sir William. He was told Signor Pallio would be returning in the morning to see his lordship and his hosts again. Thomas noticed his longing look at the marine sentry's musket and bayonet. Clearly, armaments were on the Neapolitan's mind.

The morning brought the rest of the small fleet in from the offing. They had beat to and fro all night to form a line of defense across the inner bay. His lordship could establish a line of eighteen powerful ships, flanked at each end by groups of the twenty-two smaller gun and mortar vessels. It was from this showing of formidable strength that Commodore Troubridge and Captain Ball went ashore to present to

Cardinal Ruffo His Lordship's written observations on the armistice. These were, of course, a repudiation of the document and required the unconditional surrender of Nuovo and Uovo. When the two returned, Commodore Troubridge spoke for them.

"My lord, the Cardinal has seen our strength but still declines to sign or send the revised requirements into the forts."

"So, what does he propose to do, other than sit on his dignity as a jumped-up Prince of the Roman Church?"

His lordship's tone indicated no criticism of his emissaries.

"He announced he will shortly come aboard for a discussion with your lordship," replied the Commodore with the hint of a smile.

"What did you make of his intentions and reasoning?" pressed His Lordship.

"I do not believe he has become a rebel himself. Rather he believes by showing mercy to the rebels he will be able to reconcile them to the return of King Ferdinand."

The Commodore turned to Captain Ball, who nodded hisagreement.

"Well, we shall have to parley with him. If God Almighty does not aid him to see sense, perhaps the promise I have given to Egidio Pallio to arm his Lazzaroni will aid him to see his duty."

It sounded as though his lordship was almost looking forward tothe encounter.

"Tom," he called down the companionway, "a jug of water and glasses to the cabin, and ask Sir William and Her Ladyship to join me. We must not tempt such a holy man by offering him wine."

His subordinates on the quarterdeck laughed.

Two hours later, no one was laughing, even though the ship had nearly completed reprovisioning. His lordship was exasperated by failing to agree to first principles with the Cardinal. Sir William had become exhausted with the strain of interpreting. Her ladyship had totake over that function. The Cardinal must have realized Nelson's patience was about to snap.

He announced he must withdraw to consult his Russian and Turkish allies. He would inform the castles of St. Elmo, Nuovo, and Uovo that he could not answer for Lord Nelson allowing the armisticeto stand.

His prophecy was there would be a night of terror in thecity. His lordship sustained his silent fury until this difficult man had gone.

"Clear away this water, Tom, and bring wine for us, Thomas. I swear I was within an ace of exercising my authority to arrest himand pack him off to Palermo to answer to King Ferdinand."

"My dear Nelson, your restraint was admirable in the face of provocation. I believe you will prove to have kept all the royalist factions together," Sir William contributed in a very tired voice.

"He did agree that the documents you have drawn up to send tothe sea forts and St. Elmo could be sent if you wish," added her ladyship anxiously.

"Well, we shall do that in the morning. I shall order a careful watch to be kept on the city tonight. Thank you, Tom and Thomas. Allow usan hour's rest before you serve dinner."

The next morning proved Sir William's assessment more accurate than Cardinal Ruffo's prophecy. The overnight disorder in the cityhad mainly been caused by inhabitants fleeing. They believed their homes would be destroyed in the cross fire between Fort St. Elmo and the ships. There had been murders of Jacobins and suspected ones. Others had been seized and brought out to the ships. Those could be handed over to the custody of the king's law court inoperation on the small, rocky island of Procida.

Sir William sent an assurance to Ruffo that Lord Nelson would not bring the armistice to an end without instructions from Palermo. The Cardinal asked for marines to be landed to protect the city from the Jacobins and French troops believed to be marching from Caserta. Upon this reversal of his position the previous day, his lordshipconfirmed Sir William's assurance. The Cardinal and his Turkishallies then moved their forces back into the city to keep order. By theday's end, the two sea forts had surrendered, their garrisons had evacuated, mostly into boats held in the bay. Ruffo not only sent his congratulations but also news that a group of his irregulars hadcaptured the turncoat Commodore Caracciolo.

Very early the following day, Thomas was called into the great cabin to ready all for Mr Tyson to begin taking dictation. Tom had already seen his lordship dressed and breakfasted. He was ready to work once his secretary appeared and ordered Thomas to remain onstandby. His first message was to Cardinal Ruffo. He advised that if his eminence thought proper to deliver Commodore Caracciolo, to join the other rebels, on board his flagship, he would dispose ofthem. At this point Sir William walked in.

"Do I hear you dictating a message to Ruffo, my dear Nelson? I have just received a note from him myself. He is going to a service of thanksgiving at the church of Santa Maria del Carmine, well away from the cannon of Castel Sant' Elmo!"

"Exactly where is that, my dear Sir William?"

"Why, around the shoreline from Castel Nuovo in the opposite direction from Castel dell' Ovo. I deduce Commodore Troubridge isat Nuovo from what I see there."

"Indeed he is, Sir William. I shall send him a covering note for delivery of Ruffo's note and urge him on to lay siege to Castel Sant' Elmo. He has thirteen hundred marines and sailors ashore and all the cannon and stores captured in Nuovo and Uovo. Could you show Mr Tyson how to spell these various names? Thomas, you can go with these to the commodore."

Once again, he found himself in a boat on the bay, this time being rowed in toward a mole close by the Nuovo fort. The early summer sun beat down, so the heat and noise on shore were considerable. Sweating gangs of seamen were now wheeling cannon that had been lowered from their gun platforms. They trundled out toward the narrow, rising streets of the old town. There were also some exotically dressed darker men, armed with curved swords and pistolsin their waistbands. Some of them wore long boots and others went barefoot. They looked like Thomas imagined the Caribbean piratesto have looked nearly a hundred years ago. Yet more were soldiersin some kind of green uniform.

Briefly, he looked up the steep, rocky slope that rose above the old town to the solid-looking fortress perched on the crest. On the mole, the crenulated, round towers of Castel Nuovo rose before him. He walked swiftly around it to the landward gatehouse. Commodore

Troubridge in his shirtsleeves was directing an officer and guns on squat carriages were being pulled by rope teams. Powder and shot on a variety of carts rumbled past.

Thomas picked his way between them to come within earshot of the commodore. He waited behind the lieutenant, who was following the line in which his commander's arm was pointing. However, he straightened, saluted, and left. Thomas also saluted.

"Ha, Spencer, messages from his lordship," the commodore said, squinting in the sun and holding out his hand.

Thomas passed over the two sealed notes. The commodore's open face registered first surprise that one was addressed to Cardinal Ruffo. After he had torn open his own note and started to read, he was amused.

"The church of Santa Maria del Carmine," he repeated, "he is not exactly putting himself in harm's way there! I shall deliver this in person."

He tapped the note to Ruffo, and Thomas could hardly do lessthan smile himself.

"First, I had better give you a reply to his lordship and point out sights I will name."

He took Thomas by the shoulder and pointed him to the right of thefort high above.

"You see that building a distance to the right of the fortress, Spencer? That is the San Martino Monastery. Can you remember that?"

"Yes, Sir, the San Martino Monastery," Thomas replied.

"Around that is where most of the guns are going. Captain Ball is up there now, placing the first of them. We shall work some round to the left of the fortress under cover of darkness. Come, I will write inside this fort."

Thomas obediently followed the commodore through an archway set in elaborately carved, pale stonework. It didn't match the rest of the fort. A table in a small room, little penetrated by the sun's rays, was furnished with paper, a quill, and an inkwell. Still standing, the commodore started writing at the top of a sheet and seemed to go on a long time. Halfway down the sheet, he paused.

"I am also telling his lordship that some of the locals pulling our guns are former rebels who prudently changed sides before welanded.

Never mind, even cowards can help pull a gun. Of greater importance is the number of men who slipped away home from here and Uovo last night, rather than surrender."

He began scratching across the paper again, with more frequent dips into the inkwell. Eventually, when he had nearly filled the sheet, it was done, and he paused for drying.

"I have no means of sealing, so be sure to take it straight to his lordship. Preferably when no one other than Sir Edward or Captain Hardy is with him."

Thomas stood up straight and said, "Yes, Sir." He fully understood the veiled desire that her ladyship should not be present when his note was read.

"Off you go then, Spencer,"

The commodore folded the note and handed it over. Thomassaluted and strode out into the sunlight back to the mole.

There was no difficulty back on board. His lordship and the two Captains were already on deck observing movement ashore. Her ladyship, as Tom later said, had not yet deigned to get out of herbed. He saluted and handed over the note.

"Commodore Troubridge instructed me to point out two sights,m'lord."

"Very well, Thomas, point away," His Lordship replied absently, scanning the note.

"Up there, m'lord, to the right of the Sant' Elmo fort, the building at a distance is the San Martino Monastery."

Telescopes moved around to that point. He waited while the monastery and approaches were studied.

"And the second?"

"Up the slope to the left of the fort is where guns will be hauled at night."

This time he waited only a second before Captain Hardy spoke. "Looks difficult. Steep and rocky, so they will be noisy."

"It will take several days to position sufficient cannon to force Mejean out. We can at least block the road behind the monastery with sufficient force to prevent the French in Caserta from marching to his aid," predicted His Lordship.

"I do not believe they will come, any more than I believe Ruffo will truly be of assistance."

There was indeed no message of heightened cooperation fromthat quarter, when Commodore Troubridge came on board to report progress. The following morning, events conspired to put even that into reverse. One of the small Neapolitan warships left behind in Palermo entered the bay under a full press of sail and headedstraight for *Foudroyant*. Her commander had been told his mission was urgent. The letters he brought on board from the *Colli,* especially that from Sir John Acton, bore this out. Thomas was sent to call for Sir William.

There was no doubt his lordship was also in a hurry, when the elderly knight entered.

"Good Sir William, here is a letter from Sir John Acton saying that no conditions other than unconditional surrender are to be made with these Neapolitan Jacobins. The vessels on which the men taken out of the forts are waiting must be brought under our guns. We shall have to remove the ringleaders to send direct to justice."

"It should demonstrate to Ruffo your wisdom in not allowing themto sail, my dear Nelson. It is as well that the dungeons of the fortresson Procida are commodious. We have provided Speciale with more new cases to decide in two days than he has dealt with in as many months."

"It is as well Troubridge is not here to be reminded of the problems he had with that pathetic excuse for a judge! I believe I must also issue a proclamation for those who slipped away from the forts in thenight. I cannot be seen to deal with them more favorably. Bring Mr Tyson, Thomas."

"Indeed not, my dear Nelson. Let me assist with the wording ..."

Thomas heard no more. The outcome of Mr Tyson's endeavors for his lordship and Sir William was swift in coming, once Cardinal Ruffo received his copy of the proclamation. The first sign was Commodore Troubridge being rowed to the flagship.

His troubled look had Sir Edward sending straight down to

thegreat cabin. An excuse to escape an over-warm cabin was all the admiral needed. Troubridge was surprised to be greeted by him on the quarterdeck.

"I see by your expression, Troubridge, that something troublesome has occurred."

"My lord, the Neapolitans have been withdrawn by Cardinal Ruffo. He has issued an order that no one may be arrested in the city except by his command. The Russian contingent is above the old town, so I have sent to Captain Ball to prevent any officer from Ruffo reaching them."

"This is intolerable, Troubridge, but you have done well. Let us go below and confer with Sir William."

Listening from the pantry, Tom and Thomas heard the arguments rage to and fro. It was eventually the view of Sir William, supported by Troubridge, that prevailed. An urgent request was to be sent for the king, queen, and Sir John to sail to Naples. They could take charge of the government and this would avoid a decision to arrest Ruffo and send him to Palermo.

Sir William feared a bloodbath if Ruffo were arrested. His followers would revolt and Egidio Pallio would then be unable to prevent all-out war between the Lazzaroni and Ruffo's men. Troubridge said that the English would be blamed for any repressive action taken by the fleet or his force on land. Once his lordship accepted the validity of their arguments, Captain Foote was sent for. On this occasion, he had a far better reception.

"Captain Foote, I have an urgent and vital task for you to perform, which Sir William and I consider essential to drive out the remaining French and deal with the rebels."

"Yes, my lord," responded the captain eagerly, seeing a chance to redeem himself.

"You have no doubt heard that Ruffo has withdrawn hiscooperation again. It is the belief of Sir William and myself that only the presence of their majesties and Sir John will cure the dissension among the Neapolitans."

"Yes, my lord," repeated the captain, adding hastily, "my problems showed that too."

"Quite so, but no matter. Here are two packages of letters, one for Seahorse and one for the cutter that will accompany you. Speed is of the essence. If Seahorse cannot keep up with the cutter, you are to transfer to her and present the letters personally. It is only necessary to send Seahorse so that their majesties may sail here in reasonable comfort. Do you have anything to add, Sir William?"

"Only that Captain Foote should use the excellent narrative of his dealings with Ruffo to help convince his majesty and Sir John of the need to sail here," he responded.

"Just so. We shall not have all the guns in position around Castel Sant' Elmo for a week. You must endeavor to be back in that time," concluded his lordship.

"If it can be done, I shall do it, my lord," said the captain, grasping his chance.

It seemed only a few minutes after his dismissal that Seahorse and the accompanying cutter were sheeting home in the heat haze of that Friday afternoon.

The fleet dwelt little more than overnight on how long the mission would take. The series of events that began in the morning, with Captain Hardy on the quarterdeck, overrode all else. He was doing no more than watching the Portuguese liner Rainha and the brig Balloon coming into the anchorage. There were a host of Neapolitans on board *Foudroyant*. Sir Edward and Hardy were united in refusing to have any of them cluttering up the quarterdeck.It was enough that they were consuming at a prodigious rate provisions paid for by his Britannic Majesty. A hullaballoo broke out among a crowd of them in the waist. This apparently started with a call from one of their fellows on the shore-facing gangway. Thomas had come up to do the emptying after Sir William's morning ablutions. he saw an overloaded boat being pointed out. It washeaded straight for them from the quarter of the city occupied by Ruffo's army. He couldn't follow what was being said but a number ofthe men were armed. They had to be from Ruffo's army, so he slipped below to ensure his lordship and Sir William were told.

The elderly knight was out of his own cabin, heading for the great cabin, when Thomas reached him. Once aware there was a boat approaching, he was animated.

"Come my boy, we must go up and see what is to do."

Thomas didn't mind deferentially following him up to thequarterdeck. Sir William most assuredly was allowed there. CaptainHardy had scarcely realized their presence before Sir William spoke."The boat is bringing the captured Caracciolo on board, Captain Hardy."

The captain swung on his heel and took in their appearance. "Thankee kindly, Sir William. Get below and advise His Lordship, Spencer."

He turned again and roared for the officer of the watch, marineofficer, and signal lieutenant.

Mr Tyson was with his lordship when Thomas arrived. He gave Captain Hardy's compliments and the news Sir William had gleaned. "Thank you, Thomas. We heard Captain Hardy's orders so realized something was afoot. He has the matter well in hand and SirWilliam is there to interpret. I shall not interfere, and you may return with that message."

His lordship's measured and relaxed tone left little doubt this was something he had been prepared for. His words to Mr Tyson as Thomas left confirmed that view.

"Ruffo has turned again. We must have the wardroom cleared for acourt martial."

Back on the quarterdeck, Thomas could see armed ruffians dragging an exhausted, pale, and bound prisoner. A few days' growth of beard added to the unkempt appearance. His once-fine uniform was now sadly soiled and torn. There was a look of shock onSir William's face. Captain Hardy, straight-faced as usual, simply ordered the marine officer to take possession of the prisoner and have his arms unbound. There was an ugly murmur amongst the armed ruffians and the other Neapolitans. This was when it showed that the marines were professional soldiers and the others mostcertainly were not. A file of marines had worked their way between the ruffians and the crowd of Neapolitans. Then jostled the ruffians away from Caracciolo and surrounded him.

"Lieutenant Parkinson, you will see the prisoner taken to a cabin. You will ensure he is confined with a marine guard, beyond the reach of his countrymen."

The threat in the captain's voice was unmistakable and emphasized by Lieutenant Parkinson's drawn pistol. He made his way to where the prisoner, surrounded by the red tunics of the marines and unbound, swayed as he stood. The lieutenant led a tight phalanx to a midship's companionway and down. Captain Hardy turned to Thomas.

"Prepare a platter from the remains of breakfast, and take it for the prisoner, Spencer. There is still some coffee in my pot too."

"Aye, aye, sir," Thomas responded smartly and left for the pantry.

He quickly assembled a palatable breakfast platter and the coffee pot in Captain Hardy's cabin was still warm. He made his way down to the lower gun deck. Curious seamen, engaged in their routine morning tasks were gazing toward the timber hutch that served as the carpenter's cabin. Marine sentries with fixed bayonets stood at each side of the door. Lieutenant Parkinson, still holding his pistol, was directly in front.

"Breakfast for the prisoner, Sir, as ordered by Captain Hardy." "Very well, Spencer. I will advise him it is here," conceded the lieutenant and unlocked the door. "Here is food," he said.

From the prisoner there was no response. Thomas could only see from his feet that he must be sitting on the carpenter's cot. He peered around the lieutenant to see Caracciolo's dark hair and eyes and tried what he hoped would be a helpful

"Colazione?"

At this, the dark eyes focused on him for a moment before Caracciolo mouthed an emphatic, "No."

He turned his head sharply to face the blank, timber partition of the hutch's side wall. Lieutenant Parkinson locked the door again.

195

"You elicited a clear enough response, Spencer. You had betterreport back to Captain Hardy. "What next, I wonder?""

"Court martial, I think, sir," whispered Thomas, and the Lieutenantmerely nodded.

Back at the door to Captain Hardy's cabin, he was met by theoccupant. He heard Thomas's report in silence.

"A proud man, but foolish. Count Thurn is with his lordship."

Thomas knew what that meant, but said nothing, then found his expression read.

"I see you know there is to be a court martial, Spencer. The other captains from King Ferdinand's ships are here, so it will be entirelyan Italian affair. We shall just have to abide by the verdict and do ourduty."

For Captain Hardy, this was a speech and spoken in a somber manner. He believed the outcome was already decided and it weighed heavily upon him. For a man accustomed to applying harsh naval discipline, it showed he was capable of deep feeling, even if hedisliked displaying it. Once again, he read Thomas well.

"Get along, Spencer. His lordship requires Allen and you to serve refreshment to the captains when the wardroom is cleared for them to consider their verdict. You will have to be prepared to get in very quickly and out again."

So, it proved to be. The forenoon watch was no more than half gone when the court martial convened. Mr Midshipman Parsonscalled Tom and Thomas urgently to bring their wine to the wardroom when the noon bell had only just sounded. The Italian captains sat instony-faced silence, especially Count Thurn, captain of the frigate *Minerva*. Caracciolo was said to have given the order to fire on that ship the previous month. Without speaking, but silently communicating their anxiety to be gone behind impassive faces, Tomand Thomas fled the wardroom after serving. All Thomas could think about was Caracciolo having been the captain of Sannita with sufficient seamanship to carry Mary safe to Palermo. Yet when the marine sentry at the door of the great cabin required them to enter forthwith, it was to find his lordship now entertaining Sir William and her ladyship. He was in a mood to regard Caracciolo as already condemned.

"Good. They will not be long over the verdict, having disposed of the hearing in reasonable time. Then, we can dispose of the traitor tohis king altogether. Bring us wine before dinner to celebrate Balloon's good news. Ask Mr Tyson to step in, so we can see to it that Troubridge and Ball let their Russians know of Suvorov's great victory over MacDonald."

Her adyship was smiling at this, and Tom assumed an enthusiastic smile. Thomas did his best to emulate them, although Sir William stilllooked vaguely troubled. When they were out and back in the pantry decanting wine Tom's smile dropped.

"Ers Lordship 'as got ther bit 'tween ers teeth, good an' proper," hewhispered.

"So, Caracciolo will surely hang," Thomas mouthed back."Soon."

Tom then sidled out to go and fetch Mr Tyson.

That worthy man was already penning his lordship's note to go ashore when they served the wine. The marine sentry's rap announced the arrival of Count Thurn, escorted by another marine and Mr Parsons.

"My lord, Caracciolo is condemned to die," the Count announced inheavily accented English. He burst into a flood of Italian directed toward Sir William.

"My lord," Sir William began formally, "Count Thurn does not believe he can give all the detail accurately in English. He asks to give the full account in Italian."

"Please proceed."

His lordship did not look quite so pleased upon hearing that two of Thurn's fellow captains had not voted for Caracciolo to die.

Thurn was belatedly invited to sit and given a goblet of wine. Tom and Thomas withdrew to listen to the rest from the pantry. Hislordship had Mr Tyson pen an order for Carraciolo's execution at fiveo'clock that afternoon. Both Count Thurn, in Italian, translated by Sir William, then Sir William himself, counseled that the condemnedman should be allowed twenty-four hours in which to prepare his soul. Her ladyship remained unusually silent and his lordship would have none of it.

"He is to be hung from the yard arm of Minerva, the ship upon which he traitorously fired at the time I have directed. I will not hanga man on a Sunday, so it is best done this afternoon," he all but shouted in the high-pitched voice that showed his agitation.

Thereafter, he spoke in such a low-pitched voice that the words could not be heard through the partition, a sure sign he realized he must not shock his audience.

Mr Parsons was called in for a note to Lieutenant Parkinson then Tom and Thomas for separate notes to Captain Hardy and Sir Edward. When Thomas knocked on the door of Captain Hardy's cabin, it was to find him fully dressed with sword hanging from his side and bicorn hat in his hand. He read the note.

"Come, Spencer," he ordered.

On the quarterdeck, Sir Edward, with Tom still by him, had assembled the entire ship's company of marines. He gave an order to a junior lieutenant.

"Call in *Minerva's* boat."

Captain Hardy then spoke quietly to Thomas."Spencer, tell His Lordship all is ready."

He arrived at the door of the great cabin just as Lieutenant Parkinson had persuaded the marine sentry to admit him.

"I trust your prisoner is securely guarded, Mr Parkinson," was his lordship's greeting.

"He is, my lord. It is at his request that I am here to beg the mercy of not dying by hanging. He says even the French would have given him the honor of death by firing squad had he refused to command the rebels' ships."

"Had he gone to such an honorable death and not turned traitor, hewould not be facing death by hanging. He has been fairly tried by theofficers of his own country. I cannot interfere," his lordship replied severely.

"Could he not be given time with his priests to compose his soul?" persisted Parkinson.

"He will hang today, not on a Sunday. Go, sir, and attend to your duty!" his lordship shouted at Parkinson.

The abashed Lieutenant withdrew. "Thomas, what news from the deck?"His lordship's tone was milder.

"Captain Hardy advises that all is ready, m'lord," he replied sheepishly.

His lordship turned ruefully to Sir William and her ladyship with alopsided shrug. "Perhaps I was a little hard on the young fellow. Hanging a senior officer, even one of a foreign service, is a rare event. I do not begrudge him his humanity."

"I rejoice to hear you say so, my dear Nelson," responded Sir William, still uneasy.

"He will get over it, seeing you, my dear lord, do not hold it against him," her ladyship declared robustly.

A din arose outside, rising to a crescendo.

His lordship went up to the quarterdeck. The furious, thwarted mobof Neapolitans were railing against the marines. They had seen Caracciolo delivered, with a small guard of their number and a priest sent by Cardinal Ruffo, into the waiting boat for his final journey. His lordship, a lover of order, looked on contemptuously.

At the appointed hour, the entire crew of Foudroyant lined the deckand quarterdeck. The admiral's little crew were all ordered to be with him on the quarterdeck. All other ships in the defensive line were similarly manned. Only Sir William and her ladyship were left below. Topmen of the Minerva urged Caracciolo up the rigging to the foreyard. Once there, his hands were bound and the noose placed around his neck. He was guided along this horizontal timber towards its outer edge. Thomas stood behind Captain Hardy, who was separated from His Lordship by Sir Edward. He was flanked on his far side by the Reverend Comyn, who was silently reading from a prayer book.

Count Thurn had brought Minerva almost parallel with the center ofthe line. The small amount of offing needed for all the fleet to see made the moving figures on the frigate look like marionettes. Thomas knew they were all too real. A man to whom he believed himself beholden, for Mary's sake, was about to die at the order of a great commander he idolized. Never in his years of service had his emotions been so mixed.

Captain Hardy was not seeing marionette-like movements. He wasimpassively viewing the scene through his telescope.

"The noose rope is knotted to the yard, my lord," he called.

There was silence, and time seemed to be suspended for a long moment before a single cannon banged. Caracciolo was flying downward until the rope's full extent was reached. His body seemed to jerk upward a little, then swung and spun.

"A clean break of the neck, I believe, my lord," Hardy called out. Then, he snapped his telescope shut and spoke in an undertone."A good seaman, right he suffered no more."

Thomas wondered if anyone else had heard those words. A murmur had arisen all around once it was obvious Caracciolo's headhung at an unnatural angle.

His lordship's voice broke into a strange sound.

"He will be left to hang while it is yet daylight to show the fate of a traitor to his king."

Some men stared, others looked away, but no one wanted tocheer.

CHAPTER 17

THE MARRED TRIUMPH AND
A FRAUDULENT PAINTING

In the days following the trial and execution of Caracciolo, his lordship's decision to act swiftly seemed to be vindicated. The Reverend Comyn at church the following morning preached on "not knowing the day or the hour." Only felons or traitors received notice. Everyone else was better off living a virtuous life, in harmony with their fellow men. Loyalty to their King and those placed in authority under him made a man continually prepared to meet his maker. Thereafter, the crew were treated to the sight of Cardinal Ruffocoming aboard a second time. It was hard to view him as a Prince of the Roman Church in a belted coat and equally military-lookingbreeches. Only the round hat on his flowing, dark locks did not look military. He was far from looking the well-fed prelate one usually expected to see. He was an energetic, fit man in his early middle years.

His lordship and Sir William met him on coming aboard. it was only when they brought him into the great cabin that Thomas was required to take the round hat into safekeeping. The cardinal's observant dark eyes roamed around the cabin until her ladyship made her entrance. Then it was elaborate courtesy again. This was all in Italian and flowed at too great a speed for Thomas to understand. Only his lordship's interventions communicated that Ruffo had withdrawn his opposition to the forthcoming assault on Castel Sant' Elmo.

After he had gone, Tom and Thomas returned to clear away. Sir

William, on rising to have a later-than-usual afternoon nap, commented before he left.

"It does seem, my dear Nelson, that the swift justice you saw carried out yesterday has had a salutary effect. I will still not be easy until their majesties arrive."

"My dear Sir William, I assure you I shall tread especially carefully, as befits a foreigner to this land, until their majesties arrive."

The work to invest Castel Sant' Elmo closely went on at a greater rate with the extra manpower However, they would be disappointed by the week's end in the expectation that both their majesties were en route to join them.

It was another Saturday when the cutter sent off with Seahorse returned alone. The benefit of a following breeze saw her skimming to the seaward of Capri in the clear light of early morning. She heaved to a cable's length from *Foudroyant*, well before the noon bell. The fresh-faced lieutenant who was rowed across was soon stood before his lordship. He handed over letters from Captain Footeand Sir John Acton. Tom hovered, in case he was ordered to providerefreshment to the young officer in one of his lordship's quixotic gestures. However, the order, when it came, was far removed from that.

"Have Thomas ask Sir William and her ladyship to join me before dinner. Now, young man, how far behind you are *Seahorse* and *Sirena*?"

Tom had not stayed to hear the reply. When the lieutenant left the great cabin only a minute or two later, he looked pleased enough, sohis answer must have been accounted satisfactory. When Thomas joined Tom and they were busy organizing the small table for dinner. His lordship and both confidantes were in conversation across the cabin, grouped around the desk for Sir William to read the letters.

"What it amounts to, my dear Nelson, is that his majesty has no intention of allowing his wife to influence any decision he makes here. Sir John is left behind to ensure her majesty makes no decisions, other than purely household ones. I trust we shall find himapproving of all your actions."

"His majesty can scarcely complain, now that we have made such progress in emplacing cannon around Castel Sant' Elmo. I have taken eighty seamen off every ship of the line, in addition to most marines, to do so. Even the ships sent by Lord Keith with Commodore Duckworth have provided their quota. I imminently expect his promotion to Rear Admiral to be confirmed, in recognition of his capture of Minorca."

"Surely his promotion would remove him from your command?" queried Sir William.

"Not immediately. I would still be the senior Rear Admiral. Only when I detach him back to Lord Keith, will he be lost to my command," explained his lordship.

"Then, we shall have to hope you will not need to do that in a hurry, my dear Nelson. We still need to take Capua and Gaeta, once Castel Sant' Elmo surrenders."

"My dear Sir William, your grasp of strategy never ceases to amaze me. Capua, of course, is too far upstream on the River Volturno to readily return seamen to their ships. I shall take the precaution of sending Duckworth's marines and seamen only to Gaeta."

"How much longer do you expect to campaign, my dear Lord Nelson," asked her ladyship, looking very rosy cheeked as the day grew hotter.

"We shall have to cooperate with the Russians along the Roman and Tuscan shores. Field Marshal Suvorov's victory at Trebbia has prevented the French from sending any relieving force here. It is also compelling them to abandon Lombardy. We must keep faith with him in the hope he can drive them out of Piedmont and Genoa too. We may not necessarily sail north ourselves, my dear lady," his lordship hastily concluded.

"My duties require me to stay in this kingdom," Sir William hastened to add.

"Just so, Sir William. If the soon-to-be Rear Admiral Duckworth is lost to me, there is still the option of having Troubridge hoist his broad pennant again."

Thomas noticed the relief on her ladyship's face. He wondered if this might mean a return to Palermo. He, for one, would welcome that.

The poignancy of his speculation was brought home to him early in the evening of the following Tuesday. Two frigates, one flying the Neapolitan royal standard, ghosted into the anchorage in the late afternoon heat haze. They were followed by a number of larger ships showing little armament. Captain Foote was rowed across from *Seahorse* to report. The aftermath of this was that his lordship calledin all of his little crew to organize a great reshuffling of cabin allocations. His majesty would be taking up residence aboard in the morning. after settling what they were all to do, he casually referred Thomas to a letter for him from Mary.

All he could do at that stage was secret it on a shelf in the pantry. Itwas one space in which they would not have to work the rest of the daylight hours. The first problem, which involved the carpenter, was the partitioning of the great cabin. His Lordship's furnishings had to be moved and the three of them had to be served supper in Sir William's cabin. It had been decided he should remain where hewas, handy for monarch and admiral. Everyone in the little crew was uprooted. Tom and Thomas were bottom of the heap. Their only fortune in moving down a deck lay in *Foudroyant* being a new and clean ship.

Late at night, Thomas crept back to the pantry with a candle and recovered his letter. The privacy it afforded meant he could stand and read. He first looked at the inscription *Thomas Spencer*, in a large, childlike hand on the front of the folded sheet. He turned it over to pull the bottom third away from the blob of sealing wax. He opened it out and read.

"My Beloved Husband,

I know from what Captain Foote has told Mrs Cadogan that youare safe. I was very happy to heare his lordship did not beleave the French flete wood dare attacke his ships at Naples. Pleese do not get in the fyhting on land because you are very deare to me. It isonly days since you left, but I miss you grately. Pleese rite soon.

Yore loving wife, Mary"

He found he was blinking back a tear in his left eye. He knew how she struggled with writing. The care she had taken with forming her letters and coming so close to correct spelling showed how much she loved him. He felt very humble that the good Lord had directed the great gift of her love to him. He carefully folded her letter to place inside his shirt, next to his heart. Quietly, he made his way to his new berth with Tom. Reply would have to wait for some spare daylight moments. Hopefully, a vessel carrying messages back to Palermo would soon leave.

The next morning provided no hope of spare time. A first boat from the frigate *Sirena* brought some kind of chamberlain. He reviewed the accommodation being made available to his royal master and suite. The carpenter and his mates had worked wonders knocking upcabin partitions, but there was still a great deal of sniffing over the Spartan appearance of some enclosures. Eventually, with both Sir Edward and Captain Hardy in attendance, Sir William had to provide interpretation. Those in his majesty's suite who did not find theaccommodation offered to their satisfaction could no doubt remainon board *Sirena*. That seemed to quell argument. The chamberlain's return to the frigate brought the rapid descent of his majesty to a boat. He could be rowed across before the morning became too warm.

Receiving him with all due ceremony on the quarterdeck was the better for not being in the full heat of the day. The awning hislordship had required to be rigged for the monarch's greater comfort did channel the cooling breeze. King Ferdinand saw his standardrise above them with a look of appreciation. He greeted even the lesser members of his welcoming party like old friends. The process was brought to a sudden end by the outbreak of explosions fromhigh above the shore. These seemed to roll around the bay and thenbecome overlaid with fresh ones. His lordship hastened to explain.

"Your majesty, the bombardment of Castel Sant' Elmo has begun."

No interpretation was needed. His majesty mastered his initialshock to shade his eyes to look up toward the fortress and say, "Verygood," in accented English.Tthe occupants of the second and overloaded boat from *Sirena*, midway between the two ships, did notrecover so quickly. Garishly dressed courtiers stood and turned, thenlost equilibrium in the moving boat. It rocked furiously as their falling bodies destroyed the oarsmen's stroke.

Captain Hardy stepped forward and proffered his telescope to the king. He took it to seek a better view from the awning's shade of the effect of the bombardment. He was oblivious of the danger in which members of his suite had placed themselves. Hardy drew backalongside Sir Edward and muttered sideways.

"Will we be sorry if the gilded popinjays out there get a ducking?"

Tom and Thomas on the companionway, level only with the feet of the two captains, could afford to grin at each other. When the boat did arrive and the gilded popinjays were assembled to be taken to their quarters, amusement quickly turned to irritation. There wassquabbling over the allocation of cabins. Fortunately, the noise of thebombardment penetrated everywhere within the ship. The crest ofthe slope was over seven hundred feet higher than the shoreline.The lieutenant in chargeof allocations demonstrated his inability to hear and strode away.

It couldn't be said this afforded any respite for Tom and Thomas. His lordship had said they were to hurry back to attend to anyrequirements of his majesty, Sir William, her ladyship and himself. That, indeed, was the way of things for three long days. The bombardment of Castel Sant' Elmo seemed to continue beyonddaylight hours. The downdraft from the heights carried dense clouds of mixed dust and smoke over the old town and out onto the waters of the bay. It did nothing to disrupt the endless procession of boats bringing Neapolitan worthies to seek audience with their king.

That so many of them felt the need to do so no doubt had much to do with the disembarking from the larger ships. These had entered the bay behind the two frigates the day of arrival. The boats that left their sides were full of royal troops. It rapidly became clear, once squads of these had been landed and purposefully marched off into inhabited areas, that there was an air of retribution about them.Nothing more clearly demonstrated this than the visit of Cardinal Ruffo. He came aboard early with a few of his senior aides, this time dressed as a churchman. His majesty was quick to surround himself with his lordship and a number of other naval officers to receive the dissident, clerical commander of his irregular army. Sir William was summoned to ensure his lordship was kept abreast of thediscussion.

As Tom and Thomas served refreshment, there was no meeting of minds. From what Sir William was saying in a low-voiced translation, his majesty thanked the cardinal for all his exertions. Now that regular royal troops were being landed, the cardinal's irregular forces would be best employed moving northward to confine the French in Capua and Gaeta. The cardinal responded by protesting his loyalty and expressing the wish that his majesty would be merciful to all those who had been merely foolish. It was easily possible to identify and punish those who had actually risen in arms against their King and murdered their fellow citizens. King Ferdinand's reply was only to the effect that his courts were being reconstituted within the city. That on Procida, would deal with the prisoners already there. Suspects arrested by his troops would have the same chance to establish their innocence. There matters would have to be left while King Ferdinand saw other loyal subjects.

Harassed midshipmen had the task of taking names of boat occupants seeking to board for audience with their monarch. They had to be fended off until their turn was reached. The hubbub from those allowed on board to wait, made the waist a place to be avoided by any sensible sailor. Up on the quarterdeck, her ladyship had now joined the royal party, prompting another round of refreshments. Thomas heard her whisper more than once to her husband.

"They were speaking favorably of the French."

This about personages who had reached their turn and were swearing undying loyalty to their king. If his majesty suspected any of them, he wasn't showing any inclination to question them at this stage. One early visitor who did not come into this category was Egidio Pallio. He was thanked by His Majesty for his continued loyalty. A proportion of his Lazzaroni would be armed in support of the King's troops. They should identify Jacobins and collaborators with the French for interrogation at the *Castel di Carmini*. Eventually, dinner was called. King Ferdinand and his chamberlain had clearly had enough for one day. No more were allowed from their boats.

That still allowed no respite for Tom, Thomas, and others pressed into service. King Ferdinand expected his hosts to seat all of his considerable suite in the great cabin. His lordship and Sir William took the opportunity to impress on his majesty that the first day's arrangements for receiving his subjects had been unsatisfactory. They would have to be amended by his chamberlain taking responsibility for settling who should be allowed on board. The wine that flowed during dinner did not allow a good long siesta for all. The artillery bombardment up the steep hill rumbled incessantly. Respite for Thomas to begin his reply to Mary could not be gained.

His chance only came midway through the third day of bombardment. Commodore Troubridge, standing braced in a boat that appeared out of the smoke and dust, was up the ladder at speedonce his bowman had hooked on. The royal party was still in mid- levee under the quarterdeck awning. The commodore in full, dust- streaked uniform, with a smile on his face, brought the proceedingsto an abrupt halt when he came forward and spoke.

"Your majesty, my lord, I believe the capacity of the French garrison to hold out is broken. One of the mortars brought up fromthe bomb, *Perseus*, has broken their main water cistern. Water was heard gushing in a brief lull for want of cartridges."

Sir William was still translating for King Ferdinand when his lordship spoke.

"Have you a sufficiency of cartridges, round shot, and mortar shells to bombard ceaselessly for a few hours, Troubridge?"

"Most certainly, my lord. Captain Ball was seeing fresh supplies distributed."

"Very well, Troubridge, give them hard pounding and the most mortar shells you can. If their water is gone, anything that will burn brings surrender closer."

King Ferdinand gulped at this last direction from his lordship, even before Sir William translated what he thought he had heard. The contemplation of his hilltop fortress being returned to him as a blackened shell obviously didn't appeal.

In the absence of any comment from the Monarch, Troubridge shaded his eyes.

"I believe a signal would be visible from Captain Ball's position just now, my lord. It would save the time it will take me to regain the heights."

"An excellent suggestion, Troubridge. Sir Ed'ard, send for that signals midshipman."

It seemed only moments before Midshipman Parsons arrived, clutching his signal book. A signal for continuous firing was quickly bent on. Troubridge was not yet down the ladder to his boat when the pace of cannons banging increased. It was interspersed with the "whuumps" of mortars, followed by the cracks of their fused shells.

Dinner was late, but speedily over. Participants were eager to try and view the effects of the intensified bombardment. That gaveThomas his chance.

He used the pantry shelf and neatly wrote in the middle *"Mistress Mary Spencer."*

Turning over the stiff and coarse sheet of paper, when the ink was dry, he wrote:

"My beloved wife Mary,

It made me so happy to read your letter. Dozens of cannon are up the hill bombarding the fort there. The noise is terrible. Sometimes the smoke and dust roll down over the shore. We are safe here on board. There are two more forts to take after this one. His lordship may then decide to sail back to Palermo. The day we are together again cannot come too soon.

Your ever-loving husband, Thomas.

He was thankful he had learned his letters so well. He was blowing on the ink to dry it. After fastening the container, he would place it back in his lordship's stationery store.

His mind had just moved on to sealing when he heard from a shout.

"A white flag."

Now was a good time. As it turned out, he was not a moment too soon. The arrival of a sloop he could see through the stern lights was also attracting the attention of the quarterdeck. He heard anothercall.

"She brings orders."

He pressed the bottom third of the paper down onto the cooling blob of sealing wax. He replaced the red stick of wax in its place and rapidly left with his letter. The sloop's small boat was already in the water, with a lieutenant sitting in the stern sheets. When Thomas reached the deck, he obeyed his lordship's sign to attend him.

"I shall meet this Commander below, Thomas. He comes

fromLord Keith. You attend me below, while Tom remains with His Majesty's party."

In the recently partitioned remnant of the great cabin, his lordship had the commander sit. He had handed over the oilskin wallet in which Lord Keith's letter was contained. Breaking its seal, he immediately had a question.

"I see this is dated the twenty-seventh of June, off Minorca, soyour passage has taken seventeen days. Why was that so?"

"Sixteen days, my lord. I was handed the letter in the evening, so could not sail until the following morning. The winds were contrary throughout the voyage."

"No matter. I believe I must ask you to remain on standby for my reply to His Lordship. mMy steward will provide you with some refreshment in the wardroom."

He turned to Thomas.

"Have Lieutenant Parkinson and Midshipman Parsons summoned for me first."

It transpired they had been called to signal *Powerful*, requesting Commodore Duckworth to repair on board. Arriving back from the wardroom, Thomas was required to decant a bottle of his lordship's finest Sicilian wine to serve in goblets. The admiral went on deck to greet the commodore and present him to King Ferdinand. Thomas wondered what this portended. Would it give an opportunity for his letter to be carried to Mary? He would listen very carefully.

"His majesty looks very comfortable on your quarterdeck, my lord," said the guest.

"My dear commodore, I will shift him ashore at the earliest. Pour some wine, Thomas, before we die of thirst," his lordship quipped.

"So, the one in your servant's rig above is Tom, and this one is Thomas. How do you remember which is which, my lord?" asked the Commodore, apparently serious.

"Why, this is Thomas Spencer from Nottingham, while the other is Tom Allen, a family retainer from Norfolk," his lordship returned witha smile.

"Very smart rig," said the Commodore, looking Thomas up and

down in a not unfriendly way, "but isn't Nottingham a long way from the sea for a seaman?"

"Not for a man whose father is a tenant of Lord Howe's son-in-law," His Lordship answered for Thomas.

"Ha, the Curzon in Leicestershire, isn't he? Your health, my Lord," he added after Thomas had handed him a full goblet. His spoken English was refined, but this powerfully built man had any nothing of the fop about him. He was older than his lordship, but slower toreach flag rank.

"Remain within call, Thomas," his lordship ordered by way of dismissal.

"Now, my dear commodore, I need to advise you that only this morning I sent to Lord Spencer at the Board. I gave my belief that I was likely to be ordered to the defense of Minorca, before my task of restoring this kingdom was complete. I expressed the view I should be allowed to remain. Now, however, I have an order from Lord Keith, dated the twenty-seventh of June, saying he has lost contact with the combined fleet for three weeks. He requires me to send eight or nine of the line for the defense of Minorca. Lack of contact tells me they are skulking in a port!"

There was a moment's silence before the commodore responded in measured tone.

"Sixteen days for the message to reach you, my lord, says that the combined fleet will already have made its move or never will. If it has done so, I believe Lord Keith has the means to drive them off."

"Thank you for that assessment, my dear Duckworth. I did not believe my own reasoning along the same lines was faulty. I am reassured in my decision that I must advise Lord Keith of my inabilityto release ships until I have secured his Sicilian majesty's kingdoms. Rest assured, I shall take sole responsibility, in my reply to LordKeith for that decision. I cannot do otherwise, now I have increased the number of seamen taken from each ship to one hundred and twenty for the siege of Capua."

"I am sure you are right in that, my lord," Commodore Duckworth contributed thoughtfully, "but is it enough to send merely a baldwritten reply to Lord Keith with the lieutenant who commands *Bulldog?*"

"I see what you mean, my dear Duckworth," His Lordship came back after only a few moments thought. "A messenger of the seniority to explain why I can do no other until Capua and Gaeta alsofall would be better. I have it; Sir Ed'ard Berry can go, seeing CaptainHardy is available. I shall, of course, release you with ships forMinorca once we have all His Majesty's domains, just as I must release Captain Ball for Malta, now that his appointment as Governor has been confirmed. Perhaps your overdue promotion has also been confirmed and is waiting for you."

"I shall believe it when I see it, my Lord, my second name being Thomas, but I do believe Sir Edward will serve very well as your messenger in person."

Well that was it, thought Thomas. There was no chance of Bulldog going anywhere near Palermo. Sir Edward would come chasing back here once his mission to Lord Keith was fulfilled. He ceased listening, thinking about the number of days it would take the regular Neapolitan sloop to beat back from Palermo. It would cost him a silver coin to send his letter to Mary on that vessel, if he thought the man was reliable.

In the days he waited after Bulldog had sailed at the spanking pace her Commander felt was necessary to impress his distinguished passenger. The lack of noise from both the bay and around Castel Sant' Elmo meant that the roar of the crowd at *Piazza del Mercato* was always audible when it came. All the fleet knew thatmultiple gallows had been erected there. From his place of levee under *Foudroyant's* quarterdeck awning, King Ferdinand had established ashore a provisional *Giunta.* Sir William was careful to spell the word, although the naval officers just called it the *Junta.*

The small group of nobles and royal officers who composed thisbody were both the King's ministers and his judges. They seemed to divide into smaller groups for interrogating prisoners in the *Castel di Carmini.* The sight of tumbrels rolling from that direction out of sight into the *piazza* began to be distressing. The victims were no longer those who had risen in arms against their king and garrisoned

Nuovoand Uovo or manned vessels of the republican navy. They were elderly men and wailing women.

Little happened in the anchorage to distract crews left on board theships. Captain Foote's flotilla and the country frigates had gone tothe sieges. Likewise the troopships for the mouth of the Volturno andGaeta. The seamen and marines who had ransacked Castel Sant' Elmo for movable cannon, after the surrender, had departed down the far side of the plateau for Capua. The word was that the interrogating groups of the *Junta* did not operate as proper courtsand had no consistency. Some who were strongly thought to have taken up arms for the Republic were seen to swagger away from the *Castel di Carmini*. They simply informed on others, who the royal troops then arrested. Others survived by paying large bribes to *Junta*members.

Thomas had seen enough when the chamberlain started controlling the flow of supplicants to their king. Those with the deepest pockets were the ones who reached the quarterdeck to bowand scrape. A good many on *Foudroyant* had shaken their heads in despair or exchanged angry looks. Loaded purses were passed up the ladder to disappear in the chamberlain's coat pockets.

The day came when a *polacca* arrived from Palermo to indicate that all was well there. Her majesty was already planning a great celebration of the kingdom's complete restoration. The vessel was tocarry back word of General Mejean's surrender and the other two sieges. Thomas waylaid the mate, who came on board with the master to deliver letters. He wrote *"Palazzo Palagonia, Via Quattro Aprile, Palermo,"* under Mary's name and pointed to the address. *"Conoscete?"*

The man squinted at the address, then looked Thomas square in the eye, and said, *"Si."*

In a way, Thomas was reassured that the dark eyes told him the sailor saw the prospect of money. He pulled out a silver coin and held it up while holding out the letter.

"Prendere?"

The mate took the proffered letter.

"Si, sono content."

Thomas handed over the coin, saying, *"Mille grazie."* Swarthy and scruffy, the mate was, but he looked trustworthy, and he knew Mary would treat him reasonably.

A couple of days after this, the strangest incident of the entire period in the bay occurred. It started with a hail from a Neapolitan fisherman, just after dawn. He coasted into harbor close by *Foudroyant's* stern anchor cable. The watch on deck struggled to make sense of what he was calling. One of King Ferdinand's courtiers, who had slept badly and come on deck, became very excited. He managed to convince the officer of the watch that the corpse of the executed Caracciolo was floating upright toward the harbor. Captain Hardy was called, then his lordship. He had Thomas attend on Sir William, so he could confer with his majesty.

While Thomas laid out the old gentleman's clothes, he expressed a surprising view.

"I fear this may be a portent, young Thomas. Many will say retribution on the rebels has been so swift and hard because the English have done it, and this is God's reply."

Thomas did not trust himself to make any reply. Everyone knew his lordship had encouraged King Ferdinand to take firm and swift action against the rebels. What was happening ashore was not a topic of conversation, even on the infrequent visits on board of Commodore Troubridge. He always looked askance at the activity under the quarterdeck awning, but said nothing. Thomas stropped the razor.

"Are not the decisions being made by his majesty, Sir William?" he ventured.

"That is so, but consider where he is sitting to order the retribution," the elderly knight wheezed, now in his shirt and breeches, and plumped down in a chair for Thomas to lather his face and shave him.

Thomas concentrated on the task in hand, despite hearing sounds of running feet. Unmistakable sounds of capstans being emplaced followed. When he reached the point of seeing Sir William into his coat, they could hear the loud "clacks" of the pawls.

"Do my ears deceive me, young man, or is his lordship about to make sail?"

"From the sound of it, we will be under sail within minutes, Sir William."

"Then, we must haste to his majesty."

The wisdom of this was proven when the monarch was found to be ready to go on deck and approved of His Lordship's decision to take the ship to the claimed sighting. Very few sails were needed to give steerage in the calm conditions. Little offing had been gained when a freak of the current was seen to be bringing a shrouded, upright figure. Directly toward the starboard side of the ship it came.

Deathly pale, King Ferdinand seemed to have his feet involuntarily drawn toward the rail. Her ladyship had come on deck to stand next to his lordship. Sir William, had arrived separately with Thomas and promptly made forward to the King's shoulder. He spoke to him in clear and relatively slow Italian. At this, the king's demeanor changed completely. He turned and faced Sir William, much heartened, and spoke with the elderly knight. Thomas caught her ladyship's belated translation to Nelson.

"My husband said Caracciolo was unable to rest until he had implored His Majesty's pardon. His majesty replied that perhaps a Christian burial was appropriate."

"Thank you, my dear lady. I shall carry out his wishes. Captain Hardy, a word."

The captain hurried over from where he had been muttering to Lieutenant Parkinson.

"Would you please have a boat lowered, Hardy, and have the corpse towed ashore? Santa Lucia is nearest and will not inflame opinion within the city. Have Lieutenant Parkinson take the boat. He can care for Caracciolo in death the way he did for him in some of the final hours of his life."

There was an interesting sequel to the execution of this order. When Lieutenant Parkinson returned, he brought with him in the longboat an elderly priest. He had come on behalf of the church of *Santa Maria La Catena*, where the priest in charge of the parish was willing to provide a final resting place for Caracciolo. This other priest had been selected for the visit to king and admiral because he was bilingual, being an Irishman. The offer was well received by the king. The priest needed to be rowed back to shore and gave strange thanks to his lordship for ordering this.

"I bless your lordship for this act and wish your ships Godspeed to capture Rome."

"I was not aware the Tiber is navigable so far upstream for vessels of this size," his lordship responded, smiling.

"The Lord works in mysterious ways his wonders to perform," the priest added.

"Fare you well, my lord."

After this strange day, Thomas found himself involved in another outcome, only revealed to him when he was summoned to herladyship's cabin.

"I have an important errand for you, Thomas Spencer. Prince Castelcicala tells me that a painter called Cercone is anxious to paint the scene on the quarterdeck when the corpse floated toward us. He will be coming on board tomorrow to make sketches. I wish you to give him this letter."

"Yes, m'lady," he responded, feeling uneasy. Even with a breeze flowing through the cabin, she looked hot. He thought this made her look plumper than when she was cooler and standing.

"You will be glad to return to Mary," her ladyship added, sensinghis unease.

"Oh yes, m'lady," he swiftly averred.

"I doubt we shall remain here more than another week. The sooner Signor Cercone is organized for his work, the better."

His heart silently sang so fervently he really didn't care what shewas plotting.

Cercone, when he arrived, was an odd, darting, little man, with bigears and eyes. He had small hands, badly stained by paint dyes. He carried several large sheets of course, off-white paper and sticks of charcoal. He wanted to do standing sketches of King Ferdinand, Sir William and his lordship. It was when he made a similar request in respect of her ladyship, who had kept to her cabin, that Thomas managed to slip him the letter. He noted the obviously feminine hand then slipped the letter inside his coat. Via Sir William came theindication he would first sketch a view of *Foudroyant's* quarterdeck. Thomas was left to take him to a good viewing point.

Thomas showed him the view from the starboard side gangway. For each person named, he gave the approximate position, then the distance away in the sea the corpse had been. The painter wasn't interested in sketching Captain Hardy and Lieutenant Parkinson,once Thomas showed him they were nearest the stern. He took out her ladyship's letter and read it.

"*Si, la Baronessa vuole ...*"

He outlined with his hands the body shape of a slender woman, before trying English words.

"Go to Baronessa?"

Thomas led him to the cabin, knocked, and announced the visitor. Her ladyship was seated, but cooler than the previous day andwearing a loose, flowing gown. She gestured Cercone to a chair opposite her before she spoke.

"You may leave us, Thomas, but please remain within call."

When he was called, it was to show the artist back to the deck and hail a boat for him. He now had a head and neck sketch of Her Ladyship on top of the others and was weighing in one hand a drawstring purse. When he saw Thomas eyeing that, he laughed.

"Per la storia, Tomaso,"

The days drew on to the anniversary of the Nile. there was still no sign of King Ferdinand going ashore. His lordship's own correspondence had intensified after receiving another order from Lord Keith. It took ten days to reach him and said the combined fleet had left Cartagena, bound for the Atlantic, and he would give pursuit.It was imperative his lordship or Duckworth take an adequate force, which meant nearly all of those in Neapolitan waters, to protect Minorca. Another consultation with Commodore Duckworth followed,but this time, he had left in *Powerful*, taking with him *Majestic*,*Vanguard* and the corvette, *Swallow*. Where *Bulldog* had got to, no one knew, but she had clearly not reached Lord Keith by the ninth of July and would struggle to catch up. Letters to Lord Keith, Lord Spencer, and the Secretary to the Admiralty followed thick and fast. The officers of the stationary flagship planned a Nile anniversary dinner in the wardroom, with his lordship as guest of honor. The day came, and it got off to a very good start with the benefit of fresh produce and wine from ashore.

His Lordship was quiet while others gave their reminiscences. He seemed somehow expectant. He smiled and drank a little wine when a call from the deck was heard.

"Culloden, away."

Once Commodore Troubridge was announced, and space was hurriedly made for him to be seated, he walked in and remained, standing to report.

"My Lord, they have both surrendered."

"Pray do be seated, my dear Troubridge, at the invitation of the President of this mess, of course. Well, gentlemen, I do believe his majesty will now request that we convey him home to Palermo."

CHAPTER 18

SICILIAN CELEBRATIONS CLOAK A DECEPTION

For his return voyage, King Ferdinand was content to sail in *Foudroyant*, his comfortable home on the water for nearly a month. By the time he was ready to depart, it was Monday, the fifth of August. It had no kind of religious significance that the flagship and consorts did not sail on a Sunday. The king declined to go ashore, even for a service of thanksgiving in his cathedral. In truth, therespite was useful for his lordship. He ensured the squadron Commodore Troubridge would lead in Culloden was well-found in crews and all supplies.

Moreover, he was once again acting Commander-in-Chief, Mediterranean, with all the correspondence cares that accompanied the role. Dispersal of the fleet began with the sieges of Capua and Gaeta. Detachments to Minorca and Malta continued the process. He divided the rest between Troubridge's squadron, a continued presence in the bay and his reserve force returning to Palermo.

The three ships with Sir Sydney Smith were impossible to controlat such a distance. Nevertheless, communication had to besustained, however slow. Then, there were the allies, Kadir Bey and his Turks, Admiral Ouschakoff and his Russian squadron, and the Portuguese ships of the Marquis de Niza. Even with the Austrians, who kept their naval forces in the northern Adriatic, communication was needed. With those who were closer, considerable tact had tobe employed. That included *La Marina Militare,* as the navy of King Ferdinand was called. His lordship might be the effective Commander-in-Chief of that force, but he still needed to exercise tactin the requests he made. Some of these ships whom were to accompany Troubridge, while the frigates *Sirena* and *Aretusa* were sent to join the blockade of Valletta.

The moderate breezes that accompanied *Foudroyant's* flotilla south helped them all cope with the summer heat until landfall the final morning. A swift sailing *polacca* had gone ahead the previous day. They knew their arrival was anticipated but were still surprised

by their welcome on reaching La Cala in the midday heat. A carriagebearing queen and royal children was waiting on the mole. Also highly visible the short distance away on the shore opposite *Porta Felice* was a mocked-up landing stage, finished in stucco and gilded.The Roman pretensions of this structure were emphasized by the Senators of Palermo. They were grouped on it and dressed in togas.Those who had nothing to shade their heads would be uncomfortable waiting for their monarch to come ashore. Her majesty and children came aboard immediately *Foudroyant's* rope fenders had ground against the mole, and a gangway had been swayed out.

Tom, Thomas, and numerous helpers had only a brief time to look at the welcome that waited ashore. Most of the morning was taken up by arranging the newly reunified great cabin for a royal dinner. Sir William had grumbled to Thomas over his toilette about the expense his lordship was bearing. It was well known in the ship that MrSherwin, the purser, was wringing his hands. The expense of the month-long stay of his majesty and suite on board was calculated. His lordship had absolutely refused to allow the monarch to make payment for this, with no certainty that the Admiralty would reimburse him. It was due to get worse. Every presentable chair on board had been required to be grouped around the pushed-together tables, covered by all his lordship's table linen and that her ladyship had brought on board. Young Prince Leopold, who hero worshipped his lordship, had to be seated next to him. The king did not mind having his eldest son one side and a younger daughter the other. It placed his wife at one removed from him, so he could not be readily questioned about his time at Naples.

His Lordship worked hard at being the gracious host, and Tom was parsimonious with *his* wine to ensure he continued in sparkling form. Sir William manfully did his share as Minister. The cr food was of the highest quality the ship's cooks ever achieved. Hosts and principal guests were well pleased with the occasion. Captain Hardy wasbeing particularly gracious to members of King Ferdinand's suite. Thomas suspected the imminence of getting them off his ship was the cause. They were the only ones to be leaving. His lordship had already announced that he and his little crew would be returning to *Palazzo Palagonia* for a week or two.

However, unlike himself, the little crew would be participating in restoring the great cabin after the diners had departed.Thanks to the additional helpers for the dinner, Tom and Thomas made rapid progress. Mr Tyson looked on in a kind of supervisory capacity. He did spend much of the time with his hands over his ears. *Foudroyant's* upper gun deck fired a twenty-one gun salute, answered by every fort set in the city walls. The seaward-facing fortsmounted very large cannon and the cartridges used for blank firing were of commensurate size. The noise over and the work nearly done, Captain Hardy reappeared, still in his dress uniform. His gaze roved around the great cabin, and Thomas realized he was notdispleased with the progress. Mr Tyson had shaken at thesuccessive explosions. His nose twitched at the smell, to the captain's amusement.

"Well, Mr Tyson, I dare say that after such a prodigious expense of powder, you will be wanting to march these men up to the shore base."

"Only when the work is finished to your satisfaction, Sir."

"These others can finish what little is left, so you may as well go. The gun smoke should be dispersing nicely now," the captain declared, still looking amused.

The prospect of having the ship restored had put him in a benign frame of mind. Tom and Thomas speedily knuckled their foreheads and departed, just ahead of Mr Tyson.

The gun smoke had merely drifted on the slight breeze and fetched up against the city wall. The mocked-up landing stage was both deserted and enveloped.

"I imagine they all took to their carriages to follow the royal party tothe cathedral for the service of thanksgiving," Mr Tyson managed, despite choking and coughing.

But, without the advantage of their carriage horses trotting away atthe start of the gunfire, as the royal party did, thought Thomas. The togas of the laggards would be stinking of gunpowder when they entered the cathedral. Tom winked at him, and they allowed Mr Tyson to rush past them through *Porta Felice.* If anything, the powder smoke was initially worse, thanks to the cannon discharged on each side of the gate towers. Fortunately, it hadn't reached *Piazza Marina,* so the final approach to the *palazzo* had air that was no more noxious than normal. Thomas was more than eager to match Mr Tyson's pace toward the *palazzo's* entrance arch. Reaching it first by a short head, Mr Tyson spoke.

"Good day, Mistress Spencer."

Thomas felt his heart give a leap as Mary rose unhurriedly fromthe stone step on which she'd been sitting in the shade. Her eyeshad taken in Thomas, but she still replied to Mr Tyson first.

"Good day, Mr Tyson. Mrs Cadogan asks me to tell you there iscorrespondence come for his lordship. She has left it all in his study."

"Do I take that to mean more than one vessel has called in to leave mail?" he asked.

"Most certainly. They run from the left in order of arrival. The port from which they have come has also been noted by each," Mary answered primly.

"I had better familiarize myself with what is there,"

Mr Tyson bounded away up the staircase. Tom winked at Thomas again, bowed to Mary, cheekily blew her a kiss, and walked offtoward the kitchen.

At last, Thomas had his arms around Mary and pulled her toward him. There was a slightly mischievous look in her eyes as she lifted them the short distance to meet his. It was only at that point he realized her breasts were scarcely touching his chest, and theirthighs weren't touching at all. There was a protruding, but strangely yielding, feel to her belly. He scarcely knew what to think.

"My love, you're ... you're not with child after all, are you?" he whispered hoarsely.

"Of course not, silly Thomas," she scolded quietly.

"This is only a cushion sewn under my dress. Her ladyship wrote toher mother asking for this to be done before she came home again."

"That is not all she has done," he confided seriously and went on ina low voice to tell her all he had seen and heard on the proposed painting by Cercone.

"So, she will be slender in the eyes of history, but only in this painting. There will be too many descriptions of her to the contrary for anyone to believe it," Mary chortled.

"What are we doing standing here when we could be in our room and this no longer between us?" she then slyly whispered.

He needed no further exhortation to dash up the stairs with herand along the corridor to their own room. No sooner had he shut the door behind him than she had his belt buckle undone. She then set about his breeches. When she had them around his ankles, she undid the top buttons of her dress and pulled it over her head to reveal she was wearing nothing underneath. She watched him comeerect as he cupped her breasts.

"Now, that is truly a sight for sore eyes," she whispered, standing on her toes to playfully nibble his earlobe.

"I do believe your titties are a shade bigger than I remember. Your face is fuller too."

"Mrs Cadogan's doing, I fear. She said I couldn't look like I should be eating for two, if I wasn't actually doing so. She's been feeding me royally."

At that, he felt he would burst if he waited any longer. He pushed her back into the edge of the bed, then promptly tripped. He fell on top of her, but they neither felt any hurt, nor removed any more of his clothing. Not before he had exploded inside her and they were both sated.

"Dare we lie here any longer when we don't know how long they will be in the cathedral?" he asked, shoes and shirt now gone.

"They will be there a while yet, and the queen will insist they go to the *Colli* before they return home," she soothed, rubbing the hairs onhis chest, "and I do not wish to put that hot thing back on until I have to."

With her flame-colored hair framing her face so close to his, there was almost a sense of a little girl pleading. The playful look in her wide eyes spoke of her having something else in mind than just staying out of the padded dress.

"You will get just as hot without it," he joked in a more lighthearted way than was usual for him. He began to kiss her tenderly, working down from her lips.

The city had gone stiller than usual in the early evening. Theexuberance of the day had worn out its inhabitants. They heard the hooves of the team of horses and the rumble and grind of the coach wheels from afar. Refreshed with tepid water from their bowl and neatly dressed, they joined Mrs Cadogan, Mr Tyson, and Tom at the foot of the stone staircase. The coachman steered the team through the arch at a wide enough angle to give the coach clearance. Mrs Cadogan had looked at them quizzically when Thomas had been handing Mary down the steps. Her black and white clothing looked severe, but her few words weren't.

"Here we all are, present and correct."

They stood expectantly in a line, while the coachman haltedand gentled the team. He climbed down to open the half-height door. His perspiring lordship stepped down first, then offered his left hand to her ladyship, who was clearly very hot and tired. Her mother went forward and embraced her, looking up into her daughter's eyes with concern. This seemed to impart some strength to the lady, whobriefly looked Mary up and down and seemed satisfied. Sir William stood briefly on the step of the coach, looked at the tableau just below him, and smiled.

"How good it is for the weary travelers to be welcomed home at last."

In truth, he looked the least weary of the three and stepped down unaided. Mr Tyson moved hesitantly to his lordship's shoulder and spoke with a regretful urgency.

"My lord, there is considerable correspondence waiting."

"For someone who is left to act the Commander-in-Chief on his station, there is always considerable correspondence. From where away?" His lordship concluded by asking.

"From virtually every quarter, including their lordships," the Secretary summarized.

"Well, it will not do to fail to read their lordships' instructions, or anything else for that matter!

Would you join me, Sir William, once I have given all a first reading? Tom, bring up some wine, and prepare some coffee for later. Thomas, assist Sir William in any way required, and stand by for my call."

He turned to the listening females.

"Pardon our excessive attention to duty, my dear lady. I fear you are too weary to be kept here."

"My dear Lord Nelson, the sight of home and my dear mother is reviving me. Please do not concern yourself for my comfort. My mother and Mary will see to that."

She turned for the staircase, Mrs Cadogan and Mary dutifully following. The males courteously allowed them to proceed first. Sir William was next to go.

"I find the cool and quiet of the night the best time to read and writein the heat of high summer, my dear Nelson. I shall rest a little and await your call."

The admiration of the elderly knight's listeners for his ability to recover from the heat of the day only increased later that evening when Thomas brought him into the study.

"My dear Sir William, here is a happy piece of news to start with. Duckworth's promotion was waiting for him back at Port Mahon.Pour some wine, Tom, so we may all toast the good fellow's promotion and the success of the first commission under his flag. Then you may leave Sir William and myself for discussion before we start on some replies."

This was clearly going to be one of his lordship's quixotic gestures. Five glasses were duly charged, and they all echoed the toast,"Admiral Duckworth: Success to his first commission." Thomas did this with sincerity. He had formed a high opinion of the newly promoted rear admiral.

Then, out they trooped, staying close to await the call back. Tom made a trip to the kitchen to ensure the coffee was simmering, ready for serving when the call came. It was upwards of half an hour before they were called back in. Sir William was still seated comfortably, so Tom went straightaway to bring the coffee pot and cups for the two of them. His lordship indicated what he now wished to do.

"We shall do two tonight, my dear Tyson. Ready the seals, Thomas."

The first was to Admiral Duckworth with heartiest congratulations and requesting him to nominate his successor for the naval defense of Minorca. His lordship also requested to be informed of his proposed date of departure. The second was to Sir Sydney Smith, thanking him for details of the intended Turkish invasion of Egypt, now that General Buonaparte had retreated. It enjoined Sir Sydney not to hazard any of His Majesty's ships in support of the Turks.

This set the pattern of work in that high summer period. Celebrations were given added impetus a couple of days later, whenher ladyship returned late in the afternoon from one of her tête-à- têtes with the queen. She was in a state of high excitement. His lordship and Sir William had just started reading newly arrived mail and she was oblivious to Mr Tyson and Thomas being there.

"Wonderful tidings for you, my dear Lord Nelson, given me by her majesty. His majesty is not only presenting you with a great Sicilian estate from crown lands but also the title of duke. You are to beDuke of Bronte. He has received the consent of our own gracious king to confer this title on you."

"I dare say it is some compensation for my victory of the Nile only providing a barony, while Duncan's victory at Camperdown gained him an earldom,"

He realized he should not be voicing those thoughts with Thomas and Mr Tyson present.

"You may both leave us to discussion and return later."

They looked at each other once through the door, and young Mr

Tyson had a thoughtful look on his long face. On this occasion, he felt able to mutter an order.

"Give them half an hour and then meet me back here."

Thomas went to the small sewing room, where he knew Mary was working yet again on some of her ladyship's gowns to ensure they masked her thickening belly. He found her sitting with a section of gown in her left hand, needle and thread in her right and a mouthful of pins.

"Her ladyship is back, saying King Ferdinand has made his lordship a Sicilian duke. He will be called Duke of Bronte."

Mary's face was a picture. She had been hot before he came in with his news, but now she frowned and became more red in the face. She bent to lay the gown neatly on the floor after securely inserting the needle into the fabric. With hands free, she carefully removed the pins from her mouth.

"You will have to pardon me if I do not cheer, my love. It merely slows my work."

"He is being given a landed estate out of Crown lands with it," Thomas tried again.

"Which I suppose is at this Bronte place. Well, it may be more pomp than substance."

Thomas must have showed on his face the shock at her very cool reception of the news. Mary's next words were spoken in a much kinder tone.

"No doubt it is a cause for celebration, but remember that I know the ways of this court. It will be land taken from some other owner and neglected for years. Now, let me get back to making sure his paramour's condition remains hidden."

"They have sent out Mr Tyson and myself. He says to give them half an hour."

"There is nothing we can do with what remains of that," Mary declared, "so let me finish my work here, and you can tell me more later."

"Do not tread on the gown," she shrilled as he stepped forward to bend and kiss her.

He filled in time going down to the kitchen for a drink. Tom had been summoned to the study with wine for *Tria Juncta in Uno* to celebrate, so he was in on the 'secret.'

"Durss we call 'im m'lord or y'r grace?" he asked Thomas with a grin.

"Stick to what we know until we ask Sir William," said Thomas, returning the grin.

Then he was on his way back up the steps to rendezvous with Mr Tyson. When they knocked and went in, his lordship was just concluding the discussion.

"So, you believe your man Graeffer would consent to be my land agent, my dear Sir William, despite the summer heat on this island?" "It is really no worse in a normal summer than Naples. In fact, being inland and on higher ground, it will be a drier, more bearable heat than here. It is the damp heat just now that is prostrating my dear lady and yourself."

"Now that you mention my prostration, my dear husband, I believeI should wish both you noble gentlemen good night and leave you to your correspondence. My chamber has been shuttered all day and should be cooler this evening."

Her ladyship rose slowly as though her joints were stiff.Thomas held open the door for her, after she had received appropriate wishes for a more comfortable night. It was her growing bulk and weight that made her movement difficult in the heat. It had been hot in Naples last September!

When she had gone, his lordship turned to Mr Tyson.

"I fear I must rely on you completely tonight, John. I am unable to see well by candlelight in this heat. First, we must advise my fellow Rear Admiral in Port Mahon that I am sending Captain Hardy in *Foudroyant* to Malta. I hope there is something he can do to assist in the siege of Valletta. While dear Duckworth is still there, he must be kept informed of my dispositions."

So it went on, religious feast days and celebrations of the kingdom being reunited by the heat of the day. A mid-afternoon respite, then work in the evening. Mary's view, in the privacy of their bed, mirrored that of Thomas. Her ladyship had coped perfectly well with the heat of the previous summer and the one before that. Childbearing and her age made her unable to cope.

The next day but one after the private glad tidings, a visitor arrived by sea from the direction of Messina. He was in a well-worn naval Lieutenant's uniform His Lordship had seen the sloop tack into the bay and sent for Tom and Thomas. Although it looked ungainly with glass raised by left hand to right eye, the hold was steady enough.

"That is one of the smaller vessels with Sir Sydney Smith and very well handled. See how she has a boat in the water within seconds of heaving to."

While the boat was drawing closer, he rested his arm and then played the glass again. "Why is that officer in the stern sheets not wearing a Commander's epaulette? I do believe it is young Drake returned from the east. Show that young man straight in when he arrives, Tom. Thomas, find Mr Tyson, and bring him here."

They both realized he meant *Goliath's* fourth lieutenant. He hadbeen sent overland from Aleppo to Basra on the way to India afterthe Nile. It struck Thomas that the secretary may not have met thislieutenant before he took ship from Alexandria to Aleppo. Nor was hesure their master had quite remembered the name fully. He seemed to recall it was Drake-something else. The main thing was to give Mr Tyson a quick explanation of who his lordship believed had returned. "Thank you, Thomas," that earnest young man said gravely as they reached the door.

"Thomas, it would be helpful if Sir William could spare the time to join us," his lordship called through the open door.

The sun-darkened, alert young man brought to the top of the steps by Tom had a confident, ready smile. By the time Thomas returned with Sir William, the smell of coffee wafted from the study door, and his lordship was speaking in an excited tone.

"So, it is good-bye to Mr Buonaparte's grand design, however his troops fare against the Turks. Ha, Sir William, it is good of you to joinus to hear excellent news."

Afterward, he helped Mr Tyson seal the various letters. There was a report to their lordships of the admiralty, dictated after interview with the lieutenant and reading the report he'd brought from SirSydney Smith. The young man had been at sea for over threeweeks, coming from Sir Sydney's forward base at El Arish. This was at the eastern end of the Egyptian coast, but perfectly safe. The rate at which French soldiers had died from disease during the siege of Acre and the retreat meant that General Buonaparte could only hold the valley of the Nile. The surviving Mamelukes were raising revolt against him in the south. A Turkish army was about to land atAboukir to attack his forces in the north.

Moreover, his lordship was commending the lieutenant as "a very clever young man," thanks to the success of his mission to Bombay. It had started just over a year ago with the benefit of documents captured at the Nile. Thomas recalled his lordship's agitation atfinding there had been secret correspondence between General Buonaparte and some Indian ruler with the name Tippoo. Mr Tyson, encouraged by Thomas mentioning his recollection of this, describedhow word had been sent from Bombay to both Calcutta and Madras. Tippoo, who was Sultan in a place called Mysore, intended to raise arevolt against the rule of the East India Company in southern India. Lord Mornington, who was the company's Governor, had authorized prompt military expeditions to deal with the threat. He had been able to negotiate the support of another powerful Indian ruler, the Nizamof Hyderabad. Lord Mornington's younger brother, Colonel Arthur Wellesley, started organizing the force in Madras with great energy. Mysore was a long way inland from Madras, but the force set out early. Tippoo's lands would be reached at about the same time asthe Bombay and Hyderabad columns. The attacks from northwest, north, and east were sure to eliminate Tippoo as a French ally.

If Thomas's head was spinning with the effort of absorbing these strategic consequences of that night in Aboukir Bay, the festivities of the following fortnight wore him to a frazzle. The same could also be said for Mary. She was altering one gown after another for herladyship. She had to attend festivities without comment on her distending belly. Mary had already been required to extend the padding to the front of her own dress. This made it more cumbersome and hard to wear. They neared the end of the celebrations organized by Queen Maria Carolina.

The final event planned was a midnight *fete champetre* for the evening of Tuesday, the third of September, in the grounds of the nearly completed *Palazzina Cinese*. Tom and Thomas were required to ride the rear of the coach so Tom could attend His Lordship and Sir William during the evening. Thomas was to remain with the coachman to ensure all was kept secure. The night before, Mary lay naked under a thin and nearly transparent cover when Thomas entered their chamber, after evening correspondence was done. She had spent most of the day on a final fitting of her ladyship's gown for the event.

"Will it ever be cool again?" she asked sleepily as his candle illuminated the bed.

"Perhaps when the seasons change, my love."

He seated the candle carefully on a chest while he stripped off shoes, breeches, and shirt. Placing them neatly in a pile, he blew out the candle and got into bed.

"You looked so very tired when I came in," he said, sliding his hand over her flat belly and down to the top of her triangle of hair in a light caressing movement.

"It was more the whims and fancies that tired me than the work," she whispered responsively, turning her head toward him.

"I don't know how you keep face with her for so long each day."

She turned on her side, slid a leg across his thighs, and pressed a hand on his chest.

"Oh, it is not difficult when I see her naked and reflect how gross she has become. My body remains firm and smooth. No, stay on your back; I am on top tonight."

With that, she heaved herself upon his torso so her breasts hung over him and her erect nipples brushed his face. His mouth reached for each of them in turn, then she speared herself on him. They climaxed together and she breathed out long and hard.

"That for her high and mighty ladyship."

Reluctant though he was to be away from their bed the next evening, he could not describe himself as unable to enjoy the occasion. He just wished Mary could have been present to see the fireworks display. It was supposed to depict the blowing up of *L'Orient* and illuminated the lightweight "Temple of Fame." The great crowd of invited guests thronged into this. He didn't know whetherthe goddess blowing a trumpet above the portal was male or female.There was no chance to move closer with the amount of gentling the team of horses needed. The other trumpets that blew to a warlike crescendo didn't help either. They began to calm while the bands played "See the conquering hero ..." more or less in time with each other. Storms of applause gave way to the babble of conversation that accompanied serious drinking. All the officers of his lordship's vessels had been invited. A good proportion of those from *La Marina Militare* and the Portuguese, Russian, and Turkish allies were there too.

The point was reached at which Thomas and the Sicilian coachman had nothing to do. Eating had overtaken the volume of conversation. A line of his majesty's foot guards stood with groundedmuskets between the drawn-up coaches and carriages and the scene of the entertainment.

Very smartly they were turned out, too, thought Thomas, looking at their silhouettes in the illumination blazing from the "Temple of Fame."

Some time after the babble had grown in volume again, Thomas noticed a group of young men huddled together. They engaged in some kind of discussion, punctuated by furtive glances at the soldiers. It did cross his mind they were up to no good, but he wasn'tsure who they were at a distance. The group began to break up, andthere appeared to be hesitation, but then one drew a dirk and faced the foot guards, followed by another and another. Soon, there was a short line of them in their best uniforms with dirks drawn. Theystarted to scream a drink-fuelled challenge and lumbered into a run.

Thomas realized the charge was by Foudroyant's entire midshipmen's berth. He watched in horror. The Sicilian coachman reacted fast and ran to the heads of the lead pair of horses. Thomas realized he had better go to the heads of the second pair.

The foot guards drew their muskets up to the port, content to deflect the short daggers. Sustaining that discipline all along the line when the charge was only feet away was too much. A couple brought musket barrels down to the hip and fired. One ball musthave hit no target, because only one of the youngsters went down. The noise of the shots made the horses buck and stamp in the traces. They would surely have run had it not been for the coachmanand Thomas holding their halters so tightly. As it was, the unattendedteam of two with a light carriage pulled it out of line and ran. When the horses had calmed, Thomas risked a look toward the foot guards. They had retreated a couple of paces, muskets still at the port. The young "gentlemen" were uselessly clustered round their fallen colleague.

He decided the coachman would have to cope, released the halters and slipped quietly away from the horses. Going past the footguards, he saw shock on the faces of the standing midshipmen.Swift action was needed.

"Stand aside, young sirs. We need light to see where your fellow ishit," he called.

One or two looked up and seemed to recognize him. Hesitantly, they began to move. He saw welling dark blood on the white, breeches-clad thigh of the young man lying on his back. Fortunately, he had passed out, so Thomas was able to kneel beside him andfeel under the leg. Happily, there was an exit wound, so he looked upat the others.

"Do any of you young gentlemen have large handkerchiefs?"Once a few were proffered, he knotted a couple.

"Now, a dirk scabbard, please."

He made a tourniquet just in time for His Lordship to arrive with Captain Hardy.

"Would one of you 'gentlemen' care to explain the disturbance and gunshots we heard. Also, why one of your number is lying wounded?" His lordship icily enquired.

Mr Parsons stepped away from the huddle and spoke for them. "My lord, we were foolish enough to mount a mock charge on his majesty's foot guards with drawn dirks. One leveled his musket and shot him."

"So, it was by your discreditable foolishness that one of youmumber lies seriously wounded. Only the intervention of my steward stemmed his loss of blood. One of you kneel there and keep the tourniquet tight.

Another find the first lieutenant and surgeon, whoare together, and bring both."

They were almost falling over each other to obey these orders. "One only for each task. The rest of you will stay here until

Lieutenant Parkinson arrives to escort you back to your berth forthwith. You will parade before Captain Hardy and myself in the forenoon watch for punishment."

Relieved by one of them, Thomas stood."The ball went through m'lord."

"Thank you, Thomas," his lordship said quietly, "you may return to the coach. I do not intend to allow any of our people to stay longer."

Stony-faced he was on the drive back to the *palazzo*. In the great cabin by the light of day, he stopped the leave of all the paraded midshipmen and their wounded fellow in the sick berth for no less than six months!

Thomas had been required to accompany his lordship and Tom, being a witness to the foolish affray. Once the midshipmen had been marched out, the admiral looked moodily seaward out of the stern lights and voiced his thoughts on their situation.

"That is the trouble with being too long in a friendly harbor, Hardy. High-spirited young men will get into mischief. Shall we see the wounded one to say the same?"

"I believe his lesson has already been administered, my lord. He came round while a piece of his breeches' cloth was being extracted from the wound. He seems likely to heal cleanly."

"Then, he may learn from the experience. Is that not the brig from Troubridge coming in?"

Minutes later, his mood was transformed by the letter from the commodore that he held up in positive joy.

"Suvorov has won a great victory at Novi Ligure in the mountains north of Genoa. The French field army is destroyed and Joubert killed. Now, we can drive them out of Italy, Hardy. I must go and givethe glad tidings to Sir William and his majesty."

CHAPTER 19

DECEPTION CONTINUES WHILE
AN ENVOY VISITS

The allied success in the north did nothing immediate to help his lordship in the south. There was nothing maritime power could do, while the division Field Marshal Suvorov had detached to clear the French out of central Italy was advancing through Tuscany andUmbria. The heat in Palermo continued to be crippling. His lordship was nearly as badly affected as Lady Hamilton, although for rather different reasons. The stump of his right arm became extremely sorewhen he sweated profusely. For a man with sight in only one eye, eye strain which would not abate became worrying. Of course, he worried himself to the extent of having John Tyson or Miss Knight read over to him much incoming correspondence. Likewise, lettershe had dictated could be read back to him before signature. Often, it seemed in the heat that his good eye filmed over, like his blind eye. This was especially noticeable in the evening. The nearly invisible smoke of candles troubled him greatly. He was at his best in the evening only when he was simply having a discussion with Sir William. It helped, of course, that he was talking to a gentleman of great intellect. One with a grasp of strategy and a prodigious knowledge of inland Europe.

Thomas served coffee on one of these occasions, a couple of days after the ignominious end of the *fete champetre*. He withdrew to a corner to await further instructions. His lordship bemoaned his limited number of ships.

"I cannot augment Troubridge's squadron further without weakening Ball's blockade of Valletta. *Foudroyant* is my only liner in reserve."

"So, what would you do, my dear Nelson, if his squadron were called on to blockade one of the larger ports?"

"If Leghorn were hostile to us, he could cope with that. Genoa is much too large for such a small number. If we still had the thirty of the line and the frigates that Lord Keith took away in pursuit of Bruix, then we could do it. I have every hope of forcing the French out of Civitavecchia, but Genoa is beyond us."

The Knight steepled his hands and thought for long moments before his next words.

"I wish the Field Marshal would nonetheless place Genoa under close siege before winter. He should not give priority to this other aim of clearing the French out of Switzerland. The Austrian and Russian armies already there will obtain no aid from the Swiss. They hate the Austrians and have been soundly beaten by the French under this Jew, Massena."

"I share your anxiety, my dear Sir William. He should not march all his Russians up into the mountains. Yet to place them all around the walls of Genoa until spring invites disease and disaffection. We are unable to prevent supplies flowing in."

His Lordship made a gesture of helplessness.

"Even a premature retirement to winter quarters, but still in Italy, would be better than removing himself to the mountains. I have no expectation that the Austrians can force the French to surrender Genoa," Sir William insisted.

"If their lordships sent me another dozen and a half of the line this month, I dare say we could put some fire in their bellies. Failing that, I am compelled to share your view, my dear Sir William."

No wonder his ordship now felt ill and looked at least ten years older than his real age, thought Thomas.

This lack of the means to do something really decisive was nogood for a man of action, who needed to be at sea with his flagship once again at the head of a fleet. One problem was seriously causing him to feel ill. The way in which all his upper teeth had rottedthis year was to blame. Years spent at sea, often consuming food that was far less than fresh, would no doubt have taken its toll. It wasstill a mystery why his lordship's lower teeth hadn't rotted at thesame time. Thomas wondered if it could have anything to do with thewounds to his upper face, most recently the one above his eye at theNile. The banquets at the various celebrations had been torture for him. Her ladyship had been concerned to help overcome the torpor and sick stomach caused by his rotted teeth.

The outcome of a conversation with Queen Maria Carolina on the subject was that the surgeon for the royal teeth called at the *palazzo.* An elderly, cadaverous man in a dark, shiny coat, he carried a large, black bag. It proved to contain an apron that looked suspiciously like a butcher's apron and a number of extraction tools. This did not initially inspire confidence. He poked around in his lordship's mouth and caused him additional pain. Her ladyship sat anxiously nearby, translating the surgeon's sparse words. Some of the lower teeth needed treatment with a substance he made from mercury and othermetals. In his judgment, all the remaining upper teeth needed to be removed, so he could make an upper set of false teeth. Withoutmore ado, he donned the apron and some covers for his coat sleeves. These were visibly covered in the dried blood of earlier patients. Tom and Thomas were then required to hold his lordship oneach side. This was not easy in the case of a man with only one full arm, who was their master.

"Hold me firm; you can do me no more harm than these teeth are doing," he croaked, looking from one to the other trustingly.

He shut his good eye.

Thus reassured, they held him against the back of a chair, while the surgeon, directly in front of his patient, held his head back with nostrils pinched between thumb and forefinger. It was then t hedemonstrated his great dexterity with his tooth pulling pinchers. He seemed to be able to judge from the feel of the handles which wayhe should pull for each tooth to come out with the least resistance. The teeth seemed to have shockingly long roots. Each one that came away was accompanied by a gout of blood. The surgeon couldonly manage two at a time, before having to bring his patient's head forward to choke and spit blood into a bowl. Eventually, a salt mouthwash was allowed The surgeon said, through her ladyship,that half of them were enough for one day.

No more work was done that day, nor the next when the surgeon returned. The day after that, his lordship began to revive. He could scarcely chew, but mouthwashes began to heal his gum cavities. His stomach was no longer being poisoned. It was just as well.

A serious incident in the port occurred on the Sunday following the *fete champetre*. It began in the hot, narrow streets behind the *Castello a Mare*. A sailor of the Turkish squadron was knifed in the back by a Sicilian. He claimed the Turk had made free with his woman against her will. When the sailor's comrades sought to arrest the culprit, his friends attacked them. A number were knifed to death and the remainder fled. They regained their ships and sought to gather shipmates and weapons for a sally ashore in retaliation. Theirofficers were firm that it could not be allowed. Kadir Bey, the commodore of their squadron, was called and strongly affirmed the views of his captains and lieutenants. at this point, their crews mutinied.

The start of this was the firing of shots in the air by Turkish sailors who had already picked up firearms. His lordship was alerted by the volley of shots from the Turkish moorings, before a messenger arrived. Tom helped him into his uniform coat and buckled on his sword. He was ready to order *Foudroyant's* marines paraded and marched around the shore. He needed to board Kadir Bey's flagship with a show of some force. By now, there was a sullen silence. Assembled, armed officers of the Turkish flagship watched their crewmembers in the waist and vice versa. His Lordship went straight up the rope ladder with no sign of fear. Captain Hardy, clearly felt the need to protect his Admiral in any eventuality. So did the rest ofthem. The marines drew up in an extended line ashore, facing the ship. Already, his lordship had called for an interpreter and asked Kadir Bey if he would allow him to address the entire crew. At least, they listened.

"Brave mariners of the *Sublime Porte,* I know your compatriots have suffered at the hands of assassins.

"He waited for the translation, at which there was a collective sigh.

He then filled his lungs with air to continue, high pitched.

"Yet, you do not suffer alone. English sailors have also been murdered, month after month." There were loud expressions of anger and outrage as this was translated, but he had their attention, so once more drew breath to continue.

"My ships' crews could have rampaged through this city to hunt down the assassins, but I am forced to order that we rely on King Ferdinand's officers arresting them."

There were jeers at the translation of "King Ferdinand's officers," but no movement.

"It is not want of diligence that makes bringing the murderers to justice slow. Foolish citizens obstruct officers in finding the guilty and seeing them hung."

When these words were translated, there were a few cheers at the prospect, however remote, of hangings. Emboldened, His lordship continued.

"I only ask you, brave mariners, to show patience and put your trust in your commander, Kadir Bey, and in myself. The assassins will be apprehended."

There were a few more cheers, and more significantly, the sailors started to return their arms to the racks on deck. The officers sheathed their swords.

"Will the other crews follow their example?"

"My best way to ensure that is to put to sea and signal them to follow," Kadir Bey replied by the interpreter.

"Will you return? I value your support."

"I thank your lordship for that mark of confidence. I will only return if ordered, once I have reported these events. It is my belief my men will be subjected to attack again if I come back here. I believe also the great Sultan, may Allah heap blessings upon him, will have need of this squadron elsewhere. I have just received sad tidings. The army landed at Aboukir was defeated by the French."

All this took the interpreter some time. It was clearly a double blow to his lordship. He quickly expressed commiseration for the defeat and sadness at the departure of the squadron. Assurances he would write to

239

Constantinople to explain the incident was not the fault of Kadir Bey or his men were accepted. All told, they parted on good terms. His lordship obtained a translated account of the Aboukirdefeat and its aftermath. The whole episode only made worse the bitter taste in his mouth left by root cavities.

"It was a triumph of diplomacy," declared Sir William, on hearing the whole story that evening, "but I wish there was more could be done about the murders. I suppose we do not know whether the culprits were Greek Sicilians or Genoese?"

"I fear not. Even if we knew, it would not bring the culprits tojustice. The Greeks here look after their own. It is well known that theGenoese Jacobins murdering our seamen are well supplied withFrench gold. They have no difficulty buying safety amongst the local populace. It is a waste of breath asking his majesty to declare war onGenoa and take all of them prisoner. Sir John says it would not be popular. I cannot even gnash my teeth at the corruption and indolence of this Court anymore!"

"How are you recovering from the ministrations of Tortorici, my dear Nelson?" Sir William enquired solicitously.

"I am trying hard not to think of him as the torturer. His prescription of saltwater mouth washes is beginning to improve my gums. The suggestion of cloves to hold against painful parts of my mouth does help. He says he cannot have a plate and ivory teeth fashioned until my gums have hardened. Then it will cost me a pretty penny."

"I dislike this of the exchange of prisoners after Aboukir," said Sir William, returning to business. "It may result in Bonaparte learning how poorly things go for France."

"You fear he may see his duty lies in abandoning his army inEgypt, Sir William? If he should try, all I can hope is that the Swedish Knight is keeping a close eye on shipping along that coast. I have no doubt he would crow more than usual, if he made such a capture."

"I can imagine hearing him, even now. We cannot sit here and speculate on what might be, my dear Nelson. There is the letter to compose to Spencer Smith in Constantinople, exonerating KadirBey. You know he is due to be relieved as our minister there by LordElgin.

He, so far as I know, has no knowledge of the way in whichthe *Sublime Porte* is governed.

He then realized the irony of his remarks might only depress his lordship further.

"We should allow ourselves some relaxation at La Nova tomorrow night. I have promised my lady some hands of Faro. Let us hope she does not lose!"

According to Tom, the evening at the public rooms was a success. It appeared to take his lordship's mind off his pains to stand or sitand watch her ladyship seated at the Faro table. Thomas knew full well why her ladyship so much preferred gaming to any other kind of public appearance. It gave her the opportunity to remain seated for long periods. Very little upright movement was required. He saw the party ascend from the cobbles into the coach and was amazed at theoutward jut of her breasts. Her gown was relatively low-cut, but not immodest. In their chamber, watching her undress, he asked Mary about it.

"They do grow bigger when a woman is with child. She is blessed with a fine pair in the first place and I have altered a number of her gown bodices to support them better. With very high waists and flowing lines below, she believes it conceals her belly and keeps attention off it. It clearly worked with you."

"That is what works with me."

He gasped as her thin shift came over her head and her breasts jiggled with the brief, strenuous activity.

"So I see."

She looked down at his male appreciation, coming to him. She pressed her nipple-hardened breasts to his chest and tilted up her mouth to his.

"You may have a better night than his lordship. He can only look atwhat the dressmaker's art has improved."

She breathed into his mouth. Her tongue playfully entered and her hand gripped him.

That the evening had been a success was evidenced by his lordship sleeping well into the morning. Tables for Faro were set upin the *palazzo's* large reception room. Mary kept to the room where she did her sewing. The bulky padding she was required to wear made her feel she should keep out of the way.

Tom knew what was required, so he and Thomas got on with that. They brought up wine for the evening's reception before respectively rousing his lordship and Sir William. When guests arrived, it was obvious his lordship did find it soothing to look over her ladyship's shoulder and follow her cards. From that position, his eyes did swivelto her breasts now and again. No man in the room was quite immune to that tendency. Eventually, watching the sequences of cards on which his paramour gambled was too hypnotic for him. He took a chair, positioned to her side, where he occasionally nodded off. This was the pattern for over a fortnight. Correspondence was dealt with late afternoon while his lordship's mouth steadilyimproved. He lived on soup, soft bread, and fruit.

Partway through this time, Tortorici reappeared and pronounced himself satisfied with the rate of healing. He subjected his patient to the nauseous procedure of taking a clay mould of the roof of his mouth and uneven gums. It would help to make a plate of comfortably fitting, polished hardwood, he explained to her ladyship. The patient washed his mouth in saltwater yet again to rid himself of the small pieces of clay lodged in his root cavities.

The first day of October brought mail from home by an unusual vessel. It had been too late in the afternoon when this fine ship rounded *Monte Pellegrino* for any of her passengers to come ashore in the dusk. Her captain came ashore with a bag of mail and announced he was carrying Lord and Lady Elgin to Constantinople. When he returned aboard, it was with pressing invitations for his passengers to attend separate post-midday dinners at the *palazzo*.

His lordship and Sir William settled down to reading mail. The admiralty came first.

"Well, here is a mixed bag," his lordship eventually commented, "firstly, one advising that his majesty has conferred a baronetcy on Thomas Troubridge. John, start a list for replies tonight with one to Sir Thomas. Secondly, a rebuke from their lordships for failing to follow Lord Keith's orders in June. Thirdly, a personal letter from LordSpencer. He seems to accept as valid my reason for not doing so."

"May I look at those two letters, my dear Nelson."

The elderly knight read in silence before commenting. His Lordship read private letters.

"They have had Nepean pen the least serious rebuke they thought they could justify. Lord Spencer's letter is so much soft soap because he needs you to be here and active. I wonder what he will do regarding the position of Commander-in-Chief?"

"I have been little active for nearly two months. I trust Troubridge and Ball to be as active on my behalf as our resources permit. However, should they order Lord Keith back into the Mediterranean as my superior, I shall not be happy."

"My dear Nelson, you have been seriously unwell on account of your teeth. Do you believe Lord Keith will bear a grudge, should he return?"

"That is a possibility I must face. My real concern, my dear Sir William, is his failure to carry the fight to the French. That makes himless suitable than myself."

"There I must agree," Sir William stoutly declared. "Shall you dictate to Troubridge?"

"I shall not send until we meet Lord Elgin, only make a draft. You may go, Thomas."

At this order, he quietly left, but Mary was not in their chamber. A silent approach close to the door of her ladyship's chamber told him both Mary and Mrs Cadogan were still with her. Considerable care was going into the arrangements for receiving Lady Elgin! Silently,he returned to their chamber to wait by candlelight.

The letter of congratulation did not get sent the following day. Firstly, due to his lordship's appointment in the morning with Tortorici. Secondly, as a result of the very considerable time spent entertaining Lord and Lady Elgin. Thirdly, a fast-sailing sloop was seen approaching from a long way north, just before night. The ivory teeth might have looked fine, but the plate made his lordship's gumsbleed. It had to be discarded while his mouth recovered. The meal Lady Elgin was to share with her ladyship was to be a tête-à-tête, mainly attended on by

Mrs Cadogan, but with a brief appearance by Mary in her well-padded dress. She observed to Thomas this was just for show.

That for Lord Elgin was a little more formal. His lordship and Sir William were joint hosts in the large reception room. It was rather toolarge for the occasion. Their words echoed around as Tom and Thomas sought to make little noise while serving them. Lord Elgin was a vigorous-looking young man of military bearing. That he was taller than both his hosts put them at an added disadvantage. He looked Tom and Thomas up and down, although they were both smartly turned out in their best rigs. The way they walked around thetable did not appeal to an officer used to being served by soldier orderlies.

He was superficially solicitous when his lordship explained theproblem with his teeth. He seemed dismayed that the younger of his two hosts was so prematurely aged. It was his attitude toward Sir William that Thomas thought was far less than positive. He seemed willing to pick the elderly knight's brain for his knowledge of the Turkish empire. His manner implied the ministry would have little usefor someone so elderly, once he had passed on his accumulated knowledge. He ate very well and listened between his comments on how much the Ministry had changed and modernized. He opinedhow much better constructed and effective against the French the present coalition was proving to be.

Not quite sufficient recognition of how His Lordship's success atthe Nile and Sir William's patient diplomacy had brought about the change in fortunes, Thomas thought.

No wonder this Earl looked so unlined. His face and nascentpaunch showed he was in the early stages of running to fat. There was a protuberance about his brown eyes that made him appearless and less attractive while he spoke of the secret expedition the ministry had planned. This would surely have the French begging forpeace. He did not share Sir William's fears about the Austro-Russianplan to clear the French out of Switzerland. He regarded the Turkish defeat at Aboukir as just one more step in the wearing down of Bonaparte's army. His Lordship steered the conversation back to more recent successes.

"You may be interested to know, my dear Lord Elgin, that my ships have now secured the surrender of Rome. Also, the coastal fortress and port of Civitavecchia, with no assistance from our army. I asked Sir James Erskine for twelve hundred men but was refused, pending the arrival of General Fox, who will supersede him."

"I believe we are still building up our forces on Minorca, so their dissipation is not to be lightly contemplated," Lord Elgin began responding, "but General Fox is very experienced and will bringmore troops with him. Is he not related to the wife of our Consul in Naples, Mr Lock?"

Now, it was the turn of his lordship to try and hide his discomfiture. Thomas knew this arose from the great dispute two months ago over victualing the fleet for the Bay of Naples. As he understood it, Mr Lock had been so keen to make money as to have implied his lordship tolerated frauds by his captains and their pursers. His lordship's coherent and righteous indignation, expressed in correspondence, had resulted in Sir William being able to persuade Mr Lock to give an abject, written apology. The old gentleman shifteduneasily on his chair, but his lordship carried the talk back to Rome.

"It was represented that the weather was still too hot for our men. The Russian division detached by Field Marshal Suvorov to march south to aid Sir Thomas Troubridge did not suffer. The sailors who rowed Captain Louis of *Minotaur* up the Tiber to take the surrender of the French garrison also thrived. Captain Louis is governor of the city as we speak."

"I am greatly impressed by the achievements of the officers and men of your fleet, my Lord," began Lord Elgin in diplomatic retreat, "so much so that I am anxious for the Ministry to maintain a powerful squadron in the Levant."

"You will continue to have Captain Sir Sydney Smith with three ships of the line and a number of lesser vessels, my dear Lord Elgin.I shall be happier when the ministry sees fit to send an army to Egypt to take General Buonaparte's surrender."

"That is a recommendation I shall, of course, support now that you have informed me of the Turkish defeat at Aboukir," Lord Elgin went on diplomatically.

"Not before an adequate body of soldiers is landed on Malta. It is one thing for my ships to take Rome and fulfill a prophecy made to me by a priest. The French there knew a force of Russians lay to the landward. The French who sit snug behind the walls of Valletta know only half-starved Maltese wait outside."

His lordship showed a vigor he'd seemed to have lost in past weeks.

"I believe you will have to prevail on General Fox for that, my lord. Iam not sure the Ministry wish to give great priority to the siege of Valletta. This stems from the commitment that has been given to support the Czar as Grand Master of the Knights of St. John. I do accept the islands have strategic value."

There, his lordship had to leave the discussion of strategy and move to matters social. "To more immediate matters, my dear Lord Elgin. Tomorrow, Sir William and I must present you to their majesties and their principal minister, Sir John Acton. You and Lady Elgin are invited with ourselves to their Chinese fete the following day."

"Ha, Sir John is the recusant who became General Acton, I believe. He must have some claim to competence. Why, my dear Lord Nelson, are their majesties holding a Chinese fete?"

"That is to celebrate the completion of a new royal home called the*Palazzina Cinese*. It is a matter of some dismay to Sir William and myself, when they should now be returning to one of their numerous palaces in Naples. I shall take the opportunity of tomorrow to impress on his majesty once again that a return to Naples is essential. The French are cleared out of all Italy, bar Genoa, but itwill be an uphill battle in this corrupt and indolent court. Do notexpect too much of Sir John. He has ability, but has also become affected by indolence. Moreover, Lady Acton's health is failing."

With this piece of pessimistic analysis from the admiral, Lord Elgin had had enough.

"I see Sir William and yourself are of one mind on this, my dear Lord Nelson. Would it be too soon to see whether the ladies are ready for our company?"

Thomas had only briefly seen Lady Elgin. He had only viewed her as young, pretty, and demure. He was, therefore, surprised to hear Mary's assessment that evening.

"She only pretends to be demure, just as she pretends to be inawe of her ladyship. The way she dresses, to show off a very fine bosom on such a slight frame made me think she is no stranger to using feminine wiles. A good dozen years younger than her ladyship!"

"Do you think she has realized her ladyship is with child?"

"I don't know from being in the room with them a short time. Lady Elgin has not been married for long. She may not know the signs."

"I'm not sure we shall find out what she thought. No ladies tomorrow, and I am only riding on the rear of the coach the next evening," he said, taking her in his arms.

The next day did not seem to be productive for his lordship. Thomas only became aware of the exception when the two lords andSir William returned to the coach. He was outside the *Colli* a very long time. Lord Elgin was looking very thoughtful and withdrawn, but his lordship was speaking with animation to Sir William.

"Her majesty was gracious enough to ask if I had been well servedby Tortorici. When I told her I believed his work would eventually restore me, her response was to promise payment out of her own pocket. She told me it was the least she could do for the savior ofher husband's kingdom. Naturally, I replied I was overcome."

"That is indeed very generous of Her Majesty. I suspect she will pay him far less than he was asking you to pay, my dear Nelson."

The knight's cynical comment produced a sideways glance from Lord Elgin.

The following morning brought a great burst of activity. This had noconnection with preparing for the evening's Chinese fete. A fastsloop from the west with a following wind had rounded *Monte Pellegrino* and come pell-mell into the harbor. The sails came off her in disarray. A boat was lowered even as her anchor cable rattled out.Her master and commander brought warning of an enemy fleet of fourteen ships of the line, including a three decker, which had been sighted off Finisterre. This immediately had his lordship sending an order to Captain Hardy to be ready to sail the following morning. Oneletter after another followed.

"First one to Sir Thomas, John. Most of the ten of the line I must gather are with him."

There then followed letters to Governor Ball and even to Sir Sydney Smith. They explained his lordship would have to sail from the Italian coast to Minorca to complete his assembly. He wwouldsail on for Gibraltar to protect the outward convoy from home. Some seven hundred merchantmen were protected only by a few frigates.

"We are so short of supplies on Malta," he said, while Thomas sealed letters.

The following early morning's leave-taking of Mary was brief and fervent in their chamber. His lordship had opted to go on foot with hislittle crew. He was breezy and cheerful. Thomas found it hard to match the mood, owing to what he had overheard by the coach the previous evening. Lord and Lady Elgin had hired an open carriage to take them from the mole the four miles out to *Palazzina Cinese*. It stood close to the garden, where the huge party was being held. The *Palazzo Palagonia* coach was parallel to it. It happened that the Elgins returned to their carriage sooner than *Tria Juncta in Uno*. Thomas was concealed by the coach and heard Lady Elgin clearly.

"I was so glad Mrs Charles Lock was able to rescue me from Lady Hamilton. She may have a very good singing voice and in Italian too, but she is so *gross.*"

Her Scottish accent had almost been refined out of her speech. Lord Elgin's reply, he having been a military man, had only theslightest inflection when he replied.

"They are a charming couple, the Locks, and I could see what Mr Lock meant when he said Lord Nelson is ruled by Lady Hamilton. Both he and that old fool of a husband absolutely dote on her. Mr Lock challenged me to a wager that Nelson would not be able to tearhimself away from her to put to sea tomorrow."

At this, they had both squealed with laughter. Thomas felt angered and ashamed at the same time. What right had they to run down his lordship! Why did he set himself up for malicious gossip! He cautiously remained hidden while they drove off. That they had been equally cutting about King Ferdinand and Queen Maria Carolina did not assuage his feelings. He had not yet shared these with Mary.

His wait to do this was a long one. A week after *Foudroyant* had sailed on time, his lordship had assembled nine of the line. They were sailing southwest of Minorca when the familiar sails of the sloop Bulldog rose above the horizon. She tacked toward them rather slower than the small fleet bore down on her. Presently, she came level with the flagship and tacked around to come alongside and make fast. The first man up the ladder was an eager and familiar young gentleman in the uniform of a post captain. His lordship was delighted.

"You are a most welcome sight, Sir Ed'ard. Please come up and join us with your news."

Up the quarterdeck ladder he came to shake hands with His Lordship and Hardy. The package the Captain was carrying was duly received.

"The great cabin, I think, while Bulldog is still lashed on. Bring wine, Tom."

His lordship, tapped the packet.

"I believe you will wish to see the one from Admiral Duckworth first, my lord. He gave it to me himself."

Sir Edward recovered the packet and removed a first letter to carry into the great cabin.

"This is capital. Admiral Duckworth, in command of his new squadron, sailing for the Caribbean, sights the enemy fleet. They are Spaniards, who promptly put into Ferrol. We also know Bruix is blockaded in Brest," his lordship declared, scanning the letter.

"How far behind you was the convoy at that point, Sir Ed'ard?"
"Less than a day, my Lord, although we have had a fast passage since, until today."

Effectively, his lordship's decision was then made. He went through the ritual reading of their lordships' convoy and protection vessel details. He set aside his personal correspondence and quickly dictated a letter of thanks to Admiral Duckworth. It could go in Bulldog to Gibraltar. His little crew were ordered out.

On the sail back to Port Mahon, the reason became clear. The frigate *Princess Charlotte* was signaled to come under *Foudroyant's* lee.

Captain Hardy transferred into her to relieve her sick Captain.He was ordered by his lordship to relinquish command and go ashore to await passage home. He put his view to Sir Edward, his resuming flag captain

"Hardy will make a man of war of her!"

At Port Mahon, a private letter from Sir William awaited. It hadbeen forwarded by Sir Thomas Troubridge, who had been left in solitary charge of the Italian coast. His lordship looked troubled whenhe read it, but had to keep an appointment ashore with Sir James Erskine. He required only that the ship be ready to sail on his return.

"I shurd say err ledyship ers ready t'sprog," Tom muttered toThomas.

"Likely," he muttered in reply.

They both knew the arrangement that Sir Thomas was to open anddeal with all letters, other than those from Sir William and her ladyship. If she was not writing herself, something was up.

His Lordship's talk with the General was a waste of breath. He would refer the request for troops to be sent to Malta to General Fox, on that superior officer's arrival. Mr Tyson had gone with his master and needed to file copies of letters to the port captain. Also, one to Captain Brenton, in command of the convoy escort vessels, who would receive his on arrival. This ordered that those merchantmen who were willing to sail south to sell their cargoes on Malta be escorted there and back. Even as he filed in the letter book and Thomas tied it up again for him, the capstan pawls were clicking. His lordship was up on the quarterdeck with Sir Edward in a fever to get underway.

One day out from Palermo, a *polacca* floated out of the early morning mist. Her Sicilian master waved furiously. Coming to within hailing range, he was bellowing.

"Una lettera da Barone 'Amilton."

He was allowed to come alongside and make his delivery. It appeared all was now well at the *palazzo*. A smile of relief lit his lordship's after he had read the letter through. The *polacca's* master was given a couple of gold coins and asked to sail back to Palermoto give *Foudroyant's* expected time of arrival. It was no surprise the next day to see the coach waiting on the mole.

Sir William and her ladyship descended as the ship's dying motion carried her in. There also stood by the coach an apparently heavily pregnant Mary.

CHAPTER 20

A CHILD IS BORN, BUT DECEPTION IS INCOMPLETE

Once *Foudroyant* was moored to the mole and the gangway swayed into position, his lordship was off the ship. He embraced Sir William and her ladyship in turn before all three mounted the coach steps. A sharp word from her ladyship had the vehicle moving landward. This left Mary looking rather forlorn. The little crew had to pack up and carry with them all the items their master would need for headquarters ashore. Sir Edward appeared in the doorway, obviously keen to see the job done.

"You had better go now, Spencer, and walk your wife home. She is perilously close."

Thomas knew the observation was kindly meant. He simply knuckled his forehead, said, "Thank you, Sir Edward," and departed with the bundle he had collected.

On the paving, he leaned over Mary's bulge to kiss her on the lips to ironic cheers from topmen. He ignored the occasional lewd remark, took her hand, and started to walk. Alongside him, Mary moved with a pronounced waddle.

"You see how in your absence I have remembered how to walk as though this were real."

She placed her hand on the limit of the bulge and rubbed it.

"I have missed you so much. What was the business with the letters about?"

"The babe had a prolonged kicking bout inside her. She panicked, thinking she was about to give birth. She had Sir William write the letter before her mother convinced her that all was well. Then, hehad to write again to say so," Mary explained quietly.

They were virtually beyond earshot of the ship. He could speak aloud caressing her hand.

"How long, do you think, before the birth?"

"Mrs Cadogan, whose knowledge of these things is good, says about three more weeks. Why are you smiling so?"

"I was just thinking about those topmen wondering how we will manage to couple tonight. Little do they know!"

"And, little do you know of what life will be like when the babe is inour chamber. Waking to be fed and cleaned at all hours of the night.""Perhaps his lordship will make some allowance for that in my duties."

His attempt to deflect her vehemence on the subject failed.

"That would defeat the object of passing off the babe as ours. What happens when you go to sea?"

"All the more reason to make the most of things now," he blustered.

"It is easy for you to see it that way, being a sailor. When you go back to sea, you will have a rest from it. I shall get none"

They were inside *Porta Felice*. He pressed her hand and did not pursue what he could not refute. "I need to tell you what I heard at that *Palazzina Cinese* the night before we sailed."

She heard him out in silence. They slowly walked along the marble paved *corso* into *Piazza Marina* and she thought as they turned up the slope.

"Perhaps his lordship would be best advised to take you all back tosea. I doubt that will do any good for the cause of Sir William," she ventured.

"He may yet do that. The sea voyage has done him good and his gums have healed. I do not wish to leave you at the time of the birthing, and he will not wish to."

"So, why do you say he may yet do so, my love?"

"It is driving the French out of Valletta that he has set his mind on.It will take ships, supplies and thousands ashore. The islanders are nearly starving,"

They had passed *Palazzo Chiaramonte* and were halfway up Via Quattro Aprile before she gave her enigmatic conclusion.

"We shall see."

The first letter his lordship sent was one with a replacement liner up to Sir Thomas. He ordered him to bring Culloden to Palermo for a new expedition. He clearly had Malta in mind. What proved upsetting to him in the session of mail reading was the letter he had to open first. This came from their lordships of the admiralty.

"I fear they will send Lord Keith to lord it over me."

He handed it to Sir William and the knight read it through carefully. "My dear Nelson, the accusation is wholly untrue. I have seen you send dispatch after dispatch telling them the king will not return to Naples and is not living up to promises to send men and supplies to Malta. I am surprised Nepean signed it!"

"I shall not attempt an immediate refutation. There is no point. Let us get on with something worthwhile."

Sir Thomas confirmed that the Marquis de Niza and his squadron had been recalled to Lisbon. This did not surprise his lordship. Admiral Ouschakoff had written to explain his ships could not be expected to keep the sea in winter storms. They would have to withdraw to Adriatic bases. His lordship was amused.

"I have not noticed them being keen to keep the sea up to this point. The weather this autumn has been fair. It is still set fair, so something else must be ailing them."

Of far greater concern was the situation on Malta. Governor Ball reported that lack of blockade in the summer had allowed some supplies to reach the French garrison of Valletta. At five thousand, this considerably outnumbered the two thousand armed islanders and five hundred marines, some of whom were Portuguese, who made up all the force he had ashore. They were seriously short of rations. The islanders were starving and corn was desperately needed from Puglia or Sicily. He could not invest the fortress fromthe harbor. The French had blocked it with the Guillaume Tell, one of the two liners to have escaped from the Nile.

However, the prospects for having food delivered from Puglia or Sicily might improve. A letter from the English Consul in Tripoli explained that the Bashaw of the North African state was willing to make peace with King Ferdinand. He needed paying to lay up his cruisers. Once again, his lordship was amused.

"It seems we will have to make him an offer, my dear Sir William. WWe cannot readily find him an alternative foe. Nor can we provide enough escorts for grain ships. Would you be so kind as to ascertain the availability of grain and ships to carry it to Malta? The harvest here and in Puglia must have been good; such a hot summer following a wet winter."

"I entirely agree, my dear Nelson. I believe I should best approach Prince Luzzi for organizing the supply of grain and merchantmen."

Sir Thomas Troubridge took only a few days to respond to His Lordship's summons. He brought with him a disturbing rumor that had spread around the north from Corsica. This was that General Bonaparte had deserted his army in Egypt. He had somehow evaded Sir Sydney Smith's ships and won through to the island of his birth. It was reported he had been seen there, despite trying to conceal his presence. That lent the rumor credence. Moreover, it was also claimed he took another vessel for mainland France after only a few days. His lordship was not concerned by this.

"The situation of the French revolutionaries remains very poor against our present coalition."

His lordship and Sir William were consulting after the commodore had departed to lead his squadron, with the promise of *Foudroyant* to follow.

"I would be happier if I knew how our allies are faring in Switzerland and where Field Marshal Suvorov is now." said the elderly knight, looking troubled. "My information from Prince Luzzi is that the Puglia grain merchants believe they will obtain higher prices from the Austrians and will not send any to Malta. I deduce there is a risk that the merchants here will try to follow their lead."

"The devil they will, the greedy rascals. We must keep ourselves informed of the whereabouts of their grain ships."

The truth was that his temper was growing shorter as the time of her ladyship's confinement approached, thought Thomas.

He knew from Tom that Sir Thomas had pressed his lordship tosail with him, or at least to bring *Foudroyant* himself. The admiralhad declined the former suggestion. He had to remain on shore to obtain further news from the north and secure adequate supplies for Malta. He took no view on the latter suggestion. Her ladyship was now hardly to be seen during the day. Both Mrs Cadogan and Mary were spending a lot of time in her chamber. They reassured her that everything was going well.

Giving birth was rather more complicated and risky than it was for farm animals, Thomas reflected, when he thought about it alone. His own mother had survived giving birth to himself and William well enough. However, he knew enough from village funerals in Gotham to realize that conditions like childbed fever could as readily carry off the mother as a badly positioned babe. Tearing and internal bleeding could carry off both of them.

Mary, on the other hand, said all was going well. Her ladyship had done it before and survived. The fact she was older and fatter would make no difference. The babe need only be well-positioned for a headfirst delivery. Mrs Cadogan and herself should be able to cope without any doctor. There would be time in hand, if there were any unforeseen difficulty, to summon one. He would then have to be verywell paid to secure his silence. Her Ladyship was more frightened of being found out than she was of risk to her life. Mary thought the health of the babe hardly entered her thinking at all. He wondered how she would react when it appeared, assuming it lived.

The remaining few days of October passed and the Palermo weather was still fine and warm. Word came from the north that FieldMarshal Suvorov had taken his army up the Ticino valley to the Passof Saint Gotthard. More worrying was the revelation from Sir John Acton to his lordship that her majesty had received a letter from her sister in Vienna. This spoke of a reverse suffered by a joint Austrian and Russian army at the city of Zurich in Switzerland. The news was a month old. Naturally, Sir William's opinion was needed.

"Did the letter say where this joint army is now positioned?" asked the Knight, unrolling his map of Switzerland.

"Only that they would winter in the Canton of Glarus, Sir William."

"Depending on which side of the lake they retreated, that suggests

a retreat of at least forty miles. It indicates a defeat, not a reverse. Who are these commanders?"

"Prince Korsakov is the Russian commander, and Friedrich von Hotze, the Austrian."

"Korsakov I have heard of. Was it he who drove part of Massena's army out of Zurich?"

His Lordship thought for a moment about this second question from Sir William. "I believe that was Archduke Charles. I see what you are driving at, my dear Sir William. Massena must have concentrated his entire army to counterattack. He is a man of energy!"

"Worse than that, he will be in control of the lowland road from Zurich to Lucerne. Field Marshal Suvorov must use the road around the eastern side of Lake Lucerne when he comes out of the mountains, for his army to join with Korsakov's."

"So, he will have to fight a superior force in the onset of winter, either to retreat or go forward. a Well, I do not see him to be of a mind to do other than press forward. He is lost to us in Italy."

Temporarily, reverses seemed to be the order of things. Prince Luzzi had regretfully informed Sir William that only a small amount ofgrain could be spared for Malta. His lordship had intelligence that no less than thirty ships loaded with grain had been assembled atMessina. The location was a sure sign the grain would be going to a northwestern Italian port for the Austrian army of Melas. Sir Thomas Troubridge would be able to land another thirteen hundred marines and seamen from his ships. Sufficient extra to deter the timid French garrison from sallying out of Valletta to attack. Still not enough for an effective siege.

The first of November arrived. His lordship now had to make a decision on who would sail in *Foudroyant*. Sir Edward was summoned to the *palazzo* for a private conference but left alone. His lordship then gave instructions that his little crew would accompany him at first light the following day to lower his flag in *Foudroyant* and raise it in *Samuel and Jane.* An order was sent to the merchantman for her boat to rendezvous at the warship to convey passengers. The admiral's barge and crew would be sailing for Malta.

The predawn promised another fine day. The barge crew rowed lustily to where the flagship had been warped out. The sails could take the breeze, so soon as her anchors were up and down. The barge was speedily hoisted in and stowed. *Samuel and Jane's* boat waited below for the ceremony to be over. At the leave-taking, hislordship had only a few low-voiced words for his flag ccaptain.

"Remember, Sir Ed'ard, give the location of the grain ships. Godspeed."

Samuel and Jane was moored only a short distance across the bay. The pull was not too hard for the smaller number of oarsmen. His lordship wasted little time.

"I and my little crew will go ashore again, Captain Hopps. All messages must be sent on to me at *Palazzo Palagonia.* Should I need the ship for a voyage, I shall need your full crew. If there isneed for us to be on board at anchor, some shore leave will be possible."

"I understand, my lord," responded the master, walking him to the side.

Nearly a week went by with very little news. Word arrived via the Austrians and the court that Field Marshal Suvorov had fought a short, successful battle against a French detachment at Andermatt. That was a short distance beyond the Pass of Saint Gotthard. He had pressed on for Altdorf. Sir William was even more apprehensive. Massena should have been unable to make an attempt to block the Russian army so far forward. Conversely, the word from Mary was that her ladyship was now less anxious. The babe within her was still kicking. Mrs Cadogan was sure that was a good sign. Each time she felt her daughter's belly, the babe's position was good. If she went out for cards now, it was with her husband and his lordship in the coach. This ensured she had minimal walking to the table.

To Thomas and Mary, it began to feel as though they would have months together ashore. Then, one or two messages arrived by dint of the occasional sloop, leaving a letter out at *Samuel and Jane*. His lordship could now bear having his false teeth plate in his mouth long enough to finish dinner. It was strange he should be waiting soinactively for things to happen. The Neapolitan negotiations with the Bashaw of Tripoli over payment had gone well. The great convoy had safely reached Minorca on the last day of October. A report to his lordship, including arrangements for merchantmen to Malta, was to follow from Captain Brenton.

What seemed at the time to be a bombshell arrived the day before the event that would bring a new dimension to the lives of Thomas and Mary. A *polacca* from the direction of Messina came alongside *Samuel and Jane*, with a signal of "urgent message."

Thomas had been on watch and reported on the direction from which it had come.

"Meet the boat, Thomas, and bring it straight to me," was all his master had said.

The letter, when he brought it in, was from Governor Ball. His lordship read it.

"Will you see if Sir William is able to join me now, Thomas?"

When he returned with the elderly knight, his lordship wasted no time.

"Thank you for joining me so promptly, Sir William. We have a diplomatic crisis. You may leave us, Thomas, but have Mr Tyson ready to be called."

The only letter written later was a reply to Governor Ball. It transpired he had sent his first lieutenant in *Alexander* to Messina. He requisitioned all the supplies of grain in the thirty ships and had them sail to Malta to unload. This was not an unpopular action with the crews and ship owners, nor even with the corn merchants. The simple reason was they were being *paid* in gold and silver far sooner than would have been the case. Prince Luzzi and others would no doubt have creamed off a percentage. Sir William had left the study looking unworried, after John Tyson had finished copying out the reply. His lordship had walked out too. It was virtually time for "dinner." Thomas was ready to do the sealing. While he carefully folded the sheet ready for the hot sealing wax, Mr Tyson had a tight smile on his face and spoke enigmatically.

"I think we sit on our thumbs and wait."

That could mean different things to different people, Thomas thought.

After all, what were they doing now with her ladyship? He just returned the smile as though he was in on this further secret. No doubt he would be, before long. said That evening in their room,Mary gave a prediction.

"I believe we are nearly there."

He knew instantly what she meant but was still unprepared for the rapid reaction needed.

The trouble was that it started like any other day at the *palazzo*. Tom was heard whistling early in the courtyard before he brought up his lordship's coffee. This preceded his shave and wash, before helping him into his uniform. Thomas washed and dressed himself, prior to collecting Sir William's coffee. Mary went off to attend to her ladyship. Thanks to Sir William's invariable habit of sitting up in bed to read, Thomas usually had time for other tasks. This morning, Mary was waiting just beyond the door to the knight's chamber. She urgently pulled Thomas away as he emerged.

"Her waters have broken, and I've had Tom tell his lordship," she whispered urgently."He needs you to carry a message out to Samuel and Jane."

"What about Sir William?"

"Tom is staying behind to take care of him, saying his lordship needed you for urgent business on board."

They went round to the study door and he entered alone. His Lordship had already penned a note and dried it. He was struggling with the folding.

"Ha, Thomas, come and finish folding this note to Captain Hopps. Then, you can take a boat out and ask him to be at the mole steps in under half an hour to embark a party. Say he, the mate and the hospital boys should come ashore with the boat. Tom will meet themand bring them here for some shore leave. The crew are to remain inthe fo'csle and we shall need the cook."

His Lordship looked and sounded harassed, but it was clear to Thomas there was a plan for this eventuality. He carefully folded the note while his lordship was still speaking. He took the coin proffered to pay a boatman, when he finished. Out he dashed to head down toLa Cala. Holding up the coin by the water's edge soon produced a boat with two oarsmen. They made it glide through the smoothwaters around anchored shipping. He had only needed to say, *Samuel and Jane,*" and the rowers to see the value of the coin. As they approached the ship, he could see she was securely anchored with the ladder ready rigged. When the boat hooked on and he paid extravagantly with his master's coin, Captain Hopps was at the side before he was halfway up the ladder.

Are you here about the cargo for Malta his lordship wishes to send?" he asked.

"No, captain, here is a note from his lordship. He wishes to bring a party aboard. These are his instructions."

The captain read the note, and a curious look came over his face. For an instant, Thomas thought he would query the order, but he swung around and bellowed.

"Mr Parry," adding, when the thickset bosun appeared on deck, "have the boat swung out and lowered; then have the mate and the hospital boys board it."

While the activity proceeded, the Captain's curiosity got the better of him on one item.

"Why the mole steps and not the foreshore, Master Spencer?"

"I assume his lordship's party is using the coach," Thomas replied, thinking quickly.

"Hmmm," the Captain ground out in a noncommittal way, "fouroarsmen, Mr Parry. Rest of crew and cook to remain in fo'csle."

When all were in the boat, bar the three of them, the bosun madeto go before Thomas.

"No, you stay here, Mr Parry. Master Spencer can con the boatback. Down you go."

Thomas went, and the captain quickly followed, taking his place atthe stern. The oarsmen poled off and began the pull toward themole. Seated across from the captain, Thomas saw the coach come into view on top of the mole as the boat left the lee of the ship's side. "Your admiral really is in a hurry. Put your backs into it, lads," grunted the captain.

Thomas moved to the prow when they neared the steps and threw the coiled line up to Tom. Only his lordship got down from the coach. "Thank you for responding so promptly, Captain Hopps. Please bring up your shore party. Tom Allen will show you the way to your quarters."

Up the Captain went, leading his party, and Thomas followed as the Captain paused.

"Will your lordship need help to load the boat?" he enquired politely.

"No, thank you, captain. Thomas Spencer will suffice, so you may lead off your party."

His lordship hurriedly gestured to Tom to lead off. The captain glanced curiously at the darkened interior. He said nothing and followed Tom.

"Quickly Thomas," his lordship hissed when the last of them had tramped away.

He went to the coach door, and Mrs Cadogan came down the step in a hurry. She leaned back in to take her daughter's arm. Mary was levering her ladyship's bottom along the seat from behind. Thomas could see Her Ladyship's face was pale and sweating.

"Lower yourself onto me, m'lady," he said urgently, alongside Mrs Cadogan.

Mary shifted her grip to the shoulders to keep the larger woman upright. She came one foot on the step, then down. Braced though he was and assisted to one side by Mrs Cadogan, he staggered under a weight heavier than himself. His lordship took a pace forward with his left arm extended and somehow restored balance. He held her ladyship by the upper arm. She swayed slightly, her mass of hair hanging loose.

"Get me down the steps and in the boat before another contraction," she ground out.

How Thomas got her down the steps going backward himself, he would never know.

Mrs Cadogan steadied her right arm by the wall and his lordship her left on the seaward edge of the steps. Thomas held her round the middle, her massive belly pressing against his. He somehow kept well enough in to prevent his lordship slipping over the edge into the water.

"When I let go and hold the boat steady, reach your right foot over to step in," her lover ordered.

Thomas did so, and her left foot followed into the space his had left. The boat was reasonably firm and he pivoted around to get his left foot aboard. Her ladyship's right foot followed. She inched one foot over the painter, then the other. The oarsmen looked on curiously from their places on the benches. Edging back onto the bottom planks, he spread his legs and allowed her feet to start running between them. He hoped she had shoes on to avoid her feet taking splinters. Now was no time to worry. His lordship, in a worn uniform coat and faded breeches, nimbly came aboard behind her head. He brought his body hard against her shoulders as she slipped down nearly into a prone position. Thomas leaned to his left without letting go to shift a leg.

"Well done, Thomas, well done. I have her head. Get Mrs Cadogan and Mary aboard," his lordship panted.

Thomas got his right leg over the top of her body, so he was standing in the side of the boat next to the steps. Mrs Cadogan anxiously stood immediately above him. Beyond her, lugging two large bags down the steps, came Mary. If the oarsmen had looked curiously before, their faces now showed complete mystification. They had seen one large woman collapse into the fore part of the boat and now saw a very heavily pregnant young woman bringing down heavy bags. Thomas got Mrs Cadogan aboard alongside her daughter. He reached beyond her for the first bag. His lordship was now cradling her ladyship's head as best a one-armed man could. Thomas carried the first bag beyond the oarsmen to the stern. Back he went for the second then handed Mary in. The weight was now poorly distributed.

"If you join me at the stern, m'lord, Mary can take your place."

Mrs Cadogan moved forward to hold her daughter's head. His lordship gratefully slipped from the seaward side of the prow to go over the centers of the rowing benches. Thomas got Mary over her ladyship's body. He released the mooring rope, threw the loose end onto the steps, and followed His Lordship to the stern. It was clear his anxiety had robbed him of his normal command.

"Pole her off."

Thomas seized hold of the tiller. Now, their eyes would have to be directed to him, not on what was going on behind them. He instructed again when clear, miming the action.

"Give way together."

He steered wide of the end of the mole to set a direct course for *Samuel and Jane*. A groan from right forward upset the stroke a little."Keep it together and watch only the bite of your oars."

Thomas had seen one of them trying to glance over his shoulder. Forward, he could see Mrs Cadogan had a pocket watch in her hand. She looked at it with concentration. He could only see Mary's auburn hair blowing in the breeze. Her head was down by herladyship. The ship was growing larger in his sight, and the strokewas steady again. He adjusted the steering to aim for the stern and then brouhtg her round the far side to the ladder. Glancing sideways,he could see the beads of perspiration on his lordship's brow. His grayed hair ruffled in the breeze. It was a mercy he had chosen notto put on his recognizable bicorn hat. Maybe Tom had been the one to think of that. The ladder was in view. It looked awfully high.

"M'lord, would you kindly go forward and secure that mooring rope to our prow when I bring her in?"

In normal circumstances, it would be strange to hear the admiral being given a task by another. This was far from normal and he looked pleased as he slid away. Thomas allowed him to reach the outboard side of Mary and looked hard at the narrowing distance before shouting.

"Ship oars."

He steered to glide the boat in toward the foot of the ladder. He hoped he'd got it right. Too much remaining speed through the water and they'd ram the ship's side. He would be the first steward in history to crush his admiral between boat and ship. If they fell short, they would wallow embarrassingly. It was about right. His lordship had a rope fender over before the prow grazed the ship's timbersand he grasped the rope. The wet rope's end came on board. Mary raised herself to lift a ring bolt, so the one-armed admiral could feed the rope through and hold on tight. Thomas eased away from the tiller between the oarsmen. He came up alongside his temporary bowman.

"Leave me to lash her on, m'lord. If you go aboard first, then Mrs Cadogan, you could throw me a lashing down for her ladyship and the bags."

They both looked down at her ladyship's face, which was composed at the moment.

"No, Mary next after you, my dear lord," was all she said.

He acquiesced immediately, handed Thomas the rope, and grabbed the ladder's side rope. Up he went and over the bulwark. The oarsmen were shifting around now.

"Keep your places for now," Thomas called.In a soft voice to Mary, he instructed.

"Lean well out and rely on your arms, my love."

She went up as though it were second nature and a lashing came down. Mrs Cadogan pointed to one of the two bags. He grabbed it, lashed it on and jerked on the rope. It began to sway upward.

Within a few seconds of the bag disappearing, the lashing came down again and Mrs Cadogan spoke.

"It has to be now, Thomas, or the next contraction will be on her."

They got her upright with no difficulty and Thomas lashed the rope underneath her armpits. He felt some embarrassment as he tied the knot between her breasts.

"Can you get your feet on the first ladder rung, m'lady? I shall be right behind you and the rope will be taken in above."

She nodded assent with a determined look and leaned over to the ship's side. She got her feet up on the gunnel and he jerked the rope. The slack was taken in carefully as she got her feet on the rung. He had to let her advance before he could start up. The size of her belly forced her upper torso backward. He prayed the ropeladder was strong as he got on. His face was level with her thighs. Surprisingly, it was then easy until she was level with the bulwark.He then had to use the timbers to climb level with her. Only byturning her sideways and going on deck himself was he able to drag her over the bulwark. On the deck, she collapsed, groaning again. His lordship knelt by her head. Seconds elapsed before Mrs Cadogan ascended the ladder one handed. She held the secondbag across her shoulder.

"Get her into a cabin quick."

She dropped that bag and seized the other. Thomas untied the rope around her ladyship and dragged her backward. He pulledunderneath her armpits to the top of the companionway. Mary followed to ensure footwear remained in place.

Before they had her upright to take down, Mrs Cadogan came past with the large bag. She went down first. His lordship came and knelt down by his lover.

"M'lord, we must get her ladyship up to carry her down to the cabin."

Thomas gently reached his hands under her back. Mary made sure her knees were raised and feet firmly planted on the deck. His lordship had hold of a hand and pulled as Thomas started to lift. With an initial wail, her ladyship managed to contribute to the movement. Otherwise, he could never have raised her. With a further effort of will, she managed to take actual steps down the companionway. Thomas held her and went down backward. He arrived to find Mrs Cadogan beside him. Together, they half carried, half walked her over the decking to the extra captain's cabin. Mrs Cadogan had already opened her bag and laid a large square of old canvas on the cot. To this she she pointed and directed her feet.

"Lay her on that, and bring her knees up. Good, now fetch your wife," she rapped.

Up on the otherwise deserted deck, his lordship and Mary hadtheir attention riveted to the companionway. They failed to see one ofthe oarsmen was watching from the top of the ladder. Thomas felt hehad to deal with him before anything else.

"You man, back into the boat, and secure it to the stern, *then* come aboard."

"Her ladyship is now on a cot, m'lord, and needs Mary," he quietly disclosed.

"How long had that man been stood on the ladder watching?" he asked softly.

They didn't know. Mary dragged over the bag that Mrs Cadogan had discarded. Descending backward, she allowed the bag to slide down after her.

"Do you think I should go down there too, Thomas."

"No, m'lord. I believe it is women's work now. I will fetch hot water from the galley for them and keep some in a pot to make coffee for you."

"Thank you, Thomas, indeed, thank you for all you have done today. Your command of the boat was superb."

"I only imitated a few captains' cox'ns I've rowed for, m'lord. I had better see what sort of pot the cook has for carrying."

He came back along the deck with a small, steaming, metal cauldron. It had handles, around which cloths were wrapped, and a flat bottom. He put it down on the deck and diverted to the few steps into what was normally the captain's stern cabin. A coffee pot stood on the desk. In a narrow, high cupboard behind it was a jar labeled "Coffee." He removed the wooden lid and sniffed. Captain Hopps drank good coffee. He went back out to where his lordship was nervously pacing and listening. The groans had resumed and were rising in volume as he dipped the coffee pot in the cauldron and nearly filled it.

"I will spoon in Captain Hopps' ground coffee, m'lord, and let it brew."

"What shall we do if there are complications, Thomas?""I shall take the boat and bring a doctor,"

He picked up the cauldron again. Down the companionway, it was a different world. Mrs Cadogan had a number of cloths on the deck by her at the side of the cot. On a sea chest were a large pair of forceps, a jug, a bottle, and a rubber teat. Her ladyship's groans subsided. Mrs Cadogan looked hard at her pocket watch again, then at Thomas and his burden.

"Put it over there and go," she ordered. "We will have to uncover her now," she then added. This last was directed to Mary, so he rushed up to the deck again.

He got His Lordship seated in the stern cabin, drinking coffee. The periods of noise from below came more frequently. They included a lot of shouts and screams. The sun passed its zenith and still the noise came. In a quiet moment, he went back on deck to find Mary halfway up the steps. "I needed some air, my love. It is a fine day up here."

He ran over to take her hand, oblivious to the presence on the forepeak of Bosun Parry. Words he didn't understand werescreamed from below.

"At least she has the delicacy to curse in Italian. She is not pushing hard enough. Her mother says all is still well. I must go back,"

For a moment, he just crouched there. He hoped the love he felt for his Mary followed her down and enveloped her. He straightened up and saw Parry right forward, raised his hand in greeting, then slipped back into the stern cabin. His ordship was seated at thedesk, reading the ship's log.

"I see this is already written for today, Thomas, in a very neathand. I should have thought to ask Captain Hopps if he writes it up himself. We are still likely to be here in the morning. Is there anyword from Mrs Cadogan?"

"Only to say she believes all is well, but her ladyship is not pushing hard enough. I could ask Parry the bosun about the log. He is doing something at the forepeak."

"My order to Captain Hopps was that they were *all* to keep to their quarters. Has he seen or heard anything?" His Lordship interrogated, his good eye narrowed.

"He can only have seen meself, m'lord. Should I ask him about thelog?"

"I believe it would be useful, Thomas, especially if he should tell you what he *thinks* is happening now—" At this point, a piercing scream halted the instruction.The crumpling of his face, each time her ladyship emitted one of these shrieks, was as hard to bear as thenoise itself. Thomas swiftly acknowledged his order with, "Aye, m'Lord," and went out. Parry was still there coiling a line, but one could see from the set of his ears that he was listening hard. Thomas walked past mainmast, fo'csle companionway, and foremast. Parry watched his approach with a suspicious stare.

"His lordship would like to know who it is writes up your ship's log so well, Mr Parry."

"You sound calm, Master Spencer, for a man whose wife is in agony giving birth!"

Although Parry's accent sounded Welsh, it was somehow clipped. Not the singsong type of Welsh accent he'd heard before. For long instants after he'd spoken, there was silence, but instead of renewed screaming, a low groan was followed by a new noise. Even the ship's timbers couldn't prevent Thomas's ears recognizing as the first lusty squall of a newborn babe.

"Your answer to the question?" he persisted.

"Oh, I write the log. The captain says my writing is so much better than his and the mate's. Are you not in a hurry to see if your wife has presented you with a son or a daughter?"

Parry asked this in a tone of such sardonic delight that he had to believe it was not Mary who had just given birth. Thomas stood rooted with transparent thoughts.

"I might have known it was for Lady Hamilton to give birth that you came aboard. I did not need our boat oarsmen telling me what they saw and heard. The orders were too strange. Why bring *your* wife aboard to give birth? We are not all potatoes that come from the Isle of Anglesey, however close to Ireland."

"Thomas Spencer, I need you here now. You are the father of a boy child," came Mrs Cadogan's disembodied voice. Thomas could tell from the clarity that she must be partway up the steps. He turned and ran. His lordship was standing irresolutely outside the door of the stern cabin. Mrs Cadogan's head came into view when he reached the companionway. He followed her down to see, at the foot of the steps, the square piece of canvas, previously underneath Her Ladyship. It was bundled up, the corners held together by a piece of ribbon.

"Carry this up carefully, and throw what is inside into the

sea. Wash the canvas in seawater," she ordered in a tired voice, "then come down and see the babe."

Up he went. The canvas was seeping slightly, so he hurried to the side, hung over his burden, released the ribbon, and held on to just one corner. The afterbirth and cut cord splashed into the bay, blood-streaked.

The crabs and fishes would make short work of it, he thought.

No wonder she wanted the canvas washed in seawater. That could wait until he went down into the boat, so he folded it and laid it down. Down the steps he went to find Mary standing in the larger 'tween decks space. She nursed the newly washed scrap of humanity, wrapped in a voluminous piece of soft cloth. He could see the door of the cabin was shut and hear groaning, overlaid by Mrs Cadogan speaking sharply within.

"She has refused to have him near her, and it is pointless for him to suck on me, except to get the idea. Her mother is milking her like a cow so she can be sure he is nourished. The wet nurse she arranged has to be rowed out."

Thomas looked at the tiny face, which Mary stroked with her finger.

His eyes were shut, but he had a contented look.

Better with us, than her bastard son, he thought.

"Her mother is a good woman and knew what she would do. She made preparations to be sure the babe would be fed," Mary whispered again, sensing his thoughts.

"Give him to me, my love, and I will take him up to show his lordship."

"Cradle his head properly."

She reluctantly allowed him to edge carefully up the steps, where at least the reception by the father of the newborn was welcoming, if stilted. He was trying to keep up a pretence.

"He is a fine start to your family, Thomas. I will stand godfather to him when he is baptized and wish him a long and happy life, Mary and yourself too."

"Thank you for your wishes, m'Lord," he responded loudly, before he spoke a whisper.

"Before I take him down again, I must report that Parry has worked it out. He is also the writer of the log."

"I must go ashore and chase after that corn factor who has failedto come out to the ship to judge for himself what quantity she can carry to Malta."

His Lordship spoke, much more loudly than was necessary for Thomas alone. The babe's face wrinkled at the disturbance, soThomas took him below again. Mary had heard.

"So, that is the excuse for being here. No doubt the swell madeHer Ladyship queasy and sent me into labor. We all had to stay the night on board and I gave birth."

She next gave voice to a distinct speculation."I wonder what they will tell Sir William?"

CHAPTER 21

THE CHILD IS FOSTERED, BUT BONAPARTE IS BACK!

The chance to form a view on what they had told Sir William did not come for three days. The babe had consumed in the night the bottle of mother's milk Mrs Cadogan had provided. Out in the larger 'tween decks space, Mary had laid out pallets on the deck with blankets she'd brought in the second bag. Before dawn, Mrs Cadogan had performed the same exercise on her daughter. She provided another bottle of milk Once again behind the closed door; this time, accompanied by swearing rather than groans. Shortly after, MrsCadogan made a request.

"Will you bring the boat to take us ashore?"

He left Mary feeding the babe and went off to find Parry. He was at the crew mess table.

"The new father, and how did you sleep?" he asked ironically. "Passing well, for a pallet on hard boards 'tween decks," he
answered casually.

He showed no reaction to tone or smiles. There was no gain in trying to be difficult with a man who knew what *he* knew. Now, he smiled before coming on to his request.

"I am in need of the boat and a crew to take her ladyship and her mother ashore."

"She being high and mighty, I must turn out oarsmen for you now," Parry retorted.

"Enough time for them to finish breakfast, Mr Parry. I haven't got them and their belongings up on deck yet. There may be a little wait on shore too," he conceded.

Parry eyed him speculatively. The "Mr" had been right, seeing he was seeking help.

"While it is you, Master Spencer, his lordship's steward, would there be time and the wherewithal for them to have a wet?" Parry queried.

"Upwards of half an hour and a shilling, if I have to leave the boat to find someone."

"Done, Master Spencer, I will have the boat brought round."

And I have been, thought Thomas, but it was in a good cause from the point of view that they would be more comfortable with herladyship gone and the wet nurse here.

Back he went and knocked on the cabin door, when he arrived below.

"They are bringing the boat round, Mrs Cadogan, m'lady," he called.

Mrs Cadogan opened the door a fraction in order to make herself heard.

"Please have Mary take the babe out of sight while we go."

He turned to look at Mary, and she looked back at him in a way he could tell was scandalized. Wordlessly, she retreated to the forward end of this long 'tween decks space. She was all but invisible.

"She's gone."

The door opened and out they came. Mrs Cadogan had her armup around her ladyship's waist. She had obviously been cleaned up facially since the previous evening. Her hair had been combed and tied somehow. All he could see was the front of her head, because the rest was covered by the hood of a cloak. It fell nearly to the deck and was wrapped around her. No doubt another resource drawnfrom the large bag.

"Would you please bring up the large bag, Thomas."

He didn't need to hurry. Her ladyship only shuffled to the steps.She started ascending with both feet on one step and labored breathing before she took the next. At one point, the babe gave a little cry. It carried from the dark, cavernous interior. She stiffened butlooked up to the bright sky and resumed. Mrs Cadogan squeezed uponto the deck alongside her and turned her daughter toward the top of the rope ladder. She saw the folded, blood-stained piece of canvas, dried stiff, in the corner of the deck. Thomas had left and forgotten it.

"Best you burn it, Thomas. It will not be of use again.""I will take it ashore later and do that."

He carried the bag ahead of them to the side. The boat was below, with the same four oarsmen, so he turned back.

"It would be best if I got you seated on the bulwark, m'lady. You can turn onto the ladder with me below you."

Her mother nodded agreement from the far side of her. He placed his arm around her ample back. Her mother continued to hold around her waist.

"Lean back, m'lady, and I will swing your legs up to go over the top."

He got his other arm under her knees and lifted with all his force. He supposed she was a little lighter than the day before. He doubted he could have managed without her mother taking some of herweight. That lady retained a grip to keep her balanced. Thomas climbed onto the ladder. This was the tricky bit. He had to lean well back, holding on with one hand. Hopefully, he could manage to edgeher round to get her feet securely on a rung with the other. Her mother helped by keeping Her Ladyship's bottom securely on top of the bulwark. They edged her round to gain a first foothold on the ladder. Down a few rungs he went, once she'd done that. He would be able to keep his face level with the small of her back this time.

"Will your leg hold you to swing right round?" Mrs Cadogan asked her.

"It is not my leg that feels tender," her ladyship crossly replied. Her mother took both of her arms and her bottom launched into the air space above the prow of the boat. Her second foot connected with the ladder. She gasped as the twisting motion exacerbated the soreness in the muscles of her belly. For a few seconds, she just hung by her arms. Her feet were held in place by the pressure of Thomas's body. Then she took a tentative step down and the worst was over. Thomas moved down at her pace until his feet wereaboard. She was relying on her own hands and feet to descend.

"I am holding the boat hard into the ship's timbers, m'Lady. Would you take my hand when you can feel the prow of the boat beneath your feet?"

She didn't answer, but followed the instruction. She turned very slowly with only a grimace. He stepped into the bottom of the boat. She followed and gingerly lowered herself to the starboard sidebench running. Up he went for Mrs Cadogan and the bag. That practical lady had already lashed the bag to the end of the lowering rope. Once he had ladies and bag arranged forward, he was able to pass the oarsmen and take command. There was nothing about their larger passenger to interfere with their concentration this time. Clearing the ship, Thomas was able to see the coach already waiting on the mole. By its side was a woman with long, dark hair. who had her head tilted up toward the coachman. Her laughter was audible as they approached. She did not interrupt her conversation when his lordship stepped down to the paving alongside her. He did not seem to regard this as a discourtesy and took the few steps to a rope tied to a ring bolt.

Thomas went through the usual procedure with his oarsmen. He watched for the accuracy of his estimate of the boat's speed and went forward to seize the rope's end his lordship threw. It was not bad for a left-handed throw.

Mrs Cadogan was first off. He lifted the bag to her and she placed it right by the wall. He got her ladyship to her feet and went up onto the gunwale. Still holding her hands, he coaxed her up as he edged backward. It went so well reaching the stonework that he just carried on in the same manner to the top of the steps. His lordship took her right hand off him.

"My dear and lovely lady, do not tire yourself by moving too fast. You must find your legs ashore."

"I believe I shall cope very well if your lordship will hand me to the coach."

She released Thomas's right hand from her left so she could pivot around. He moved around Mrs Cadogan to go down again and bring up the bag. When he got to the coach, her ladyship had not gone up the step. She was resting her hand on the side and in Italian conversation with the woman. She was not tall but had a broad, smooth face and flashing hazel eyes. Her cloak hung loose, and her appearance beneath it was blousy. She was clearly some years younger than her ladyship. She looked at him as the conversation came to an end. Her ladyship turned her head to speak to him.

"This is Marta, who you will take out to the ship, Thomas. She is Letizia's cousin and knows what is required of her. Thank you for your help."

With that, she turned to his lordship. he carefully handed her up into the coach and briefly turned before he followed her.

"I also thank you, Thomas."

The object of their brief thanks carried the bag to the coachman. Mrs Cadogan followed. In what seemed like the twinkling of an eye, he was at the top of the steps with Marta, pointing down. Shedescended with only a flash of sandals below her billowing skirt and cloak. He followed close behind, eyes fixed on the oarsmen, who swiftly faced their front. He gestured to the starboard forward bench and swallowed hard when she leaned toward him to sit. Her open- necked blouse was much too revealing. He stepped between the oarsmen. He concluded the decision to seat her behind a quartet of horny seamen was correct and faced them harshly.

"Pole off."

Arriving on board, he had no difficulty with this young passenger scrambling up the ladder. Mary was on deck, walking up and down and holding the babe close to her neck. Parry was in front of thestern cabin, checking wind direction for his log.

"This is Marta," he called, reaching the top of the ladder.

"Bienvenido, Marta."

Mary smiled and advanced toward her. There followed a conversation in Italian. Parry advanced to the side, looked down on his oarsmen, and resumed possession of the ship's boat.

"Jem, lash her to the stern again. The rest of you, back on board now."

"We should go below and show Marta the cabin," Thomas interrupted

Mary took her by the arm to the companionway, still talking. Down they went, Mary in the lead and Thomas bringing up the rear. The babe screwed up his eyes and wailed a moment. Perhaps he was upset by being taken back down into the gloom. Thuds sounded on the deck behind them as the oarsmen came aboard.

Better to keep both women and the babe away from the crew, Thomas thought. Mary showed Marta the cabin where her ladyship had given birth. It was now entirely tidy. They had agreed the night before she should have the cabin for privacy. They would stay wherethey were. Marta tested the cot for comfort and looked into the eyes of the babe. She held out her arms for Mary to hand him over. Her handling of the still tiny babe was expert and she held him nuzzling her thin blouse material.

Thomas backed out of the doorway, knowing what was coming, but Mary watched.

"She is suitably endowed for the task," he whispered dryly when Mary came away and closed the door.

"So, you had a good look did you, you rogue," she whispered back. "Her baby daughter has weaned very early, so her milk is still coming."

"I could not help seeing when she got into the boat. As well I kept her well clear of those horny sailor men."

"Well, there I agree with you. She has a sailor husband, who willno doubt be handy with a knife. She has been promised a room next to our new one in the *palazzo*. She can have her baby and her son with her when we go back."

"I did not know we were getting a new room. Do you mean she hasan older child?

Where are her children now and when are we going back?"

"She was told it was only a couple of days here. Her mother has her children for that short time. Yes, she has kept the bloom of youthso far."

"Well, there is nothing wrong with charms beyond youth," he asserted, playing his hand around her rump and pressing against her. "Why is your dress still padded?"

"Get off, you fool. A woman's belly does not go down immediately after she gives birth. What would she think if she came out here and found us rutting!"

"She would know less than the crew," he defended, still holding her.

"Wait until tonight. What do you think his lordship will do about them?"

"What can he do other than send them to Malta as he has said? Will we not wake the babe, doing it out here?"

"He will be with Marta part of the night. Now, go and have the cookprepare us some food. I am starved. So will Marta be when his hungry little mouth is done."

She was true to her word and better rested than either of them expected. Marta did little extras, like winding and changing the babe. They were glad to cling together that night and the following one. The large 'tween decks space became chilly in the small hours. They were lucky the days were still dry and fairly warm. The small supply of napkins for the babe in Mary's bag meant washing in seawater and drying on a line, from stern cabin to mainmast.

After one more night, his lordship arrived in a naval sloop's boat. It was weighed down with Captain Hopps, the mate, the hospital boys, and a corn factor. This last, the sole Sicilian in the boat party, went around the ship. Captain Hopps, Parry, his lordship and the corn factor assessed the quantity that could be carried. Mary was called on to interpret. It transpired the corn factor liked the 'tween decks accommodation. It would provide dry stowage for grain in sacks. If *Samuel and Jane* could be warped alongside the mole, delivery could be made from carts. Swaying aboard by sheer-legs and rope netting to a forward hatch would minimize carrying. The hold was reasonably dry. Some of the cargo could be risked there for such a short voyage. His lordship undertook to clear the necessary length ofmole. A convoy of carts would be organised.

"I will hold the sloop well out to advise *Foudroyant* to anchor in the bay. That will ensure a clear passage for you, Captain Hopps, once Ihave transferred my flag."

He shook hands with the corn factor on quantity and price, then spoke to the captain.

"I will provide you with the usual lading note for the admiralty to settle with your owners, captain. Now, Thomas, see your womenfolk and babe into the boat."

Thomas could see him looking very hard at Parry. He was trying togauge his reaction. Parry tried to look nonchalant, but didn't wholly succeed. He wanted to know what his lordship intended. Thomas went below to obey his order, feeling there was unsettled business between his admiral and the crew members. He had no idea what the outcome might be.

On arrival back at the *palazzo,* the coach was met by Tom. He showed them to a pair of rooms with an interconnecting door at the uphill end of the building. It was no coincidence they were as far away from her ladyship as possible. Their windows overlooked the end of the church, *Santa Maria degli Angeli.* They did catch some morning sunlight and were clean.

No time was allowed Thomas to enjoy the new room. Tom said his lordship and Mr Tyson needed him for correspondence. It did seem to have resumed with a vengeance. General Fox had arrived on Minorca and sufficiently taken stock to be willing to send General Graham to Malta. However, he would take with him only a few more than a thousand men with small arms. This would no more enable a proper siege of Valletta than the resources Sir Thomas and Governor Ball already possessed. King Ferdinand had also failed to make good his promise to send troops to Malta. A report from Messina indicated that the Russian troops there appeared to bepreparing to leave. Sir John Acton's latest note indicated no change in the refusal of the King to return to Naples. A first formal request came from the Austrian army for a blockading squadron to assist them in taking Genoa. There was much to contend with. The arrangement for Samuel and Jane's cargo to Malta was documented. His lordship then asked Thomas to beg Sir William to join him. His greeting at the elderly knight's door was far from usual.

"First, young man, I must congratulate you on becoming a father. Please lead me to your Mary and the child."

Thomas led him around the corridors to the new rooms and found Mary in the first of them. Marta had gone to collect her own babe and little son, he later learned. The ostensible babe of Mary and himself was asleep in a low cradle. After offering his congratulations to Mary and telling her how well she looked, Sir William was invited to look atthe babe.

"It looks as though he will have dark hair, not your glorious color, my dear Mary. Have you thought of names for him?"

"His lordship has agreed to stand as godfather, so he will have to be Horatio," Thomas replied, "but we have talked of a second name and favor Horatio William."

"Then, I insist you allow me the honor of being second godfather. I will prevail upon my lady to become his godmother, once she is recovered from her mal-de-mer. Is it not strange how a low swell can have a more unsettling effect than a great storm?"

Thomas risked only a quick glance at the fixed smile on Mary'sface before replying.

"The honor will be all ours, Sir William, when we reach a suitable time for baptism. Perhaps it was the failure of the corn factor toarrive that caused her ladyship's malady. The accommodation on board overnight was lacking in comfort."

"I dare say you have the right of it. I have never seen my lady return from an expedition looking so wan. A merchantman with provision for only a small crew is no place to spend a night unexpectedly. I hope the court will notice the lengths King George's subjects go to, so the Maltese do not starve."

The babe became restless with the noise above him and whimpered a little.

"His lordship is waiting for us, Sir William," Thomas said opportunistically.

"We shall leave you now to take good care of your babe, dear Mary," the knight responded. Both felt they had deceived him.

In the study, he was back to displaying an incisive mind on his lordship's problems.

"I see no harm in admitting to the Austrians you will only be able to blockade Genoa when substantial reinforcements reach you. You should advise your wish to be able to make that contribution, mydear Nelson. Please add you will press the Admiralty to provide the ships."

"Thank you for so admirably expressing the sentiments I feel, my dear Sir William. It also gives me something positive when I reply to Nepean's carping," his lordship responded warmly.

"If we draft that reply together, it might help to hit the target squarely. Perhaps later, as we have a free evening. My lady intends a visit to La Nova tomorrow," the knight added.

The morning brought the return of *Foudroyant* from Malta. Sir Edward had left all the supplies and marines he could spare. The seized grain ships ensured armed forces and inhabitants would not be hungry again before Christmas. A fair rationing system had been introduced by Governor Ball. The forces and their armament were adequate to watch and deter sorties by the French.

The flag lowering on *Samuel and Jane* had proceeded quickly. Parry, behind Captain Hopps, warily watched the admiral. He sensed this and was uncomfortable. He passed it off by saying he had to be back in the boat. The ship could then be warped alongside the mole, ready for loading.

On board *Foudroyant*, the raising of his lordship's flag was performed with all due ceremony. He lingered over Sir Edward's account of the way things were on Malta and Gozo. Sir Edward diffidently broached another's view.

"Although I believe he has the land forces well in hand, Sir Thomas expressed great disappointment that you had not sailed to satisfy yourself of his accuracy, my lord."

"If you could find no fault with his dispositions, Sir Ed'ard, nor should I have done. I do more good here, ferreting out supplies of corn. Those at Court who hope to make a fat profit selling to the Austrians would frustrate us. Sir Thomas will need more beforewinter is out."

Sir Edward was easily won over by the combination of logic and charm his lordship was so adept in deploying. He simply acquiesced.

"As you decide, my lord. Have we no word yet of troops?"

"Oh, General Fox is sending General Graham with a wholly inadequate number. Sir Thomas's organizational skills will be indemand until spring."

There the matter was left. The return of her ladyship to the late night gaming tables at La Nova, with both husband and lover, startedto cause

281

talk from that night on. That his lordship worked on Mediterranean fleet business until eight in the evening, counted for nothing with the gossips. Only her ladyship's late-night gaming, with an exhausted, ill admiral looking on and sometimes falling asleep, drew attention. Hence, the oft repeated comment that he was ruled by her.

The English community in Palermo were mostly unaware LordNelson rose early and worked on incoming reports from his shipsand force on Malta. Intelligence reports came from other islands and the north. Correspondence arrived from allies and time had to be found for frequent meetings at the *Colli,* which were usually frustrating.

It was that evening of her return to local society that Tom gaveforth a private comment.

"Err ledyship irs getting back in err stride. Tomorrer shay goes ter see err maajersty."

"I'm surprised she can cope," Thomas replied, seeing that Tom knew the truth.

"So shay should. I don't see err carin' for a babby."

It was a fact that she had lain in bed nearly all the time since her return from *Samuel and Jane.* She now expected Mary to resume working for her, despite receiving little help from Marta. She had to care for her own children, in addition to feeding the babe. Theproblem intensified a day later, when Marta's husband, Angelo, arrived back in harbor. He walked up to the *palazzo* with a letter for Sir William from the British Consul in Leghorn.

He was personable with a ready smile and a smattering of English. His first action on seeing his young wife's room was to prevail on Mary to take out the newly fed babe and his own two infants. He closed the door and made noisy love with Marta.

Thomas had brought him there and was left holding the baby girl. He was annoyed.

"I may not understand much Italian, but you succumbed to his pleading readily enough," he grumbled to Mary as she persuaded the small boy to eat.

"Be fair to him. He hasn't seen her for weeks. You know what it's like," she hefted the babe a little higher on her shoulder to wind him.

Later, he showed no inclination to leave. The time came for all of them to troupe down to the kitchen for dinner. It transpired his captain had signed off the entire crew for winter. Afterward, Thomas was summoned to the study.

"The young seaman who brought my letter, is he the husband of Mary's new assistant, Marta?" He confirmed this and the Knightcontinued.

"He seems reliable. The news he brings, of General Bonaparte overthrowing the Directory and taking the government of France into his own hands, could not be described as welcome."

"I do not see an adventurer like General Buonaparte doing much ina hurry to restore the state of France," his lordship commented. "Tell me about this seaman, Thomas."

"He speaks a little English, m'lord. Angelo Melone is his name. Hiscaptain has signed off the entire crew for winter," he replied.

"Do you also think him trustworthy?"

It hardly ever happened that a lowly admiral's steward was required to give a personal opinion on another. Thomas had to think at unaccustomed speed to reply.

"I believe he is to be trusted, while his wife and children are under this roof, m'lord."

"Now, that sounds a cautious approval. Bring him to me. I will decide if he would make a useful addition to my little crew. No doubt you can then assess the extent of his knowledge of our language, Sir William."

Thomas left to find Angelo. He and his infants were still in the kitchen with Letizia, so it didn't take long. He only showed Angelo into the study and shut the door again. He remained within call. The mixture of three voices from within went on for quite a few minutes. It seemed Angelo must be saying enough to interest his audience. When the call came, Thomas found his lordship sitting back.

"Melone is recruited to my little crew as Able. Take him out to *Foudroyant* to be signed on and fitted out, Thomas. Here is also a note for Sir Ed'ard."

"Aye, aye, m'lord," Thomas replied very formally and saluted.

It could not be said that Angelo's recruitment had a profound effect on his behavior. He was respectful to officers and all at the *palazzo*. He had some difficulty grasping the status of the various warrant officers aboard. Only Mr Bray, the bosun, had a merchantman equivalent. Over a few days and a number of conversations with Mary about correct translations, he began to understand how his lordship worked. This made life easier for Thomas. An extra man to run the admiral's errands gave him a little more time to support Mary.Sometimes, he merely watched the tiny Horatio's facial expressions while sleeping or being cleaned up. He took his turn at the latter. Ifhe cried, there was a reason, Thomas found. He slipped into the pattern of not expecting an unbroken night's sleep. Mary became more tired than he did. The strain of having to call on Marta to feed him fell entirely on her, he reasoned. The washing generated was endless. Her ladyship still insisted on Mary altering for her many items in her wardrobe. Her body shape underwent more change.

A few events that were positive in his lordship's work occurred over the two weeks when November ran into December. The first of these was the reply to the carping letter the secretary to the admiralty had sent on behalf of their lordships was finally sent off by courier brig. Immaculately penned and copied by John Tyson, His lordship had signed it with a left-handed flourish. That he now included "Bronte" somehow added grandeur.

"That should prove an education to the small-minded cheeseparers who never see a shot fired in anger, my dear Sir William."

"I hope it does, my dear Nelson. I cannot see any unjust accusation unanswered by fact."

Captain Brenton's full report arrived. He set out how he had fought off a dozen Spanish gunboats near Gibraltar, in order to bring the huge convoy safely to Minorca. He went on to deal with preparationsfor the onward convoy to Malta. It would now also be a troop convoy for General Graham's reinforcement. The account of the action and the extended size of the forthcoming Malta convoy brought a welcome injection of enthusiasm to his lordship's work. The littlecrew always responded well to a lightening in his mood. It was too prone to be cast down by his private correspondence, without them knowing the exact cause. The return of the sloop, *Bulldog*, before theend of the first week in December was a high point. She brought news that the Malta convoy had sailed. Moreover, General Graham had embarked two full regiments of foot. He would land with fifteen hundred properly equipped and trained men, plus all their supplies. Even if the other merchantmen taking their cargoes to sell had only minimal supplies of preserved food, their manufactures would prove useful to the civilian inhabitants.

Armed with this information, *Tria Juncta in Uno* rattled off in the coach to the *Colli*. Of course, they parted on arrival for her ladyshipto have a private meeting with her majesty, even if her influence on policy was minimal. It was obvious on their return that a good meeting with King Ferdinand and Sir John had been enjoyed. There was an air of sadness about her ladyship as she stepped down from the coach. Mary had just reached the courtyard, where Thomas had been waiting for orders on their arrival.

"Mary, my dear, I have just heard from her majesty that Lady Acton is gravely ill. Would you be so kind as to visit her, if I send a note?"

It was so far from her recent demeanor that Thomas thought Lady Acton must be nearly at death's door. He saw the look of concern that came into Mary's eyes.

"Of course, Milady."

"I shall say you will go tomorrow morning. We can spare the coach then, seeing we are to receive an artist, Mr Henry Barker, who has come on Bulldog. Can you also spare Thomas to go in the coach with Mary, my lord?"

"Of course, my dear lady. It is only this afternoon I cannot spare him. Poor Sir John, he tries to conduct business as usual, but I can tell he is sadly affected."

There was an underlying eagerness to be doing something urgent. "Would you find Mr Tyson and bring him to the study, Thomas." When they arrived, they were told of progress. "Come in, John, and bring Thomas with you. We have work to do. Now that the regiments from Minorca have sailed, I have at last obtained

285

a firm commitment from his majesty. Twelve hundred can be sent from this island. I am charged with organizing their transport. First, a letter to Sir Thomas. It will help to convince him I am not sunk in idleness here. I am taking steps to ensure he and General Graham have a properly equipped besieging force."

The letter made clear why his lordship had felt driven to that last remark by its reference to a letter from Sir Thomas. On and on they went with letters to ship owners. They promised a well-protected convoy and set out plans for embarkation. Finally, a note was penned to Captain Hardy advising him that Princess Charlotte would lead the escort. It was a worn-out Thomas who lighted his way by candle along the corridors to bed. Mary was wide awake, rocking thehealthily growing Horatio. Marta had been in to feed him. She lookedat his tired eyes, made sore by melting sealing wax.

"You have had a busy time today, and I shall have a bad time tomorrow," she stated.

"So, you assumed, my love, as I did, that Lady Acton is at death's door."

"I shall be as kind to her in a hopeful way as I can be. It will be the thought you are waiting for me in the coach that will keep me going," she confided.

He took her hand in both of his and caressed it. He was a lucky man to have a wife who loved him and a child for them to bring up astheir own.

Mary's visit to Lady Acton was indeed a trial, to find her so wasted. Her offspring were so lively and receiving no discipline from Sir John's niece. She was only fourteen herself. The return in the coach was her only respite. There was to be a well-attended party in the *palazzo* that evening. Her ladyship had to be prepared. Tom and Thomas had to lay in the drink, before serving. It was strange she would not let Mary bring the babe. She was quite willing for her mother to have him. She came into the large receiving room early to greet their guests. The artist, Henry Barker, was amongst the first arrivals. She introduced him to Sir William, with whom he had a conversation about their mutual enthusiasms. Thomas moved around, serving tea and wine. The person with whom Mr Barker had the most enthusiastic conversation was Miss Knight. She was something of an artist herself. Thomas smiled inwardly when Sir Edward arrived. She was obviously torn between her desire to cultivate the acclaimed artist of the Nile panorama and the alternative of enjoying conversation with the gallant flag captain. Thearrival of his lordship solved the problem. Mr Barker had to be introduced to him. On providing him with a glass of wine, Thomas heard first the fulsome thanks to the artist for keeping the fame ofHis Lordship's victory at the Nile alive. Then the artist answered the question as to what he had been doing on Minorca. He had made sketches of the three decker, *Queen Charlotte*. His following remark caused is lordship to stiffen, although his smile didn't falter.

"'Tis said that Lord Keith is on his way to make her his flagship."

"The gossip between one station and another is truly amazing," His

Lordship responded.

The following evening, Mr Barker arrived out of the rain to receive some letters from Sir William for Naples and Rome. One was particularly dear to him. It was an introduction from Miss Knight toher friend, Angelika Kaufmann, another well-known artist. His lordship kindly advised that the convoy in which Mr Barker wassailing would not leave until late the following day. He was pressedto stay this evening and to return to dine the following day.

That, of course, was a naval middle-of-the-day dinner. Mr Barker also met John Tyson, who was well acquainted with his father. The result was a jolly dinner party. It was brought to an end only by *Bulldog* making the signal that the convoy was about to set sail. Mr Barker took with him the good wishes of *Tria Juncta in Uno,* who were taking their ease while the weather was wet. A couple of days later, word came from Malta that General Graham had landed. His lordship was achieving progress even while he simply conducted paperwork from the *palazzo*. Thomas and Mary needed a period of stability to cement their new family status.

Christmas drew nearer, and the Sicilian convoy to Malta alsosailed and landed. The return of Captain Hardy brought news. Sir Thomas and Governor Ball had calculated they would need another grain convoy by the end of January. Sir William and His Lordship began casting around for information about supplies. This was whereAngelo began to prove his usefulness. The news from the north proved far less to their liking, especially that coming from France via Genoa. One evening, Sir William read aloud from a correspondent.

"The Directory has now been replaced with a Consulate of three and General Bonaparte is the named First Consul. He has imitated the Roman Republic just before it became the Roman Empire, with himself as Augustus Caesar!"

"I did warn you to beware of what he would do, my dear Nelson, thanks to there being no young military rivals on hand."

"My dear Sir William, I took your warning to heart, with MacDonald locked up in Genoa and Massena still contending Switzerland with Field Marshal Suvorov. Now, I hear from Sir John that Suvorov has retired to Vorarlberg."

"But that is Austrian territory, my dear Nelson, so the French have all Switzerland in their grip. a Bonaparte has some freedom to maneuver," the knight concluded with a depressed shake of his head.

CHAPTER 22

NELSON IS SUPERSEDED, AND SIR WILLIAM REPLACED

It was as though the gaiety of Christmas in *Palazzo Palagonia* was designed to hold at bay a sense of foreboding. This was on more than one front. The first of these amounted to the local portents that all was far from well with the Russian alliance. Admiral Ouschakoff had withdrawn his ships from the blockade of the Maltese Grand Harbor well before the gales struck at Christmas. He had also transported the Russian troops withdrawn from Messina all the way to Corfu.

The second was the supply of corn needed to sustain Malta for the entire winter. His lordship was still determined to capture or destroy *Genereux* and *Guillaume Tell*, the only two French ships of the line to escape the Nile. The latter was one of the block ships in Grand Harbor. Winkling out the block ships depended upon being able to press the siege of Valletta. That required Sir Thomas to be sustained in his command of naval land forces and cooperation with the army. His correspondence caused his lordship some disquiet. This was known to the little crew, but none saw his confidential letters. There was a discreet enquiry around the *palazzo* as to whom, if anyone, had been regularly visiting the court. The period when her ladyship had failed to visit her majesty for weeks at a time came in for particular scrutiny. The implication was someone had suggested there was a royal spy. This was not lost on members of the little crew. No-one had the finger specifically pointed at him and Angelo had joined them too late to be a suspect.

Angelo's own enquiries for His Lordship, on the subject of grain ships, were going slowly. There were captains of ships contracted to load grain at a number of small Sicilian ports but no news yet of their assembly point. This was essential to be able to seize enough at one time to keep the Maltese fed until spring.

The final corrosive influence was the lack of confirmation from the admiralty that Lord Keith was ordered back into the Mediterranean as Commander-in-Chief. The rumor mill to the effect he had been could not be ignored. That *Queen Charlotte* lay waiting at Port Mahon to become a flagship was a potent signal.

Most of the festivities were in the *palazzo* rather than invitations out. It was a mixed blessing for those who served the household. Gambling came to a sudden end. There were less desperately late nights out, but more work to ensure hosts and guests were fed and watered. His lordship still kept up a frantic hunt for intelligence as to the whereabouts of *Genereux*. That ship had become illusive. Supplies of grain were becoming so. Incoming correspondence slowed as the weather worsened. Attempts to persuade King Ferdinand back to Naples continued to fall on deaf ears.

Thomas and Mary did not mind being restricted to life in and around the *palazzo*. Their quarters were noisier with Angelo and Marta in the next room. Two babes and one small boy running and talking made the domesticity less than relaxing. Yet it was interesting to compare experiences and learn new words. The strongest difference Thomas recognized was that the other couple were more openly affectionate. He found himself beginning to copy them. Their little piece of the *palazzo* seemed to develop a unique character that excluded the other servants. In the early hours of Christmas morning, when all was quiet within and the babe slept, Mary mentioned it. "Do you realize, my lover, you said '*Mamma mia*' at that last gust of wind? You are becoming more Italian in your manner than ever I am."

"It felt as if it would take the roof off," he whispered fiercely.

He turned in the bed and reached an arm around her waist. "Should we be noisy like them?"

"No noise at all. No-one outside the room will hear us in this wind, but it will wake the babe." sh

Afterward, with the wind still howling outside, face to face, she whispered again.

"Did I tell you Mrs Cadogan brought him some more mother's milk while you were still with his lordship? It makes life easier for Marta, and he sleeps well after it."

"No, you didn't, but it's nice to have peace to start the day of our Savior's birth. Does she look at the babe or say anything?"

"Oh, she always spends minutes looking at him, and this time she said how well he is growing and what a good job we are doing."

"I find her a very good woman," he opined. "I reckon I could sleep again now."

Keeping the parties going was hard work. A large number of people came to offer seasons greetings and stayed for hours. However, his lordship relaxed his working hours for some days.Nothing of a non-urgent nature was dealt with. There was also the benefit for Tom that he did not have to get him up and dressed so early. That only gave him more time to hang around the kitchen and Letizia. She was pleased when breakfast was called for and she could send him off to serve. She had more than enough to do.

What brought the reduced working hours to an end was news fromAngelo. He had finally fallen in with a couple of old shipmates in a tavern. They were about to be taken by cart on the mountain road to the old city of Girgenti. A ship owner who was shorthanded had a ship lying in the small port below the city. He had provided the cart totake crew members hired in Palermo. This was the last day of theold year, indeed the old century. The cart would take more than the following day to cross the mountains. There was time for his lordshipto order a sloop to sail round to the west and along the south coast. Very careful orders were drawn up for the commander. Return to Palermo, if he found no convoy gathering. Sail straight to Malta and report to Sir Thomas and Governor Ball, if he found a concentration of ships.

The weather was much calmer on New Year's Day. The sloop's excellent start had his lordship and the entire little crewwaiting with bated breath over the next few days. Of course, the sloop would be slower, having to tack southeast along the far coast.It would not take long to cross the open sea to Malta if a Sicilian convoy was forming up. Any further enquiry in Palermo would be risky. It would arouse the suspicions of the merchants and nobles in the consortium that had to exist to sell grain to the Austrians. It wouldthen sail too early for Sir Thomas to descend on the ships in port.

A whole week went by and no news had come. The assumption had to be made that Sir Thomas now knew there were grain ships to be seized. Late on the Tuesday afternoon, the sloop was sighted far to the east, coming from the Messina Strait. Much closer was a brig rounding *Monte Pellegrino* from the west, flying a Royal Navy ensign. Being able to sail close to the wind, her sails filled to bringher across the bay toward the mole. In the last of the daylight, she hove to just outside La Cala and lowered a boat. His lordship looked on from his *palazzo* vantage point and took the telescope from his good eye.

"I wonder why I have a sense of foreboding. Show the commanderin when he arrives, Tom." With that, he turned and stalked into the study.

The commander, when he strode through the archway into the courtyard, looked pink cheeked and solemn, carrying a document folder tied with ribbon. Tom led him up the stone steps. Thomas let him reach the landing before he discreetly followed.

"My lord, I bring orders from Lord Keith, the Commander-in-Chief,."The door closed, with Tom outside. He fetched wine and two goblets on a silver tray. His lordship would not be inhospitable to the bearer of unwelcome orders. As later transpired, there was a method about His Lordship's hospitality. The commander had returned to his brig as Sir William entered.

"My dear Sir William, we are shortly to have Lord Keith back withus as Commander-in-Chief, accompanied by a lady it appears. Imust dictate an acting Commander-in-Chief's report. I hope you will listen in case I go wrong."

My dear Nelson, I see no chance of you going wrong but will gladly listen. When and where does he arrive?"

"He goes first to Port Mahon to raise his flag in *Queen Charlotte*. He will look into Genoa. I am ordered to rendezvous with him at Leghorn and account for my stewardship of his command." That sounded bitter, but the addition was in a much milder tone

"You may leave us for an hour, Thomas."

He gratefully fled to Mary and told what news the brig from Lord Keith had brought.

"The powers that be in London are coming down hard on hislordship. I reckon the turn of poor old Sir William and her ladyship is yet to come. There is precious little hope for this poor mite," was her forthright opinion.

"He is better off with everyone believing he is ours."

He was thankful their talking had not yet wakened the contented-looking babe.

"I sense Mrs Cadogan is uneasy about the future. Sir William is an old man, and some nephew called Greville is heir to his lands. Her ladyship has risen so high and is now so proud she cannot see the risk of a fall coming," Mary went on.

"What I heard Lord and Lady Elgin say must be what people in London believe," Thomas reasoned miserably, "but what will become of us?"

"We just watch and hope we can get home safely with somemoney in our pockets," Mary replied, took his hand and looked to thecradle.

When he went back to the study, his lordship was in a morecomposed frame of mind. The report was written out and Mr Tyson was already writing a copy.

"Ha, Thomas. It will not be long before we have a copy signed and sealed to go off in the brig. We shall not sail for Leghorn before next Thursday."

His lordship clearly did not wish to arrive days before Lord Keith. Perhaps her ladyship had exerted pressure. She would not want him tempted to arrange an assignation with Adelaide Correglia. If so, her husband had no inkling.

"I hope you are not running the risk of Lord Keith arriving a day or more ahead of you, my dear Nelson. I see no merit in getting off on the wrong foot with him."

"There is no risk at all, my dear Sir William. *Foudroyant* is much faster through the water than *Queen Charlotte*. Whatever the wind we will still be there first. Also, the brig must have gained a few days on Lord Keith's frigate between Vigo and a point south of PortMahon."

All to the good, thought Thomas. Another full week with Mary and the babe!

That, however, amounted only to the nights. Work for his lordship intensified the following morning after the sloop's commander had finally arrived in the hours of darkness. He had reported the build-up of a convoy at Girgenti to Sir Thomas. He had sent a letter to his lordship, stating his intention to remove the entire convoy to Malta. His admiral was in no doubt he should reply, giving the baronet afree hand to ensure the people could be fed. That was only the start of it. He had to call in Sir William to try and forestall any diplomatic crisis arising. Surprisingly, the old knight was relaxed about thesituation.

"Akragas it was called by the ancient Greeks. Agrigentum by the Romans. It is now much less of a port than the Girgenti of the Saracens or those more ancient cities. I should say, my dear Nelson,that assembling a fleet of merchantmen in such a quiet place was designed by someone to hide the ships. Those guilty of subterfuge can hardly complain of being found out."

"I have written to Sir Thomas, giving him a free hand. It would havebeen as well to have an account that fair play has been done to the ship owners and masters. We could not send anyone in time."

"There is an agent of mine close enough for another to send him a message by carrier pigeon. That is, if you wish to go to so much trouble."

"If you would be so very kind, my dear Sir William."

The old man took his leave to set his communication in hand. He had word back by the same means the following day. The escorting away of the grain fleet by *Culloden* had seemed to be amicable. The sloop returned from just off the south coast the following day. The word from Sir Thomas confirmed the deed was done. He would soonhave the ships unloaded on Malta, paid off and free to return. His lordship wrote to him by return, confirming approval of his action.

"One more item to update my report to Lord Keith. It shows the energy with which I am seeking to throw the French out of Valletta."

Work continued apace to ready *Foudroyant* and her flotilla for the voyage north. It would not be a particularly large flotilla. His lordship was not prepared to weaken the blockade of Valletta. aft Frigates were in short supply. Even *Princess Charlotte*, which he had tried to keep close by while Captain Hardy knocked the crew back intoshape, was now sailing out to the west. Any French relief forcewould have to come from there.

Knocked into shape was the right way to put it, thought Thomas. He reflected on the orders for the flotilla of small craft. Captain Hardy was a great one for the use of starters in the hands of bosun's mates. It was a wonder brutal methods were able to restore disciplined efficiency on a ship. No doubt Captain Hardy's reputation went before him. It would have been enough to make the goodhands realize what was coming and determined to keep their own noses clean. He would expect a hundred and twenty out of the one hundred and eighty to be fair to middling. Then there was the ruthless way the captain transferred out officers and warrant officers whom he found not up to the mark. His lordship replaced them with more promising appointments. The majority before the mast could see those in authority over them being treated no more kindly than their own minority of malcontents. The response would be to restore some pride to the ship.

In his own case, the Captain had been fair, and not just because he was one of the little crew. No doubt others felt the same way. Of course, his loyalty to his lordship would have been an influence. That would have been the same with any captain. That loyalty, on the part of many more than himself, would be needed to sustain him through a difficult time.

The night before they sailed, it was a miracle the babes and little boy slept at all. There was desperate love-making in both rooms. It had to

come to a sudden end in full darkness. A lantern-lit procession to the
ship was required before the capstans began to turn. As it was, his
lordship had been generous in allowing themmost of the night in
the *palazzo*. Sir Edward had all ready for a dawn departure. The great
cabin had been equipped with favored possessions the day before.
The coffin sat behind his desk andchair. Although it had been
there when Thomas arrived the previous day, he doubted Sir Edward
had kept it in that position during his independent cruises. The desk
contents had been renewed. Tom and he had restocked his lordship's
pantry. He always entertained some of his officers.

The plan was to send one of the smaller and faster craft to
lookinto the Bay of Naples. All needed to be as well as it could be there.
Foudroyant would stand out to sea until approaching the mouth
ofthe Tiber. At least an exchange of signals with *Minotaur* would be
advisable to check how things stood in Rome. Thereafter, a look into
Civitavecchia before bringing up *Monte Argentario* would suffice. The
strait to the landward of *Isola del Giglio* and the *Canale di Piombino*
would allow them to review how matters stood all the way up the coast
and to benefit from the easterly breeze off the land.

For the time of year, the sailing conditions for their passage to
the north were very good. *Foudroyant* was of the most recent design
of large third rates. A good copper bottom that had been in the water
less than two years made for a fast sailor. She had a taut crew at full
strength. Mr Gardner was an excellent sailing master and Sir Edward
was keen to make the ship fly with his lordship's flag aloft. Those crew
members involved in frequent castings of the log and the readings took
it cheerfully. Well they might, because gunnery practice was confined
to periods of shortened sail. King Ferdinand's *Marina Militare* and
Captain Louis respectively had matters well in hand. There was no
cause for delay and the deviation well to the west of north made the
sailing even easier. His lordship was now so confident they would reach
Leghorn before Lord Keith that he allowed more frequent shortening
of sail for gunnery practice. His sole requirement of Sir Edward was
that all firing should be offpopulated stretches of the shoreline.

Empty barrels as targets were on occasion towed by longboat to seaward and large amounts of powder were expended. Officers in charge of individual batteries anxiously consulted their watches for the speed of reloading. No one wished to be a laggard when it came to gunnery. Improvement was sustained over the final long stretch from Piombino to Leghorn. They arrived a bare half day before Lord Keith's enormous flagship led his fleet into the anchorage.

Queen Charlotte had not even dropped one of her anchors before a signal was flown. Midshipman Parsons, complete with book and glass, read off the flags.

"Rear Admiral *Foudroyant* and Captain to repair on board flagship."

The admiral's barge had already been lowered in anticipation of such an order. Both were on the quarterdeck, dressed for the pull across. The terse wording did not seem to bode well. His Lordship looked at Sir Edward.

"So, that is how it is going to be. Tom Allen to me."

Thomas and Angelo, on the larboard gangway, watched the boat pull across. His lordship was met at the entry port by a slim officer. They had half an hour watching to be sure they were on hand for the boat's return. The coastal strip the other side was fairly flat and uninteresting. Thomas already knew from Angelo that the buildings of the town offered some good entertainment. The place was known as Livorno to its inhabitants, and just about everyone other than the English. That wouldn't make them any less welcome. Thomas, however, had a feeling in his bones that there would be no opportunity.

When they saw Sir Edward and his lordship go down the ladder into the boat, they waited only until they could see the expressions on faces at the stern. Thomas led quickly down to the passage at the break. Their status allowed them past the first marine sentry to arrive alongside the second at the door of the great cabin. His lordship's face looked like thunder, Sir Edward's extremely concerned, and Tom's just glum. When they arrived and the marine sentry came to attention, they were noticed.

"Some wine for Sir Ed'ard and myself, Thomas. You may leave, Angelo. I doubt I shall need you this side of Palermo. Call for dinner, Tom."

Thomas followed them into the great cabin.

"At least Lord Keith is instituting a proper blockade of Genoa, mylord."

"He has the ships, Sir Ed'ard, that I never had when it would have been best done."

Thomas poured two glasses of wine out of His Lordship's decanter.

"Now, we have to accompany a quarter of his fleet. First to Palermo where he will do better than I in persuading King Ferdinand back to Naples. Then to Malta, for him to improve on my dispositions or those Sir Thomas has made."

"His lordship will be hard pressed to improve on anything with no more troops," Sir Edward stoutly supported.

"Well, he has enough lordly advisers to help him come up with something. Even his flag lieutenant is that young Lord Cochrane, although I did see some promise in his attitude. Let us hope Lord Keith does not kill it. You may leave us the decanter here, Thomas."

Thus dismissed, Thomas went to His Lordship's pantry and squeezed in with Tom and Angelo. It was smaller than what passed for the three-berth cabin they slept in but better for holding a whispered private conversation.

"Fair upset, errs lordship, werth Lord Keith questyernin' all he ars done," Tom said.

"Zees Lord Keef, e come to Palermo?" asked Angelo.

"Yes, he intends to persuade King Ferdinand to return to Naples," Thomas informed.

Angelo looked incredulous and then started to laugh, the volume rising.

"Quiet, or ers lordship and Zur Ed'ard ull 'ear urs."Tom, like Thomas, also started laughing silently.

The collective opinion of all three of them, on the persuasive power of Lord Keith over King Ferdinand, proved correct in the days after their Palermo landfall. This was Tuesday, the fourth of February and they found on arrival nothing to cause them further amusement. The coach was waiting on the mole. Lord Keith's one concession to his lordship had been that he should proceed inshore and send word ashore for himself as Commander-in-Chief to meet King Ferdinand. *Queen Charlotte* and the other liners anchored in the bay. There was a sense in which even this was demeaning. It reduced his lordship's role to mere messenger. He could not go ashore without first having himself rowed out to *Queen Charlotte*.

The barge crew were ordered and the barge lowered into the waterof La Cala. Tom had been given a letter to her ladyship, as well as one to Sir William. The little crew were mustered to go ashore. His lordship had no doubt that days would be spent trying to persuade King Ferdinand to return to Naples. Once the gangway was lowered into position, her ladyship descended from the coach, looking very solemn. She looked positively stricken when she saw it was onlyTom walking down to the mole's paving, followed by Thomas and Angelo.

"Where is His Lordship?"

"Milady, ers lordship murst report to Lord Keith," Tom replied, waving an arm in the general direction of *Queen Charlotte* andpulling out the letters for her.

"You had better come in the coach, all three of you."

She took the letters and put the one addressed to her into a cloak pocket.

Only when they followed her to ascend the step did they realize that Sir William was in the coach, resting with his head back in thefar corner. The three of them sat across from the knight and his lady,cramped and not knowing what to say. Her Ladyship engaged Angelo in an Italian conversation that Thomas thought was about Marta when they were nearing *Porta Felice*. By that time, Sir William had read the letter addressed to him. He then looked across at Tom and Thomas searchingly.

"Does either one of you know the content of this letter?"

"I believe it asks you to arrange an audience for Lord Keith with hismajesty, to persuade him to return to Naples," Thomas ventured.

"Lord Keith obviously does not believe his lordship and myself. Wehave tried the same with as much determination as any two men canmuster."

"Then we must assist him in making a fool of himself," her ladyship intervened in a brittle voice.

"One of the last useful things we do here," said Sir William with theghost of a smile.

By that time, they were halfway up *Piazza Marina*. They fell silent for the seconds it took them to reach the entrance arch. Mary and Mrs Cadogan were waiting by the steps. They looked surprised to see the three sailors step down, before assisting her ladyship and SirWilliam in turn.

"His lordship is away to Lord Keith's flagship," her ladyship offered by way of explanation. "We will wait half an hour for dinner in casehe arrives."

"I will send to Sir John in the meantime," added her husband.

Mrs Cadogan went with her daughter to her chamber. Tom went toassist Sir William. Angelo went off to their room, where Marta hadthe babes and their son. This left Mary and Thomas to dash to the kitchen and advise Letizia of the need to slow down the cooking of dinner.

"What did Sir William mean about one of the last useful things he will do here?" Thomas asked Mary, his arm around her as they walked into the kitchen.

"A vessel came a few days after you sailed, bringing Sir William's letter of recall from the ministry. Someone called the HonorableArthur Paget is being sent in a fast frigate to replace him," Mary replied before a brief conversation with Letizia.

Then, they were free to follow Angelo up the stairs.

"What will they do when this Paget arrives?" Thomas wondered aloud.

"Why, go home to England, I suppose. Sir William has estates somewhere called Pembrokeshire, doesn't he?" Mary speculated.

"I believe that is in the far west of Wales, my love. It is a very long way from London, where a gentleman of learning like Sir William would want to live. Even that is much colder in winter than here, for an old gentleman."

"I am more worried what will happen to us when they go home

to England. I do not believe his lordship will keep this place on when they go."

Mary brought an air of cold reality to bear on their situation.

"The way it is shaping, I do not believe Lord Keith will allow him to. Where will you and the babe go while I am likely at sea with His Lordship? He does not want to leave before finishing the French ships."

"You must speak to him about our situation, my love."

Finding an opportunity took a little time. His lordship had to accompany Lord Keith repeatedly to the *Colli* and *Palazzina Cinese*. When King Ferdinand was hunting, the *Colli* was Sir John Acton's chosen venue. When he was with his family, they were now spending more time in this new residence. There was no doubt this was wearisome to both their lordships. King Ferdinand's evasions were supported by his queen. She continued to be anxious over the security of her family.

A new evasion was the need to remain closer to the action to evict the French from Valletta. While this was useful to wring a promise of more troops for the siege, it did show the extent to which Lord Keith was wasting his time. The point arrived at which he and his accompanying lady availed themselves of the opportunity to dine at *Palazzo Palagonia*. The invitation for this had been given by Sir William at the outset of their stay.

Thanks to there being two hosts and a hostess, joint consideration of the guest list and preparation was needed. This gave Thomas his opportunity to see His Lordship in the study. A copy of the table plan was needed so Tom and he could show the principal guests to their places.

"Here you are, Thomas. Go over it carefully. Ensure Tom's understanding and your own agree. It is important this dinner goes well."

"Aye, m'Lord, we will make sure to get it right. Could your lordship spare me a moment about Mary's worry for herself and the babe when Sir William and her ladyship leave for home?"

His Lordship's face looked troubled at the very thought. His good eye concentrated on Thomas and he spoke very carefully and sincerely.

"No doubt you expect this residence will have to go when Sir

William and his lady leave. That is certain, but the timing is not. Sir William's replacement is not yet here, and I must take *Genereux* and *Guillaume Tell* before I lower my flag. If I am unable to discharge you with a passage home for all three of you, I will find a place for you on my estate at Bronte. Please assure Mary she is not to worry. I will see she has a roof over her head."

"I am most obliged to your lordship. It is my hope I can carry on in the service," Thomas replied with relief.

"Your loyalty does you credit, and I will do what is best for you all."The obvious meaning was that he could say no more at present.

Mary's view was succinct when he recounted the response he had received.

"I would prefer not to be in a hovel halfway up a mountain. It would be better than nothing, if I had you to myself."

"Better if it works out he can find us a passage home. Then, there is no passage fare to eat into the money we have saved, my love."

"Then we must seize the opportunity, if it offers. It would suit both him and her if we were tucked away in your Gotham with our money."

The day of the dinner came and both of them were engaged in serving. As usual, Mary supervised the carrying in of hot dishes by serving girls from the kitchen. Thomas was with Tom and Angelo on readying and serving wine. Before they started, the uniformed members of the little crew were lined up to show the principal guests to their places. The first to arrive were Lord Keith and lady with the admiral's flag lieutenant, Lord Cochrane. His lordship escorted them in, and Lord Keith halted. "I recognize your body servant, Lord Nelson, but who are these two others?"

"This is Thomas Spencer, my steward, who can read and write in afair hand, and this is Angelo Melone, who speaks a fair amount of English. Both are prime seamen."

"They are well turned out, Lord Nelson, but I see you have abandoned the pigtail. Do you not also have a Secretary?"

"Yes, my lord. He is John Tyson and will join us shortly."

Lord Keith sniffed slightly as though to indicate Mr Tyson should have been there. "Is Spencer also one of your Norfolk men?" he enquired.

"No, my lord, he is from Gotham by Nottingham. His father is a tenant of Lord Curzon."

Nelson was keen to turn the subject away from his absent secretary.

"Ah, yes, his son married the late Lord Howe's daughter but died young, although I believe there is a grandson."

"I have only lately heard of the death of Lord Howe, my lord. A grievous loss to the service," Nelson hurriedly responded.

"I believe he never recovered from the government's refusal to honor the terms upon which he ended the mutiny at Spithead. Perhaps he should never have accepted the commission in the first place,"

Lord Keith noticed that his accompanying lady was becoming restless, although still attentive to the conversation.

"No doubt we could now be shown to our places at table."

Tom bowed, indicated the center of the top table and led off. It was an unusual line up to have Lord Keith and lady seated between his lordship and her ladyship, who normally cut up his meat for him. It had seemed politic to place her ladyship one side of Lord Keith. She was next to her husband. His lordship was the far side of the guests of honor and Lord Cochrane beyond him. Accordingly, when all the guests were seated and meat was being served, it was Mary who arrived with a plate of ready-diced meat for him. It was his, "Thank you, Mistress Spencer," that showed how sharply retentive was the mind of the Scottish lady next to him.

"Is that the wife of your steward, Lord Nelson?" she asked languidly.

"Yes, my lady. She frequently assists Lady Hamilton's mother, Mrs Cadogan, and is also an excellent seamstress."

"Quite a domestic establishment you share with Sir William and his lady. I am surprised that Lady Nelson has not come out to join this household. The climate is so much warmer here."

Thomas, serving wine on a table nearby, could see that his lordship was positively squirming at this. Tom, who had just replenished Lord Cochrane's glass, moved behind his master, but forbore to pour him more wine before he made a response.

"I fear my wife is a poor sailor, madam. She would have to cross

Biscay in a small ship in winter. Even here in the Mediterranean, sudden storms blow up."

It was surprising how this older, angular Scotswoman could so readily get under His Lordship's guard. She didn't even knowing the true extent of his commitment to Lady Hamilton or the real nature of the "domestic establishment," Thomas thought.

She resembled the thin-faced, dour admiral, who was older than his lordship but looked a well man. Could she be the Commander-in-Chief's sister? He did not seem to be a man one would feel inspired to follow. The demeanor of Lord Cochrane, in earnest conversation with His Lordship a little earlier, had shown that.

Funnily enough, it was Lord Keith himself who saved his lordship from the acute observations of his accompanying lady.

"Storms or not Lord Nelson, we must take whatever the wind and the sea throw at us the day after tomorrow. We shall sail for Malta with King Ferdinand's troops before he finds an excuse not to send them. Have Sir Edward embark one company."

There was nothing the rear admiral could do but accept the order.

CHAPTER 23

OFF MALTA, NO NELSON TRIUMPH
SO CLOSE TO BLOODLESS!

King Ferdinand had in fact excelled himself. His officers and ministers had equipped no less than twelve hundred troops to be embarked for Malta. They were to replace a mere five hundredPortuguese. Their commander had been prevailed upon by his lordship to remain ashore, until replacements arrived. Whatever the reason for King Ferdinand's new contribution, Lord Keith could only seize the opportunity with both hands. Soldiers and their equipment were loaded in no less than five ships.

The Sicilian company of soldiers aboard *Foudroyant* wereseriously crowded. All their equipment and supplies were stacked around them down the centers of both gun decks. For the short voyage to Malta, it was hardly worth stowing their property in the hold. Some of the men had to accept the claustrophobic conditionsof the orlop, to ensure all was loaded. For the first full day's sailing, the February weather was surprisingly kind. Open sea allowed the small fleet to sail on with riding lights throughout the night. The usualpre-first light procedure of beating to quarters aboard *Foudroyant*was slightly ahead of the other ships, being in the van. It appeared this day would go well too. The weather was still kind and the ships bowled along. *Queen Charlotte* flew a signal for his lordship to repairon board, shortly before nine o' clock in the morning. The recipient's reaction was quick.

"Have my barge lowered and the crew mustered, Sir Ed'ard. I shall go across."

The row across took longer than he was on board the flagship. It was only as the boat returned that his watching loyalists realized how put out he was by his meeting with Lord Keith. Seeing the looks of concern on the faces around him, he seemed to rally and threw out an invitation.

"I believe we shall take advantage of these clement conditions and have a dinner in the great cabin tomorrow, Sir Ed'ard. As many officers and young gentlemen as we can. It is, after all, the anniversary of the great Earl St. Vincent's triumph."

Tom, Thomas, and Angelo now had their work set out to prepare atable for numerous occupants. The cook in his galley would beanxious.

Well into the afternoon the occasion ran. His lordship's wine and reminiscences of the battle of a mere three years ago flowed around the table. Many of them had been there. Their careers, like their host's, had carried them higher since that day. Their admiral was more like his old self, incisive, but kindly to the youngsters. Theironly knowledge of the events their elders were describing came fromlistening. The happier atmosphere was not dented by the initial events after first light the following day.

They had a landfall off Saint Paul's Bay. This had at its landward end one of the small ports used to supply the besiegers, also called Saint Paul's. His lordship chose to signal the flagship to ask if he should lead the small fleet in. The bald reply was, "No." There was scarcely time to register the affront this implied. A distant frigate signaling was being observed by Sir Edward with his eye to theglass. Young Mr Parsons had been summoned with his signal book, ready to read off the entire signal. Sir Edward swung his telescope round to the nearest liner, *Lion*, a sixty-four, and then on to the flagship, which was unsighted.

"I see *Lion* has begun repeating Captain Peard's signal to *Queen Charlotte*, which absolves us, Mr Parsons. Read out the full signal so soon as you are able."

"It says *French convoy led by a seventy-four sighted west of Sicily bearing southeast,* Sir Edward," the youngster got out, hesitant and high pitched.

"Well, there should be adequate time to find them northwest of Gozo, while the wind is against them," Sir Edward observed, turning to his lordship.

"It seems General Buonaparte, or First Consul Buonaparte, as we must now call him, does not wish to allow his garrison to surrender," was his admiral's first reaction.

"Signal from flag," Mr Parsons interrupted, shouting into the stiffening breeze.

Sir Edward paced to the other side of the quarterdeck, accompanied by his lordship. The captain's glass was raised. He smiled even before Mr Parsons sang out the order. He recognized the numbers of the ships being given the order.

"Flag Officer *Foudroyant* to detach with *Alexander, Audacious, Northumberland,* and *Success* to seek French convoy to windward," the youngster sang out.

"Now, there is something for us to do. I am sure the Frenchseventy-four is the *Genereux,* eighty," His Lordship preempted Sir Edward.

"Wait, my Lord, there is a second signal. Ah, it is for *Lion* alone," the captain added.

"*Lion* to detach to the Kemmuna Straits and prevent use by French convoy," the youngster sang out again.

His Lordship lifted his glass toward *Queen Charlotte,* which had turned southwest.

"What is Lord Keith doing now?" he asked no one in particular.

"I believe he is going into the bay to land troops," Thomas heardSir Edward reply.

Angelo and he had been assigned to the crew of a quarterdeck long gun as sponger and rammer. They still stood ready after beating to quarters.

"H'm, the wind has shifted from a few points east of north to a few points west and strengthened. Lord Keith will still leave the approach to Valletta wide open for another day. He sends one ship to block two straits," his lordship criticized.

"I will have the guns double-lashed and ports closed, then stand down the crews for breakfast, my lord. We have a rising sea and head winds to contend, bad enough without these troops cluttering the gun decks," Sir Edward advised.

"Signal *Success* and *Alexander* to take the Malta Strait. They will both be quicker than the rest of us, seeing that *Alexander* carries no troops," His Lordship ordered.

He made toward the top of the ladder, where Tom waited for him on the steps. His only assignment was to go to His Lordship's aid, if need be, once the ship had beaten to quarters.

"It is as well Lieutenant Harrington is used to command. No doubt it will aid him to be made post the sooner," Sir Edward commented to the Officer of the Watch.

The signal sent, his lordship had gone down to the breakfast Tom would serve him. Thomas dawdled, while Angelo and the gun captain were checking the double lashings on their gun. Being partof the little crew, Thomas and Angelo ate with Tom, so were in no hurry. The wind was bringing low clouds and the sea was getting steeper. The three heavily laden liners tacked northeast to give themsea room to round Gozo to the north. To larboard, *Success* had already disappeared into the murk. *Alexander* was stern on, following the frigate. Thomas smiled as he went below, rememberingagain the towing of *Vanguard* off the Sardinian lee shore. There was nothing wrong with Lieutenant Harrington's seamanship; he had been well taught by Captain Ball.

A very bumpy and dismal passage they had that day and during the night. The smells from the troops blew aft each time the ship changed tack to edge a little further west. It was that vile mixture of vomit, urine, and excrement that sailors were mostly able to avoid. Even the bilges in *Foudroyant* didn't smell that bad. The problem wasn't that the troops didn't know their way to the heads. They had coped very well on the sail southward in better weather conditions. The growing number who were incapably seasick created the smell. Initially, the surgeon's loblolly boys had carried the worst cases down to the orlop. The sickbay space was soon overflowing and the soldiers had to be kept away from obstructing the smooth running of the ship. An action would have to be fought.

"Errs lordship irs worrit it might be like urntin thet Buonyparte's fleet," Tom had confided over breakfast.

That was something else to worry about.

That worry increased in the afternoon of the second day. *Success* and *Alexander* emerged from the cloud ahead of them and signaled there was no trace of the convoy to the west. His lordship's anxiety was almost tangible.

"Signal them to search east southeast, Sir Ed'ard. I fear we have been humbugged by the convoy using the following wind to press far south. They must turn north at fourteen degrees east and may separate to cover more sea."

"Yes, my lord. What should our own course be?"

"Signal *Audacious* and *Northumberland* to follow us round to aim for a mile off the Malta coast south of Marsa Scirocco, once the course is plotted," was the order.

Thomas and Angelo looked at each other over the top of their gun. Only dumb gunnery exercise had been possible this afternoon. It was a relief to know they would be putting some land between the ship and the wind, however small it might be. Sir Edward and Mr Gardner also looked at each other, but rather less happily. Two dayshad gone by with no noon sight. Their present position had been arrived at by dead reckoning from the last glimpse of land. Now, theyhad to give a course that would not run three liners ashore. They needed to be close enough to at least hear the waves hitting the shore. They conferred, as the crews departed the lashed guns. The hoist was made and the ship heeled over to turn and run before the wind. Down in the pantry, they could hear His Lordship's footsteps. He restlessly paced the great cabin. At least the ship's motion was more comfortable. It didn't remain so that night, because the wind veered several points more westerly. A number of calls to adjustsails in these poor conditions had to be made.

The wind continued to veer the following day until it was some points south of due west. Poor visibility persisted, showing howextensive the area of low cloud must be. His lordship, when he cameon deck, fretted more. A convoy to the south of Malta would have an easier run up the eastern coast to Valletta.

That night, Sir Edward posted listeners up by the prow and relieved them each change of watch. Several times, he went forward. His lordship was equally restless, never taking to his cot without his breeches and waistcoat still on. He called for Tom each time he needed coat and hat to go on deck. The final time, all hands were beaten to quarters, ready for first light. This time, he called for Thomas.

"I have had Tom out of his hammock half the night, Thomas. Help me on with my coat and hat. We shall let him rest a little longer."

The coat sleeve was easy to slip on his lordship's extended left arm. It sat well upon his slight shoulders. It was placed on wooden shoulders, mounted on a stand, while he rested. Thomas fastened the single button that held it on, then placed his lordship's hat firmly athwart on his head. There was a ribbon that tied it on in a blow. He slipknotted that and stood back, looking hard in the candlelight.

"I do believe you have me presentable, Thomas. Follow me up, you have your gun to serve. Angelo will doubtless be there already," his lordship averred, smiling.

"Aye, m'lord," was all Thomas said, but he responded to the smile. He knew full well it was when his lordship was about to lead them into danger that he was at his most charming. It didn't alter the fact that he would follow, just so long as he was needed. Up the steps they went and found the strong wind had lessened.

"My lord, I can pick out one wake on station, but the other has dropped back some distance," Sir Edward reported anxiously.

"If you can still see it, Sir Ed'ard, we should have a day of better visibility," His Lordship responded with a confident ring to his voice.

The guns were now unleashed, ready to be run out. Thomas took his place by the aftermost larboard gun. Below, the ports were raised. Here on the quarterdeck, the order to run out the guns would result only in the muzzles being run forward.

Somewhere distant, fine on the larboard bow, came a single, deep gunshot. The whole ship went silent, listening, but no more came.

"A ranging shot and it had the sound of a thirty-two," his lordship pronounced.

Sir Edward nodded his agreement and sent men with glasses up main and mizzen. The light was strengthening and the order came.

"Run out your guns."

Even as the rumbling was drawing to a close, a shout came from the mizzen-top.

"Land astern, well to larboard."

Sir Edward grimaced in discomfort that they should have overshot the southeastern corner of Malta by a margin. Before anyone could speak, a different shout came.

"A two decker to larboard giving chase to another two decker anda merchantman. Other ships beyond, all bearing nor, nor'east."

This came down from the maintop.

His lordship walked to the larboard rail and steadied his glass. Sir Edward followed.

"I will swear the one in pursuit is Alexander, Sir Ed'ard. Look, sheis signaling!"

The excitement on the quarterdeck was palpable, and another shout came down.

"The stranger is evidently a man-of-war—she is a line of battle ship, my lord, and going large on the starboard tack."

"Ah! An enemy, Mr Staines," exclaimed his lordship to the officer of the watch. "I pray God it may be *Le Genereux*. The signal for a general chase, Sir Ed'ard."

In the strengthening light, the signal was flown, and Sir Edward reported the response. "*Northumberland* responds with alacrity, my lord. *Audacious* responds but is some distance astern."

"I doubt we shall need her, Sir Ed'ard. See how the starboard tack shortens the distance for us. Make *Foudroyant* fly!"

Northumberland had indeed responded with alacrity and was pulling level.

"This will not do, Sir Ed'ard; it is certainly *Le Genereux*, and to my flagship she can alone surrender. Sir Ed'ard we must and shall beat

Northumberland," his lordship insisted in a high-pitched voice, audible across the quarterdeck.

The result was a great flurry of orders from Sir Edward to gain a knot or two more.

"I will do the utmost, my lord. Get the engine to work on the sails, hand butts of water to the stays, pipe the hammocks down, and each man place shot in them, slack the stays, knock up the wedges, and give the masts play. Start off the water, Mr James, and pump the ship."

Not quite the right sequence, thought Thomas.

The pumps needed attaching to the engine. The ship would be pumped so as to play water on the sails. His lordship was now by the larboard rail, between his gun and the next one forward. The stump of his right arm twitched incessantly. That was a bad sign for anyone who failed to do his bidding smartly. There was no doubt that all the measures ordered were being energetically pursued, more due to the lure of prize money than anything.

"*Foudroyant* is drawing ahead, my lord, and at last takes the lead in the chase," Sir Edward called across the quarterdeck. Then, in an aside to Mr Staines, he added, "The admiral is working his fin; do not cross his hawse, I advise you."

It was true that emptying the bilges and freshwater casks to lighten the hull and using some water to stiffen the sails was giving the ship a slight edge over *Northumberland.* It was growing in effect, but his lordship prowled to the center of the deck.

"I'll knock you off your perch, you rascal, if you are so inattentive," he screamed at the hapless quartermaster. "Sir Ed'ard, send your best quartermaster to the weather wheel."

There had been only the barest slackening for seconds. In such a wound up state, a momentary lapse was all it took to send him into a rage.

"A strange sail ahead of the chase," was the call from above.

This accompanied the helmsman being replaced and diverted his lordship's attention.

"Youngster, to the masthead," he snapped at Mr Parsons, who darted for the ratlines then recalled he had forgotten his glass and darted back for it.

"What! Going without your glass and be damned to you? Let me know what she is immediately," his lordship ordered tartly but without venom.

"A sloop of war or frigate, my Lord," Mr Parsons called down a few seconds later.

"Demand her number," was the next peremptory order.

There followed by a brief delay for flags, before Mr Parsons called down.

"The *Success*, my lord."

"Captain Peard," his lordship enunciated almost to himself and smiled.

"Signal to cut off the flying enemy," he called out, adding to the quarterdeck at large, "great odds though, thirty-two small guns to eighty large ones."

There followed an excited Parsons commentary from the mizzen top.

"The Success has hove-to athwart-hawse of the *Genereux* and is firing her larboard broadside. The Frenchman has hoisted his tricolor with a rear admiral's flag."

"Bravo, *Success*, at her again!" his lordship called out, thus encouraging Parsons.

"She has wore round, my lord, and firing her starboard broadside. It has winged her, my lord—her flying kites are flying away altogether. The enemy is close on the *Success*, who must receive her tremendous broadside."

Even from the quarterdeck, it could be seen that *Genereux* had turned thirty to forty degrees to larboard, so that her starboard guns would bear on *Success*. The hammer blows of a rolling broadside reverberated across the water a few seconds after their view of the frigate had been blotted out by the smoke of forty guns, most of them thirty-two pounders. His lordship's expression, which had been indulgent during the Parsons commentary, was now grave, despite *Foudroyant* having made good progress in closing the gap on *Genereux*. The smoke cleared to show, amazingly, *Success* still sailing and trying to bring her guns to bear again. Her topmasts and upper yards had been shot away and her rigging mostly lay in tatters.

"The signal for the Success to discontinue the action and come under my stern," his lordship ordered. "She has done well for her size. Try a shot from the lower deck at her, Sir Ed'ard."

The signal flags rose on the halyard instantly. They had already been bent on in anticipation of this moment. The first bang of a forward gun on the larboard side sounded only seconds later. Sir Edward had his glass to his right eye.

"It goes over her," he observed.

"Beat to quarters and fire coolly at her masts and yards," hislordship ordered.

Nothing remained to be done to open a fire of aimed shots, asguns could be brought to bear. *Genereux* opened a ragged cannon fire, with balls going harmlessly high. Of these, one tore through the mizzen staysail with a wonderfully accelerated ripping sound. This quite unnerved one of the younger midshipmen. His reaction happened to be seen by his lordship, pacing close by.

"How do you relish the music, my young fellow?" His Lordship asked, smiling and patting the stripling's head.

Seeing the look of alarm still there, he reassured.

"Do you know that King Charles the Twelfth of Sweden ran away from the first shot he heard, though afterward, he was called 'The Great' and deservedly from his bravery? I therefore hope much from you in the future."

There, thought Thomas, *was the way in which His Lordship inspired devotion in the youngsters who served him.*

He winked across the cannon at Angelo, who had been listening intently. Their gun was not yet bearing. *Northumberland* also opened fire with her forward guns. The tricolor at *Genereux's* stern floated down as she struck her colors.

"I think we may cease fire, Sir Ed'ard. It is only right you should have the joy of taking the ship's surrender, after your unhappy experience aboard her when *Leander* was taken. Have my barge lowered for the purpose."

"Thank you for that honor, my lord," Sir Edward replied and gave the orders.

On his return in the barge, he came up to the quarterdeck bearing a sword. By now, the guns were being secured before the crews could leave, but all were curious.

"This is the sword of Rear Admiral Peree, my lord. He was blinded by a splinter on the first broadside from *Success*, and his leg was taken off by the second, so I am afraid he has bled to death," Sir Edward reported.

"And what is her butcher's bill otherwise?"

"That is the strange thing, my lord, a few splinter wounds and bangs from falling blocks and other items from the rigging. Nothing her surgeon cannot put right. She is in a condition to sail under close escort up to Valletta," Sir Edward responded.

"Well, Sir Ed'ard, I am encouraged that, with the sole exception of their rear admiral, none of them were moved to die for First Consul Buonaparte. What of the other ships ahead, which ran out to sea to escape us?"

"I have the papers here, my lord. They were mostly troopships, bringing no less than four thousand troops to reinforce theValletta garrison. The frigate *Badine* and two corvettes were additional escort. It was *Badine* that led the escape."

"Well, they will show us a clean pair of heels while *Success* isbeing jury-rigged. We had better ask the other captains to join us during preparations to get underway with a view to appointing a prize agent. The merchantman, *Ville de Marseilles*, was taken by *Alexander*. I believe she is richly laden, while *Genereux* will surely bebought into the service. Then, we shall hope to report to Lord Keith off Valletta."

Queen Charlotte was indeed off the besieged citadel, safely out of the range of block ships and fortress guns. It was an obvious pleasure for his lordship in his dress-uniform coat, with all his decorations affixed, to be on the quarterdeck leading in his squadron. Both an additional ship of equal force to his own and a fat,heavily laden merchantman flew the ensign above the tricolor. The signal for him to repair on board the flagship was duly flown. He wentoff with a look of satisfaction.

He returned in no better humor than on his last visit to Lord Keith. "Bring me wine, Tom. Ask Sir Ed'ard to join me, Thomas."

He flung his cockaded hat onto a side table and himself into a chair.

When Thomas returned with the Captain, His Lordship was already halfway through his first glass of wine, but his humor was scarcely improved. "How pleased I am you could join me so promptly, Sir Ed'ard. A glass for Sir Ed'ard please, Tom. Nothing drives me to drink more readily than a visit to Lord Keith. No, do not go, Thomas. I may need you to make some notes now that John Tyson has gone."

"How did Lord Keith take to our appointment of John Tyson as prize agent, my Lord?" Sir Edward asked anxiously.

"He gave him a black look. You know his own brother is hissecretary. I believe he wanted him to be appointed agent for any prizes. there are no more rapidly in prospect as the captain of *Badine* decided he and his charges should live to fight and die for Buonaparte another day. If he manages to get them back to France, no doubt they will be welcome. I imagine Buonaparte will be short of seasoned troops this spring. It appears he will not have to fight Suvorov or any Russians at all. The Czar Paul, who is reputed to be mad, admires Buonaparte and is in correspondence with him. Suvorov has gone to Prague to await orders."

"For a monarch to admire a man who owes his rise to regicides does sound like madness," Sir Edward responded after a moment's thought.

"Very apt, Sir Ed'ard. I am not sure it will yet come to the Russians allying themselves with the French. A revival of the armed neutrality that applied in the late American War is possible. To get back to John Tyson, I took him to *Genereux* and found he will have a draughty passage to Minorca. The French smashed all the cabin lights before they were taken ashore."

"For people who had no stomach for a fight, they have been truly spiteful, my lord."

"Just so, Sir Ed'ard, and Lord Keith has compelled Tyson to make the passage under the command of his acolyte, Lord Cochrane. Cochrane's younger brother, who is a senior mid on *Queen Charlotte* is with him. Seeing that he is also providing the main part of the prizecrew, and the young man shows promise, I did not feel I could object."

"Poor Tyson, he is bound to have an uncomfortable passage in all senses, my Lord."

"There may, of course, be a way to ingratiate himself with them, but I fear it will be at the expense of his own pocket if he does," his lordship observed dispassionately, "but we must first see to the landing of our guests from Sicily. Their comrades in arms have already come south from Saint Paul. Have your pencil ready, Thomas."

King Ferdinand's troops had been landed in a sorry condition. They would be fit for nothing other than a rest camp for some days. Sir Edward settled the changes needed to cope with being shorthanded. He had provided the initial prize crew for *Genereux* and nearly all of those were still required by Lord Cochrane. It was common knowledge in the ship that his lordship had suggested he lower his flag to go home. Lord Keith had only reacted by requiring that he remain on station off Malta. He had to take an active part in bringing the Valletta garrison to the point of surrender. The written orders to that effect arrived by boat from *Queen Charlotte* on the day he sailed away to the north. He took all the liners that had sailed south with him, other than *Lion*. The requirement that his lordship cease to base his command on Palermo, but remain no further away than Syracuse or Messina, also became common knowledge.

What His Lordship had written in his reply to Lord Keith, that also went by boat to *Queen Charlotte* just before she sailed, was not common knowledge. Two days later, he collapsed with pain around his heart on the floor of the great cabin. Tom had to carry him to his cot to revive him and a sense of unease spread through the ship. His lordship then wrote another letter in his own hand to Lord Keith, which was sent off by sloop.

For the next ten days, *Foudroyant* was at anchor in the inlet north of Sliema. His lordship was frequently visited by Sir Thomas and Governor Ball. Sir Thomas wished to press the siege more aggressively, but General Graham was unwilling to risk heavy casualties when the French were losing men daily to disease and starvation.

Governor Ball had reports from a Maltese spy working ashore in the port that *Guillaume Tell* was being surreptitiously prepared for sea. The ship was very close to being ready to sail. There was no doubt that both of them wished he would stay until *Guillaume Tell* emerged from the harbor to be captured. There was no sign that the French ship had bent on her yards., The brig, *Speedy* arrived withletters for him from home. There was no real improvement in hiscondition. His mind was made up to take up the grant of a fortnight'ssick leave, already obtained from Lord Keith. He wrote again to theCommander-in-Chief and ordered Sir Edward to set sail for Palermo.There was a feeling of spring in the air, although the first week in March had only just ended. A breeze from the east with no bite to itcarried them comfortably past Marsala. Officers and crew wouldhave been more comfortable had his lordship's mood improvedduring the passage. He kept to his desk much of the time, writingprivate letters, one of which Thomas noticed was addressed to hisold mentor Admiral Goodall. Thomas thought he had recognized theold admiral's writing amongst the letters delivered by the Speedy. Hefell to wondering what the admiral had written. Did it have anybearing on his depression? WWas simply the belief he had a fatal heart condition, which Tom said was the problem?

On arrival in the Bay of Palermo, his mood was temporarily buoyed by seeing her ladyship waiting with the coach. The wind having been contrary, the final tack out in the bay had been to the east of the city.They were able to coast in with the wind and his lordship gave an order. "Have *Samuel and Jane* signaled to come into La Cala and anchor, Sir Ed'ard."

They waited some time for the small ship to raise a yard with sail furled on and haul up her anchor. Each activity took too long, so his lordship was critical.

"What is wrong with Captain Hopps? The yard is being raised in a most lubberly fashion. I do not see enough hands hauling to do the job properly."

"There is no one directing them, my Lord," Sir Edward reported, with glass raised.

Then, they were past and gently coming in toward the mole. The little crew were mustered to follow on foot after the coach left. When the gangway had been positioned, Tom was by his side for the walk down. His lordship reacted badly to the near cessation of the ship's motion and swayed so much that Tom had to steady him by his left arm. Her ladyship came forward imperiously to take his hand and draw him to her.

"My dear lord, it saddens me to see you suffering so. All is prepared for your comfort and the coach will quickly take us home. You may leave the care of his lordship to me, Tom Allen," she said loud enough for those on deck to hear.

Wisely, Tom allowed her to put her arm around his master and lead him to where the coachman waited by the step. The coach was out of sight beyond *Porta Felice* before Thomas and Angelo set off with Tom. They did not waste time threading their way around the side of *Piazza Marina*. Inhabitants thronged around the numerous market stalls spread out across its slope. At the lower end of *Via Quattro Aprile*, Mary and Marta waited, both holding their babies. The little boy rushed into his father's arms to be swung high. Tom realized this was a husbands-only occasion. He simply smiled and walked past them. Ashore, this mid-March day was warming up nicely. Both women had dispensed with cloaks and Thomas moved easily to put his arm around the waist of Mary's dress. He kissed her and the babe in turn. He could not help noticing how he had changed in their month away. How he smiled and how natural he and Mary looked together. He kissed her again, holding her tight.

"You do not know how good it is to be back with you," he said shakily.

Angelo and Marta were all tangled up with their son and baby daughter. Mary looked hard at Thomas.

"What has been happening to you?"

Angelo leaned back from Marta and said, "*Mamma mia,* a sea fight."

Mary's face took on an anxious look. Thomas knew he had to explain quickly.

"Not a real fight at all, except for the frigate *Success*, which took on *Genereux* all by herself until *Foudroyant* and *Northumberland* could come up. Then *Genereux* only fired token shots before striking. There will be prize money."

"An' all others run before Lord Nelson, pouf!" added Angelo.

"There was a French troop convoy, but their frigate and corvettes led them out to sea, and only one fat merchantman was captured," Thomas explained.

"Even token shots can kill, and some must have died on *Success*," Mary observed.

"Only a few and they killed the French Admiral!" Thomas protested.

"Well, it all sounds very lucky," Mary retorted and turned to walk to the *palazzo*.

"What has been happening here?" asked Thomas, catching upwith her.

"Oh, the Honorable Arthur Paget has arrived to replace Sir William. He is a younger son of the Earl of Uxbridge, very grand," Maryreplied cynically.

"Has nothing else worthy of note happened?" Thomas asked incredulously.

"That depends on whether you believe what happens at Court is worthy of note. You remember Lady Acton died after Christmas. Well, it appears that Sir John is now to marry his niece. She is not fourteen, as we were told, but still only thirteen."

"I believe such a marriage would be contrary to our Book of Common Prayer," Thomas rejoined in disbelief. "How can such a thing happen here?"

They passed below the archway and fell quiet, although Angelo and Marta conversed energetically up the steps and round to their rooms. Later, Thomas was called for by Tom to go and make some notes for his lordship, prior to a set of orders being drawn. He then realized the same subject was the cause of dissension with her ladyship. She was about to leave the study.

"My dear lady, how can we with a good face provide a banquet in celebration of a marriage that is within the prohibited degrees of consanguinity. Particularly now that we know the girl is so veryyoung?"

"The Roman Church has granted him a dispensation, and my husband says that diplomacy requires we smile and wish them well," she replied smoothly.

"All my feelings that he is merely a courteous old rogue are confirmed," he added.

"He is still the chief minister of a monarch allied to King George." She turned to the door Thomas held open.

"Do not let his lordship work too long, Thomas Spencer; you know he is much too poorly!"

"If I were not so unwell, I should soon put to sea with *Foudroyant*. As it is, I must raise my flag again in *Samuel and Jane*, slovenly though she is now. That man Parry, her erstwhile boatswain, has run."

"I did not know he had run, m'lord," Thomas said neutrally.

"No, of course not. It was while we were off Malta, where I shall have to send you again, Thomas, and Melone. Sir Ed'ard is soshorthanded. I cannot truthfully say I need more than Tom while I amonly here on sick leave. Now, the orders ..."

CHAPTER 24

A SAVAGE BATTLE FOR THE GUILLAUME TELL

Those few nights spent in the *palazzo,* before *Foudroyant* sailed on the twenty-fourth of March, were seen by Thomas as blissful. He hadno doubt that Angelo felt the same. The horrors they endured on this cruise brought the joy that immediately preceded it into sharperfocus on recollection.

They took to their rooms with their loving wives and saw how the babes had developed. For Angelo, listening to his son becoming more coherently vocal was a great blessing. It didn't matter how much was audible through the wall between their rooms. Both couples knew they had only a few nights. *Foudroyant* was being sentback to give Sir Edward the opportunity to pounce, once *Guillaume Tell* emerged.

Other than the prospect of a battle when the ship returned toMalta, only one topic of serious conversation arose between Thomas and Mary. This was the absconding from *Samuel and Jane* of John Parry. Thomas repeated his lordship's words about him and Mary added some information of her own.

"I met him on *Piazza Marina* one market day when you had just sailed for Malta. He said 'Good day' and asked how we and the babe fared. When I said it was for Malta you had sailed and could be there many weeks, he told me he would be gone before you came back."

"Did you ask him where he was going?"

"No, I asked him if *Samuel and Jane* was sailing for home. He said he was leaving the ship. He feared all in the crew who had been on board when Horatio was born would be pressed into men of war."

"I find that hard to believe. The ship needs a crew to sail home," heexclaimed.

"Well, he did say either here or when the ship had been sailed home," Mary clarified. "He said he would find a berth on a merchantman."

"I shall ask no more."

Thomas did not want to know anything that might work to Parry's disadvantage. Instead, he drew Mary closer in their bed.

The first four days of the cruise seemed to presage nothing other than backbreaking toil happening in a hurry. Once *Foudroyant* sailed beyond Trapani and into the open waters between the islands of Levanzo and Marettimo, the wind was seriously contrary to their heading. Endless westerly and easterly tacks in succession were needed to gain any southing. Thomas and Angelo, in keeping with their gun station, were attached to the deck party for bracing round the mizzen sail. This had a yard only a little less massive and heavy than the mainsail yard. There were very few landsmen in the crew, only the problem of being shorthanded. The combined experience of their team had to compensate for the raw pulling power. By day and by night, the careful coordination of sail handling was wearing on hands, arms, and legs. The only consolation was that they were eating and drink well.

Thomas allowed his thoughts to stray back to the previous late spring. His lordship's small fleet had beat up and down on a north to south line, just to the west. That had been in fine conditions with afull crew. His hands had not been blackened with the tar off the rope he was now joined with shipmates in hauling. He was pleased how well his hands had hardened again. His arm and back muscles had responded to the resumption of a proper seaman's life. Initially he had a lot of leeway to make up in comparison with Angelo. It was a strange thing, that the short time he had been relieved of the normal work of a well seaman had made him instantly acceptable to the rest of their team. No doubt his ready wit and quips in accented English had much to do with that. The best thing about his acceptability was that it galvanized Thomas to come up to the same standard. He could sense the others rapidly coming to take him more seriously. On the present cruise, it only mattered that he be regarded as useful in sail handling team and gun crew. How life had changed since he was last out in these waters!

Sir Edward followed his lordship's example in encouraging themidshipmen to hone their navigational skills. Some watery sunshine on the fourth day had a number of sextants poised for the magic moment. Mr Gardner calling the compass bearing a moment before he and Sir Edward took their own sights. Low voiced, they agreedthe sun's angle and set to with chalks on their slates.

"Land distant on the starboard bow," floated down from the lookout high above.

They had been on an easterly tack for some time and hands had been assembled in preparation for going about. Both captain and master looked pleased with a look at each other's slates.

"Now, which of you gentlemen can identify the land just called?" SirEdward asked.

Thomas saw a smile spread slowly over the face of Mr Thomson. He and the officer of the watch kept their mouths shut. They looked skyward at a first reply.

"Pantelleria, Sir Edward," called a gangling youth.

"Did you consult the last dead reckoning figure for our easting?" asked Sir Edward.

"No, Sir Edward," the youth replied, now looking worried.

"If you had, you would have realized your calculations were mistaken," the captain said in a severe tone. "Has anyone a better suggestion?"

"Might it be Gozo, Sir Edward?" Mr Parsons asked very tentatively. "Let me see your slate, Mr Parsons," his captain ordered in a clipped tone.

"As I expected. Your sight was not accurate. Your calculations would have put us beyond Gozo to the north, not still approaching. Has any one of you arrived at a position close to that on Mr Gardner's slate?"

The master duly held up his slate and swiveled around. At this, a couple of them called out numbers that were not far removed from the master's.

"Then you should have called your numbers promptly. The service cannot afford officers who hide their lights under a bushel. What if there had been no one else to make the calculation!" Sir Edward commented no less severely.

"We shall stay on this tack until after dinner, Mr Thomson. Have allthe sail parties stood down. As for most of you gentlemen, more study with Mr Gardner, I think!"

However, the rest of the cruise offered no opportunity for more study. Practical examples of the benefits it conferred on their elders were the only education provided. The visibility deteriorated again. Mr Gardner spent an anxious late afternoon and evening listening to the outcomes of the log casts. He observed the compass and plotted their dead reckoning course on the chart. He conferred with SirEdward before darkness fell. They concluded there was sufficient sea room to come about on a westerly tack for the night. Hopefully, the morning would see them several miles off St. Paul's Bay. That would allow the hours of daylight to work inshore. There, the latest intelligence of French intentions for *Guillaume Tell* should be available. All night, Sir Edward and Mr Gardner shared alternate watches with successive officers of the watch. The log casts were accompanied by forward plotting of the dead reckoning course. It seemed likely that, by first light, the ship would be close to the edge of St. Paul's Bay.

Mainsails were furled and topsails reefed, prior to beating to quarters. The ship was moving more easily through the water withthe cannon run out. Eyes and ears were straining.

Ears gave the first intimation of activity not far distant when theship fell quiet, and it was the sound of a ship ahead of them going through the same evolutions.

"That has to be a King's ship, but how far ahead and on what course?"

The answer to Sir Edward's question came from above.

"Two-deck ship of war anchored fine on the larboard bow," called the lookout.

"Take your glass aloft Mr Parsons, and see if you can identify her. Also, call down a course to take the ship parallel to her. Send the topmen aloft to take in our remaining sail, Mr Thomson."

Mr Parsons was rapidly on the small platform, disdaining the lubber's hole. He had his glass trained before the topmen came past him.

"I am sure she is the *Lion*, Sir Edward. She is not pierced for as many as seventy-four. Ah, she is asking us to make our number," Mr Parsons shouted.

"Then, come down and make the reply. Ask her to confirm her ownnumber and captain to repair on board."

"I could see the land beyond her, Sir Edward," the youngsteradded breathlessly.

He had slid down a backstay at perilous speed to reach the quarterdeck and his signal book.

"You forgot to advise how the ship should be steered to come parallel, Mr Parsons."

"I am sorry for my omission. Three points to starboard will be ample, Sir Edward," the midshipman replied, his face reddening. He hurried to make his signal.

"Helmsman, three points to starboard. Send a lookout forward, Mr Thomson. I should not like to risk our bowsprit running into Lion's rigging. Then, you had better make ready to greet Captain Dixon and bring him to my cabin. Thomas Spencer, I need you below in your best rig. Coffee, I think," Sir Edward ordered.

The sprit sail and staysails would have to come off her too, Thomas thought, as he went below. His thoughts turned to cleaning up his hands to grind coffee beans and get into his best rig. Rancid butter in His Lordship's pantry would do the trick. He could finish witha rag and hot water from the galley before grinding the beans. A big enough pot would keep hot to pour some into a smaller coffee pot. Just as well his lordship's supplies were still on board. The worst of the tar smell and that of the rancid butter had gone before he left the coffee to brew. He got cleanly into his best rig.

Captain Manley Dixon, a well-rounded and weathered bundle of energy, was a shade disappointed his lordship had not returned. He was clearly anxious to work comfortably with Sir Edward.

"I am so pleased to meet you again, Captain Dixon. Some coffee? Can I offer you some breakfast?" his host enquired.

"Coffee would be most welcome. I fear I must return to breakfast with my first. We have an urgent matter to attend to if we are to be ready for *Guillaume Tell*. Other than ourselves, there are only the brig, *Minorca*, Commander Miller, and the frigate, *Penelope*, Captain Henry Blackwood, available," Captain Dixon reported with some relish. "*Minorca* is close in, and *Penelope* out of sight."

"Would you pour the coffee and leave us, Thomas? Now, the latest intelligence from Villa San Anton, Captain Dixon," Sir Edward pressed.

"She will sail either tonight or tomorrow night ..." Captain Dixon was saying as Thomas left the great cabin.

No alarm was sounded during the night that followed. *Foudroyant's* crew had two full days to pursue preparations that would hopefully make up for their shortage of numbers. The wind shifted a few points but remained favorable for *Guillaume Tell*. The clewing up of *Foudroyant's* sails was carefully done with slipknots to minimize the manpower needed to sheet home.

All of her ball, chain, and case shot was brought on deck and carefully examined for fit. Removal of rust and filing into shape was undertaken. Stockpiling close to hand followed. The gunner had a party of experienced men in felt slippers behind his screen. They made up a large supply of cartridges, ready for the powder monkeys to supply all eighty guns. The number of these had not been depleted for *Genereux's* prize crew. Safety in avoiding excess powder on the gun decks would not be compromised. Each gun was checked to eradicate barrel and vent deposits and for the reliability of its carriage.

The wind eased a little in the afternoon. *Lion* raised her anchor, let sails fall, and edged a few points south of east, out to sea. She could sail a fraction closer to a contrary wind than *Foudroyant*. It made sense for her to be positioned off the coast between St. Paul's Bay and Valetta. All these preparations and arrangements stemmed from Sir Edward's discussion with Captain Dixon. Both captains believed *Guillaume Tell* would put up a stiffer fight than Genereux. She was a stronger ship and running for home.

Sir Edward offered a toast to his officers.

"Good hunting. Whatever precautions Rear Admiral Decres takes, he cannot prevent a signal from shore that the ship is leaving. So long as Commander Miller responds quickly, we should be within range before dawn."

Thomas smiled as the officers drained their glasses and filed out. This enabled him to replace the wine decanter on his lordship's sideboard. His expression was noted.

"What is it that is causing you to smile, Thomas Spencer?" "Only that none of us will sleep tonight, Sir Edward," he replied.

"Well, we shall all eat and rest once our preparations are complete. It will be enough for men eager to make a capture."

A late, ample dinner was provided by the ship's cooks before the galley fires were doused. Who knew how long the French would wait after darkness fell? The ship's anchor was raised and replaced witha sheet anchor to prevent her drifting too far on the current. Once word came, it could be cut loose at no great cost. The ship fell unnaturally silent in the last dogwatch. This continued into the first few bells of the first watch. Only the lap of the swell against hersides, the working of the timbers, and the pacing footsteps of the officer of the watch were to be heard. In the final hour before midnight, there built up the hum of conversation that Mr Bray and hismates found hard to quell. Sir Edward had posted nighttime lookouts, who had been told to report anything they heard, particularly if it came from waters to the south or east. Past three bells into the middle watch, one of the listeners thought he heard the faint sound of cannon fire to the southeast. The sounds were intermittent and the intervening silences long. Sir Edward had come up to the quarterdeck to listen in frustration.

The time for the morning watch to rouse themselves and prepare for duty drew near. They were already wide awake and fully prepared when a fine spread of sails loomed out of the darkness. They were close, but swinging to cross *Foudroyant's* stern. Had the mastheads not indicated a much smaller ship, there would havebeen alarm. A stentorian voice sounded from aft of the sails. "Millerof the brig *Minorca*, Sir Edward. *Guillaume Tell* is out and being engaged by *Penelope*. I advised *Lion* at two bells of this watch."

"Thank you, Mr Miller. How far offshore? When do you suppose

Lion will engage?" Sir Edward urgently enquired.

"About six miles, but she is still a little south, so the distance will increase. As to *Lion*, by daybreak, I am certain," Miller shouted in reply.

"Very well, I shall make sail. Keep station on me, Mr Miller," Sir Edward called.

Rapid orders to cut the sheet anchor cable, sheet home the courses and topsails, and steer east then followed. Sprit and staysails improved movement through the water. The listeners heardanother burst of gunfire. The course was adjusted a couple of points.Gun crews not needed to sail the ship were directed to stand to their guns. Gun ports remained firmly closed while speed of sailing was the priority. The sky forward was still dark. Occasional flashes were followed by percussions that sounded a little closer.

"Those are mostly eighteen pounders. Penelope is making herself a difficult target," Sir Edward exclaimed.

The minutes drew on, and the sky before them seemed to be lightening. There was suddenly a vivid series of distant flashes. A deeper, more powerful series of explosions sounded from ahead. Sir Edward strode to the starboard corner of the quarterdeck and gripped the rail to peer forward.

"Lion has surely engaged. Extra lookouts aloft," he called to Mr Thomson.

The order was given, and Mr Thomson also spoke quietly to Mr Parsons, who slung his glass from its band over his back and made quickly up the mizzen ratlines. For a minute or two between gun flashes, Mr Parsons was silent. Then, he shouted over gunfire.

"The battle is still moving north, Sir Edward."

"What do you estimate our best interception course to be?" the Captain shouted back.

"About four points to larboard," came the reply. "Make it so," Sir Edward rapped to the helmsmen.

"I believe our present sail setting will suffice," he then observed to Mr Thomson.

Suddenly, all was changed by the call of the mainmast lookout. "Sails in view. Two ships close together. Smaller ship several
points to starboard."

"Stay aloft, Mr Parsons, and call it as you see it," Sir Edward sang out.

There was no immediate reply. The light had begun to strengthen. The cannon fire seemed to become sporadic. The noises were from only one or two guns at a time. High above, Mr Parsons' voice sounded high pitched with excitement.

"I believe *Guillaume Tell's* bowsprit is embedded in *Lion's* rigging. The French are trying to board *Lion*. Oh, there go a couple into the sea."

"We must have more speed. Topmen aloft to sheet home thetopgallants, Mr Thomson. Mr Parsons, you did not indicate the direction of their drift."

"Begging your pardon, Sir Edward, it is still north."

The ship heeled as the wind caught the additional sails, but young Mr Parsons had obviously managed to keep hold of his glass as wellas the mast and shouted again.

"The *Lions* have beaten off the boarding, but there is another party gathering on *Guillaume Tell's* fo'c'sle, Sir Edward."

"Alter two more points to larboard. We must close the distance more quickly," Sir Edward snapped at the helmsmen. "Entire starboard battery to be triple shotted, Mr Thomson. Larboard gun crews to assist starboard battery for first broadside."

With the gun well inboard on its tackles, they set to in company with all the other starboard gun crews. At this point, Angelo had nothing to do. The gun had been carefully cleaned out the daybefore. Thomas had to ram the cartridge home. The gun captain checked by hefting that it was full, and placed it inside the muzzle. A wad, chain shot, another wad, and a final ball followed, all carefully checked by the gun captain before Thomas rammed them firmly home. Well-aimed from its elevated position, it could do a great deal of damage to the upper works of an enemy.

"*Lion's* men have nearly cut away the rigging that is holding *Guillaume Tell's* bowsprit, Sir Edward. The boarders are being shot down by *Lion's* marines. Well shot, that man! I am sorry, Sir Edward;

a boarder had crept up on one of the axmen dealing with the rigging but fell away shot," Mr Parsons commentated.

"No need for apology, Mr Parsons. Just keep calling it as you see it," Sir Edward called upward with a remarkably boyish grin.

The distance must have closed. The sound of musket fire was carrying.

"Lion is free, but she is drifting. Her foremast rigging is very poor, and most of her sails are in tatters. *Guillaume Tell* is bearing away north, but there goes *Penelope,* closing the range," the youngster called down again with excitement.

There was now reasonable early morning visibility. *Foudroyant* was undoubtedly closing the range on her converging course. The overhauling still seemed slow to those watching from the quarterdeck.

Pity those on the main gun decks, thought Thomas.

They would be able to see nothing with the gun ports still closed. *Penelope* had now sailed within range of *Guillaume Tell's* stern and turned to bring her larboard broadside to bear. Even a rolling broadside of eighteen pounders, as the guns came to bear, might hit something vital in the larger ship. Captain Blackwood had to bear away to reload and bring his other broadside in range. He dare not expose *Penelope* to the huge weight of metal in *Guillaume Tell's* broadside. The stern chasers were an acceptable risk.

The range was closing. The French ship had clearly suffered some rigging and masts damage. Her lower sails were well holed. Sir Edward looked intently through his glass and watched *Penelope* loop around for her starboard broadside.

"Now is the time. Reduce sail to fighting topsails. Bend on a signal for her to surrender," he cried.

Topmen went right up to take in the topgallants. The lower yards swarmed with men taking in sail and swiftly lashing it tight. Thesignal went up, but in vain. The only reply was a splash as a ballfrom a stern chaser landed alongside. Whether the target was themselves or *Penelope* wasn't clear. She was now coming past Foudroyant's stern after her rolling starboard broadside. Guillaume Tell kept plugging north.

"Raise gun ports," Sir Edward called out.

He waited while his order was relayed along both gun decks and heard the sounds of it being obeyed.

"Bear away two points," he ordered the helmsman. Then, he added "The guns may fire as they bear, Mr Thomson."

Although it was a rolling broadside, cannon on both main gun decks fired together. The huge weight of metal from eachconcentrated from midships to the Frenchman's stern. It tore mostly through her bulwarks and lower rigging. They waited, crouched and peering into the gun smoke, virtually the last gun to bear. Thomas saw both main and mizzen masts on the Frenchman shiver from direct hits. They held; such a strongly built vessel!

The gun bore and their gun captain touched his port fire to the powder cone in the vent. It spluttered into life, and the gun roared, flinging itself back with a fury that threatened to snap the restraining ropes. Instead, they exposed a surprising elasticity, so the gun barrel ran itself out again. The extra men from across the deck proved their worth. They hauled it back from the firing slot in the bulwark.

"Quick, the sponge, Angelo," Thomas called across.

He could see how unsettled his shipmate was by a first experience of man of war gunfire.Down the barrel the long reaming tool went. The larboard sponger, who clearly had more experience, laid on with Angelo, twisting it around. The gun captain spoke.

"Missed the wheel. Went through timbers right across. Next time, maybe."

For a moment, Thomas wondered how many on the Frenchman's quarterdeck had been scythed down by the resulting splinters. The gun captain was being handed another cartridge. Sponging wasdone and he had to be poised with the rammer. At that point, all momentarily froze, starting with a shout behind him.

"She has eased for her guns to bear."

The sustained firing of heavy guns other than their own was punctuated by the whistling, tearing, and crashing sound Thomas so dreaded. His eyes met those of the gun captain. They crouched over the muzzle of their gun. A crash behind Thomas, followed by a huge thud, caused something wet to spray across his back. An object rolled past the gun truck toward the stern bulwark. It was the way in which the gun captain's eyes moved that made Thomas look sideways. He realized it was a man's head taken off by a ball through the neck. Right up to the bulwark alongside the petrified Angelo it rolled. He stood rigid, holding the reaming tool across his body, as if it offered some kind of protection.

"Throw it overboard, Angelo," Thomas yelled at him.

He moved to ram. The gun captain had resumed his cartridge loading. The wad and a single ball followed. Moments later, he straightened to look behind as his gun captain spoke.

"Mizzen is hit and cracked but still stands. We draw ahead."

The headless corpse behind must have been crouched by his gun, because the same ball had knocked the gun on its side, trapping another man under it. Already, a party from the larboard battery were trying to raise it enough to free his legs. The cannon ball was embedded in the mizzen mast. The crack in the timber ran above and below it. Close by the helmsmen, Sir Edward was being supported by Mr Thomson. A splinter protruded from his far arm. They hauled their gun back into its firing position. Another member of their gun crew had slapped Angelo's face to get him moving again. The severed head had been thrown overboard. What other guncrews had done with the headless corpse, Thomas didn't know. He saw the trapped and moaning man dragged out from under the overturned gun and carried below. He would not have his smashed legs for long!

Despite his own injury, Sir Edward was still giving orders to Mr Thomson.

"We must come about ahead of her, Mr Thomson, and come down on her starboard quarter. I saw her mizzen rock under the force of our blows. It will not stand long."

"Thomas Spencer, you and Melone come and attend Sir Edward, while I go around the divisions," called Mr Thomson.

Thomas found a willing pair of hands for the rammer. He pointed to another seaman and shouted.

"Give him the sponger, Angelo."

He rushed to the two officers. The shock must have been abating. Angelo did as he said.

"Allow Sir Edward to steady himself on you, but do not touch the splinter. It needs the surgeon to remove it. I shall not be long."

Mr Thomson gently detached himself and headed down the ladder to the upper gun deck.

Sir Edward was swaying a little. Beads of perspiration stood out onhis forehead. His wits were clear enough, and he called Mr Bray.

"We must make more sail before we come about, Mr Bray. Just themain course."

Hands were mustered for this. They were no longer troubled by *Guillaume Tell*. Only a bow chaser would bear and its last ball had just been fired harmlessly to larboard. Up they went; the sail droppedand caught the wind. The ship surged, but reasonably upright. Hopefully, the gun decks were still dry. Mr Thomson did not say otherwise on his return. He did confirm the entire starboard battery was reloaded and ready to run out.

"Sir Edward, I am ready to bring the ship about and engage again. I beg you to allow Spencer and Melone to take you to the Surgeon. The hands will fight far better for seeing you mended," he advised.

He was not the least discomforted by their situation, although he would have been safe on *Genereux* had Lord Keith not superseded him with Lord Cochrane.

"I do not wish him to deal with me before those with more serious wounds," Sir Edward resolutely affirmed. "Spencer and Melone can take this man laid here. His foot was run over."

It was not just the ladder to the upper gun deck they had to negotiate without knocking the man's leg. They half carried himdown two companionways in the gloom. The orlop was now a noisy and stinking candlelit space. For a moment, Thomas feared Angelo would lose his wits again. Their wounded man was in screaming agony. The surgeon's table was happily clear. His loblolly boys took over and deftly placed the injured man on it. The leather strap was between his teeth and his breeches cut away to above the knee in a trice. Examination of the mangled foot and splintered lower calf bonewas only to decide the level of the cut. On went the tourniqet and theloblolly boys continued to hold the man down. His eyes bulged in terror, but the surgeon kept the knife out of his line of sight. The first cut had the scream curtailed by teeth clamping hard on the strap. Round the shin bone the surgeon went at some speed. His patient must have gone into a limp faint at some stage. His jaws no longerbit firmly on the leather strap between his teeth with the bone saw at work. The tourniquet was certainly effective in exposing the wound and the surgeon's work. The smell of blood, urine, feces, burning, rum, and the bilges all mingled together was virtually unbearable, butso were the noises.

He was through the bone, pulled the flesh with both hands gently, so his tying off of blood vessels and ligaments stood out, and raised the lower flap of skin so he could start sewing. It did not take himlong to reach the point where he could release the tourniquet and look critically at his work to check if the tying off of blood vessels had been effective. Fortunately, seepage around his stitches was minimal.

"Reasonably below the knee. He will live to do nicely with a wooden leg, if it does not fester," he commented on his own handiwork. "I will bandage, and you will carry him gently to a cot in the far bay," he then ordered the loblolly boys.

Angelo had watched the amputation fascination. Thomas was amazed he reacted so coolly. Once the surgeon was free to be told about Sir Edward, he shook his head and checked the small table laden with his tools.

"He must believe he can stay to win the fight."

The ship lurched upon coming about. Even this far below deck, thebrief sound of sails slapping was to be heard before they filled again. The surgeon had time to check which of his patients lived. Thomas and Angelo set off up the first companionway to the lower gundeck.They were too late for the second rolling broadside. On thecompanionway to the upper gundeck, there was the sound ofcheering from above. It cut off very quickly. The answering broadsidesmashed into *Foudroyant*. It seemed there was no division betweenthe booming of the guns and the arrival of the heavy balls. This time,some of them hit the hull. That was more terrifying than it would have been on deck.

When they reached the upper gundeck, it had ended. The pumps were still going and the shambles was being cleared. They reached the quarterdeck by the starboard gangway. The sight of their captain still standing was a positive sign. When they reached their gun it could be seen astern that *Guillaume Tell* had cut away her downed mizzen. but had her mainmast trailing in the water. Mr Thomson returned from below with a report.

"Sir Edward, we were holed close to the waterline in this lastbroadside. I have had the hole covered by sailcloth and the bilges pumped. We await only the carpenter's word that he has finished a temporary repair within the hold. Then, we can come about to attack again."

"Lion's success in downing her mainmast has bought us sufficient time," responded his suffering captain. "What is our butcher's bill so far?

"Six killed outright, two more dying, and over fifty wounded. Some are back on deck again, Sir Edward."

"This Rear Admiral Decres seems determined to press north on only fore, sprit, and staysails. I must confess she is a stout ship, and her guns are still being well served. Captain Dixon's information that she was carrying nine hundred must have been close to the mark.He is right to dash in, and wound, then bear off," Sir Edward reflected soberly.

He paused to think through the next order. The splinter in his arm remained painful.

"When the carpenter says his repair is holding, we will attackagain. *Lion* and *Penelope* can help to draw her fire, while we aim to down her foremast. Signal our intentions so soon as we can managea hoist."

It was a sad fact that the rigging was still in the early stages of restoration. A halyard that would take a hoist was identified. Mr Parsons was dragged back to his flags locker from temporary command of a subdivision of guns. The other ships acknowledged the signal. Word from the carpenter was impatiently awaited and an hour dragged by.

The hammering below could be heard throughout the ship. The many minutes' wait, when it ceased, was agonizing. All who were fit enough desired the opportunity to finish off *Guillaume Tell*.Eventually, the carpenter appeared at the head of an upper gun deck companionway. He was disheveled and his damp clothing was covered in sawdust. He made for the quarterdeck ladder, but Sir Edward called down.

"Put us out of our misery. Is the repair holding?"

"Aye, Sir Edward, with hardly any seepage. It is well braced," replied the carpenter. "I have been informed that the mizzen needs my attention."

"Not now, when we are still short of blocks to repair the rigging. If the mizzen stands coming about, it will have to take its chance in battle," his Captain ordered.

Men were going aloft. Others on deck were manning ropes before the order was given. A very satisfactory turn was made. Sir Edward only once had to place his good arm on Thomas's shoulder to steady himself. The aim this time was to bring the larboard battery to bear. It had few damaged guns and would use all men still available. The most experienced gun captains had now been deployed to the forward guns on both decks. The hope was to down the Frenchman's foremast before his main battery would bear. Sail was reduced as the ship closed. *Guillaume Tell* was reduced to a snail's pace and overhauling had to be avoided. *Lion* made as if to attack her starboard side. *Penelope* crossed her stern again, firing her eighteen pounders at will.

The range closed, and Mr Thomson went forward on the upper gun deck. Each loaded gun was being manhandled to achieve the correct elevation for strikes below the yard. On the first shout, "She bears," the foremost gun banged and hurtled back on her ropes. An instant later, her partner below followed. Mr Thomson went back from gun to gun, and one after another they fired. Whether it was an upper or lower deck gun that finally set the Frenchman's foremast slowly toppling was hard to say in all the powder smoke. Her rudder still answered as she turned to try and bring her guns to bear. The sudden increase in collapsed rigging quickly made it clear that virtually none of her upper deck guns were capable of being served. A few of her lower deck guns banged out, but their aim was poor.

"I believe they may now be short of experienced gun captains. Look how her scuppers run with blood!" exclaimed Sir Edward.

"Come aft again, Mr Thomson," he shouted. "Now is the time touse our upper deck elevation to finish her lower guns."

A happy situation, thought Thomas.

The helm order was given to ease off a point or two to limitdamage from the French lower battery. *Foudroyant's* upper deck guntrucks had their height lifted to plunge fire into the French hull. This unequal contest went on for some minutes more. *Lion* joined in to starboard of *Guillaume Tell*. Thomas suddenly noticed the French ship was rocking from side to side. In excitement, he pointed and spoke out.

"The Frenchman is rocking in the water, Sir Edward. I wonder for what reason?"

"Let me lay my glass on your shoulder, and we shall see," Sir Edward said keenly.

"Yes, his ballast must have shifted. His gun ports could be swamped," he continued after Thomas had obliged. "They are starting to close them."

Mr Thomson also raised his glass and trained on the mizzenstump.

"They have finally struck, Sir Edward." "Then, you may cease fire, Mr Thomson."

A couple of lower deck guns banged again before the order could be passed down, but then an unnatural quiet descended as *Foudroyant* and *Lion* eased closer to *Guillaume Tell* on each side. A pair of forlorn figures stood on the Frenchman's quarterdeck.

"Have we an undamaged boat for you to take across, Mr Thomson? We must know their butcher's bill and the number of prisoners."

"The gig is intact, Sir Edward. I will muster a crew."

"Do so. In the meantime, I shall signal Captains Dixon and Blackwood to come aboard and confer. We must decide all thepressing matters," Sir Edward flustered.

Mr Thomson departed, and Mr Parsons was summoned. The signal was duly hoisted and barely acknowledged before three boatswere in the water for their short pulls.

"Attend me down to the cabin, Thomas. You too, Melone."

Sir Edward rested his hand more heavily than before on Thomas's shoulder.Thomas saw his face was very pale and gestured to Angeloto go first to the head of the companionway. Fortunately, damaged items had already been cleared. With relief, Thomas got the captain down the steps and up to the door of the great cabin. When Thomas helped him to his chair at the desk, he collapsed into it, muttering, "Bring wine."

Angelo saw to this. He had the sense to load the tray with twomore goblets. Sir Edward struggled to raise his to his lips. A few sipsof the Sicilian wine revived him enough to reach out his arm to Thomas and be assisted to his feet to greet his fellow Captains.

The contrast between the condition of Sir Edward and his unwounded colleagues could not have been more marked when they entered. Captain Dixon spoke up.

"I give you joy of our capture, Sir Edward. You are not about to emulate our dear Lord Nelson in only having a left hand to shake, have you?" he asked, taking in the protruding splinter and right arm hanging uselessly.

"No, the surgeon will see to its removal shortly. Please do be seated, my dear captains, and take some wine with me," Sir Edward replied with a wan smile.

Captain Blackwood, a younger, watchful, and lithe officer, who looked exactly how one expected a frigate Captain to look, also sat with an expression of concern.

"What are we to do to bring our prize into harbor, Sir Edward?" asked Captain Dixon.

"My first lieutenant, Thomson, is aboard her now, assessing her life-saving needs and number of prisoners to be transferred," Sir Edward responded, sitting back.

"He clearly did well this morning. I can take my share of prisoners. I regret the state of my rigging precludes towing the prize. Captain Blackwood advises me that *Penelope* alone should be adequate for the task," Captain Dixon briskly stated.

"We have covered a considerable distance north," mused Sir Edward. "Where do your calculations put us, my dear Captain Dixon?"

"Less than thirty miles south of Cape Passero, in which case, Syracuse is the best harbor within easy reach. A noon sight will give us a course," the captain averred forcefully.

He turned his head to receive Captain Blackwood's nod of assent. "Repairs will take me at least that long to get underway," Sir

Edward reflected tiredly, "but it would be remiss of both of us, my dear Captain Dixon, if we did not express our especial thanks to Captain Blackwood for the great skill with which he hampered *Guillaume Tell's* escape and gave us time and opportunity."

"Just so," said Captain Dixon.

He turned to smile at Captain Blackwood, who looked embarrassed to be the focus of attention.

A knock came at the door. Mr Thomson returned with the swordsof Rear Admiral Decres and Captain Saulnier. The figures he gave were high. "Sirs, there are no less than two hundred dead out of an original nine hundred. Their Surgeon is overwhelmed with severely wounded. He begs assistance."

"I shall send my surgeon and a pair of his assistants. He is a good fellow," contributed Captain Blackwood, to the relief of his fellow Captains.

The meeting broke up. The surgeon was waiting to attend to Sir Edward There was a lot to be done in a short time. It did not extend to a noon sight being taken from *Foudroyant's* quarterdeck. Mr Gardner and the youngsters were just preparing for this when the damaged mizzenmast started to topple. There was only a splitting sound by way of advance warning. Another five had to be assisted orcarried down to the overflowing orlop. Just as well the other twoships advised that the distance to Cape Passero was barely twenty- four miles!

Chapter 25

A Babe Thrives—His True Parents Cruise

The change of attitude which had come over his lordship in the wake of *Genereux's* capture deepened with the transfer of his flag back to the damaged *Foudroyant*. Her repairs were still temporary. The lack of an adequate replacement mizzenmast at Syracuse meant that a spliced lesser spar and lighter yard were used. The major internal hull repair near the waterline had been left as it was. The sailcloth fother had been cut to shape, secured, and painted over. The ship needed a dock where she could be stripped and leaned over for an external hull repair. A full-sized, new mizzenmast would need lifting gear of the heaviest kind. They all knew that Port Mahon was the closest dockyard where these tasks could be attempted. The carpenter and his mates had done scores of lesser repairs in just a few days. Their newly fashioned blocks had been put to good use by sailors renewing the rigging. Despite the successful passage of the Straits of Messina, it was still obvious she had been badly knocked about. Not, of course, as badly as the dismasted *Guillaume Tell*, which still wallowed in Syracuse harbor. That was like a battered, but solid, prison hulk. This she was no longer, since all her people had been sent to captivity ashore.

When his lordship came aboard, he merely looked curiously at the repair work.

"Well, Sir Ed'ard, I can see you had to fight hard to bring final compliance with my orders from our blest Commander-in- Chief,

Lord St. Vincent. My flagship lives to fight again, unlike QueenCharlotte. Ah, I see you have not heard."

Sir Edward, now much better, had looked mystified, so his lordship continued.

"Lord Keith sent Queen Charlotte to survey the Isle of Capraja. Why he sent his flagship on such an errand, I do not know. She caught fire and burned almost to the water line before her magazine blew. Worse still, the abandoning was too slow, and most of her creware lost. Now, we have no first rate and near seven hundred prime seamen have gone to the bottom. The blockade and siege of Genoa go on. I have written giving Captains Dixon and Blackwood and yourself full credit for your capture. I am in no doubt you havebrought the surrender of Valletta much closer."

"I thank Your Lordship for those kind words. Every man and boy aboard did his duty in fine style. Many are still sore wounded," Sir Edward replied.

It was not the praise that produced a slight discomfort but that his own recovery was swift.

"Then, we shall shift them ashore to a commodious hospital in the *palazzo* with doctors from the city. Our prize crewmen are back. I have in mind a cruise that does not require a full crew, but my little crew can now be reunited."

His lordship smiled in the direction of Thomas and Angelo. Behind him, Tom grimaced at the mention of a cruise and then winked at his messmates.

The result was that Mary and Marta were kept waiting. They helped move the seriously wounded onto hastily summoned carts forthe short, bumpy ride. The April weather still wasn't too hot to impede recovery. The pain of being moved would take time to overcome for a few of them. They finally arrived, walking alongside the carts with loblolly boys. Both wives were pressed into service by her ladyship and Mrs Cadogan. They received the wounded into freshly cleaned-out spare rooms. These were still in the process of being sparsely furnished with cots by Sicilian workmen. Sir William looked in but retreated again. His lordship went round and spoke kindly to those who were not delirious.

Her ladyship was confidently in charge of the entire enterprise. Mary gave Thomas a tight smile, and squeezed his hand in passing, but said nothing. It was Tom, on returning to a cart to carry in another man, who gave an inkling of how things stood.

"Err edyship ers rehseevin' errs ordship agin an' we ers goin' home an' therr will be ther devil ter pay when we arrives," he muttered.

"How soon the passage home?" Thomas enquired in an urgent whisper.

"Next month orr month after. Err majesty ers forr Vihenna," Tom replied quietly.

Eventually, they were done with seeing the wounded installed. Thomas was able to join Mary in the kitchen, where the babes and the little boy were being minded. Horatio was making progress toward being weaned and would now suck on a biscuit. This was justas well. Marta's milk was drying up. Her own little daughter was now sitting up. She had a few teeth with which to chew. Marta wasoverdue a rest from feeding babes at her breast! Once in the privacy of their own room, Mary revealed that her ladyship still had milk to express. Mrs Cadogan coninued bringing her a small, covered jug two or three times a week. They had done well up to this point. Horatio kicked his legs in pleasure as Thomas gazed down on him.

"I fear it will be warmed cow's milk and biscuit when her ladyship comes away with you on this cruise he is planning," Mary concluded quietly.

"How do you know about it, my love?" he asked. "His lordship only mentioned it to Sir Edward this morning."

"From her ladyship, of course. His lordship has it in mind to take their friends amongst the courtiers to see the places you have come from," she replied.

"But we have only just arrived back!"

"True, but Sir William hands in his recall papers on the twenty-second, so he will then be succeeded as minister by the Horrible Arthur and be free to depart. We have a few nights before you go again. It will not be to a battle this time,"

There was a slightly aggrieved note to her voice.

343

"Have I done ought to offend you, my love?" he asked anxiously. "No more than put yourself in harm's way again. I could have been

a widow and him fatherless." she pointed down at the babe, who justgurgled happily.

"His lordship is determined to go home with Sir William and her ladyship. If Tom is any guide, we should be done with battles for some time,"

He picked up Horatio, who put a little fist on his rough chin.

"You must do all you can to gain us passage home with hislordship's party, my love. Be wary of promising to join him again. Even Tom is thinking of retiring from his service," Mary urged anxiously.

"Ah, so that is it! You have been talking to Tom. He has put the wind up you."

"He has put the wind up himself," she said with a sad smile. "He reasons that his lordship's luck will not last forever. If you can call it luck to have his injuries."

"I see what he means," Thomas commented thoughtfully. "Doesn't his lordship believe he is too ill for further service?"

"He is not too ill for what he does with her ladyship. Like a ferret chasing a rabbit, he is," Mary indignantly asserted.

"I'm feeling a bit like a ferret myself," Thomas said laughingly. "Well, first you had better get our son to sleep," Mary replied tartly.

"I wonder why the babes next door haven't been got to sleep."

"The battle well nigh unhinged Angelo. He was a little better down in the orlop, but he's still not right. Treat him gently."

"I had better slip to their door and speak to Marta."

Whatever Mary and Marta cooked up between them, Angelo was more like his old self the following day. Thomas wasn't complaining either. That was until Marta relayed to Mary all the sights and sounds of battle she had teased out of Angelo.

Mary gave him a hard time on the subject. He had to shrug andsay he'd experienced it a few times before. Angelo had only seen ships of King Ferdinand's navy pound corsairs at a distance.

"He will be happy to be discharged when his lordship lowers his flag. So should you be."

This was her parting shot on her way back to the wounded, afterhe had unsuccessfully tried to change the subject.

"Is the Honorable Arthur Paget really horrible?"

In one respect, his lordship was a little more like his old self. That related to the work on board *Foudroyant* to ensure his guests were accommodated comfortably. Sir Edward, Mr Thomson, and the carpenter were summoned. A whole string of decisions were taken in their morning conference, before the carpenter was sent to get on with the work. Both flag captain and first lieutenant stayed to talk his lordship through the entire running battle over dinner. To hear his own small contribution receive favorable mention while he was waiting on the party troubled him a little, but his lordship's placid response put him at his ease.

"So, Angelo near lost his wits, Thomas, and you steadied him. Well, we need not worry about him. I dare say he will be back to a merchantman when I discharge him."

It seemed to take precious few days for the carpenter and his mates to knock together all the extra cots and cabin partitions. They would provide cruise guests with comfort and privacy. With John Tyson back, the process of issuing invitations also went on apace. Thomas was busy with extra stores being laid in and Mary with daytime care of the wounded. They had only the evenings withHoratio. Fortunately, he slept well. The nights were their own before exhausted sleep overtook them. They didn't do a great deal of talking, but Mary did finally answer the question about Arthur Paget. On his first visit to the *palazzo,* he had affected not to notice anyone he believed to be a mere servant. That included Mary. He had been very distant with Mrs Cadogan and formal to the point of beingstandoffish with her ladyship.

"Worst of all, he could hardly bring himself to ask Sir William's viewon anything. He set up his own rival establishment," she ended.

"How does he behave toward His Lordship?"

"Oh, he is anxious not to offend him. Each time his lordship sayshe will soon be lowering his flag to go home with Sir William and her ladyship, he feigns anxiety." Mary observed.

Thomas leaned toward her in bed and stroked her thigh.

"I suppose their majesties are in no danger from the French if there is no squadron here. They can't be if we are going on this cruise."

"That is another thing with Horrible Arthur. He doesn't like any of the friends they have made at this court. How will *he* ever get help from any of them?"

She pulled his hand around the back of her thigh into the cleft, and rolled tighter to him, a conversation stopper if ever there was one!

A week later, Thomas was beginning to think the Honorable Arthur might be right about Sir William and her ladyship's Neapolitan and Sicilian friends. At any rate, those on the ship. he was not the only one harboring such thoughts. His attitude wasn't helped by the snooty Miss Knight. She had accepted the invitation to join the party at the last moment. Most of the nobles themselves treated the little crew reasonably. They were simply so demanding and had so little English that he was lost without Mary. Angelo had his own group of passengers to serve, so there were occasions when the only available source of interpretation was Miss Knight. This didn't pose any real problem for the first few days, thanks to the purely coastal sail to Syracuse. This was the place Miss Knight really wanted to see.

For a completely different reason to hers, his lordship was also keen to reach Syracuse. However, ruined masts and rigging were his interest, not ancient ruins up the hillside. When they sailed into the harbor, he detached himself from the shore party to be led by Sir William. He concentrated his attention on the work being undertaken by the skeleton crew Sir Edward had left behind.

"I see now the desperation with which she was fought, Sir Ed'ard. I had thought the butcher's bills of Captain Dixon and yourself were high. Now, I believe you did very well."

"Thank you, my lord. Now that I look at her hull, I see we did not inflict enormous damage. Naturally, we were seeking to disable," Sir Edward replied gravely.

"We must have her repaired and jury-rigged for the passage home, Sir Ed'ard. I am sure she will be bought in and refitted. Civilian labor must be hired. Leave carpenter and a few mates here to see it all done. Captain Blackwood can have the pleasure of providing her escort."

"Very well, my lord. We must also complete the restowage of the ballast I reported had shifted during the battle," Sir Edward reminded him.

"Have it seen to, Sir Ed'ard. I must prepare orders to relieve you of Mr Thomson again. This time for some months, I believe."

Thomas, attended his lordship because Tom and Angelo had been sent with the shore party. He permitted himself a secret smile. The other purposes of the cruise and his nocturnal forays to her ladyship's cabin did not prevent him displaying his decisive best. The ship's overcrowding would be relieved a little. Those left behind would be happier. Mr Thomson would have a cruise home as commander and *Guillaume Tell* would be ready to sail the sooner. Captain Henry Blackwood was also likely to be well pleased. Captain Dixon, who had returned to Malta for the siege, would feel the captains' interest in the prize money was well represented. Thomas thought all of them were less likely to be shortchanged with Captain Blackwood on the spot when the ship was bought in. However, it was as well *Foudroyant* was not intended to be involved in a fight again. They would be lucky to fight off a single determined frigate!

The ruins of ancient Syracuse took a full two days sightseeing. This at least saved the crew from daytime pampering of passengers. It did not save them from work. Boatloads of them were sent over to *Guillaume Tell* to speed the work. Those left were mainly in support of the galley's preparations for a late and ample dinner. No doubt Captain Blackwood and Mr Thomson were well pleased. They had been his lordship's much-praised guests for dinner the night before *Foudroyant* left them. The servitors were rather more weary. The pleasure of listening to the company's rendition of Miss Knight's song in praise of her ladyship to the tune of "Hearts of Oak" had already begun to pall. So, for that matter, had listening to her ladyship accompany herself on the harp. By the time they were done, young Mr Parsons, who always listened to her in rapt attention, had to be nearly carried down to the orlop. Here, the midshipmen had now been relegated.

The passage to Malta was not so slow as that to Syracuse had been. It was not without incident on the quarterdeck, when the landfall off St. Paul's Bay was made. Sir Edward sent for the signals midshipman. Mr Parsons, coming up the companionway in haste, quite overran Sir William. This left the old gentleman lying bemused on the steps. It was his luck that the lady to whom he was devoted was on hand to restore her husband to his wits. She excused the youngster from blame for a pure accident. The source of the exculpation meant Sir Edward and his lordship graciously assented.

Not so the following night, off Valletta. The ship had been anchored safely away from the French shore batteries, it was thought. The holding ground for the anchor could not have been sufficiently good. A breeze off the sea sprang up and the anchor dragged. Mr Bolton, officer of the watch in the middle watch, was compelled to wake Sir Edward. He advised him the ship had drifted a distance inshore. The Captain could have decided to rouse the crew to raise the anchor and make sail. That would have meant disturbing his passengers' sleep and would have been hazardous in darkness. He ordered this action to be taken at daybreak. Moving a shorthanded ship, with a less than favorable breeze, rapidly became apparent to the French gunners.

Thomas was shaken awake by Tom to the whoosh of a missing cannonball, followed by a loud splash.

"Ers Lordship needs urs on deck quick. Frenchies ars opened fire," he cried.

Angelo too, pulled on breeches and smock. He looked terrified as another distant gun banged. Thomas listened for whoosh and splash then spoke reassuringly.

"It's all right, Angelo. French gunners ashore haven't got the range yet."

Up the companionways they dashed. His lordship was in a complete fury that French gunners were able to use the ship for target practice. The real reason for his fury was that her ladyship hadgone on deck for some air. She refused to go below while the ship was sailed out of danger. There was an atmosphere of anger and anxiety in the group around the wheel. Sir Edward's face wore a hurtlook. Her ladyship was alone aft.

"Ha, Thomas and Angelo at last. You will escort her ladyshipbelow."

He tried hard to bottle the fury he had obviously unleashed on Sir Edward.

"Aye, aye, m'lord," said Thomas for both of them.

"M'lady," he began, "his lordship has instructed us to escort you below to safety."

"Then, he is wasting his breath. Those French gunners have neither the range nor the aim."

She turned to stare at the French batteries.

"There might be a lucky shot, m'lady," he tried desperately.

As if to mock him, a couple of guns winked orange fire, and the balls splashed short.

"As I told you, Thomas Spencer. Also, the sails are now beginning to draw."

She turned regally to view the set sails.He gave up and returned tothe command group.

"Her ladyship declines to go, m'lord," he reported. "Are we to use main force?"

"No, of course not. I am surprised you should even ask the question! I will go and speak to her ladyship myself."

As his lordship walked to the aft rail, Sir Edward smiled sheepishly at Mr Bolton, who had no doubt been joint recipient of the tongue lashing.

"She will calm him down eventually, so let us just get out of range," he murmured.

A few hours later, *Foudroyant* nosed into Marsa Scirocco, which was full of shipping. A boat came out bearing letters of invitation fromGovernor Ball, Commodore Troubridge, and General Graham. The governor as the civil authority represented the Grand Master of the Knights of St. John, the Czar of Russia, so he took precedence. A further short sail round to the south was the preferred approach. The entire cruise party was invited to Villa San Anton. This was the firstof many jaunts ashore. The little crew were detailed to attend the party. The atmosphere was relaxed and the crew were heartily pleased to be rid of the passengers.

Thomas found he rapidly lost interest in these visits ashore after the first couple. He respected both Captain Ball and Commodore Troubridge. The problem was there was only so much news to be gleaned. Also, much of the island was rocky and barren. That first visit was notable for celebrating the award of decorations from the Grand Master to both the governor and her ladyship. Unlike hislordship's other firm friend on the island, Alexander Ball did not seek to draw him away from her ladyship. He enjoyed such a warmrelationship with her as to call her "my dear sister" during this celebration. A debonair and reserved gentleman, he was not naturally prone to showing his feelings. Yet there was no doubt that he, as much as the Commodore, wished his lordship to remain and see the fall of Valletta.

Far removed as they were from other areas of Coalition action, they were avid to hear the latest news from his lordship. Dismay was the reaction to the extent of withdrawal made by the Grand Master.

"Suvorov has withdrawn to Prague. It is now said that he is in disgrace with the Czar Paul, because his army was so depleted, ragged, and starving when he withdrew from Switzerland."

"That is preposterous. He was ordered to effect a junction in Switzerland with a defeated army. He had to fight his way out in winter!" exclaimed General Graham.

"His marshalling of the Coalition armies was superb until he was ordered into Switzerland in September," added the commodore.

"Just so. Such is the gratitude of rulers! Now, Suvorov's erstwhile adversary, Massena, has become the recipient of the Corsican bandit's gratitude. He has been sent to be shut up in Genoa," His Lordship commented with amusement. "He is now the ruler and doesnot want any rival who is successful on the battlefield."

"He cannot relieve Genoa by skulking in Paris," the Commodore declared.

"Do not rely on First Consul Buonaparte doing that for long. He willtry something he believes we do not expect. After all, the man is a gambler," His Lordship reflected sadly. "The Czar Paul's misguided admiration of him merely encourages him to gamble again. At least we have now rejected Sir Sydney Smith's misguided Convention with Kleber. The army he abandoned in Egypt is doomed, but he will not care."

This gave his listeners pause for thought, from which the governor recovered first. "At least he has shot his bolt here, my lord. His garrison will continue to starve until they surrender. We may overwhelm them first."

"Which we shall do if they are too starved to man their guns," General Graham added quickly, just to dispel the notion he would sanction any reckless assault.

Indeed, there was none. The ship was sailed back to Marsa Scirocco to lie there another nine days of visits ashore. Nothing morethan pleasant dinners ensued. The commodore kept seeking to involve his lordship in stratagems to mount assaults. The lack of his appetite for confrontation with General Graham was obvious. The French artillery positions were strong and mutually supportive. The manpower that would be thrown away in a sufficiently powerful "forlorn hope" could not be afforded. There seemed little prospect of more soldiers. The Convention of El Arish had been repudiated by Lord Keith on Admiralty instructions. There was a general assumption that the government would have to send an army to Egypt to force the French to surrender.

So far as Thomas was concerned, his lordship's nightly forays to her ladyship's cabin were merely delaying their return voyage. It was not a sentiment he, Angelo, or anyone else with a sweetheart back in Palermo could openly indulge. Quite apart from discipline, a good many other members of the crew would not have sympathized.Shore leaves gave access to Maltese women, some of whom were young, comely, and grateful for being saved from starvation! It was not a moment too soon for him when the indication came that dinner the following day at Villa San Anton would be their leave-taking for the return to Palermo.

It was like any other Mediterranean day in May. Clouds and rain showers drifted, interspersed with short spells of hot sunshine. On board *Foudroyant*, the early routine of the crew had given way to languid preparations by those who were to make the last trip ashore.Tom came to the pantry with news.

"Err Ledyship ers poorly thers mornin. I fear ters the mornin sickners."

"Surely not again!" Thomas burst out.

Angelo heard and looked on curiously. Swiftly, he realized he had better curb his tongue. There was no good reason to get anyone other than Tom and himself involved.

"She ers not to go with ers loordship's party an you murst stay, Thomas," he added.

His lordship had confirmed the order in a distracted manner before the party left.

"Do whatever her ladyship requires, Thomas. Do keep her quarters aired but not cold or draughty. I am hopeful she will improve and we shall not be late returning."

It was not to be. Her ladyship was not merely sickly but clammy with a light fever. She had not lost all the weight she had put on before Horatio had been born and looked a flabby, unhealthy color inher night attire. She craved large amounts of a cooling lemon and sugar drink, once her bouts of vomiting had subsided. Her separate chamber pots had to be emptied and washed and kept smelling sweet to comply with the command. It was in his nature for Thomas to carry out these menial duties with a good grace. The thought of Mary, the babe, and himself getting home to England underpinned allof his ministration. Her ladyship was never easy to serve when she didn't feel well. She did seem to appreciate that so much loyalservice had come in her direction from him. Even with a low fever on her, she made some effort to retain his goodwill.

"You will be wishing you were back with your Mary. How I wishboth she and my dear mother had come on this cruise!"

"I am sure we will see them soon enough, now that we are to sail, milady," he replied.

"It cannot come soon enough. That is not to say I do not appreciate your loyal support, Thomas," she panted with the exertionof suppressing the fever to speak.

"I understand, milady. It is the care of a good woman you need when you are unwell," he contributed smoothly.

He suppressed his joy that she would press his lordship to sailback to Palermo as quickly as possible.

This also was not to be. The winds were from the north and northeast, so contrary for a vessel sailing into the northwest. Of course, as the wind veered more in an easterly direction, *Foudroyant* could have made some northing close hauled. The admiral was so anxious not to have the ship heeling over and worsening her ladyship's condition that he had Sir Edward sail west. They gained hardly any northing by day and absolutely none at night. They ran before the wind on a reduced spread of sail.

In the first few days and nights of this, it didn't seem to bring any improvement in her ladyship's condition. The onset of the sickness, ifit was what Tom said, must have been a shock to her system. Small wonder it had made her so ill. His lordship wandered the quarterdecklooking doleful while she showed no improvement. Sir William shuffled around the great cabin, looking lost. Thomas wonderedwhat he thought the real cause of his wife's illness could be. Hecould only serve the old gentleman politely as normal. He simply asked him each morning if her ladyship was any better.

The princely and noble passengers enjoyed the tranquility of the cruise westward. They could scarcely do otherwise. The ship heeled only a little during the day and not at all at night.

The frustration Thomas felt did not appear to be shared by Angelo. Among those serving the passengers, he derived the greatest benefit from this prolongation of the cruise. It restored him to his sunny best. He became so popular with the courtiers aboard, withhis cheerful service and quips, that Tom was moved to comment.

"Angelo wull soon find a new persishon, when errs Lordship derscharges 'im."

Not knowing what the future held for Mary, the babe, and himself, Thomas could not help feeling a little envious.

A couple of days before the end of May, the wind had veered round to a warm southerly. Her ladyship felt so much better that her lover was galvanized into directing a proper course for Capo San Vito be set. The ship heeled to the wind with her yards far over. They all had their sea legs and the cruise would soon end.

Chapter 26

Marengo Overshadows a Royal Arrival at Leghorn

The first few days of June were ones of feverish activity. It all started with the departure of the princely and noble passengers. They had nowise been anxious to depart the ship for their mansions at the dead of night. Why should they indeed, when they could be providedwith an ample breakfast on board? Their carriages were summoned. They could still be home and settled in before the day became too hot. For those waiting on them, it was mostly a case of feeling they could be tolerated an hour more. They would soon be gone. The arrival of the next lot, and royalty at that, would only give them a respite of a few days. The scuttlebutt had worked overtime on what Tom had imparted to Thomas regarding the queen.

Thomas and Angelo had to hide their impatience. They got through the work of clearing up behind them. Some semblance of order was brought back to his lordship's stores. Finally, the order was given to send them up to the *palazzo*. Tom had been sent early to have the coach brought down to the mole, so *Tria juncta in uno* were away, along with the first passengers to depart. Sir Edward graciously bid farewell to the remainder. A large group of the wounded who had recovered were already trooping back to the ship when Thomas and Angelo were released. Like long-lost brothers, they were greeted by those cleared out by his lordship.

"Thy wives are eagerly waitin' thy return. Angels of mercy they've bin."

"Get away with ye, Rob," Thomas returned with a smile to their principal spokesman. "Doin' no more than any sailor's wife would. Are many shipmates still there?"

"Only a few. Nary enough to deprive ye of your wife's attention," came the reply.

The ribald laughter that accompanied this assurance was something they took in good part. They lengthened their stride to get beyond *Porta Felice* the faster. The returning sailors headed for the ship slowly picked their way along the mole. They would be put to work soon enough on stepping aboard!

Swiftly, they hastened to the corner of *Piazza Marina* and up across it to the mouth of *Via Quattro Aprile*. Coming up to the familiar archway, a small, barefoot figure launched himself at Angelo, yelling, "Papa," to be swung aloft. Then, framed in the archway's center, babe at hip, was Mary.

Thomas scarcely noticed Marta emerge from the direction of the kitchen. He was straightaway up to Mary and folding her and the babe in a tight embrace. He was hardly aware of the much noisier reunion going on alongside them.

"Oh, my love, so many long weeks," was all he could get out. Little Horatio had grown and changed again. Now, he smiled and chuckled at the sound of Thomas's voice.

"I am afraid he wants you already," Mary said in a low voice. "We shall not be far away once you are done. I must see to one whose stump is slow to heal."

Instantly, Thomas was embarrassed by putting first his own need for her. He gave her a quick squeeze with his left arm. He stroked her face and that of the babe with the back of his right hand.

"Whatever it is, I shall make it swift as I can," he promised.

He took the stone steps at speed to arrive before the study door. He knocked, and entered to find his lordship stood behind his desk. It was covered with unopened letters.

"Ha, Thomas. I am sorry to remove you straightaway from your

Mary and the babe. I must have you find John Tyson forthwith and come back yourself. You see my correspondents have not been idle.We must list and reply in some order."

"Aye, aye, m'Lord," Thomas responded.

He departed with speed equal to that of his arrival. His lordship had not given up his own correspondence, even during the cruise, so it was not surprising that routine and other correspondence loomed large.

It didn't take long to find the secretary. He was also on his way back from the ship. He had been helping Sir Edward document the minor modifications needed to cope with the royal suite. Into the study Thomas went with him. They found his lordship struggling with a paper knife.

"Good, you are both here. You open them, Thomas, and hand to me. I will call out from whom while you list them, John. Then, we can start on replies."

He picked up a first letter, which had her majesty's seal and carefully prized it open. His lordship dictated the origins of the naval communications he had managed to open. Thomas opened out the letter without reading it and passed it over.

"A note in her majesty's own hand, with her secretary's list of her suite below. There must be fifty names here. Make a note, John, that I must order *Alexander* here at utmost speed. We must send a fast sloop if we are to be gone in five days."

Thomas opened the next and handed it over.

"Here is one from Lord Spencer," His Lordship commented. "I shall read it later."

So, it went on for nearly half an hour until there was a neat pile on one corner of the desk. John Tyson had a list that filled a side of paper. He perched by another corner, with his inkwell and a spare quill before him.

"I think we must begin our letters, John. Have Tom bring in some wine, Thomas. Come back yourself just before dinner is ready," His Lordship ordered.

Thomas inwardly exulted as he acknowledged and saluted. That would give him well nigh two hours, most of which he could spend with Mary and the babe. He hurried away, found Tom, and left him toserve the wine. He could deal with the kitchen folk over the timing of dinner. He scurried along the corridor to where the remaining few wounded were housed. Mary was still with the little Sicilian doctor, Mrs Cadogan, and the gunner's mate whose amputation was slow to heal. A musket ball had shattered his wrist. *Foudroyant's* surgeon had left him a significant length of forearm, but something must have been wrong with the tying-off of blood vessels. The forearm stump had seeped. Angelo had been holding him down while the skinny Sicilian doctor had painfully operated. Mary and Mrs Cadogan had just dressed the wound.

At least it didn't smell bad, thought Thomas.

He looked at the man's face, pale beneath the tan. Mary was translating the Doctor's instructions.

"If he has an onset of the fever, we must bleed him for ten minutes every three hours. We must send for him again, if the fever does not come down the first day," she reported.

The poor man would then look even more bloodless, thoughtThomas.

Come to think of it, the Doctor looked pretty bloodless himself. Perhaps he was given to following his own advice. Mrs Cadogan was evidently of the same mind as Thomas.

"I will bring some broth to feed him, my dear. Now that the doctor isdone, you can go with your man back to the babe."

She also waved out Angelo.

Back to their own rooms they went. Marta was minding the babes and little boy. Horatio gurgled happily again at the sight of them. Thomas held him while Mary prepared a bowl of crumbled bread and milk to feed him in their own room.

"Is he fully weaned now?" Thomas asked her, bouncing him on hisknee.

"Oh yes, he will eat anything soft and milky that I can spoon into him. He fills his napkins much faster, and I only have so many to wash and dry."

Mary came over to him with filled spoon, at which the little mouth opened obediently, a process which was repeated until it was all gone.

Thomas rubbed his little back to wind him. A few minutes later, the telltale grunts started. Mary went over to a small wooden chest and threw a napkin to him.

"You may as well start on your domestic duties, my love. When he is clean and dry, he may rock to sleep in his cradle."

All considered, he coped well with that chore. The rocking to sleep took so long that no time was left for just Mary and himself. He hadto go to the kitchen to be sure how long he had before the dinnerwas to be served. The message from Letizia was "only minutes." Back to the study he hurried, to find his lordship signing "Nelson and Bronte" on one letter after another.

"Here is my seal. Start sealing these, Thomas. I am nearly done now," he ordered, wrinkling his nose. "I have not smelt that infant smell since last at my sister's house. It is good you do your parental duty."

"Aye, m'lord," Thomas replied with a wry smile.

He busied himself with lighted taper and sealing wax. Deftly, he positioned the melting wax over a letter's fold. He had to accurately drop a blob of wax, withdraw the flame, and impress the seal. One after another he sealed, while his lordship watched. John Tyson slowly gathered up those on which the seals had cooled and hardened until interrupted by Tom entering.

"Y're lordship, dinner errs served, and Sir William and err Ledyship await."

"I will attend immediately and Mr Tyson shortly. Finish here, Thomas, before you come to serve. I have matters to discuss with Sir William and her ladyship."

So he had, and most of it was about planning four continuous days of visits and farewell meals.

They seemed concerned only with the social fripperies of the days before their removal into *Foudroyant's* cabins. He still did not know what would happen to Mary and the babe when they left. He had to maintain the appearance of being untroubled, because he had agreed with Mary that it was best to await an opportunity to ask His Lordship privately. The turn taken by the conversation gave him a pleasant surprise. The change of subject came when Mrs Cadogan joined the dinner party.

"How are the last of our wounded faring, my dear Mrs Cadogan?" Thomas hurried to serve her some food.

"All bar one could be taken on a cart back to the ship. I am hopeful even for him in a couple of days."

She smiled all around the table, including Tom and Thomas asthey served her wine and food.

"Let them rest where they are for the two days then. I have no wish to merely put them in Sir Ed'ard's way while the ship is loading forour voyage. I have sent off a sloop to fetch *Alexander*, and that is just to take the excess passengers! *Samuel and Jane* will follow with the household furnishings we shall not need before we reach home. She can carry one or two household members."

His lordship looked meaningfully at Thomas when he reached this last point.

"How long will it take our party to reach home? We shall scarcely know what to consign to Samuel and Jane's hold without knowing if we need linen for weeks or months," her ladyship exclaimed.

By this point, Thomas was inwardly smiling because he had his answer for Mary. His lordship now went on to create new uncertainties.

"That will depend on whether we continue from Leghorn by land or sea. Also, whether Lord Keith will allow me to sail for home in my own flagship."

"Of course, we could accompany Her Majesty all the way to Vienna, where I know Prince Esterhazy would be delighted to be our host," her ladyship wheedled.

"An admiral would normally expect to sail home in his own flagship, my dear," Sir William intervened.

Thomas noticed she pulled a face at this.

"It will need further consideration. Travel by land would need us to gain the Adriatic. We would have to cross the mountains to Lower Austria," his lordship hastened to add.

That was the unsatisfactory way it was left, so far as Thomas was concerned. Mary was far less worried when he recounted the conversation that evening.

"A good quantity of their linen and furnishings is to be stowed in *Samuel and Jane*. Little Horatio and me have a cabin to Leghorn. Surely, his lordship will detach you there for the voyage home to see their property safeguarded."

"So I would hope, my love. If he takes the royal party in a king's ship round to the Adriatic Sea, I should not be released soon enough," he worried.

"Would he not need Lord Keith's consent for such a voyage, while these sieges of Genoa and Valletta are going on?" she questioned.

"Well, there is that. Perhaps I should not worry about it now," he reflected, sliding his arm around her and drawing her body tight against him.

"So, it's a case of seize the moment, seize the woman," she said, lifting her face.

However, there came a gurgle from the cradle, and she arched her back to look. The babe was looking at them with a happy expression on his face.

"The moment is gone," she then added, "at least until he is changed again and rocked to sleep, by which time it may well be dark."

Four days of farewell dinners, one at the *Colli*, tested the stamina of *Tria Juncta in Uno*. Those who served them were tested more. Packing up their home and seeing the goods safely stowed on board the ships was tedious labor. First, the three of them and Mrs Cadogan had to decide what was merely going home and what they would need at some point during the entire journey. Everything packed had to be labeled as to which ship it would go aboard. The only saving grace for items to travel with them on *Foudroyant* was that these would go to cabins only. *Alexander* only arrived the night before they were due to sail. It scarcely mattered, taking only the overflow from the Queen's suite. Their baggage could be loaded the day of departure.

The final full day had involved a banquet in the *palazzo*. The fine morning of the intended day of departure was lost on the bleary-eyed servitors. Also unnoticed was the arrival of a Neapolitan country vessel tacking into the bay. She dropped a boat urgently to send a message up to the *Colli*. The response from that quarter was highly noticeable. A royal messenger on horseback clattered into the courtyard in a hurry.

He noisily demanded care for his horse. He wastaken to Milord Nelson, for whom he had a letter.

His lordship emerged from the study, grim faced and holding the letter. He called for Tom to have the coachman ready the coach and Thomas to find Sir William and her ladyship quickly. This was easily done, seeing they were ready to depart.

"Word has come from the north. The Corsican bandit has brought an army over the Great St. Bernard Pass. He is behind Melas, who is about to capture Genoa. Her majesty is now unwilling to sailtoday," his lordship reported hotly.

"We must away to the *Colli* and reassure her we will keep her safe," her ladyship promptly rejoined.

"Do we know the size of this French army?" Sir William asked calmly. "It must be very strung out if it has come that way through Switzerland."

"The numbers seem to matter less than the panic Buonaparte causes his intended victims. I am sure you have the right of it, Sir William," His Lordship replied bitterly. "I have sent Tom to the coachman. We must do our best."

Despondency prevailed on their return. Her majesty was so fearful as to be immovable until some further information of a more comforting nature arrived. The next two days were spent living in as few of the clothes retained for the voyage as they could manage. Only furnishings not already struck down into the 'tween decks large space on *Samuel and Jane* remained. A close eye was kept by his lordship on the horizon to the north for a sail bringing news. He was not the only one who was afire to sail, but also Sir Edward and most of his officers and crew. The feeling had developed that the transportof the royal party was to be a one-way passage. It was best to get started and make the voyage a swift one!

Darkness was close to falling that second doleful day when aNeapolitan brig, with all sails set, came in at a spanking pace out of the northwest. A signal came from the city wall. His lordship called inThomas and Angelo to run down to the mole with a note for Sir Edward.

"We must intercept the messenger and have his tidings before he disappears to the *Colli*," he instructed them, handing over the note.

They managed a cracking pace, only to find that Sir Edward had anticipated them. He already had a boat in the water. Thomas ran up to the quarterdeck, lungs burning, to hand over the note. Sir Edward merely scanned it by the light of the binnacle.

"Down to the boat that Mr Staines has in the water. You question the messenger, Melone. Be sure Mr Staines has all of it."

All of it was that Genoa had been on the point of surrendering five days previously. The number of Austrian troops surrounding its wallshad been sharply reduced. General Melas had turned most of his army around to face the threat from the mountains This, his army apparently outnumbered. It was the seaward blockade by Lord Keith's fleet that had made all the difference. Supplies to the French garrison had been cut off. Back to the ship the boat went aftermaking this productive interception. Mr Staines had written it alldown and Sir Edward countersigned it as seen. Thomas and Angelo carried the news back to his lordship. He enthused upon reading it.

"I think we may safely allow their majesties to sleep on these tidings and take the coach to the *Colli* early in the morning. Her majesty should be prepared to sail the following day at the latest."

"The news is considerably better, but it does not rule out some stroke by Bonaparte," cautioned Sir William.

"Perhaps not, but it is to Vienna her majesty is travelling. Her route from Leghorn is well to the east of any action, Sir William. I shall be careful not to put her and her children in any danger," his lordship reassured.

"So, we can all press her to sail and have a clear conscience about it," added her ladyship. "Are you really happy to remain another full day, dear Lord Nelson?"

"The westerly wind may swing round to a more favorable direction after another day. It seldom blows long from the west this time of the year," his lordship advised with a smile. "If I am correct, we should set a spanking pace to Leghorn."

In the event, he was correct. Thomas fretted inwardly about the extra days it would take for *Samuel and Jane* to reach Leghorn. She followed far behind in *Foudroyant's* wake. Mary and little Horatio were in the 'tween decks cabin in which he'd been born. Mr Parsons and one or two more in the midshipmen's berth were glad of the extra two days' choppy weather off the port. This prevented the queen, princesses, and prince being landed by boat. They were especially struck with the eldest princess, who was a delight to behold. It was hard to believe the unprepossessing King Ferdinand was her father.

The informality of the four-day cruise northward had to give way to the formality of the leave-taking from a regal daughter of the late Empress Maria Theresa and her Bourbon-Habsburg princely offspring. Presentations were made to his lordship, Sir William, and Sir Edward, also to her ladyship and the ship's officers. When he brought up Her Majesty's baggage the morning the weather abated, Thomas bowed to her. He was amazed by her reaction.

"For my dead child," she murmured.

She pressed something into his hand. He was too stunned to do more than bow again and stammer, "I thank your majesty." Then she was gone into the bosun's chair to lower her to join her children in the boat. It would take them to the ducal palace of her Tuscan son- in-law. She had a daughter already married, in addition to the three travelling with her. They would, no doubt, soon have husbands found for them too!

He kept his hand clasped tight around the hard object the queen had placed there until he regained the pantry. To his further amazement, she had given him a Maria Theresa gold thaler, pierced for a delicate chain, so it could be worn around the neck. For now, he looped it over his own head. It would be safe until Mary arrived and he could give it to her. That was less time coming than his lordship's first orders from Lord Keith. It was late afternoon on the eighteenth of June that the bluff bow of *Samuel and Jane* came into view, flattening the little waves running ahead of her. This was long after her mix of red and buff sails had become visible under a clear sky. It had been a case of drying out that day. The choppy and wet weather that had prevented the royal party going ashore had also exposed the temporary nature of some of *Foudroyant's* repairs. Sir William and her ladyship had gone ashore with the royal party. They had taken up residence with the British Consul in the port. His lordship had returned that night to a leaking ship rocking on the swell. Even the great cabin had been awash, despite the best efforts of his little crew to keep the water out. He had been laid low with a severe cold during the voyage north. His recovery had been set back and his little crew found their work cut out to make all clean and dry again.

Thomas had little time to keep watch on *Samuel and Jane's* progress, until Angelo informed him. "I see Mairee on deck look for you."

He stopped to take a look and saw the small ship anchored a couple of cables away, Mary was holding little Horatio in her arms. Her red hair still blew in the lessening breeze. It was then he saw beyond her the sails and colors of a naval sloop beating in on a long easterly tack.

They seemed to have been starved of real news since their arrival at Leghorn. The surrender of Genoa had been confirmed. The rumors of a great battle between the Austrian and French armies had not been substantiated. His lordship's commitment to the queen meant that he could not move from their present anchorage.

He waved to Mary from the gangway just below the break of the quarterdeck, and she caught sight of him. Once she had waved in reply, he blew a kiss to her. He pointed to the other vessel now rounding *Samuel and Jane's* bow. Then, he gestured toward the great cabin, so that she would not be hurt by his disappearance. It was obvious that a messenger would be on board within minutes. He would need to be on hand for any call from his lordship. The darkness of the short night was beginning to fall, so Mary would not mind having to retire to her cabin. She would have been drier in there these past few days than all on board Foudroyant!

As it happened, his wait to be called was rather longer than Tom's. The commander of the sloop was offered a glass of wine. He had handed over his package and been asked to sit and tell all he knew of recent events. It was after he had departed again that Thomaswas called in to assist.

"Come here, and seal this order for *Alexander*, Thomas."

His Lordship, looked up as he entered. His desk that was bright with candlelight. John Tyson was seated the other side from him, putting the finishing touches to a copy.

"Now, we must quickly do a separate order for *Santa Dorotea* before I respond to Lord Keith. I must tell him the force I have sent toSpezia, why I am sending Sir Ed'ard and am unable to go in person."

Just then, the door opened again for Tom to show in Sir Edward. John Tyson, using his copy of the order to *Alexander*, was busy writing the order for *Santa Dorotea* as Thomas completed the sealing of the first order. His Lordship resumed.

"Thank you for joining us, Sir Ed'ard. I fear I must ask you to shift your berth to *Alexander* at first light. All our gains in Italy have been put at naught, by Melas losing one battle to General Buonaparte. I am ordered by Lord Keith to take control of Spezia, before Genoa is surrendered to the French again. I cannot send less than *Alexander* and *Santa Dorotea,* and cannot put Harrington in command while a Neapolitan post captain commands the frigate. I will reply to Lord Keith that my duty to the queen prevents my going and that you will take my place."

"I shall very gladly take control of Spezia in the hope it will somewhat restore our fortunes, my lord," Sir Edward replied, looking anxious and bewildered. "Do we know where this disastrous battle took place?"

"Near Alessandria, Lord Keith writes, a place called Marengo. It appears controlling Spezia will only be a short-run measure to aid further evacuation. Melas has signed a convention to remove all his forces from Piedmont and Lombardy. Here is your sealed order you may share it with Harrington," his lordship lamented.

"Even though Alessandria is none so far north of Genoa, surely it was craven to surrender all of Piedmont and Lombardy," Sir Edward declared hotly.

"That may be, Sir Ed'ard. It now seems victory on land was only possible while Suvorov and his Russians were still here. If Lord Keith had blockaded Genoa last summer ..."

Here, His Lordship sadly and lamely broke off, leaving the strong impression he wished he was no longer on this station.

John Tyson had now written out the order for *Santa Dorotea's* captain, which his lordship read through approvingly and signed. Thomas saw to its sealing.

"I shall see a boat delivers the order tonight, my lord."

Sir Edward saw that nothing more could be achieved by himself that night and left.

"Now, for the reply to Lord Keith, John. There is one of my little crew who will benefit from not having to shift our berth in the morning, eh Thomas!"

He grinned and replied, "Yes, m'lord."

"You shall take a boat in the morning and check that our property stored there is clean and dry. A letter for Captain Hopps will give the requirements of Sir William, her ladyship, and myself. You may stand down for half an hour while we finish."

Bar two more sealings, he was done for the night. He had to rouse himself very early to secure a seat in the boat that took the dispatch for Lord Keith over to the naval sloop. He was deposited on *Samuel and Jane's* ladder, on the way back to *Foudroyant*. Up he went, with the letter tucked in his shirt. Captain Hopps waited for him on deck. Wordlessly, he pulled out the letter and proffered it.

"Good of thee to keep it warm, lad."

The captain broke the seal and scanned it.

"Thee'll be down there some time, then. Not that the 'tween decks cargo ull take much checkin, seein as we sails dryer'n most. His lordship ull want thee t'see t'the comfort o'passengers!"

This last was said with a very large wink, which had Thomaswondering exactly how the instructions had been framed. Still, hehad better not overdo it.

"Thankee, Captain," he replied politely.

He knuckled his forehead, and took the steps of the companionway at a good pace. Mary was in the cabin doorway, finger to lips.

The babe was in his cradle, fast asleep in the gloom, rocked by theship's motion in the swell. Mary was still in her night attire. One upright embrace against the door frame was enough to set them afire, after this last week's separation. He shuffled her back to her cot's edge and lowered her as quietly as he could, following her down.

"You've not been too damp in here, my love?" he asked her quietly, when they were sated, but still joined.

"Not until a few moments ago," she giggled. "If you move, we may manage to get dry again. You can tell me what it is you are supposed to be doing here."

He detached himself as quietly as he could. Now that his eyes had adjusted to the gloom, he could see Mary's expression was fond. Little Horatio's face had a contented look in sleep. A few minutes more to rest beside her and talk would do no harm.

"I am to check that the belongings of his lordship, Sir William, and her ladyship are unharmed and dry," he whispered.

"I can save you a deal of effort there. I walked Horatio around the whole cargo last night when he wouldn't settle. Captain Hopps had a hatch cover over they top of the companionway during the storm," she whispered in reply.

"Weren't you afraid, sealed below deck, with water swilling around the bilges below?" he asked her urgently, and little Horatio stirred at his louder voice.

"It didn't sound to be getting any deeper, and Captain Hopps had promised to bring us both up to his cabin if the ship was in danger," she whispered evenly.

Now, the sound of their voices woke Horatio and he whimpered. Thomas slid off the cot onto his feet and stooped to pluck the babe from his cradle. He held him close and spoke soothing, meaningless words. Whether it was the sight of him close to or the familiar sound of his voice, Horatio gave a happy sounding gurgle. Mary lay with her hands behind her head. She luxuriated in not having to respond immediately to the infant's needs.

"So, are all three of them still aboard *Foudroyant*?" she asked him.

"No, only his lordship, who is miserable with a cold. After the queen, her son, and daughters went ashore, Sir William, and herladyship went to the British consul's house. Mrs Cadogan has followed them," he replied, looking down at her.

"He will be especially miserable with her ashore and him afloat," she mused. "No word yet on when and which way we carry on for home?"

"Not yet, my love. He is weighed down with tasks connected with pulling back from Genoa. He worries about the queen since Buonaparte's victory," he conceded.

"That was the first thing we heard about when we arrived lastnight. It seems clear I must sit here with the babe until he remembers us," she sighed.

"He has not forgotten, my love. Otherwise, he would not have sent me across, but I must not be away overlong. Sir Edward is due to weigh in *Alexander* for Spezia. I had better cast an eye over their cargo and ask Captain Hopps if he could have the boat lowered to take me back," he said anxiously.

She levered herself off the cot and ruefully held her arms out for little Horatio. When he came back, Mary was at the door again.

"Come back to us soon, my love," she said huskily, and he thought he saw a tear.

"When any chance comes my way."

He clasped her to him and kissed both her and Horatio, before dashing up the companionway to hide his own tears.

Captain Hopps had forestalled him, and the boat, with a couple of oarsmen, awaited.

"Did thee find all to thy satisfaction, lad?" he enquired with a broad smile.

"Very much so, thank you, Captain Hopps. I shall so inform his lordship," he replied.

"Good man! Try and slip us word of what's due to 'appen. Sittin' at anchor wonderin' what Frenchies be up to is unsettling," the captain added.

"I will," Thomas promised and swung himself over the side onto theladder.

The other warships were heeling over to the breeze when hereached

369

Foudroyant's deck again. His lordship had gone ashore, so his report had to wait until nightfall. It was received absently inrespect of the cargo. When he mentioned Captain Hopps's wish tobe kept abreast of events, his lordship was more forthcoming than usual.

"When I next hear more, Thomas, I will send you over again. Iknow you worry for Mary too and both of you for the child. We are safe for now. The Convention Melas has made with Buonaparte leaves all Tuscany under the control of the Emperor's troops. Sir William tells me there are hotheads here who wish to use the queen as a figurehead for an attack on the French. I cannot allow that while the Emperor's armies are withdrawing here and to Venetia. It would give Buonaparte an excuse to invade Tuscany."

"Thank you, m'Lord," said Thomas.

There was nothing more he could say. His lordship hadunburdened himself of his own anxieties so frankly. That Sir William was acting as his eyes and ears ashore was useful to ensure they were not caught unawares by events there. The next couple of days,with no news other than bellicose rumblings from the Tuscans, were trying. Only during the afternoon of the third day did a brig-sloop come bowling in from the northwest to disgorge a young man with a commander's epaulette into her boat. He was not with his lordship more than a few minutes. Tom then relayed the order for both Mr Tyson and Thomas to attend him. One package the familiar-looking brig-sloop's commander had brought still lay unopened and waslabeled "Most Confidential" in a corner. Another lay open on thedesk.

"We must set to work at some speed before I go ashore to her majesty. Hold this down while I open it, Thomas," His Lordship ordered, wielding his paper knife. He read through the letter and sat back thoughtfully.

"We must write to Sir Ed'ard, John. He must return forthwith when Spezia is secured. Lord Keith's fear that the Brest fleet may have sailed for this sea is to my mind fanciful. What he says regarding her majesty's safety is not. Happily, it lends force to my advice to her. This other order, which missed me at Palermo, denies me the use of any vessel from the blockade of Valletta to carry her. Fortunate that *Alexander* now carries out one of Lord Keith's other tasks given to me!"

Why did his lordship sail so close to the wind with Lord Keith?

thought Thomas.

CHAPTER 27

A BAPTISM AND DEPARTURE
ON A FAMOUS SHIP

Lord Keith's view was no help whatsoever in the combined efforts of *Tria Juncta in Uno* to persuade Queen Maria Carolina that the onward journey to Vienna should be commenced now.

It became common knowledge throughout the ship that the queen was obdurate. She was also hysterical about the risks of travelling across Italy. His lordship went ashore repeatedly to see her. She hadbegged to be taken back to Palermo in *Foudroyant*. His lordship wasas much forbidden to do that as he was to sail her right around Italy to Trieste. She might have been persuaded of that! Two full days passed by with no sign of any new development to break this impasse.

On the second of these, Thomas was sent over to *Samuel and Jane* with a note for Captain Hopps. It explained why they could onlywait at anchor. This meant some private explaining to Mary was alsoneeded. The Captain's view was brief.

"What a pickle, bein' tied to a queen's apron strings. Best get thee below, lad."

He didn't really require any urging, despite the worry he knew his news would cause Mary. Horatio was awake and fractious but calmed at the sound of his voice. He couldn't stay long with theboat's crew standing by. Their conversation with the babe in his armswas unusually fraught. Mary showed this by twisting the Maria Theresa thaler hung around her neck time and again. She had so loved it when he first gave it to her. It seemed ironic the giver was now the cause of her anxiety.

"Why can't the queen be taken by loyal soldiers across to the far coast?" she asked.

"I doubt there are any of his majesty's ships there. I don't know if the Emperor in Vienna has any ships on that sea either," he replied.

"Is there no one friendly to her with ships there?" she questioned in a rising tone.

"Well, there are Russian ships, his lordship says. He's not sure how helpful they would be It's not an easy journey over the mountains," he lamely justified.

"Perhaps his lordship should put her on one of King Ferdinand's ships back to Palermo and have done with where she goes," Mary suggested, holding him.

"He refuses to abandon her, my love. That means he must take her where she goes."

She reflected a few moments on this reply then gently took his hand.

"You may have no choice but to speak to His Lordship for all three of us. We need to know what will be done for us. Do you know my beloved, loyal Thomas, what is her ladyship's hand in all this?"

"Tom is convinced she is with child again. She does not want to travel home by sea, so is anxious to set off overland."

He held her as close as was possible with the babe between them. "Well, if she cannot convince the queen, the poor woman must be mad with fear."

Little Horatio seemed to sense the lessening of tension between them and quietened himself. Thomas kissed them both and handed him back to Mary. Her final words came as he went up the companionway.

"Do not forget, speak to him if nothing changes in a few days."

Two days later, a great deal changed. A flagship of three gun decks sailed in, leading a small fleet. His lordship and assembled officers keenly observed.

"Why, that is the old *Victory*, Lord Hood's flagship on this sea. She looks very worn now and see the water pouring from her scuppers.

She must need pumping with great regularity. She must be all their lordships had to replace *Queen Charlotte!*"

"Rear Admiral, *Foudroyant*, repair on board flag," sang out Mr Parsons, happily reading off the signal. Then, he added, "there is a second signal calling for captain, *Minotaur*, my lord."

"*Minotaur* was flagship for the siege of Genoa. I suspect Captain Louis is about to be called on again," his lordship announced to all present. "To the boat, Tom."

Thomas was able to view the passage of the barge from *Foudroyant's* stern gallery. The barge hooked on well ahead of *Minotaur's* boat. His lordship had been greeted and whisked awayby *Victory's* captain well before Captain Louis ascended the ladderto be greeted by a saluting lieutenant. Tom had disappeared too. No doubt he had just been taken to wait and be supplied with a wet. Thomas stared across to *Victory's* faded stern gingerbread. He felt uneasy about his lordship's interview with Lord Keith. There was potential for an outcome that would do no good for Mary, the babe, and himself. Whether he would have been reassured to be listening at that point was doubtful. His lordship was only gaining the germ of an idea that would help them travel home. So far, Lord Keith had merely been negative regarding the queen.

"You will see, Lord Nelson, that I cannot spare a ship for you to sailher majesty all the way around Italy and up to Trieste. She must either go overland or sail back to Palermo in one of her husband's ships. *Foudroyant* must go to Port Mahon for proper repairs once Sir Edward Berry is back," the Commander-in-Chief determined.

"I cannot just leave her, my lord, even though I am firmly resolved to lower my flag and return home with Sir William and his lady. It is not yet settled how we should travel," Lord Nelson responded quietly but resolutely.

"I can undoubtedly consent to you lowering your flag, Lord Nelson. If you wish to be taken home by sea, you and your servant may have passage in *Seahorse*, so may Sir William, his lady, and her mother. Even passage to Palermo for her majesty and her suite is quite beyond the capacity of a frigate. I cannot spare a single ship of the line," Lord Keith spelled out with dry, Scottish logic.

"*Alexander* must return to the siege of Valletta. I have summoned Captain Louis to arrange for *Minotaur* to fly my flag again. This leaky old tub must return home. she is no use to me or any station in His Majesty's service in this condition."

This was as near to emotion as Lord Keith was capable of coming. Nelson was not slow to pick up on his demeanor as an idea began toform.

"I did notice the sad deterioration in her condition, my lord. It will beeither the breakers or a rebuild in dry dock once home."

"Of course, you were here when she was Lord Hood's flagship. Well, I agree with your assessment, Lord Nelson. Let me know your decision as to how you are to travel home. Please impress upon her majesty that, if she decides to cross Italy, the sooner her party sets out, the safer they will be."

Lord Keith was making it quite plain he wished the interview concluded.

"How soon are you intending to send *Victory* home, my Lord?"

Nelson's good eye looked a little brighter as he considered something.

"In just a few days, when crew adjustments have been madebetween ships. I need Sir Edward Berry back here before all can be concluded. Please ask Captain Louis to come through as you leave,"Lord Keith answered pointedly.

He need not have worried. His subordinate had heard all he needed and bowed politely.

"Good day, my Lord."

Out he went with a sympathetic expression on his face for Captain Louis. In the outer cabin in which he waited, he grinned mischievously for a moment.

"Your turn now, my dear Louis,"

The grin was returned but suppressed as Louis went in.

"We had better go ashore to the Consul's house. Bring Thomas to me when we regain the ship," his lordship ordered Tom as they walked out onto the deck.

Hours later, Thomas was called into the great cabin, Tom letting him in and going.

"Thomas, I have been giving some thought to the best means of sending Mary, the babe, and yourself home when I lower my flag. I had thought to discharge you at that time and send you together in *Samuel and Jane*, but that would provide you with no pay for the duration of the voyage."

"Yes m'lord," was all Thomas could say to that obvious piece of reasoning.

"However, Lord Keith has just advised me that he will be sending *Victory* home in a few days because she is unfit for service. It appears I shall have to lower my flag in this ship at the same time for her to go to repair dock in Mahon. so I can discharge Melone and yourself, and you and your family may take passage on *Victory*."

"Why, I am indebted to Your Lordship for giving thought to our future," he managed to say. He was not truly sure this was going to be the best way of getting home.

"You will have to work your passage, mark you. Lord Keith will have to approve the arrangement. *Victory* will pay off on reaching Portsmouth. I will provide you with a protection, so you may carry Mary and the babe safe to your home."

"I had hoped I could continue serving you, m'lord, when we reach home," Thomas averred, painfully speaking from the heart.

"You will be doing so by winning safe to your village home, Thomas. Listen to me very carefully. I will make arrangements to have the lad taught, when he is old enough. This will fit him for me to provide a place as a midshipman, once he reaches the right age. It will be your task, and Mary's, to see him nurtured for that. Now, we must make some plan for his baptism, and you must tell Mary."

There was the whole plan laid out before him, thought Thomas. His lordship had obviously thought long and hard about little

Horatio's future and his and Mary's part in it. No doubt he had also talked it through with her ladyship. Mary said she had concealed a long-ago childbirth. She had concealed this one. She would surely try and conceal the next. He only stammered an assent. He wanted to secure his release to take a boat over to *Samuel and Jane* and tell Mary his news. He realized that His Lordship had plenty of other concerns to deal with. He awaited the return of Sir Edward to put this particular plan into operation.

When he had recounted the whole plan to Mary, she sat on the cot for some time. She absently winded little Horatio while he gripped buttons on her blouse front. He had been fed just before Thomas arrived.

"It could be better than sitting here. We would be waiting for release of this ship and then waiting for a convoy," she reasoned slowly, "but will it be safe?"

"*Victory* will still be able to defend herself, even with a smaller crew than usual and will have a consort, if only a frigate. She is a solid ship, if leaking and slow. Pumping will get her safely past Spain and France," he justified.

"You are not just saying this because his lordship has put words in your mouth to suit her high and mighty ladyship?" she agonized.

"No, I am not, my love. *Victory* is our best chance of reaching home this summer before gales start blowing in the Atlantic," he replied gently.

"So, all I have to be worried about is crossing England, when we land, and how I shall be received in your Gotham."

She looked at him trustingly over Horatio's head. The trembling when he had mentioned gales was now diminishing.

"Have no doubt about being well received in Gotham. As for traveling across England, it will not take much of the money I have put by. His lordship will see I have a certificate for the prize money still to come," he reassured.

"How did I come to deserve a man as steady as you, my loving Thomas."

Tears glistened in her eyes. She leaned over to kiss him. Horatio gurgled happily beneath both their heads.

Events began to move at speed. Another letter arrived for his lordship from Lord Spencer on an incoming courier brig. A second within a month from the first lord of the admiralty could have been taken as a mark of favor. Reading it seemed to leave His Lordship in a morose state. *Alexander* sailed in from Spezia. A signal flew from *Victory* for her Captain to repair on board. Sir Edward had no chance to confer first with his lordship. He returned from his interview with Lord Keith and announced he had been ordered to supply parties of seamen to *Alexander* and *Minotaur*. He had to sail for Port Mahon and major repairs no later than the twenty-ninth of June.

"That settles it, then. I shall lower my flag in *Foudroyant* for the final time on the twenty-eighth. I will take John Tyson and Reverend Comyn, and of course Tom Allen, into *Alexander*. Thomas and his little family will sail home on *Victory*. Melone will take a country ship home,"

His lordship decisively revealed all this over a glass of wine withSir Edward. Thomas hovered to serve more.

Sir Edward glanced at him while he thought, obviously prey to conflicting emotions.

"An arrival home before winter, set against endless toil pumping ship on the voyage. I dare say it will be more worthwhile thanwintering in Port Mahon, my lord. Is there no chance that you might sail with us there?"

"Lord Keith offered for me to establish myself there. Influenced, no doubt, by his unjustified fear that the Brest fleet might come into the Mediterranean again. It would not be an unworthy command. I was obliged to refuse because I am committed to the safety of her majesty and to accompany Sir William and her ladyship home," he responded with a frank smile.

There was the quandary, thought Thomas.

It was just as Mary said. He had to dance attendance on her ladyship, now she was with child again and very likely didn't wish to return home by sea. He couldn't break his promise to her majesty, who was too frightened to continue on her way to Vienna. Sir Edward sensed the dilemma.

"Is there no prevailing on her majesty to resume her journey to Vienna while her party may do so safely?"

"Her ladyship, who has more influence over her than any, sees her daily with reports obtained by Sir William on the safety of possible routes. It is really a matter of gradually calming her fears," Hislordship indicated to Thomas that his goblet was in need of replenishing.

"I fear it would overtax my patience to be in such a position, my lord," Sir Edward confessed.

"As I grow older, I sometimes think patience a virtue. I may yet wear down Lord Keith on the use of *Alexander*, on which subject and others I must away to see him, Sir Ed'ard."

He rose from his seat and caused Sir Edward to do the same. "Please do be seated again and finish your wine."

Half an hour later, Nelson was seated before a tired-looking Lord Keith again.

"To avoid impeding Your Lordship's orders for *Foudroyant*, I shall lower my flag in her on the twenty-eighth and rehoist in *Alexander*," Nelson was saying.

"Does that mean you have decided against quitting the station, Lord Nelson?"

Lord Keith was sharper than might have been expected from his tired look.

"I remain unwilling to allow you to sail her to Palermo or into the Adriatic."

"I may not be aboard for more than days, my Lord. I have also received a letter from the First Lord, who considers I should travel home soon. There are others who would prefer to travel overland and are still seeking to persuade her majesty it is safe."

Nelson was so much the model of a loyal subordinate that Lord Keith was unable to avoid a look of suspicion crossing his face.

"If you mean Sir William Hamilton and his lady, I must point out they have been trying to persuade her majesty for so long, that I have little confidence in their success," Lord Keith pronounced with a humorless laugh.

"Her majesty is almost as fearful of the Tuscans who wish to place her at their head. As they become more enraged against the French, it may change her view on how she should travel. If I have to lower my flag again, so be it. Your Lordship will then have *Alexander* entirely free for action. Before that is resolved, there are two small favors I must seek for seamen in my little crew,"

Nelson petitioned so humbly that Lord Keith's look of suspicion returned.

"And, what are those, Lord Nelson?" was all he asked.

"Firstly, my lord, to allow the Sicilian I enlisted into my little crew forlocal information to return home to his family in Palermo," Nelson humbly requested.

"Well, let it not be said that I am against returning Sicilians to their homeland," expostulated Lord Keith, "and the second small favor?"

"My steward, Thomas Spencer, justifiably rated able, now has a wife and infant. I ask that they be given passage home in *Victory*. Spencer will, of course, work his passage in any capacity required," Nelson again requested humbly.

Lord Keith's eyes narrowed, while a question formed in his mind asto what lay behind this request. However, he also reflected howmuch he wanted the lucky popinjay in front of him off this station, so merely posed a question.

"Tell me what this virtuous steward has done to prove himself a right seaman?"

"He helped to save *Vanguard* the Christmas before last and fought in *Foudroyant's* running battle with *Guillaume Tell*, my lord," Nelson asserted.

"Hm, and he was with you at Aboukir Bay?"

"Yes, my lord, and in the storm off Sardinia when *Alexander* towed *Vanguard* off a dangerous lee shore. He has always been a steady man," Nelson affirmed.

"Very well, he will likely be a useful support to the limited numberof officers I can afford to send home with her. He will have to work the pumps with everyone else," Lord Keith allowed. "Where will hego when she pays off?"

"To take his wife and child home to Nottingham. He does thenhope to rejoin me, my Lord," Nelson assured.

There, Lord Keith left the matter and moved on to his own arrangements.

"I shall shift my flag the day before your shift, Lord Nelson, and have the crewmen move the same day. Of course, your party to *Alexander* will be considerably smaller than mine to *Minotaur*, but the proportion of prime hands will be greater in both. I shall provide a post captain for *Alexander*. If Harrington wishes to sail *Victory* home, he is welcome to that alternative acting command."

That it wasn't much of an alternative to an officer who had distinguished himself in action was obvious, but Nelson did not contest the decision. He had achieved what he wanted for one day.

The day the crew of *Foudroyant* was reduced, he had gone ashore early to visit the queen and his friends. Thomas begged a ride in one of their boats to *Samuel and Jane*. He would help Mary pack ready for a boat the following morning. He clambered on deck to find the news had spread.

"Thee be sailin' home on *Victory*, lad," Captain Hopps greeted him. "That we are, captain, not that we wouldn't have been comfortable on this ship. His lordship arranged it all to get us home the quicker," Thomas answered.

"Which means he intends to keep me dangling," the captain said heavily.

"Not once he is able to leave himself," Thomas replied defensively. "Well, there be a convoy formin' in less than a fortnight, and we should be in it. Will thee take a note to his lordship," the captain requested.

Thomas agreed and went down to see Mary while it was written. She had Horatio on her knee, feeding him something milky with a small wooden spoon. Hearing his feet clatter on the companionway steps, she looked up expectantly.

"Well my love, it is all settled. We go aboard *Victory* tomorrow morning."

"I heard you speaking with Captain Hopps and only waited for you to tell me how soon," she responded with a little smile and turned back to putting another spoonful of the milky mixture in Horatio's mouth. He opened it to make a happy sound.

"All you need to do is to have all we are taking on deck, ready for the boat."

He came to sit beside her on the cot and tickled Horatio under the chin.

"You will put him off his food, and I have enough to do, getting ready to obey your orders for the morning."

Her mock severity didn't reach her eyes. He put his arm around her waist and watched her feed another mouthful to Horatio.

"Are you happy we are leaving to go home, my love?" he asked, leaning his head on hers. "Really happy that we are going home as we are?"

"Oh, these years in Naples and Palermo have been good to me. I would not change any of it, especially you and this babe, but I feel this part of my life has run its course. I am also sure there will be a day of reckoning for his lordship over his relationship with her jumped-up ladyship. I do not want us or little Horatio near them whenit comes."

"I think I understand how you feel," he said very slowly. "We willjust have to get used to cold winters again. Can you manage to get all ready for the morning?"

"There is not more than will fill three canvas bags. This bedding, my clothing, Horatio's, and a few pots and bowls. Not much to show for our time here," she ruefully admitted.

"Except I do have money and the certainty of more. We can buy what we need when we get home. Tomorrow, we share the same cot."

He kissed her and the babe and stood up. He felt he must leave but looked reluctant.

"In which case, let me see to all that needs to be done before I enjoy a good night's sleep," she rejoined coquettishly, waving him away.

In the morning, he was up at the second bell of the morning watch and soon in his best rig. His money belt was strapped snug beneath his shirt and breeches. Even as Tom departed to see to his master's toilet, dressing, and breakfast, he was bundling his slops and rough weather gear into a piece of canvas with eyelets. He could rope it together to form a rough bag to sling over his shoulder. Angelo was doing the same, with even less to pack. The ship he was to join was already loading at the mole. As Thomas wondered how to say farewell to him, Tom returned, grumbling.

"Errs Lordship sayss ars on'y 'alf errs barge crew need row. Naow 'oo sayss which 'alf?" he ground out with a shake of his head.

"The cox'n?" Thomas ventured, while Angelo just laughed.

"An' ee'll not thank 'ee for the taask, seein' ars ee'll still be 'ere tomorrow. Well, I'll do the tellin and get urs off thers ship," Tom scoffed and stumped out again.

The flag lowering ceremony required not just his lordship in his dress uniform, with all decorations on display, but also Sir Edward and all his officers. Even down to the warrant officers, a great effort had been made. The entire remaining crew crowded the main deck to bid farewell to their admiral. Thomas and Angelo did not see it all, because they were sent down the ladder into the waiting barge. They certainly heard the hearty three cheers the crew gave him. Looking across to both *Alexander* and *Minotaur*, former shipmates and long-standing members of the crews of each ship were lining the sides. Many of those started to wave and cheer once his lordship descended the ladder and entered the barge.

Once he was seated, the order for the pull to the mole was given. Standing there were the three reasons for that being the barge's first call. Sir William and her ladyship, with Mrs Cadogan, were to be helped aboard as Angelo departed. When they neared the stonework, Thomas leaned to him.

"*Va bene,* Angelo."

He, by way of reply, hugged Thomas. "Farewell, my friend."

"I wish you a safe and speedy voyage home to your family, Melone," his lordship called from the barge's stern.

"Zank you, milord, and farewell," Angelo replied.

Then he was on the mole steps, politely handing her ladyship over the painter before doing the same for Mrs Cadogan and Sir William. Way was made for them to progress to seats at the stern. Thomas realized how sad it was that he was unlikely ever to meet Angelo again. Marta and he had become so much a part of their lives, the infants too. The sight of him trudging up the steps was confirmation that the partings begun in Palermo were final. One day, he would talk to Mary about it. Not today, for the barge also had Reverend Comyn on board. They were now headed to collect Mary and little Horatio from *Samuel and Jane* for more than one purpose.

Mary's eyes widened when she saw over the ship's gunwale that Sir William, her ladyship, and Mrs Cadogan were present. She gave nothing away as she followed Thomas and their belongings down the ladder. He was holding the babe, and her ladyship was looking on benignly. He reached the foot and took his seat amongst their belongings. Mary also reached the point of turning away from the ladder when she was addressed.

"Why, Mary, it is so good to see you and your infant son thriving."

"Thank you, milady."

A brief inclining of her head was all Mary managed by way of response. That was perfectly reasonable in a boat moving to the swell. Mary had to sit down for the oarsmen to get underway.

His lordship also smiled at Mary, slightly nervously, Thomas thought. What was noticeable during the pull to *Victory* was that his left eye kept returning to little Horatio. Thomas pretended he hadn't noticed. He reasoned his lordship was trying to make up his mind on the subject of resemblance. When the time came to hook on at the prow, the cox'n delayed the party's transfer to the ship just long enough to present a loyal address from the barge's crew to their admiral. Clearly, a great deal of thought had gone into its writing.

"I thank every one of you for your loyal service and your fellow oarsmen who have missed this last occasion together," his lordship thanked them very prettily.

He made his way to the ladder he would rightfully ascend first. Thisbarge would not wait for them. It would be replaced by a newly designated admiral's barge from *Alexander.*

Thomas was sufficiently down the order of ascent not to have seen the confusion on deck. The first lieutenant belatedly realized hislordship was actually coming aboard and hurriedly summoned his captain. Admittedly, he was only an acting captain, but it would notdo for an admiral to be received by less. It was noticeable that jaws had dropped further when Sir William, her ladyship and her mother, Reverend Comyn, Mr Tyson, Mary, Tom, and Thomas, holding the babe, had followed. All accompanied by a shout to haul up thedunnage. However, his lordship was master of the occasion.

"I bring you one extra crew member and two passengers, captain. First, I must beg the use of your quarterdeck for an unusual purpose. It is not fitting an infant should be taken to his parents' homeland without baptism."

Thomas, the ostensible father of the child, had doubts about the theological correctness of this. An acting captain who aspired to be made post was hardly going to argue with the admiral before him. Upto the quarterdeck they all went. Reverend Comyn strode over to the binnacle to place his bag upon it. Out came his robes, which he donned, then a dish and a stoppered bottle. Finally, out came his *Book of Common Prayer.* The bag was then wedged by the quarterdeck rail, so that the dish could take pride of place on the binnacle. The bottle was unstoppered and water poured into thedish.

"The water is from the spring at a shrine dedicated to Saint Francis of Assisi," he explained while pouring.

When he straightened, he was ready to begin, and Mary placed Horatio into his outstretched arms. Once he had started the baptism service, Thomas and Mary stepped forward as the parents bringing their child to be baptized. When the point for the godparents toparticipate arrived, all three of *Tria Juncta in Uno* stepped forward. This was to the noticeable surprise of the ship's officers compelled tobe part of the small congregation. They could not vacate the quarterdeck while the ship was preparing to put to sea. There were afew seamen on the main deck and up the masts, with the unsupervised time to stop and stare. However, the work of readying the ship for sea went on as though nothing out of the ordinary was occurring.

Thomas felt self-conscious to the point of believing all eyes on the ship were on them. He felt a surge of pride that Sir William should bewilling to stand as godfather. his lordship and her ladyship had to be here out of conscience. Continued concealment of Horatio's true parentage was their wish. Sir William would only be showing respect for Mary and himself. For that, he felt a profound gratitude to the old gentleman. He clasped Mary's hand when the Reverend Comyn signed the cross in the holy water on Horatio's forehead.

That the three of them had rehearsed their participation with Reverend Comyn became clear from their responses. Thomas had a good recollection from home of the parental role in the service. This left Mary trying to follow his words as he spoke them. Fortunately, it seemed to work right up to the point where the Reverend poured the entire dish of water over Horatio's head. He briefly bawled until handed back to Mary. A quick drying with her shawl was all it took to reduce him to bemused silence. His lordship soon filled this. Reverend Comyn rummaged in the bottom of his bag and handed over a large book.

"It would give me great pleasure to stay here with you longer, as it would Sir William and her ladyship, but we must call *Alexander's* boat now."

A midshipman scurried off to make the signal and his lordship resumed.

"There is time while we wait for me to give you this Bible for Horatio. Keep it safe for him, Thomas. You will see that it is inscribed to serve as his family Bible. It will remind you of my promise for his education and later employment."

"My dear Mary, I shall never forget your loyal service. Your needlework will be sore missed, but care of your infant comes first," her ladyship emotionally declared.

She embraced Mary, rather to her embarrassment, Thomas thought.

For him, she only shook his hand and bade him farewell. The way in which she first looked at little Horatio, whom he now held in one arm, and then into his own eyes showed the trust she reposed in him and Mary. Then, Sir William shook his hand.

"Farewell, my boy. I see what a good parent you are become. I know you will do very well by this little man."

"I am greatly honored by her ladyship and yourself joining with his lordship in becoming his godparents," Thomas thanked Sir William.

"Well, you know we call ourselves *Tria Juncta in Uno*. You could not have less than all three of us," her ladyship interposed with a laugh.

His lordship and Sir William both kissed Mary. His lordship took Thomas's hand.

"Farewell, Thomas, I will send for you when I have need of you."

Alexander's boat was near for hooking on, and he turned on his heel to go down the ladder into the waist, followed by the other two. Seconds later, they had gone over the side. Thomas opened the front cover of the Bible to find that his letter of protection and prize money certificate lay just inside. He removed those and placed them inside his shirt. Mary took Horatio from him again. He found that His Lordship's inscription took his breath away. Mary, standing by his side, looked down and also read it.

"No good will ever come of that," she whispered, looking to the receding boat.

Thomas would have watched it to *Alexander*, but the first lieutenant was by his side.

"After that, I had better rate you master's mate, so you may be given a cabin to share with your wife and infant. You must still do your turn at the pumps," he decreed.

"You will not find these wanting, Sir" replied Thomas, showing his seaman's hands.

"I dare say not. The bosun will show you where to go," indicated the officer.

With that, Thomas, Mary, and little Horatio left *Victory's* quarterdeck.

Chapter 28

Lordly Indiscretion

There was something incongruous about the two gentlemen crossing Birdcage Walk to skirt the eastern end of St. James's Park in the low sunshine of an early November afternoon. They both walked into the breeze cutting across them from the left with an upright martial bearing. Both were very soberly dressed in dark coats and breeches, white silk stockings, and buckled shoes, with high stocks around their necks. The disparity in their heights was one of head and shoulders. The taller of the two also towered over passers by and was of a stately bearing. His shorter companion was having to make his legs work at a faster rate to keep up. Yet it was primarily to him that passersby were doffing their newly fashionable, tall, black hats.

The disparity was heightened close to and face to face. The tall gentleman of craggy features was fully able-bodied. His companion, despite a slightly more youthful and regular face, had an empty right sleeve pinned to the front of his coat, an opaque-looking left eye, and a scar running down to just above his right eye. This was only partially covered by the rim of his hat. One similarity was a slight expression of anxiety as they turned inward to ensure their words to each other were not snatched away by the breeze. It had already stripped most leaves from the park's trees. A listener would have heard the louder voice of the shorter man first.

"I do hope our support for the proposed peace treaty, in especial the return of the Cape of Good Hope to the Dutch, will cause no loss to our mutual friend, Davison, my dear Moira."

"Do not trouble yourself about that, my dear Nelson. We are telling him this afternoon what we have just said in the House of Lords. That will give him several months of our troops still in occupation. Heis unlikely to be the loser," the tall gentleman replied.

"He will still have to find alternative buyers for his manufactures. I should not like to see him lose money in so doing. He was generous enough to make me an advance to purchase Merton Place," added Nelson.

"He has sufficiently deep pockets to send ships on to other markets, my dear Nelson. Not all of the India trade is in the hands of the East India Company. An ever greater quantity of goods is being absorbed there, thanks to the expansion of our interests by theWellesley brothers," Lord Moira replied with a smile, which softened his features.

"I confess I was impressed with the way in which *Tippoo Sahib* was dealt with, after my message from Egypt. I did not know Mornington's brother had a hand in it," Nelson admitted, returningthe smile.

"He is a very promising soldier, the younger brother, Arthur. Hewas with me in the retreat across the Low Countries in the year Ninety-Three. Of course, he had only a battalion then and still called himself *Wesley*. I understand it was Richard who changed his name to *Wellesley*, so all of them had to follow," Lord Moira reminisced.

They turned into the park, the wind now in their faces, to follow the path slantwise towards The Mall. Nelson looked at his House of Lords colleague quizzically.

"Have you also received an advance from Davison, my dear Moira?"

"Not for myself, you understand, but for a deserving cause I felt impelled to guarantee," the Earl responded with another smile.

Nelson nodded sagely. Lord Moira's involvement in charitable causes, and the debts he incurred to fund them, were as legendary as his military ability. It was back to the latter that he now steered the conversation.

"It must have been hard on you, after you had rescued the Duke of York, to find that both the Austrians and the Dutch were in a state of utter collapse. I know how hard I took it, when General Mack could do nothing with King Ferdinand's army, and we had to flee Naples."

"Ah yes, General Mack, not a singularly fortunate commander, but you, my dear Nelson, recovered Naples with irregulars and sailors. Our continental army of Ninety-Three could only retreat to safety in the Electorate! As for rescuing the Duke of York, well he is the brother of the Prince of Wales, whose interests I have long sought toprotect," Lord Moira commented philosophically.

"It is fortunate our continued successes at sea, in the siege of Valletta and securing the surrender of the French in Egypt have, for the time being, blunted the Corsican bandit's appetite for war," Nelson observed.

"The assassination of the Czar Paul, and the accession of Alexander, would have helped a little," Lord Moira added with some amusement. "I agree with you that his appetite is only blunted for now. That is why, with our forces spread so thinly around the world, Ihad to agree with Henry Addington's concessions. Making ourselves secure in India is far more important than the Cape of Good Hope. That only consumes bodies of useful soldiers, to watch restive Dutchcolonists."

"Who we can cut off from Holland and the French at will," added Lord Nelson.

They had reached the entrance to The Mall, to take them past the eastern side of St. James's Palace They began their approach to St. James's Square via Pall Mall. A downdraft carried chimney smoke briefly across their path.

"God be thanked, this is my last task in this city, before I head offto the pure air of Donington Park for a week or two!" Lord Moira exclaimed.

"Exactly where is your country estate, my dear Moira?" inquired Lord Nelson.

"Why, set on the most northerly hillside in Leicestershire,overlooking the Trent valley. It has views of the near parts of both Derbyshire and Nottinghamshire. You must come and visit me there,my dear Nelson, even though I keep only a bachelor establishment," Lord Moira invited in a self-deprecating way.

However, his listener seized on another point in the location's description.

"You mentioned a view of the near part of Nottinghamshire, my dear Moira. My former steward, Thomas Spencer, went home to Gotham, outside Nottingham."

"Indeed, that lies only a little over five miles from Donington Park. Are you in need of re-enlisting his services, my dear Nelson?"

"Not now my active service is coming to an end. It is just that I discharged him in Leghorn, to bring home his wife and infant son, forwhom I had stood as godfather at his baptism. My chaplain of that time arranged with the Rector of Gotham to educate the boy, once he is old enough to be taught. I have promised Spencer I will take him as midshipman, when he has made sufficient progress," Lord Nelson confided.

"I deduce that Spencer must have been a very reliable steward, my dear Nelson. It occurs to me that I may be able to assist you in ensuring your arrangement for the lad's education comes to fruition. The adjacent parish, East and West Leake, is in my gift and the present incumbent, Theophilus Hastings, is my kinsman. He is reliable, if elderly. I often invite him to dine," Lord Moira informed.

"Then I should be very much obliged if you would mention my interest to him, and request his good offices," confirmed Lord Nelson.

"Consider it done, my dear Nelson. Who else stood as godparents?"

"Sir William Hamilton and his lady kindly consented. That is whythe infant was named Horatio William Spencer," Nelson instantly replied.

Lord Moira nodded sagely and thought for a few moments, before speaking again.

"Well, he has a fine-sounding name. Does your former steward own some property?"

"Oh no, his father is a tenant of Lord Curzon, the one whose son married Admiral Lord Howe's daughter," Nelson responded.

"Yes, I was acquainted with the couple, but Assheton Curzon died young, about four years ago, as I recall. Lady Howe, as she is called since her father, the Admiral, died, has not re-married. Her son, Richard, is growing up a fine lad and he is Lord Curzon's heir. His lands march with mine in places," Lord Moira observed.

"Then it seems you are well placed to aid me in my concern, my dear Moira. I shall most certainly take up your kind invitation at the right time for the lad's education to begin. That is if the war has not begun again and my active service resumed," Nelson indicated hesitantly, sounding reluctant to say more.

Lord Moira looked slantwise at his companion. *There was rather more to this than met the eye, but Alexander Davison's house lay just around the corner. He thought it all too likely that the war with France would resume in the next few years. In that case, his brave friend would be called to command a fleet again. Addington had said as much privately to himself, as confidante of both the Prince of Wales and the Duke of Clarence. The latter, he reflected, continued to be a Royal Navy man himself. He was Nelson's most fervent supporter in the Royal Family. The Prince of Wales admired Nelson too, although he perhaps also admired Lady Hamilton more!*

It may have been his short silence that brought a request from Nelson pouring out.

"If I should fall in battle, or become so disabled that I am unable to look to the lad's future, will you do so on my behalf, my dear Moira?"

"My dear friend, I gladly give you my solemn promise I shall do so. I pray that the need never arises," Lord Moira assured him, and knocked on Davison's door.

There he had the confirmation why this infant was so important to his friend, he thought.

They waited for Davison's doorman to respond. The butler was called and attended. Yes, Mr Davison was at home and would gladly receive their lordships. If they would wait in the drawing room, he would bring some refreshment. Mr Davison would attend them shortly.

Mr Davison was as good as the word he had sent and greeted them initially in the reserved and respectful way a well-mannered commoner would be expected to greet members of the House of Lords.

"My dear Lords Moira and Nelson, you honor my house with your visit. I believe the House has been sitting today and my man tells me that you arrived on foot. We shall have some refreshment shortly."

The smile on his thin-lipped, narrow face indicated they were both friends of long standing. He shook their hands in turn, as was customary amongst masonic brethren, although a rather different approach to normal had to be adopted for a man with no right hand.

"You are well-informed, as usual, my dear Davison. We have indeed come straight from the House," Lord Moira opened, as they sat to await the butler's return.

"Doubtless you will have been discussing the terms of the proposed peace. Is there something I should know about these?" Davison asked quietly.

He had only the faintest trace of a Durham or Northumberland accent.

The reply he received from Nelson was more firmly that of a Norfolk man.

"We need to tell you what has been decided on the Cape of Good Hope, Alex. The government have decided not to oppose its return to the Dutch, even though they are only puppets of *Buonaparte*. We felt that we had to support the government, because the troops to hold it cannot be afforded."

Davison looked from one to the other and noted Lord Moira's nod in confirmation. The butler knocked and came in bearing a tray, with decanter, glasses and plates.

"Some hock and sweet cakes after your walk should prove refreshing," Davison proferred, with no hint of any alarm or displeasure at their news.

"We were concerned, knowing that you are owed considerable sums for manufactures supplied to the colony," admitted Lord Moira.

"I believe I have some months of occupation remaining, to recover full payment," Davison estimated with equanimity.

His butler served his noble guests.

"You sound as though you were expecting some such, Alex," Nelson could not forbear from saying. "We did look very hard at the Government's proposals."

Davison shrugged and let his butler serve him and leave, before responding.

"I knew they were firm on holding gains in the sugar islands, where garrison troops die like flies. John Company will give up nothing gained in India, where balance between native troops and our own must be sustained. That justifies your military judgment."

"I shall go to Donington Park secure in the knowledge you havenot been caught out, Alex," Lord Moira contributed with a smile, now more relaxed.

"That is what a man of business can never afford to be, my dear Francis," riposted Davison. "Do you have pressing concerns at Donington Park?"

"None greater than Horatio has given me, regarding the infant of his former steward in Gotham, now he knows it is close by," Lord Moira answered with a laugh.

He did not notice the look of concern which flashed across Davison's face and was wiped away instantly. Nelson, thanks to his poor eyesight, couldn't have seen it either. His happy demeanor at Moira's words didn't falter.

"What is the particular cause for concern with this infant?" Davison asked, his mind racing.

Nelson had been at sea, during and after the ill-fated attempt on Santa Cruz de Tenerife, which had cost him his right arm, when the political furore over the conspiracy to depose Pitt as Prime Minister had erupted. Therefore, he was not to know that the entire debacle had been caused by the indiscreet manner in which Lord Moira had gone around those Tories who he believed could be counted on by the Prince of Wales. He had let it be known that Charles James Fox and other leading Whigs were willing to join a new Government, with the Duke of Northumberland as compromise candidate for Prime Minister.

He, Davison, had been required to put the Duke in the right frame of mind for Lord Moira's approach.

Forewarned, it had been child's play for Pitt and Dundas to frighten wavering Tories with dire warnings about the direction in which Charles James Fox would lead the titular head of government and the rest of an ill-assorted cabinet. The conspiracy had been dead in the water, even before the Duke gave it the coup de grace, byrefusing to allow his name to be put to the King, as an alternative Prime Minister.

All this flashed through his mind, before Nelson replied.

"Why, to ensure that, as my godson, he receives a fitting education."

"And, do not forget, as a future midshipman. All with the aid of his Gotham parson and my kinsmam of the neighboring parish, Theophilus Hastings," added Lord Moira.

There you have it, thought Davison. *Concealment of the infant's likely parentage, until he was at least making something of himselfas a young gentleman. That was until he had confided in Moira! It would be foolish to say any thing privately to Nelson and worry him. For one thing, it would be repeated to Lady Hamilton, who might provoke him into taking the completely stupid step of asking Moira totell no-one. As for the alternative of speaking to Moira himself, it would just confirm what he must believe already, and lead to greater indiscretion! He told himself that hopes of Moira sometime paying back the unsecured thirty thousand he'd loaned him had no bearing on his decision, but it was hard not to take it into account. As for now, there was nothing he could do, but dissemble.*

"Will you go down there and see that all is well with the infant and his parents, my dear Horatio?" he asked, in what he thought was a suitably naïve-sounding tone.

"No, Alex. I am determined not to trouble them until the lad'seducation is due to start. At that point I shall need to be satisfied it is adequate. If war has broken out again and I am away, then our dear friend, Francis, has agreed to see to it."

"And I have invited Horatio to stay with me at Donington Park, when the time comes. Sooner if he wishes, but he seems reluctant for now," added Lord Moira.

"It is not so much that I am reluctant, my dear Francis, but rather that I have so many commitments. Chief of them for next year is my promise to Sir William, to make a progress to inspect his lands along the Milford Haven. It cannot be done quickly. Towns along the route expect me to tarry, be entertained by their mayors and aldermen and to make speeches for them."

"Well, there you have it! The price of heroism in a war which we have at least won on the sea, my dear Horatio," declared Moira, articulating what Davison had thought.

The latter now added a completely unworthy thought.

He would be very glad to see the pair of them out of his house thisafternoon.

CHAPTER 29

THE DEATH OF A LADY IS REPORTED

"Shall I turn over the page now, Uncle William?" asked Horatio.

"Aye, go on, lad, while there's a mite o' daylight left," he replied from his armchair.

It wasn't much beyond mid-afternoon on a Saturday. At this time of the year, it was Uncle William's custom to stop work at about two in the afternoon, this one day a week, to listen to Horatio read the *Nottingham Journal*. Unlike Horatio, he wasn't much of a reader, but his ability with figures was considerable. He could always figure in his head what an entire load for sale, priced at so much a bushel or a hundredweight, would cost him. Better still, he had a great knack of knowing what would turn a profit if he sold on some or all of it. All of the sale items were in the columns on the front page of the *Journal*. Horatio had read out every last one of them, seated at the kitchen table of High Thorn Farm. Uncle William took it in by the range. In a chair on the other side of the range, by the oven door, was Aunt Mary. She had a pie of salted beef and pork baking. Chopped fine, the baking meats oozed liquid fat into the pastry, and the smell was mouthwatering. They wouldn't eat it until the light had gone and the fire in the range had fresh logs blazing.

Uncle William usually took the view these winter afternoons that they could eat by firelight alone. They didn't need to waste money on candles. He leaned his sturdy frame back in his chair, big hands gripping the rounded ends of the chair arms. His sandy hair was receding from his broad, weathered face, which was currently also fire reddened.

The shape of his hair was where his resemblance to father ended, thought Horatio.

Not that the images of father and mother were more than memories now, the amount of time they'd been gone. It was the twenty-first of January in the year eighteen-fifteen. The first report to catch his eye, on this inside page with the foreign news, was the double column in the middle. It started at the top with the headline,

Latest News From the Congress of Vienna.

He recalled Father's more wiry build. His hands were as accustomed to holding a quill as a hayfork or scythe, although work-roughened. There was often a tender look in his brown eyes, as he watched Mother at her sewing. This detained him from reading for a moment. His sickly nine-year-old cousin, John, fidgeted to his side. Uncle William made his chair creak, sitting bolt upright again.

It was enough to snap him out of his reverie, and he started to read once more. He had been reading this series of reports to Uncle William for a few months now and had become quite bored with the subject matter. Great Britain was represented by Lord Castlereagh, who was to be joined by the Duke of Wellington. It was all about settling the borders of the kingdoms and principalities of Europe, now that the Emperor Napoleon Bonaparte of France had been forced from his throne and exiled to the Island of Elba. For someone who was nearly as old as this century, it did not rank as exciting. Now France had a King again. He called himself Louis the Eighteenth, the fat brother of the one whose head they'd cut off. Her borders had reverted to those she had when last a kingdom. It was what was happening farther east in what were called the German lands and Poland and to the south of the Alps in the states of Italy that was taking so long.

He knew, from when Reverend Kirkby had been teaching him geography, what the map of Europe had looked like before the war against the French revolutionaries. It was a few years ago that he'd last studied the maps in Reverend Kirkby's library at the rectory. Now, he had difficulty relating the parts of Germany and Italy described in the reports to what he could remember from the maps. He hadn't yet seen a map illustrating what he saw in a report.Perhaps none of the writers knew exactly where these places were.

As for Poland, the Czar of Russia, who was a sort of Emperor, the Emperor of Austria, and the King of Prussia all said it didn't exist. The people who said they were Polish claimed the three monarchs had stolen parts of Poland and should give it back. They didn't appear to have any real support for their claims. There seemed no possibility Great Britain could support them. Not after taking lands outside Europe that had belonged to other countries and refusing to give those back! Some of these were needed to suppress the slave trade, which Parliament had now abolished. It was well understood across the country that the Royal Navy would have to bring the slavetrade to an end, now there was no longer a war to fight. That was, of course, a matter of concern to Uncle William. Regiments across the country were already scaling back their battalions and depot establishments. These had helped to keep up livestock prices by the sheer quantities of salted meat they had been buying.

"Not in any urry, are thee!" sniffed Uncle William. "Enjoyin theirsens at the public expense, while our ships watch Napoleon Boneyparte beaves isen on that island. Well, we ope they are doin."

Suddenly, a headline of a short single column at the top but to the side of that for the Congress of Vienna caught Horatio's eye. He involuntarily read it out.

"Death of Lady Hamilton."

"Wasn't she the one Father and Mother always talked about intheir stories of Lord Nelson?"

He looked up at Uncle William on voicing his question.

He saw a complete change in demeanor come over his uncle's face. Gone was the self-satisfied expression of a farmer who could sit comfortably before his fire in winter. Anticipating a good feed afterhe'd carped a little about the doings of the great and good. In its place was a wary alertness of the kind he displayed when his lordship's agent came round to inspect the farm or receive a payment of rent. He always required the rest of them to say no more than, "Good day,

Sir, ow de do, Sir?" He did all the remaining talking.Heweighed his words with the utmost care, lest he should give the faintest impression he was doing well.

"Yes, it was, lad," he admitted.

It was as though the words were wrung from him. Aunt Marynervously got up and opened the oven to prod her pie.

"Read it all, lad."

"It is reported from Calais that Emma, Lady Hamilton, died in a lodging at Rue Fraglais in the town on Sunday morning, the fifteenth of January. It is understood she had been living in the town since early July last year, when she was released from the King's Bench Prison, where she had been confined for a year by reason of her debts. It is also reported that Miss Horatia Nelson, the adopteddaughter of the late Admiral Lord Nelson, was with her at the end, along with an old servant.

She was the widow of Sir William Hamilton, a renowned diplomat and savant, who was for many years His Majesty's Minister at the Court of the Kingdom of the Two Sicilies. It was there that shebecame notorious for her relationship with Admiral Lord Nelson during his 1798 to 1800 period of duty in the Mediterranean. It was upon their return home in November 1800, after sojourns in Vienna and Saxony, that Lady Nelson parted from her husband. He acquiredMerton Place, where he lived with Sir William and Lady Hamiltonuntil Sir William died in 1803. Thereafter, he continued to live with the widow in an openly adulterous relationship until he was recalled to the service in the middle of that year as Commander-in-Chief of the Mediterranean Fleet. He returned briefly to Merton Place in 1805 before the fateful Battle of Trafalgar secured our country's safety from the ravening Napoleon Bonaparte, who called himself Emperor of the French, but cost the hero his life. Lady Hamilton continued to live at Merton Place for some time after his death, but this residence, upon which Lord Nelson had lavished such care, had to be sold in a vain endeavor to gain the Lady freedom from debt. It is understood that her extravagance was her undoing."

Uncle William frowned while he reflected on what he had justheard and gave his measured comment.

"A story of ow the mighty are fallen, ye may say,".

"Ah well, remember our dear sister Mary tellin ow she sewed yards uh costly silks and laces she would ave er usband buy tuh mek up er gowns," chimed in Aunt Mary.

"And the quantities of food and drink she ad Lord Nelson and er usband buy tuh feed thur guests in that *palazzo* place the shared in Palurmo," added Uncle William.

Horatio had heard the stories so many times before, direct from father and mother, that he no longer listened. This time, something was troubling him about what he'd just read. Essentially, it was a matter of arithmetic.

"If Lord Nelson and Sir William and Lady Hamilton were at my first baptism on *HMS Victory*, would that have been after they all got home from the Mediterranean?" Horatio asked tentatively.

The change in Uncle William's expression was dramatic. He had begun to warm to the task of describing Lady Hamilton's extravagance. He looked truly alarmed for a moment or two while he was furiously thinking. His chest heaved, and then he spoke in a controlled voice.

"That's right, lad. Yuh must a' bin born durin *Victory's* very slow passage ome. They must a' arranged tuh meet the ship when she cum in. Ah dare say that were after Lady Nelson left 'em."

There was something about the way Uncle William gabbled this explanation that made Horatio wonder if he was making it up as he went along. Also, Aunt Mary looked worried even when he'd finished speaking.

"What time of year would that have been, Uncle William?" heprobed.

"Oh, gettin on fer Christmas, it must 'a bin. It was well after arvest that yore father and mother brought y' ome."

His uncle answered evasively but slower, as if he had more confidence in what he was saying.

"Father said I was born on the Mediterranean. The ship must have been much faster from Gibraltar home than from Italy to Gibraltar."

401

Horatio felt rather proud of his recollection of geography.

"That's as may be, but Tommy did say the ship was leakin like a sieve, so pr'aps they did some quick repairs and got er movin. Not that they will ave eld up fer long, seeing she went intuh dry dock fer near on two year."

Uncle William's firm response was in a tone that would brook no argument with his accuracy.

"Ah remember Mary sayin the clanking uh the pump andles kept going all night, and she couldna sleep fer the fust few days," added Aunt Mary.

She rushed her words to support her husband, then looked doubtful she'd said the right thing.

Before Horatio could express any doubt, Uncle William was off again.

"Ah remember the *Journal* sayin ow much ad tuh be spent tuh make er fit tuh be Lord Nelson's flagship at that Battle uh Trafalgar. As much as a new ship ud cost."

Now, that brought another memory back to Horatio. When thenews had reached the farm that Lord Nelson had been killed at Trafalgar, Father had come in from the farmyard with tears streaming down his face. Mother had been helping him learn how to write his letters at the kitchen table and had looked up in alarm.

"Have we suffered a defeat at sea, my love?" she had asked anxiously.

"No, we have won. His lordship has won a great victory but was cruelly struck down in the hour of his triumph," father had blubbed. "Ifonly he had recalled me."

He had seen mother's eyes harden for just an instant, but hervoice had been soft.

"Then, you would likely have been dead alongside him, my love. Didn't you all love him because he put himself in harm's way asmuch as any?"

Father had pulled a rag from his breeches pocket and wiped his eyes so he could look at himself and mother in turn, helplessly, as if lost in a thicket.

"I do not know where this leaves us with the promise we made.

Who should we ask what will happen now?"

"It doesn't need to worry us, my love. We just go on quietly as we are."

Mother had spoken very firmly, putting one hand on Father's and the other arm round himself.

They had, indeed, gone on quietly for some years. He had continued to be one of the Reverend Kirkby's pupils and had done quite well at reading, writing, history, and geography. The problem had always been mathematics. It wasn't that his reckoning in mere arithmetic was poor, or even that the basic concepts of geometry, like Isosceles and Pythagoras triangles were beyond him. Only algebra beyond the simplest equations floored him. Why he could manage at the level of $x+y2=5$, to work out that x was one and y twobut then be unable to fathom more complicated equations, he didn't quite know. The time had arrived when he'd overheard a conversation between father and the Reverend Kirkby that he wasn'tmeant to hear.

"I fear Horatio is making little progress with the mathematics, Thomas. I have not even reached trigonometry, which he must master for navigation," the Reverend Kirkby had said with regret in his voice.

"'Appen it don't matter anymore, yore Rev'rence," father had replied.

His speech had been going broader over the years Horatio had been receiving his education.

"You are no longer thinking of sending him away to sea?" the reverend had questioned sharply.

"With his lordship gone, if I wrote to one of his captains, he would do no better than ship's boy. I shall leave him be until he's older," father had concluded.

"Well, it shall be as you decide," the reverend had conceded with ahint of relief.

It did not seem to Horatio that he had got an awful lot older before father and mother were no longer around. It had been when the Emperor Napoleon had made the great mistake of invading Russia that he became aware they were finding it difficult to continue living on the farm. At first, it was only little things, like mother and Aunt Mary getting in each other's way in the kitchen. Mother didn't have enough dressmaking orders to keep her busy in the small parlor she used for her sewing. In truth, there were few in the village who could afford to have fine clothes made by a seamstress of mother's talent. Lord Curzon's lesser relatives at Redhill didn't have the means to be ordering continually. Then, there was the problem that father wasn't a natural farmer. He made a good bookkeeper, but there was only so much of that to be done. So far as work around the farmyard was concerned, his skills extended only to menial tasks. He wasn't particularly good with livestock, nor with plowing. There was little doubt a versatile farm laborer would be more useful to Uncle William, except in one important respect. That was the cash float father had provided out of his carefully hoarded prize money. Uncle William was able to show to Lord Curzon that he had the means, in addition to the skills, to make a success of the tenancy.

That was also the initial source of funds for Uncle William's successful buying and selling. There had been another conversation he hadn't been meant to overhear, this time between father and Uncle William in the farmyard. He had been round the corner, mucking out the cowshed.

"Ave you got all the cash you need to buy them bullocks for fat'nin, Willum?"

"Every last penny fer the 'ole two dozen, Tommy," Uncle William had replied, the curiosity in his voice underlined by adding, "why d'yuh ask?"

"Ma prize money is close tuh runnin' out," father had admitted. "Well, us'll get by as partners. We're showin a profit an' likely tuh

do, long as this war lasts. There int any sign o'it endin soon," Uncle William had reassured.

"Not while Lord Wellington keeps beatin' the French in Spain and needin' beef tuh feed all them sojers," father had responded, trying to sound lighthearted.

"There y'ar then," Uncle William had concluded, as though the matter was closed.

Horatio had known from father's tone of voice that it was not. If father had almost no money he could call his own, the feeling he was less use on the farm than Uncle William was bound to make him unhappy. Mother wasn't getting enough work to put much money in the pot. It was no wonder they often looked careworn.

One weekday, after a Sunday when Reverend Kirkby had added tohis usual prayers for the Royal Navy and Lord Wellington's army, another for the Czar of Russia and his armies, everything changed. Itwas the halting of a huge charger with a taller man in the saddle thanHoratio had ever seen before. Father was humping a sack of grain across the yard at the time.

"Good morning, Spencer. I see you are still employed in farming," the tall gentleman called. Horatio gaped from the cowshed door and father straightened.

"Good morning, m'lord. Ah didn't know yore lordship was home," Father had replied.

Horatio had pulled off his cap and bowed to the unknown lord on the charger. The horse's head was over the farm gate, now he'd smelt the corn in the sack on Father's shoulder. This straight-backedlord was far from being a young man. His craggy, yet jowly, face would have looked quite frightening, except that he had been smilingbroadly at father and himself with obvious sincerity.

"Not for long, then it's back to Scotland, but not for many months," the tall lord had continued, answering father's unspoken question. "Have you thought any more about my offer of employment, Spencer?"

"That ah has, m'lord, weighin up ow long this farm'll show a profit fer two."

"If you come, Spencer, we shall be for hotter climes next year. If Boney comes to grief in Russia, and I believe he will, the war will end quicker than you might expect. Then where will farm prices be?"

"May we talk it over, m'Lord, then send word?" Father had politely requested.

"I am on my way to see the new Reverend at East Leake. Better still, I will call on my ride back," his lordship had pressed. "Is this yourson?"

"Aye, m'Lord, he is," father had answered simply.

"A well set up lad. You have done well," his lordship had responded and ridden off.

Father had continued carrying the sack of corn to join the others already on the cart, ready for the trip to the millers. Horatio would be accompanying him. He had pulled the canvas cover over the sacks and sighed.

"Ah shall ave to speak with yore mother. Ah doubt there's time tuh go t'millers afore his lordship is back at th'gate, demandin an answer."

"Who was that grand lord, father?" was all Horatio had managed, awestruck.

"Only His Majesty's Commander-in-Chief of the Army in Scotland, the Earl of Moira, and ee wants me and yore mother tuh work for'im," father had replied heavily.

"What, in Scotland?" he had asked father incredulously.

"No, only Donington Park, fer now, but we s'l ave tuh live in."

"But that's only a few miles off. What sort of a name is Moira?"he'd questioned.

"It's one o' them Irish names. 'Is lordship is an 'Astings really."

With that reply, father had gone in and taken mother off to their bedroom. One of the fortunate aspects of the farmhouse was that it had a sufficient supply of bedrooms for them to enjoy privacy there. They hadn't stayed there long on that occasion. Father had gone off up the field to where Uncle William had been plowing with a coupleof heavy horses harnessed. He'd been persuaded to bring the day's work to a premature end for a family conference. Mother and Aunt Mary had already seated themselves at the kitchen table when they had come in. He had been told to keep young Johnnie entertained. The result had been that he hadn't followed the conversation fully. It stuck in his memory that Lord Moira had obtained some overseas appointment. He would be bringing his Scottish lady and their children back from Scotland to Donington Park in preparation. He listened intently only when they touched on his future. Uncle William had been first questioning and then assertive.

"The lad can stay 'ere, if thee be gettin ony one room at that there Doninton Park. Ee's gettin good wi' osses an' arness."

"What abaat 'is edication?" father had questioned his brother warily.

"Well 'ow much more do ee need fuh what 'is life's goin' tuh be naa?" Uncle William had shot back.

Mother had flashed father a warning glance when he'd opened his mouth to speak again. He'd closed his mouth again with a worried look, and that had been that. The stately Earl of Moira had ridden past again in the afternoon. Father had hurried to the gate for a private word when they'd heard the charger's hooves. The very next day, a cart had come for father and mother, as though to make sure they had no time to change their minds. When their bundled belongings had been loaded, they had hugged him in turn before mounting the bench alongside the driver.

Father had hugged with a look of pride in him and mother withtears in her eyes, but he had merely clung to each of them without blubbing. He hadn't wanted them to feel he was hurt they were going without him. For the first few weeks, he'd really missed them. Uncle William had reduced the number of lessons he was sent to. At the same time, he trusted him with more jobs around the farm and took him out on the cart on every single buying or selling mission.

This increase in the outdoor life had greatly appealed to him. In those first winter months, the weather had been much like now. It had not seemed long after the first month of eighteen-thirteen that the *Journal* had brought word of the scale of the Emperor Napoleon's defeat in the retreat from Moscow. Father and mother had reappeared on the cart, bringing news of their own.

"We're to be off with his lordship and her ladyship to Bengal," mother had announced when the cart had pulled through the openedgate.

When she'd got down and Horatio had hugged her, she had held him at arm's length and found he'd grown well and pleasingly.

"We have brought what money we have to leave with your Uncle William for you."

"Will you not need it for your journey?" Uncle William had cut in. "No, Lord Moira is going as Governor General, so we'sell be all found on board a fine Indiaman," Father had replied.

His accent was noticeably changed from the local one he'd slipped back into over recent years.

"So, thee's come up int'world!" Uncle William had commented.

Father had proudly hugged him. He'd tried to get over the shock that they were going so far away without him. He'd not seen them since they'd gone to Donington Park.

"Well, so long as her ladyship's Scottish fortune survives," mother had responded.

She looked from Uncle William to Aunt Mary, who had now also come out into the yard. She then looked anxiously from her husband to her brother and sister-in-law.

They had trooped inside and heard more about how much younger Lady Moira was than her husband. How they now had young children, who would also travel out to India with them. Mother had sounded as though it was enabling her to relive the past, in whichshe had traveled out to Italy with Lady Acton and children. She felt that this time it would be grander, with the Earl and his wife, who wasalso Countess of Loudoun in her own right. Father was somehow just carried along with it all. Perhaps he'd felt that nothing could ever equal those two momentous years in the Mediterranean. Uncle William suggested that India was somehow more barbaric than even Bonaparte's Europe. Father had replied that it was much more settled since Lord Wellington's victories there.

Far different was the one letter he'd sent when the fine Indiaman had docked at Calcutta. Then, it had been a case of how crowded and stinking the Indian city was, once either the Governor General's compound or the East India Company's dock were left behind. Sacred cows and rabid pariah dogs roamed the streets. The Indian servants carried forked sticks when cleaning out rooms, in casethere were poisonous snakes. In fact, it was as well to keep such a stick and a sharp knife in the bedchamber, just in case one slithered in at night. Above all, the baking humid heat day after day was hard to bear. The smell of the funeral pyres, where the many dead were burned day and night, seemed to spread throughout the city. How these would fare when it started to rain, father hadn't known. It was said to rain continuously for weeks, once it started. The overallimpression had been they expected Bengal to be like the Sicily they remembered, and it wasn't.

That one letter had taken so many months to arrive Emperor Napoleon had already fought all his battles in Saxony and lost the final one beforehand. As a result, they hadn't worried when nothing came the following year, during the invasions of northern France by the Prussian, Russian, and Austrian armies. It was only after harvest that the lack of a further letter had become worrying.

Not that they could do anything other than get on with their lives while waiting, Horatio reflected.

His life had now taken a new and exciting turn, thanks to Uncle William trusting him to make alone deliveries and collections with the cart. It had started last October, when he'd had a cartload of stubble stalks to deliver to a farm at Costock. the bundled stalks had needed to be carried up to an empty end of a hayloft. The farmhands had all been out plowing, but the milkmaid, Mary, had been available tohelp. When he'd reached the final bundle, with her help, she'd come up behind him with some loose stalks and tickled his neck as he'd put down the bundle. Giggling, she'd run past the top of the steps up to the loft to where the hay had been stacked. He, of course, had run after her, caught his toe on a board and fallen headlong into the hay. The next moment, she had been down beside him, and it had seemed the most natural thing to kiss her.

It wasn't so much that Mary was pretty but that she had a rosy cheeked vitality. When she'd first moved her body close up to his on the yielding hay, he'd suddenly been overwhelmingly aware of the softness of her body. The kiss had lasted a long time, and her hand had inched down across his stomach toward his groin. Tentatively, at first, his hand had rested on her plump buttock then squeezed. She'd thrust her body forward, so he could feel her breasts underneath the thin fabric of her smock, tight against his chest. After that, there had been no stopping either of them. Not that they'd stayed up there too long afterward. The horse with his nosebag and the empty cart might well arouse the gaffer's suspicion.

Sat there with the *Journal* in front of him, Uncle William staring intothe firelight and Aunt Mary fidgeting with the stove, he realized he was well and truly aroused. He would have to stop thinking about Mary and the number of occasions since that first one. If he had to stand up now, the bulge at the front of his breeches would beobvious. Aunt

Mary would be scandalized and Uncle William would be suspicious. He didn't want to run the risk of his unaccompanied, cart-borne jaunts being brought to a sudden end. None of the other lads in the village who were fourteen appeared to have the powerful urges he had. No doubt, none of them had experienced the delights either. Oh, there he went again, and he must stop it!

"Shall I carry on readin the *Journal* now, Uncle William?"

He desperately interrupted the firelight reverie, thankful only that his erection was weakening.

"Aye, lad, from that there susighety page, so's us can ear the doins of lords an ladies who've not squandered all thur money like yon Lady 'Amilton."

He looked happier in anticipation of hearing the social trivia of the lives of the local great and good. Aunt Mary came to the oven to pull out her piping-hot savory pie and looked content to be done with questions. With a sense of relief that had nothing to do with hisearlier questions, Horatio started to read again.

EPILOGUE

Bright sunlight penetrated the chinks in the front room curtains of Horatio Spencer's cottage at Bag Lane, Gotham. His youngest and oldest daughters kept vigil on his coffin, which sat on the table behind them. He had only died yesterday, but it was still summer. As often happens in Britain, warmer as autumn approaches than in the very middle of the year. His grave, in what was still thought of as the new cemetery, had been dug this morning, the twelfth of September, eighteen eighty-nine. The Rector had been very kind when they went to see him yesterday morning. He had promised them a fitting service for their well-known father. He had lived so long after being brought as a baby from the Mediterranean by his parents. There would undoubtedly be an obituary in the *Deanery Magazine*.

The service was to be held today at two o'clock this afternoon. Those family members who worked in Nottingham, as well as those who worked locally, could get back in time without losing a whole day's pay. Times had been hard in the eighteen eighties, even if Father himself had lived in reasonable comfort. The sisters sat there silently with their thoughts. They were waiting for the cart from the workshop of the carpenter who served as the village undertaker. It may have crossed their minds that perhaps father's comfort had been a little too great. Plenty of time had been afforded for drinking and storytelling in the Cuckoo Bush across the road.

They were an interesting contrast, the sisters. For one thing, Ann was no less than eighteen years older than Eliza. Also, Ann well remembered the mother of both of them, also an Elizabeth, after whom her youngest sister was named. This Elizabeth could not remember her mother at all. No doubt it was the effect of all the childbearing that had carried off their mother while her last borne was in her infancy.

Eliza had been mainly brought up by her stepmother, a good woman who had done her best by the younger children.

Father had never loved her like he loved Mother, thought Ann.

She had been married herself and starting her own family at the time Mother had been snatched away from them. It had hit her hard, just when she felt the need of Mother's support. Now, she was a widow in her late sixties and knew she had aged a great deal. Eliza, however, had not seemed to be touched by personal tragedy in her life thus far. She was still good looking in her late forties, with a husband capable of supporting her. She got on well with their siblings, especially John, the second youngest, who now lived and worked in Nottingham.

Ann's husband, Emmanuel, had been a gypsum miner earning good money when he was killed in a mine accident sixteen years before. Then, Charlotte was under ten and Kate was no more than a baby. She had needed to work to finish bringing up her family. Cleaning and laundry was all she knew, but it was hard to make a living from that. She had been born at a time before his lordship had started the elementary school for the village children. She could hardly read or write, while her youngest sister could confidently do both. She was wondering what her grown-up children would do for her when she was old and useless like father. Her sister was thinking about the way her younger children were still developing and might do well in life.

Their separate reveries were brought to an end by the sounds of hooves and wheels on the lane outside. Eliza got up to take a peek through the curtain's edge by the window frame without analyzing the sounds. She fully expected it to be the cart and horses of the carpenter.

She let the curtain's edge fall and stepped back in complete surprise.

"It is a closed private carriage with both driver and rear footman," she exclaimed.

"Is it His Lordship's carriage?" Ann asked her.

"No, it's nothing like his carriage. I'm sure the crest on the door is different," her sister replied, taking another look. "It's a crest I don't recognize, nor thelLady."

There came a rap on the door, and Ann got there first to open it. Eliza came to her side. The coachman had done the rapping, but the lady stood there.

"Is this the home of Horatio William Spencer deceased?" she asked haughtily.

"It is. I am his youngest daughter and this is my eldest sister," replied Eliza. "Who might you be?"

"My identity does not concern you. I have signed proof that an itemin this cottage is Crown property. I am directed to collect it," the stranger retorted icily.

"I am not sure I am willing to let you remove anything," Eliza said defiantly.

"Shall I enter, milady?" asked the coachman, with an obvious air ofthreat.

"That will not be necessary. Here is the paper," said the unidentified lady.

She held out a sheet of paper that looked very old. It had faded writing on its upper side.

Eliza reached out and took it, focusing hard on the writing before she read aloud.

"*I acknowledge to have received into my safekeeping a Bible that remains Admiralty property for my lifetime and that of my son, Horatio William Spencer.* Signed *Thomas Spencer.* Is that our grandfather? Could he read and write?"

"He is supposed to have been our grandfather, although he'd left Gotham before I was born. I don't know what became of him. He must have been able to read and write. Uncle William said his letter home about the Battle of the Nile was printed in the *Nottingham Journal,*" Ann replied in a regretful tone.

She had hardly got the words out of her mouth when the haughty lady spoke again.

"He could not have been Lord Nelson's steward without being able

413

to read and write. He signed this on his discharge on the twenty- ninth of June, eighteen hundred. Are you going to bring the Bible to me?"

When Ann heard the date, she looked cowed and turned around toascend the stairs. Eliza stood her ground at the door. She was angry at being stared down by this lady who looked about her own age but hadn't worn very well. A shade too flabby and pale for the time of year, but well held in by a corset.

Her body looked like that of a woman who'd given birth a few times, Elizabeth thought.

Why did she have to look so censorious and severe? She heard the floor creak behind and above her. She involuntarily looked around to see Ann at the top of the stairs. She held the bulky Bible inboth hands. Slowly, she came down, one tread at a time. The lady shifted her weight from one foot to the other, containing her impatience.

When Ann reached the doorway, Eliza held up her hand.

"There is a letter inside from Lord Nelson, which we are entitled to keep."

"Not so," rapped the lady. "The letter was in the Bible when it was handed to your grandfather. It must remain inside. Hand it all to my coachman."

The burly man in his livery came up to the doorstep, holding outhis hands. The footman up on the back of the carriage looked on as though it was a foregone event.

Ann reluctantly held out the Bible. She felt its weight more with her arms extended. Eliza looked on grimly. She wished her brother,John, would appear and bring a halt to this terribly mistaken capitulation. He didn't, and now the coachman was carrying the Bible to the carriage's interior.

"I will wish you a comforting burial service and farewell," said the still unidentified lady.

She turned on her heel to follow the coachman. In a trice, he had the Bible on the carriage seat and was handing up the lady to sitnext to the volume. She looked back to the doorway with flinty satisfaction. Ann was so stupefied in her funereal black that she dropped a curtsey. Eliza just stood and glowered as the carriage moved away, up the gentle slope of the lane to where there was a turning space. When it came back down to take the Kegworth road, there was no sign of acknowledgment from exterior or interior of the carriage.

"What have we done?" Eliza growled through gritted teeth.

"Perhaps it is for the best," Ann said in a tone that had no confidence in the words.

The carriage had just turned onto the main road. The carpenter's cart, with brother John walking alongside, passed it and turned into the lane. Minutes later, the cart and principal mourners had reached the church. The rector waited with the additional pallbearers. The carriage came down from the bridge over the River Soar and turned left onto the Loughborough road. The Lady's last look northward before the turn was filled with loathing. No-one was in a position to see this. Her coachman did not see her either, although she called out sufficient directions at road junctions to show she knew the roads around here. The burial service and interment in Gotham had been succeeded by most of the mourners repairing to the favorite hostelry of the deceased. The carriage turned into a gateway with a long and nearly straight drive. It led to a large mansion on gently rising ground and had a backdrop of woodland behind it.

Where the drive broadened out in the approach to stone steps leading up to an impressive, pillared entrance, a smartly dressed, middle-aged man waited with a small case in his hand.

"Start turning the carriage to go back, James, and bring me alongside that gentleman," the lady ordered.

The standing man looked through the carriage window at her as the coach drew near.

"Good afternoon, my Lady," he started, bowing, then continued, "I am his lordship's Land Agent. He asks me to tender his apologies for not being present to meet you himself. He was required to accompany the Prince of Wales to a race meeting."

"No matter. You may tell his lordship I have carried out my instructions. The daughters of the deceased, the only ones present, have no idea of my identity. You had better open your case here on the carriage floor and put this inside," she ordered.

If the Land Agent thought two ordinary women would find it hard toargue with this one, he didn't show it. He simply said, "Certainly, my lady," and did as she said.

She lifted the Bible off the seat for him then spoke again.

"Here is also the receipt with the signature of Thomas Spencer. I believe I should have failed to convince them without it."

"Clearly a useful precaution, my lady. I wonder how they feel now about what they have done," the Land Agent pondered.

"It would have done them no good to retain the Bible and what lies inside it. Their father made no effort to lift himself away from rural squalor or to leave any mark on society. I fear he was only an indolent son and deserved no acknowledgment that he was fathered by a brilliant man," the lady said severely.

The Bible went in the case, which he then shut and removed from the carriage.

"Any more than knowing who really bore him! Thank you, my lady, for all your help in dealing with this matter," the Land Agent said warmly, stepped back, and bowed.

"Do not get me started on that notorious lady. Perhaps with her blood, he could never be anything other than indolent!" the Lady exclaimed with a wintry smile.

She leaned forward of the lowered door window, called "Farewell" to the Land Agent, and then called up to her coachman, "Take the road west from the gates, James."

"Farewell, my lady," the Land Agent quickly called.

The carriage was already moving away. He looked at the height of the sun and calculated the lady should reach home by sunset. She sat back on her cushions and smiled to herself.

Ingram Content Group UK Ltd.
Milton Keynes UK
UKHW020714210423
420559UK00015B/834